THE
CARETAKER

A novel of power, money, & murder

Roi Solberg

Cover Art: Tayle Design Studio

In Memoriam
David Zehel
1949—2013
Storyteller extraordinaire

DEDICATION
For my wonderful family
And Jeannee Sacken

La Lumbre is a fictional small town
set in the Santa Cruz Mountains.

Chapter One

~~~~~

Richard Sobrantes was out of time. Out of solutions. This meeting was his last chance to nail the bastards sabotaging his company.

The speedometer hit eighty as he raced along Skyline Boulevard toward Woodside. Dense clouds, a precursor to the storm moving in from the Pacific, hung low over the tops of the redwood trees standing like centurions beside the road.

Quick glances to the passenger seat reassured him that the blue sports bag he'd stuffed with a hundred and fifty thousand dollars was still there.

Richard slowed, then hung an abrupt left. The car fishtailed, slid sideways. He brought it under control and turned onto an obscure unpaved road, once a logging trail in the 1800s, now part of the Open Space Land Preserve. The car lurched over the rutted dirt. He parked behind a cluster of trees, hiding the car from the traffic on Skyline.

His cell phone chirped with text messages, emails, and phone calls. Endless calls. His office would demand to know where he was, what he was doing, and if they knew, they'd discourage him from meeting with this anonymous person. He tossed the phone aside where it continued to vibrate.

He got out and locked the car from habit rather than caution. It wasn't an area where you'd get mugged, but a great place for a confidential meeting or a romantic tryst.

How in the world had he gotten involved in this cloak and dagger bullshit?

Thirty years of success and respect in the electronics

industry until recently when counterfeit components slipped undetected into the industry supply chain. They'd created failures in an array of products—medical, industrial, and military. When the components continued to infiltrate the assembly process, Richard began to suspect an inside source but never found proof of who or how.

It felt personal as if someone had a vendetta against him and the company that he and his friends founded when they were fresh out of Stanford.

Richard kept walking toward the creek. He had to be calm when he met the mysterious caller. Uncontrolled anger, lack of rationale created mistakes, and he couldn't afford any more mistakes.

He pushed back his sleeve, checked the time. Five minutes.

Security had taken every precaution to prevent the continued influx of counterfeits. But a month ago, a military transport plane crashed, and the cause was traced to the printed circuit boards containing RKB's semiconductors. Fortunately, the crew members had escaped with minor injuries. Unfortunately, the 10-million dollar aircraft was badly damaged.

Tomorrow he had meetings with the DOD, NSA and a plethora of other *alphabet* agencies investigating the crash. They weren't interested in his theories. They'd want solid information, which the enigmatic voice on the telephone had promised.

The wind blew cold gusts of misty rain, stinging his cheeks. Richard pulled up the collar of his suit jacket. He made his way along the incline to Indian Rock where he'd played as a kid with his pal, Rand Bainbridge. He kicked at a stone in the path and then picked it up, slung it into the water. Startled birds took flight. A squirrel scolded from a nearby tree.

He sat on a large flat boulder and dropped his head in his hands. If word about the counterfeits got around, RKB stock would drop like the stone he'd thrown.

He stood. Paced along the bank. The Internet, social media, news shows, and stock reporters would jump on RKB's downfall like vultures to a kill.

He'd meet with the informant, hand over the money, and pray the information was enough to end this nightmare.

Afterward, he'd go home, sit by the fire, and have a glass of wine.

Then he remembered. Christ almighty, on top of everything, he had to tell his daughter what he'd discovered about her fiancé, Jeffery.

A loud thrashing from the woods brought Richard to his feet. Adrenaline raced through his body. Cougars were spotted around here last week. He hawked a laugh at the idea of being eaten by a cougar. He imagined the headlines—*Billionaire CEO eaten alive in Santa Cruz Mountains.*

A four-point buck stepped out from the trees. Richard froze and then raised his hands. "Play through, sir," he said softly. Wild-eyed, the deer stepped warily along the bank and then sprinted up the hill and out of sight.

Calmer, Richard walked back to his car. This problem would work out. It would all work out.

Another cracking sound made him pause and search the woods for more deer. He saw nothing until a figure dressed in black motorcycle leathers stepped into the clearing.

"You have what I need, right?" Richard unlocked the car.

"I have this."

Richard turned back.

Death spiraled toward him at six hundred miles an hour.

The first shot slammed into his chest, ripped his heart, destroyed his lungs, and exited through his spine—spewing blood, spinal fluid, shattered bone, and tissue.

His legs folded like a marionette with severed strings. A rapid second shot hit the center of his forehead. Brains and bloody skull fragments drenched the headlight of the car.

Birds rose in a single mass, disappearing in the cloudy mist. Circling back, they settled in an oak tree. The only witnesses to the death of Richard Sobrantes.

Chapter Two

~~~~~

Lauren Sobrantes stood at the edge of her father's grave, a red rose hung limp from her fingers. The mahogany casket was covered in a massive spray of white roses, carnations, baby's breath, and those lilies Richard detested. The fragrance of the flowers mingled with the musty odor of freshly dug earth.

Lauren fought the scream rising from her gut.

Fought the urge to rip off the flowers, tear open his coffin and yell—*Game Over!* Like the year her parents had created a haunted house in the Casa for her tenth birthday party. Richard had dressed up as Dracula with fake teeth dripping blood. When she saw him in the cardboard coffin, she'd become hysterical. Richard had jumped to his feet, wrapped his arms around her, and whispered—*Game over, honey. Game over.*

But this game was never going to be over.

Not until his killer was caught, convicted, and executed.

She drew a shaky breath as the minister read another homily, raising his voice over the wailing of her stepmother, Fiona.

Clouds with underbellies swollen black with rain spun over the mountains from the southwest. Wind bent the redwoods and pines, scattering leaves and branches. Gathering speed, it whipped the grasses in the meadow of the old family graveyard. Behind Lauren, mourners unfurled their umbrellas. The minister intoned the last prayers for Richard's soul to rest in eternal peace.

Flanked by her godfather, Randolph Bainbridge, and her fiancé, Jeffery Davis, Lauren placed her rose on top of her

4

father's casket in a final goodbye.

Marisa Montgomery stepped into the crowded foyer of Casa de la Lumbre. The smell of damp coats and umbrellas blended with the scent of women's perfume, burning candles, and food passed around by white-shirted caterers.

She worked to control the fluttery nervousness that pulsated under her breastbone and worked its way down to the pit of her stomach—fear or hunger?

The Casa was crowded with guests eating, drinking, and gossiping with an occasional burst of laughter while the overwhelming question of *why* circulated unspoken through the house. Richard Sobrantes was known to be a good man with a stellar reputation for honesty and fairness.

Who wanted him dead?

Marisa drifted through the people and paused to watch the video presentation of Richard's life with his family, Lauren and her mother, Elizabeth.

Etta Kowalski, the Casa's housekeeper, joined her and slipped her arm around Marisa's waist.

"Have you seen Lauren?" Marisa asked.

"She go to bedroom." Etta's Polish accent was strongest when she was stressed. Miss Etta looked virtually the same as she had the day she started working for the Sobrantes. Except that her dark hair was now streaked with gray, but still pulled tightly into a bun at the nape of her neck. As the keeper of the Casa, she'd run the household with iron-glove efficiency for three decades.

"I wish I knew what to say to make her feel better. How to comfort her," Marisa lamented.

Miss Etta drew her to a quiet area of the kitchen and handed her a tissue. "Words don't make pain go away. Hold her. Cry with her. She fall, you pick her up. Someday she remember her father with smiles before tears."

"Is Jeffery with her?"

Miss Etta's mouth pinched. She shook her head and nodded to the bar where Jeffery consoled a tearful young woman.

"He's rather busy," Marisa, murmured. She recognized the

woman as a receptionist at RKB.

Etta laid her hand on Marisa's arm. "He is nothing. Go to Lauren. She need you. You be strong one now."

"I don't know."

"You're stronger than you think," Etta assured her.

Marisa had doubts whether that was true. Lauren was the strong one in their friendship. The one who'd led the way and helped her overcome the loss and depression when her mother had abandoned her and her father, Kyle. She wasn't confident she had the strength and courage as Miss Etta claimed.

"Has Lauren eaten?"

"Bird-bites," sighed Etta. "I bring a plate for you both."

Marisa worked her way through the increasing mass of people. She paused on the stairs; her hand gripped the carved newel post.

The fluttering sensation in her chest exploded like a bolt of lightning. Her heart pounded, choked at her throat, drummed in her ears. Her legs went weak. She held onto the post with trembling hands. Looking back at the gathering in the foyer, the living room, and hallway, she had a sense of knowing—*the killer is here.*

What she felt was confusing, and she didn't know what to do with the information. Tell the investigators? Tell them what? That she had a feeling? Woman's intuition?

Marisa decided she'd deal with it later when she had time to think about it more clearly. She continued to Lauren's bedroom and rapped softly on the door and then slipped inside. Lauren stood in front of the cold fireplace with her arms wrapped tightly around her body. Tears and black mascara streaked down her cheeks.

Hugging Lauren, she let the silent grief bridge between them.

"I keep thinking it's a mistake," Lauren said shakily. "It must be someone else because I hear him walking down the hall. Sometimes I hear him whistling or calling me." Lauren crumpled to the floor. Marisa knelt beside her and rocked her until she grew quiet.

"I don't know what I'm going to do," Lauren whispered.

Marisa remembered Miss Etta's suggestions to take control until Lauren could manage on her own.

She wiped the tears on Lauren's face with her fingertips. "Well, first we're going to take it moment-to-moment. In this moment, you're going to breathe. Then, you'll take a hot shower and re-dress. Miss Etta is bringing up lunch. We can have a bite to eat and when you feel like it, we'll go downstairs."

After her shower, Lauren dressed in a pair of black linen palazzo pants and a gray silk tunic. Marisa had turned the bedroom lights on low; the fire in the gas fireplace burned softly and soothing jazz played.

"We should go downstairs," Lauren said.

"No hurry, your guests are in good hands. Rand, Uncle Bernie, and my dad are playing hosts."

"Where's Jeffery?"

Marisa hesitated. "He's there. Chatting up people and making sure everyone has a drink."

"And Fiona?"

"Oh, she's keeping the guy at the bar company. Miss Etta is on her way with lunch."

As if on cue, there was a tap on the door. Marisa crossed the room and Miss Etta carried in a tray of sandwiches, and a pot of tea.

"You eat everything," she commanded like she'd done when they were children.

"Yes, ma'am." Marisa handed half a turkey sandwich and a napkin to Lauren and then helped herself to the other half. They ate quietly. Each lost in thought.

"We're going to find who did this, Lulu," Marisa said, reverting to Lauren's childhood name. "No matter how long it takes."

"Dad had conflicts but not to the point where someone would want to..." Her voice trailed off. "Who? Why? What could he have done that would make someone want to kill him?"

"Have you talked to Detective Schott?"

Lauren shook her head. "He says they're investigating.

There's nothing new." None of it made any sense. With no evidence, the investigation had nothing but theories. The sheriff's report had said robbery. The killer had stolen Richard's wallet, watch, ring, and the car keys but left a very expensive car. Detectives assumed the shooter worked alone and had planned on coming back, but the storm stopped him.

"If only I hadn't been sick, I'd have had breakfast with him and maybe we'd have driven into the office together. Maybe if I had..."

"You can't do *maybe* or *if only*, Lauren. It's like a dog chasing its tail, you just get dizzy and go nowhere." Marisa knew it wouldn't stop Lauren, or her, from going over imagined opportunities that would have prevented his death.

Lauren had called the sheriff the night they couldn't find Richard. When it became evident that something was wrong. Everyone had gathered at the Casa, in spite of the storm that downed trees and blocked roads with mud and rockslides.

When the storm knocked out the power, Arlo, Etta's husband, started the generator. He'd kept the fire in the fireplace going and even walked Lauren's dog, Mr. Watson. Kyle and Uncle Bernie had joined Lauren, Jeffery, Marisa, and Miss Etta to keep a vigil. They prayed for Richard's return while battling their anxieties that something terrible had happened to him.

In the early morning hours, Detective Schott confirmed their worst nightmare. Richard had been found. Murdered.

Lauren collapsed on the marble floor of the foyer, screaming until her throat was raw. Bernie and Jeffery had carried her to the sofa where she cried with a grief that penetrated so deep that no sound remained. Unable to think, to move, to talk, or cry, she'd sat for hours in the dark, encased in a private well of pain.

"Lauren, come home with me. I don't like the idea of you being alone. I have a private art lesson early in the morning, or I'd stay here with you."

"Thanks, but Rand is staying over, and Miss Etta and Arlo will be here. Come back after your lesson."

"I can do that. Please, be careful until they catch this guy."

"Of course, I will."

"Lauren, I'm serious. I couldn't bear it if anything happened to you."

Lauren hugged Marisa. "I swear I'll be cautious."

"Promise?"

"Yes." Lauren held out her pinky finger. Marisa hooked hers onto it. "Blood sister promise."

Downstairs, laughter rose above the cacophony of voices. Rand Bainbridge stood in the foyer near the staircase waiting for Lauren. Head bowed, he contemplated questions that had no answers.

Who hated Richard enough to resort to murder?

"This is so wrong. Terribly wrong," Kyle Montgomery muttered when he and Bernie joined Rand. The men had founded RKB with Richard after graduation from Stanford but never imagined their partnership would end like this.

"What was he doing out there?" Bernie swirled the ice in his drink. "I keep going over everything. I'm not buying the random shooting theory."

Rand wasn't buying it either. It was a professional hit. But what, or who, had lured Richard to such a remote place?

"It has to do with those damn counterfeits. I know it does," Kyle declared vehemently. "Richard was adamant. He swore RKB was being singled out and sabotaged, and that he was going to find out who was behind it."

"If he'd just waited for the AZEN guy we hired to go with him."

Kyle snorted a chuckle. "Richard wait? Come on, Bernie, you know Richard was the most impatient and stubborn man alive."

"It made him a success in business," Rand said, defending his friend.

"His greatest gift." Bernie's voice was glum. "And his greatest detriment."

They discussed the whys and wherefores of Richard's death before Bernie and Kyle returned to the bar leaving Rand alone with his thoughts.

Rand met Lauren and Marisa at the bottom of the staircase when they returned to the reception. Marisa took the tray and empty plates to Miss Etta in the kitchen. When Rand confirmed Lauren was doing okay, he went to the bar for a beer.

Lauren mingled with her guests.

Pungent perfume broadcasted her stepmother, Fiona.

"You've got to rein in your fiancé."

Lauren paused to study her. She was disheveled, eyes bloodshot. Since the divorce Richard initiated had not been finalized, Lauren wondered if Fiona was still legally her stepmother? "Because?"

"He's acting like the family spokesperson, talking to the media. His fifteen minutes of bullshit fame." Fiona gestured broadly.

"Feel free to talk to him." Lauren looked over the gathering but didn't see Jeffery. Marisa joined them. Fiona waved her glass and sloshed amber liquid down the front of her navy dress.

"You might want to take it easy on the drinks, okay?" said Lauren. Fiona liked her cocktails, but she couldn't remember ever seeing her plastered.

"Okay?" Fiona mimicked in a whine. "I have enough drugs in me to anesthetize a horse, and they're not working, so I'll keep medicating, thank you." She gulped more of her drink and began sobbing. "I know you don't believe I loved your dad, but I did. I did. I don't know how I'm going to live without him."

"You'll carry on as before, Fiona." Marisa stepped in front of Lauren, shielding her from her stepmother. "You'll shop and travel until you find another rich sucker to snag."

Fiona teetered. "You're vile, both of you. Just vile little bitches. You'll get yours someday." She wobbled off toward the bar.

"She shouldn't be driving home in that condition." Lauren frowned at Fiona's unsteady gait.

"I'll get someone to take her." Marisa looked around for Rand.

Lauren joined her uncle across the room.

Bernie's gray face was deep with worry lines. "What's with

Fiona?" Bernie nodded toward the bar.

"Had a few too many. Marisa is finding someone to drive her home."

"Good idea." He hesitated as if debating whether to say more. He leaned close. "Have you seen your dad's engineering lab book?"

"His what?"

"It's that black book. His name is imprinted on the front in gold. It wasn't at the office. If it was in the car, the sheriff might have listed it as evidence."

She shook her head. "I haven't seen the list. It's important?"

"Your dad kept track of everything, ideas, meetings, appointments, conference calls. He even made notes on what he ate for lunch."

"And maybe who he was meeting that day?"

"I don't know. Hopefully. It would be a long shot."

"Did you ask Detective Schott?"

"No. I haven't mentioned it to the sheriff. Not yet. I wanted to find it first."

"You're just now looking for it?"

"I searched his office."

"Did you look in his desk or the safe in the study?"

"I wanted to wait for you."

"Come on, let's go check."

They wove their way through the gathering and walked down the hall to Richard's study in the west wing. The room was dimly lit. She paused in the doorway, confused by the sound of slapping.

Bernie flipped on the overhead lights.

Jeffery, in the throes of an orgasm, didn't even notice.

Chapter Three

~~~~~

Waking up was the worst. That drift from unconsciousness to reality. That moment when she remembered that her father was dead, murdered, left to die on a lonely road, face down in mud and blood.

Lauren ached to sink back into the void of darkness, to see nothing, to remember nothing, to return to the insentience sleep that removed her from the agony that swelled like a tumor in her chest until grief discharged in gut-wrenching sobs.

Last night, after discovering Jeffery in the study, Rand and Bernie sent everyone home, even Marisa. Lauren could not bear having anyone, even her dearest friend, near her.

She heaved a sigh. She could stay in bed all day and cry and feel sorry for herself or get up, take action—call Detective Schott to find out if there was anything new. She'd deal with Jeffery later.

Kicking back the covers, she swung her legs over the side of the bed. Standing at the window, she watched the smoke rising from the cottage chimney as if it were a normal day.

The weather had shifted from rain to sunny chill. The trees swayed in the wind. The maple tree released the few remaining yellowed leaves that floated to the ground in a gentle swirl.

She had a glut of questions running through her mind. Why was he killed? Why did Jeffery betray her?

Stop asking why. It keeps you stuck. Her father's voice was as clear as if he were standing beside her.

When her mother died, she'd hidden under the covers, virtually comatose, until the morning her dad charged into her room and ordered her out of bed. *Keep moving. Life doesn't stop because you're hurting.* They'd started traveling. Over the next few years, they'd trekked all over the world, wearing funky disguises so they'd not be recognized. They spoke her mother's name on every mountaintop, in every sacred place they visited, knowing she'd be happy they were together.

Then, he'd met Fiona. They married two years ago. Fiona hiked nowhere except bars, restaurants, and shoe stores. Lauren didn't mind most of the time. She'd been immersed in her own life—working in the marketing department at RKB and meeting Jeffery, becoming engaged, and planning for her wedding next year.

She'd had it all. Now, she had nothing except the promise she made to her father every day. *I will find out who did this.*

Lauren looked back at the bed with longing but kept moving toward the bathroom. Finally, dressed in jeans and a warm sweatshirt, she selected a pair of boots and went downstairs.

The aroma of freshly brewed coffee greeted her. Mr. Watson sat by the counter, tail thumping against the cabinet, eager for Rand to drop a morsel or two. Rand looked up from his cell phone, poured a second cup for Lauren, and passed the cream. He slipped his arm around her shoulders.

"Miss Etta made a quiche for our breakfast. I told her to go back bed. I believe it's the first time that woman hasn't argued with me," Rand chuckled. "I suggested that she let me take care of you and the dog."

Mr. Watson gave up waiting for tidbits and whined to go out. Lauren watched him tear through the garden, like a white streak among the evergreen shrubs. With his nose to the ground, he searched for the perfect spot to re-mark his territory.

Lauren thought about the many decisions that lay before her, including where to live.

It was as if Rand had read her thoughts. "You have options where to live, either here or the corporate condo downtown. They have stronger security. Or you can come to Italy with me and visit with Lillie and Alexis for an extended stay."

Chucking everything and flying off to Europe had a certain

appeal. "I have a meeting with Tully Jones this week to discuss Dad's will and the probate, although everything is in a trust. And I have to decide what to do about Dad's things." She'd not been able to bring herself to enter into his room, look at his clothes, his toiletries, or smell his zesty soap and aftershave. Bernie had selected the clothes for Richard's burial.

Watson scratched at the door and then turned in circles for his reward. "Guess it's time for our walk." Lauren set her cup on the breakfast bar and gave Watson a dog treat. She turned to Rand. "You're welcome to join us."

"In a few minutes, I'm waiting for a call. Which way are you going?"

"Down the driveway to the pear orchard. Watson likes to chase the rabbits and scare the quail."

"I'll catch up with you when I've finished. Take one of the security guys with you." Lauren slipped on her jacket. Mr. Watson danced, eager to leave.

Rand stood in the kitchen alone with his grief and guilt. He and Richard had been friends for sixty years. If only he'd kept searching for the manufacturer of those counterfeits, as Richard had asked him to do. He'd checked out several leads, but when the trail went cold, he'd gone to the Italian coast with his wife, and their daughter for a rare vacation.

He poured another cup of coffee and checked his watch, too early for his call. Pulling on his jacket, he walked outside and inhaled the crisp October air.

Gravel crunched under his feet.

He listened to the birdcalls until they were drowned out by Watson's frantic barks.

Multiple gunshots.

And Lauren's screams.

Chapter Four

~~~~~

Lauren Sobrantes, daughter of murdered billionaire, Richard Sobrantes, and heiress to the family fortune, vanished yesterday according to the La Lumbre Sheriff's Department. Ms. Sobrantes, 27, disappeared from the family estate early Sunday morning. She was last seen the previous evening at the funeral reception for her father.

Bernard Anderson confirmed that his niece has not been seen or heard from in over 24 hours.

There are no leads or suspects in the recent murder of Mr. Sobrantes. The sudden disappearance of his daughter is highly suspicious. The department is investigating all leads and asked if anyone has any information to please call the La Lumbre Sheriff's Office.

Chapter Five

~~~~~

Two years later ~
Some claim that a spirit woman in a red dress and fire in her hair
haunts the Sobrantes estate. The Spanish knew her as *Dama de la
Lumbre*, the woman of fire. The legend, long forgotten by most,
proclaimed she was the protector of mountains and found lost
children, injured loggers, and those who'd disappeared in the
forest.

Others claim the Dama put a curse on the estate and that
death shadowed the Sobrates family. First, Elizabeth died of an
unknown allergy. Then, Richard was murdered. The day after
his funeral, their only daughter vanished.

A coyote trotted down an old logging trail through the
redwood forests of the estate. Hunger gnawed at his belly. He
didn't care about legends.

The trail led to a meadow that lay alongside the Casa. At
the edge, thickets pulsated with life and death, the hunters and
the hunted.

The waning moon offered scant light, but Coyote didn't
need it. He paused along the tree line. Overhead a barn owl
glided whisper-smooth over the grasses and impaled a field
mouse with her talons.

Coyote watched. Waited. Quail stirred. A rabbit ventured
out in the predawn darkness. Coyote pounced, and with a quick
snap, the rabbit went limp. Without pausing, he carried his feast
to the greasewood bushes across from the fenced-in compound
and the caretaker's cottage.

Inside the cottage, glowing red embers were banked in the

old fieldstone fireplace. Upstairs, the caretaker, Sam Gallagher lay still, his legs entangled in blankets, arms flung wide, a crucifix on sweat-soaked sheets.

Nightmares trapped his mind. He was back in Afghanistan, high on the mountain above the Korengal Valley, miles from the U.S. safety zone. His night-goggles tinged the terrain a surreal green moonscape.

Night. Cold. Their mission was to rescue the hostage, return the man to his family.

Home. Safe. Unharmed.

Sam waited in the sniper hide he'd set up on the second floor of a blown-out building. His scout, alive again, sat beside him, grinning as he whispered the coordinate range—eight hundred, ten meters to the target.

Ignoring the sand gritted between his teeth and the stench of his sweat, Sam adjusted the gun's fine-tune ring to eight-plus-two, and then rechecked the coordinates on the scope of his M40.

Nothing could go wrong.

Not this time.

He sighted the doorway of the crumbling mud house at the end of the lane, beyond the withered mulberry tree. Behind the thick wooden door was the hostage they'd been sent to rescue at the request of Senator Riley Phillips.

National security, Phillips said when he'd hired them. Their security company was known for rescuing and returning high-level people home safely without a ripple of media attention.

A lone donkey, small and boney with a bloated stomach wandered down the path, picking his way through trash and waste.

They waited.

Finally, the donkey moved beyond the lane. The lights dimmed in the house. Jon's voice came quietly over the headset. "Go."

Moments later, an over-confident guard stepped out of the house to take a piss; his RKP light machine gun hung carelessly from his shoulder. Sam locked the crosshairs, took a breath, slowly exhaled, and gently squeezed the trigger. The bullet exploded the left side of the man's skull, spun him around, and dropped him face down in dirt and urine.

Sam ejected the spent cartridge, reloaded.

The second kill was equally methodical.

As he reloaded for the third, Armageddon exploded. The ground shook, flashes of fire and bright lights streaked across the night sky. A loud pop was followed by the pop-pop-pop of antipersonnel bomblets. The house was obliterated by a cluster bomb detonating on impact.

A hole blew open in the roof of the sniper hide. Debris fell over Sam and his scout.

Stunned, he stared at the stars through the opening. Acrid smoke filled his nostrils. Men yelled. The scout's death rattle came from somewhere in the rubble.

"Sam, you mother fuck, answer me—" Jon's voice screamed through the headset twisted around Sam's neck.

Sam wanted to laugh, but it seemed he'd forgotten how.

His body drifted upward.

Closing his eyes, he floated, immersed in music without sound.

"It's called Harmonics," murmured a voice. "The vibration of the universe."

Sam opened his eyes. Bright flecks of stars peppered around him. A woman in red hovered beside him, held him in place. He watched the men below work on his body. It wasn't so bad, this dying stuff.

"You're not dying, just resting." She brushed a hand across his brow, wiping away the blood. Her touch was hot but soothing. Her long hair drifted around them like the flames burning below. Starlight illuminated her face. "You have another mission."

She let go.

Sam woke shrieking. Kicking back the covers, he sat up, gasping for reality.

Fragments of the dream disintegrated, shoved out by pain penetrating his brain like shards of glass gyrating in his skull.

It was the nastiest hangover-headache ever but without the good-time party the night before. It hurt to breathe, much less move. He forced himself to get up and staggered to the bathroom for Vicodin. The bottle cap stuck. He slammed it against the sink, tablets scattered. Grabbing one off the counter, he washed it down with water cupped in his hand and then held on to the counter, waiting for relief from the nausea and the stabbing agony behind his eyes.

He gathered the spilled tablets and dropped them back in the bottle. He went in the bedroom, pulled on yesterday's jeans and a gray sweatshirt, and went downstairs. The headaches were stronger and more frequent, which meant another round of doctors, tests, and the constant worry that he'd never work again.

Sam was a killer, one of the best. His sniper skills were legendary among SEAL recruits. Five years ago, when he and Jon Malcolm furloughed out of the service, they founded AZEN. His brother, Flynn joined them two years later. They were a team, and he needed to get back with them.

Downstairs, Sam made a fresh pot of coffee. Then, he stirred the embers in the fireplace, added a log that sputtered into flames. Pouring a cup of coffee, he stretched out on the sofa. The drugs blunted the sharpness of the pain. The coffee relieved the nausea, but now he felt like he was moving through dense air. The morning sun filtered through the windows. A coyote yipped in the distance as Sam fell asleep.

The ax swung in a smooth arc over his shoulder and down with a loud thwack. The blow vibrated in his hands when the log split. The sound echoed through the still air. Picking up a piece, Sam placed it on the tree stump and split it again. At this rate, he'd have enough firewood for a dozen winters. Not that he cared. He'd not be staying at the estate much longer.

Chopping wood was a daily routine. It relieved the residue of bad dreams and the drugs. The exercise built up the strength and endurance he'd lost after the explosion over a year and a half ago in Afghanistan. He was flown to a private hospital in Germany where he'd spent weeks recovering from a coma, cracked ribs, a broken leg, and numerous lacerations along with pain and hallucinations about a woman who wore a red dress and had flames for hair.

The doctors had assured him the pain medication affected patients in different ways. Some experienced stomachaches or depression, and others saw things that weren't real. His migraines and night terrors had continued. His leg ached in rainy weather. Loud noises triggered the PTSD and threw him right back into the explosion.

Six months ago, Jon Malcolm arranged for Sam to live on the Sobrantes estate as caretaker in exchange for keeping an eye on the place while he received outpatient treatment at Stanford Hospital. The owner, Richard Sobrantes, had been murdered and his only daughter disappeared. Most people believed she was dead, but her uncle refused to sell until he knew for sure what had happened to her.

Jon had flown to California with Sam and helped him get settled at the estate—a hundred and eighty acres of isolated quiet and peaceful undeveloped land. In the center was the historic house, Casa de la Lumbre. The mansion, the caretaker cottage, and the pristinely manicured gardens were enclosed with a high iron fence.

Splitting the last log, Sam left the ax embedded in the stump. A familiar tingling ran up his neck. Casually, he picked up a piece of wood from the stack, held it loosely at his side, and scanned the area from the stables below, the driveway leading to the Casa, and the caretaker's cottage. He looked back along the pathway, across the drive to the broken gate of the paddock area, and the empty pasture beyond.

Nothing. Questioning the tingling that saved his life on so many occasions, Sam reversed his search. There across the clearing, about thirty feet away in the tall, dry grass beyond the paddock gate, stood a coyote with his ears up, head cocked, yellow eyes staring at Sam like a stranger trying to remember your name.

The morning sun glistened off the animal's coat, highlighting the black-tipped fur. He appeared young, a year, maybe two at the most.

"How did you get in here?" Sam's voice sounded awkward in the quiet. The gates were locked, and the fencing around the six-acre compound was too high to climb. The fence was designed specifically to keep animals and people out.

"Where's your pack, buddy? They leave you behind?"

Coyote sat as if settling in for a long chat. Neither of them moved.

"Mr. Coyote, I'm jonesin' for my breakfast, so you need to be on your way." Keeping the animal in sight, Sam walked toward the back gate beyond the stable.

Coyote watched, lifted his nose as if catching a scent, then dissolved into a haze of red, slowly rising upward, gathering lift on the current of an unfelt breeze, and spiraled into a red scarf, that floated toward the sky.

The wood dropped from Sam's grasp. "What the hell—"

He was a rational man, a logical man, a linear thinker.

Black. White. Gray could get you killed.

Hallucinate, and you're dead. Crossing the road to where the coyote had been, Sam studied the deep indention in the dry grass. He squatted down and felt the weeds; they were still warm.

There *was* a coyote.

A coyote that shape-shifted into a red scarf.

And floated away.

Sam walked back to the cottage and dumped an armload of split wood in the old brass tub beside the fireplace. He set the kettle of water on the stove, ground fresh coffee beans, and poured them into the French Press. He tried to rationalize how a coyote could dissolve into thin air.

How could he go back to work with AZEN if he was hallucinating?

A crazy man with a gun could destroy a mission and kill the wrong people.

He jumped at the ringing of his satellite phone.

"Yeah," he snapped.

"Hey, Sammy," Flynn's voice boomed over the roar of an engine.

"Where are you?" Sam poured the boiling water over the ground coffee.

"About fifty miles outside San Jose. We're coming in for a

landing."

The transmission cracked up.

"We?"

"Jon, with me...joining you. Breakfast... Got eggs? I've got bagels."

"What's up?" Sam pressed the phone tight against his ear, straining to hear, but the static and engine noise drowned out his brother's voice.

"When we get...an hour...coffee—" The connection broke, leaving an ominous quiet.

Flynn Gallagher climbed out of the black SUV, stretched his long legs, and then waved to his brother. "Good lord, almighty, Sam. Just look at you." He pulled him in for a backslapping hug. "Damn if you ain't got this mountain grunge thing going for you with that beard. You need a haircut."

Sam laughed. Flynn's long hair was tied back with a leather cord.

"Come on now, don't tell me that's a flannel shirt you're wearing." Flynn tugged at Sam's shirtsleeve, rubbed the fabric between his fingers. "Jon, we gotta get this boy out of here before he's too far gone and becomes a full-blown hermit."

The youngest and the tallest of the Gallagher brothers, Flynn wore a brown leather jacket that should have been retired a half-century ago, worn and faded jeans, and dark aviator glasses. Lanky, he gave the appearance of slow and easy until he slipped behind the wheel of a fast car or sat at the controls of a fighter jet or helicopter. Flynn's expert skills had saved Sam's life that night on the Afghan mountain, rescuing him and the other men and flying them out safely.

"How's it going?" Sam asked, fully engulfed in another hug.

"Great, what've you been up to?"

Sam shrugged. "Splitting logs, you know, mountain man stuff." *Watching flying coyotes disappear.*

Jon Malcolm shook Sam's hand and gave a quick one-arm man-hug, before stepping back to study Sam's face. "How are you feeling these days?"

"Good, doing great."

"Headaches gone?"

Sam nodded to avoid an out-and-out lie.

Jon was a sharp contrast to Sam and Flynn. Clean cut, short hair, and thin patrician face. He'd dressed in khakis and a white button-down shirt under a dark green sweater. A chameleon, Jon could be nondescript when he wanted to blend in with the crowd and equally noticeable and charismatic at an international black-tie affair.

Sam was impatient to know the purpose of their visit. He led them inside. Jon walked beside him. "Do you think the Sobrantes woman is dead or just hiding out?"

"Dead most likely. Someone will eventually find her remains. The crazies keep popping up around here to search for her. The latest rumor going around is she's a recluse and lives here but never goes out.

"Two weeks ago, a guy parked at the gate with a megaphone. He called her name over and over and played loud, obnoxious music, a torture technique to drive her out. He'd already set up his tent before I got to him."

The man hadn't believed Sam when he told him she wasn't there and he had to leave. "I called Deke Farelle, a Deputy Sheriff. He threw the guy in the squad car and took him away for mental evaluation."

"Set up!" Sam shoved aside his plate of half-eaten eggs and bacon and stared at Jon across the table. "We lost men because someone set us up?"

Unbelievable. They'd been double-crossed. His scout had died. And he'd shot two men for nothing. It made his kill shots senseless. Sam didn't hesitate to kill when he was protecting his team, but he'd never taken a life needlessly.

Jon leaned forward bracing his forearms on the table. "There was no hostage in that house. We've identified the man who was supposed to have been the hostage. He showed up in Marrakech two days ago. Now we have to find who set us up and why." Former Special Ops, Jon J. Malcolm, was not a man to cross.

"Who knew we were there? Who the hell had access to so much firepower?" Sam pushed back from the table and crossed to the window that overlooked driveway. In his head, he replayed the mission, the sniper hide, shooting two guards, and the explosion.

He stared at the Casa across the way. The wind swirled in gusts, blowing the dry maple leaves into a pile around the front steps of the Casa where a coyote sat, watching him. Sam squeezed his eyes shut, and when he opened them, the animal was gone. Pressure built behind his eyes.

Flynn collected their plates, took them to the kitchen, and brought back the coffee pot. "Someone wanted to annihilate us, that's for sure," he said, refilling the cups.

"Senator Phillips referred the project to us, right?" Sam asked over his shoulder. "Do you think he had anything to do with it?"

Years ago, Phillips had contacted them when his daughter was kidnapped from her college dorm room at the University of South Carolina. AZEN operatives quietly found and returned her to her family.

"Right now, everyone is suspect, even Senator Phillips."

"Sam?" Flynn's voice sounded far away.

"Yeah?" The new wave of pain gyrated through his skull. "Yeah," he repeated. "I have to, um, go—" He walked upstairs.

Flynn recognized the familiar indicators of pain on Sam's white face, the tense jaw, and the hard swallowing. He followed him and waited outside the bathroom.

"What's going on?" he asked when Sam stepped out.

"Can't a man take a piss without being interrogated?"

Flynn pushed by him, grabbed the bottle off the counter. Five tablets left out of thirty.

"Vicodin 300. Super strength. How many did you take, Sam?"

"What are you, my fucking doctor?"

Flynn gripped Sam's arm. "How many?"

"One. It keeps the pain from taking over."

"So, you're still having headaches which means you're not

reliable enough to come back to work." Flynn leaned against the door and watched the conflict flash over his brother's face.

"I don't know, Flynn. I don't know." Trust was the cornerstone of working together in perilous conditions, without it they were lost.

"You're no good to us if you're not a hundred percent. You'd tell me the same thing." Flynn's voice softened. Of the four brothers, Flynn had always been closest to Sam. When Sam became estranged from the family, Flynn had joined the service to be with him. Someone had to have his brother's back.

"What's the plan?" Sam asked when he and Flynn returned to the table.

Jon studied him before answering. "Flynn flies to Marrakech in the morning. The man's been on the move, and we want to catch up with him and have a little chat. Was he in on the attack or was he a stooge who was conned? I'll go to Washington and talk to Senator Phillips. Explore a few options and see what more we can find about the explosion." Jon maintained a broad range of contacts. "Sam, I'd like for you to go with Flynn to—"

"He's not going," Flynn growled, staring at his brother for confirmation.

"Flynn," Sam protested.

"You're not ready to go back to work."

Jon looked at Sam and then to Flynn. "What's going on?"

"He's having headaches, again. Taking Vicodin."

"How many missions have you flown drunk or hung over out of your mind?" Sam countered angrily.

"That's not the issue," Flynn roared. "You go out with a migraine, pop a few of those pills, we're all lost, and you fucking well know it. You can do a suicide run, but you're sure as hell aren't taking the rest of us with you."

"Well," Jon said thoughtfully, his deep voice silencing the men. "This changes things. It was my understanding you were good to go. Flynn, you go to Marrakech as we planned. Sam, you hang out here. Go to your doctor and get checked out again. We'll get back together next week to see where things stand." Jon excused himself and stepped outside to make a call on his satellite phone.

It all seemed simple and doable. So why did Sam feel like he'd been fired?

"Jon had to know, Sam." Flynn's voice broke the silence.

Sam nodded in agreement. They finished clearing the table. Working efficiently as a team came naturally from years together in a large family and from working in a profession where *leave no trace* meant survival.

"I'm going to the herb farm to see the folks after I drop Jon off at the hotel. Come with me." Flynn scraped the plates and stacked them in the dishwasher.

"Why would I want to do that?" Sam spooned salsa back into the jar.

"Mom would have your hide if she saw what you're doing."

"Yeah? Well, she'd be impressed that I first served it in a bowl." Sam handed the dish to Flynn to rinse and pushed aside memories of his mom and the family dinners.

"It's been a long time, Sam."

Silently, they reflected on the event that blew the family apart.

"Don't you want to see them?"

Sam shook his head.

"Sammy, come on, it's time to forgive and forget. Everybody says things they don't mean sometimes. I'm sure Dad's sorry—"

"No, thanks." Sam walked out the kitchen door. The last argument he'd had with his dad left a wound, one he wasn't willing to re-open.

"You're one stubborn sonofabitch!" Flynn followed.

"Seems to run in the family, doesn't it?" The door slammed shut behind them.

Chapter Six

~~~~~

Sam had one long, hard-ass day. He'd cleared the oleander bushes by the gate, dragged the brush to the area behind the stables, and then walked the fence line around the perimeter of the property, checking for holes where a coyote could slip through. If it really was a coyote.

Checking the full boundary of the compound was rough. He'd climbed over boulders, cut back briars, brush, and red-leafed poison oak vines to scrutinize every foot of the fence.

There were no openings where a coyote could get inside.

No answers for why they were attacked in Afghanistan.

No reason for his continuing headaches.

No solutions to any of his problems.

Returning to the cottage, Sam dropped his dirty boots outside the door and went upstairs to shower. Refreshed and redressed in clean jeans and a sweatshirt, he popped the top off a bottle of Gordon Biersch's Marzen and rather than swigging from the bottle, poured the golden liquid into a glass. Time to get re-civilized, he supposed. Scratching at his beard, he momentarily considered shaving, but quickly dismissed the idea as too much work.

Sprawled on the sofa Sam stared at the glass in his hand. The moisture slowly rolled down the outside. Inside, fine bubbles rose to the foam. He pondered his life—the *before* when he was active and living in Paris and the *after* as the caretaker, now moving in the slow lane like an old man whose days were reduced to fire watching, disappearing animals, migraines, and his early to-bed-nights.

He couldn't imagine living like this for years on end. Rescuing people had paid well, and his income, invested by Jon Malcolm's family brokerage firm in Milwaukee was now a lucrative portfolio. Not billions like the Sobrantes, but enough that he could have a good life, even if he never worked again.

Nevertheless, he'd miss the adrenal rush of a new rescue and afterward returning home to his apartment in Paris. The vibrant neighborhood cafés, late night dinners with friends, and their boisterous discussions fueled by wine and great food. Pseudo arguments that morphed into contentious debates that no one won, but invoked a hilarity everyone enjoyed.

The spontaneous trips to Greece, Spain, and London for pleasure were now just memories recalled while watching logs burn. He could go back whenever he wanted, he reassured himself.

Now, he rarely left the estate except for quick trips to buy supplies and food and pick up an occasional takeout order from restaurants in Saratoga. He'd thought about contacting his family—his mom and dad, twin brothers, sister, but decided nothing good could come of opening old disappointments, no matter what Flynn believed about forgiving and forgetting.

You can't forgive if you can't forget. Sam would never forget his father's words the last time he saw him—*I'd rather you were dead.*

Tomorrow, he'd call the doctor to get answers as to why he was still having headaches, and then he'd clean his guns, do a little target practice, take longer runs through the hills, hone his skills to get back to work, back to his real life with good friends, good food, good sex.

Good sex. How long had it been since he'd been with a woman?

The shrieking of the alarm ended his reverie. He padded barefoot to the small room off the kitchen, formerly the grandmother's sewing room it was now filled with a long desk and four monitors connected to the multiple wireless security cameras he'd installed around the Casa and down the driveway.

A woman, dressed in black, stood at the gate, a red Prius parked behind her. She punched at the numbers on the keypad with futile attempts because Sam changed the code every other day.

"Come on, lady, go away."

As if she'd heard him, she stopped, looked directly into the concealed camera. Her face filled the monitor's screen, exotic dark eyes, and dark hair. He watched as she stood back and studied the gates as if contemplating climbing over. She turned back to her car. A second camera picked her up as she drove down the service road that ran by the stables west of the compound.

Sam swigged the last of his beer and prayed she'd drive away. Instead, she parked, got out, and tested the back gate. Finding it locked, she walked rapidly along the fence line and disappeared into the woods.

A bad feeling ran through Sam, a drop in his stomach followed by goose bumps that darted up his neck, his intuitive signals of trouble. Big trouble. Crazy people were drawn to the estate all the time. And this woman seemed more determined than others to get inside.

He called Sheriff Deke Farelle, quickly explained the situation, and then slipped on a pair of socks, and laced up the boots he'd left by the door.

Sam knew his long, hard-ass day had just gotten a lot longer and a lot harder.

There was no sign of the woman as he jogged down the path and made his way to the west corner, beyond the stables and the paddock where the coyote had disappeared.

Dealing with trespassers was problematic. When Sam first arrived, Bernie warned him to be cautious. If you manhandle them, they'd have you arrested and sue the estate for assault and battery. If they got injured, the courts might award them damages even through they were on the property illegally.

Sam paused. Listened. And then moved quickly. She'd be impossible to find when it got darker. Striped shadows were already elongated in the late afternoon light. About six yards from Sam, the golden leaves of the sycamore tree, highlighted by the sunset, began to shake.

A squirrel chattered noisily. Birds flew straight up and then resettled in an adjacent tree.

A dark figure climbed the trunk of a leaning tree.

Advancing without perceptible movement, Sam tracked the woman quietly so as not to startle her and make her lose her balance and fall. He paused beside a large madrone tree, mutely commanding her to give up, turn back, and go home.

The woman crab-crawled on hands and feet along the sloping trunk that extended high above the fence. Then, straddling the tree as if she were riding a horse, she paused and looked around planning her next move.

Sam admired her maneuvers; it's exactly what he'd have done if he were the one breaking and entering.

Then she stood, balancing precariously.

Don't jump! Sam willed her to wait until he got underneath to catch her. But before he could move, she leaned forward.

Arms spread wide.

She threw herself off.

Grabbing a sturdy limb on the next tree, she swung back-and-forth monkey-like, and then hand-over-hand moved closer to the trunk. Still swinging, her feet grabbled in the air.

Every muscle in Sam's body strained, aching to help her find a foothold.

She let go. Grabbed the limb below.

Rocked back and forth.

Her hands slipped.

She fell to the ground.

Stunned, the breath knocked out of her, she lay still. Slowly rising up on hands and knees, her head hung low, she breathed shallow puffs of chilly air.

"Oh, man, that's gotta hurt." A voice shattered the stillness.

Startled, she screamed, struggled to stand. "Who the hell are you?" she demanded.

The man leaned against the tree with one hand. The other fisted against his hip. He was tall and unshaven and wore a long-sleeved black sweatshirt, and hefty, dirty boots. His smile was just shy of a smirk.

"May I help you?" she snapped.

"I'm thinking that's my question, seeing as how you're trespassing and all," he laughed, the kind that makes you want to laugh with him even if you don't get the joke. She resisted.

"Trespassing?" Emboldened by his laid-back attitude, she asked again. "Who are you? What are you doing here?"

"Sam Gallagher, the caretaker. And I'm kicking you out."

"I'm not leaving." Her tone was incredulous that he'd suggest such an idea.

Sam pointed to the back gate. "Lady, I'm giving you a choice. I'll open the gate, you get in your car and go home, or you can wait for the sheriff. He'll be happy to give you a free ride, straight to jail."

She pretended to deliberate the two options and nodded as if resigned. She patted her jacket pockets, pants pockets, and then looked around frantically. "I lost my car key." She pointed toward the leaning tree. "When I jumped... I, uh, it must have fallen out of my pocket. Could you look? Would you mind? I twisted my ankle when I fell."

Sam grumbled about damsels in distress but went to look under the tree where she'd fallen. As soon as he started looking for the keys, she took off running for the Casa.

The thumping of his boots close behind told her she couldn't outrun him. Halfway up the slope by the tool shed, she stopped, turned to face him, and pulled a vial of pepper spray from her pocket, finger on the button.

She was fast.

He was faster.

He knocked the vial out of her hands. It flew into the weeds.

Acrid odor filled the air.

She braced her feet in a wide stance, threw a palm strike to his nose.

He turned; the blow glanced off his cheek. "Hey now. Play nice." He grabbed her right arm.

She felt a spasm of fear. He was stronger than he looked and more experienced than she'd thought.

She bent her knees, jumped, and slammed her head under his jaw.

"Damn it—" The momentum knocked him back. Falling, he pulled her close and took her with him. They rolled down a small incline over sharp rocks. When they stopped, his thigh was pressed intimately between her legs. Her right arm trapped beneath him. The other arm he pinned over her head. Rocks stabbed her back.

His breath was warm on her neck. "We done with the foreplay?" Lifting up, he took his weight off her but held her hand captive.

She twisted her head to look at him. His eyes were dark brown like the bittersweet chocolate she hated. She steadied her breath. What was she thinking coming up here alone?

"Let me go."

"No hitting, kicking, spitting, or trying to un-man me." His smile didn't reach his eyes.

She nodded into his chest. His sweatshirt was soft against her cheek and saturated with the sweet smell of bay rum soap, smoke, and beer.

"Agreed?" he repeated, quietly.

"Yes." He got up and pulled her to her feet.

"No more funny business; time for you go home."

She studied him, this caretaker man. She'd come this far, and she had no intention of leaving.

"I am home. I'm Lauren Sobrantes."

Chapter Seven

~~~~~

"Well, that's original," Sam scoffed. Just what he needed to finish this day, a bat-shit crazy, delusional woman claiming to be the missing heiress.

"Prove it."

She brushed at the leaves and dirt on her pants. "Can't at the moment, but that doesn't mean it's not true."

"People show up here every day demanding to go inside the house or dig up the woods so they can solve the mystery of Sobrantes disappearance. But, you, you're the first to climb over the fence, get inside the compound, and then have the moxie to claim that you're Lauren Sobrantes."

He studied her—her height was about right, she had the same heart-shaped face, but her cheekbones were sharper than the last photos he'd seen. With that dark hair and dark eyes, no, she looked nothing like Lauren.

Years ago, he'd met her at a charity horse show when she was a teenager. He was home on leave. His brother, Flynn, who attracted trouble like metal to magnets, was doing community service for spray-painting slogans on the high school fence. He'd been assigned to work off his penance with two days of shoveling out stalls, watering the horses, and assisting the riders. He'd conned Sam into helping him.

Sam's job was to help the riders prepare to enter the ring, including the beautiful, and young, Lauren Sobrantes. Her sun-streaked chestnut hair had been pulled in a tight bun that emphasized her famous gray eyes—luminous and expressive with a slight tilt in the outer corners. Her eyes had pulled him in and made him want to camp there forever.

Oh, he'd been smitten all right, but she'd been too young for him; the five-year difference in ages between sixteen and twenty-one had made him feel like an old man.

This woman was not Lauren.

Definitely not.

The alarm on his cell phone buzzed. Sam punched in the code that remotely opened the gate. "Sheriff's here," said Sam. "You have about thirty seconds to leave, or he'll arrest you for trespassing."

She crossed her arms. Gave him a heart-stopping grin. "Your cheek is bleeding."

Two sheriff cars drove in the front gate and parked beyond the Casa. The flashing and rotating red and blue lights illuminated the fading light.

Deputy Sheriff Deke Farelle, hard-jawed and mean looking, gave a quick look around before striding down the path toward Sam. Another deputy followed, his hand resting on his gun. Farelle stopped a few feet from Sam. "What's going on?"

The woman broke into a broader smile as he approached. "Well, well, well, just look at you. All spiffy in that uniform and looking so rough and tough. Who knew?"

Sam rolled his eyes, swiped at the blood on his cheekbone. Now, the crazy lady was flirting with the law. He'd seen Deke in action. The man was going to slap cuffs on her and haul her away.

But Deke was silent. His head was cocked to one side, a puzzled look rutted across his brow.

"Dekie, come on, just tell this caretaker man who I am."

Dekie? How did she know his name? "She thinks she's Lauren Sobrantes," Sam said quietly.

Deke's frown deepened.

"Oh, wait a minute." Reaching up she pulled off the black wig and the covering underneath; thick chestnut hair tumbled to her shoulders. She shook her head and pushed the strands away from her face.

Deke looked even more puzzled. Sam wondered how she

kept the thing on her head during the climbing, falling, and fighting they'd done. Deke stepped closer, turned on his flashlight to illuminate the woman's face.

Wiping her hands on her pants, she reached up and popped the brown contacts from her eyes.

Deke Farelle's howl could be heard beyond the next mountain. Dropping the light, he swept the woman up and off her feet, set her down again, held her at arm's length before he pulled her in for another hug. She kissed him hard on the lips.

Sam was surprised that he didn't like the way Deke ran his beefy hands up and over her arms, smoothing her hair, cradling her face, like a long-lost lover.

"I can't believe it," Deke said as they laughed, cried, and talked over each other.

"All this time. Dammit, woman, I thought you were dead. For sure, I thought you were dead." He held her with one hand as if afraid she'd disappear if he let go.

Deke turned to Sam. "Lauren Sobrantes, meet Sam Gallagher, your new caretaker."

She. Lauren. The crazy woman gave Sam a smug gotcha smile and offered her hand. The smile turned into a grimace as Sam's hand covered hers. Turning up her palm, he saw dirt embedded in numerous cuts and scrapes.

"You can clean up in the bathroom." He nodded toward the cottage.

Sam turned on Deke the moment she'd gone. "You shitting me, man. You really expect me to believe she's the Sobrantes woman?"

"Yeah. Absolutely. I am positively sure." Deke didn't hesitate. "That's a nasty cut on your cheekbone. Did she do that?"

Sam swiped at the blood. "She could be a ringer. One of those impersonators."

"I've known Lauren since she was a kid and that's her, no doubt in my mind." Deke's voice was firm with unwavering conviction. "She always was a feisty one," he laughed.

A call came over Deke's radio. He walked away to answer it leaving Sam with unanswered questions. Deke sent the other deputy away and then returned.

"What a shock. I mean just like that, she's back. Tell Lauren I had to go. If you'd like I can send over a few off-duty guys to help with security tonight. You'll need it once word gets out she's back. I'll come by tomorrow to check on her."

Deke started the squad car and cast one last look at the cottage. "I'd sure like to know where she's been. Did she say anything before I got here?"

"We didn't get that far."

Deke studied him as if deciding whether to believe him. "Keep her safe, Sam. Because if anything happens to her, I'm coming after you."

Chapter Eight

~~~~~

A web of memories spun over Lauren when she walked into the cottage. The scent of oak logs in the stone fireplace reminded her of her beloved Nana. Her grandmother had renovated the 1850s carriage house into a cottage for herself, even incorporating the rough adobe blocks salvaged from the first hacienda. And after her death, it had become the home for the estate caretakers, Miss Etta, and her husband, Arlo.

In the downstairs bathroom, she washed the dirt from her scraped hands, splashed water over her face, and finger-combed her hair. She sighed with relief to be out of the tight, itchy wig and those dry contact lens.

"You made it," she said to her reflection. The dark circles under her eyes confirmed the terror, jet lag, and sleep deprivation of the last twenty-four hours, when she'd fled from London, the place where she'd foolishly believed that she was anonymous and safe. That safe world crashed when someone tried to kill her—again.

She'd called her godfather, Rand, who'd insisted she wait for him to come and get her. But her need to run led to her impulsive decision to book the first available flight to California under her alias, Grace Delaney. And to come straight to the Casa, instead of checking into a hotel.

This evening when the caretaker found her, she'd thought it was all over. He looked like a derelict living in the woods. Thankfully, Deke confirmed Sam was an ally because she'd obviously lost her common sense.

Lauren turned off the light in the bathroom and wandered

through the familiar open-space living and dining room. The dark pine floors, milled on the estate decades ago were wide planked and solid. They reminded her of her shop in London.

Her stomach rumbled loudly, the last time she'd eaten was on the flight from Heathrow. The offerings on the plane were a pathetic excuse for food. She found cheese and salami in the refrigerator and rolled the cheese in the slice of meat and ate as she walked about.

Nana's photos, quilts, and needlework pillows had been packed away long ago. There wasn't even a hint of Miss Etta and Arlo in the cottage. Now, a solitary framed photograph was displayed on a small table by the telephone. The caretaker man was standing by two men in full combat gear, military weapons propped beside them. Their arms were thrown over each other's shoulders, big smiles on faces covered in camouflage paint. Who was he, what was his story, and how had he become the caretaker?

She ran her fingers over the hand-hewn dining table that her grandfather had constructed from one piece of a fallen redwood tree. Memories of good times and bad were layered deep in the worn surface.

Returning to the living room and the fireplace, she picked up the iron poker and stirred the fire. Footsteps crunched on the gravel outside, followed by a long pause before the door opened. Sam stepped inside, boots in one hand.

The boots dropped. Sam flipped the switch and the room blazed with lights.

He saw Lauren with the poker. "Oh, please. Not another fight. Just whop me over the head and be done with it."

Lauren passed the poker to him. Sam threw two pieces of wood on the fire. The logs quickly flamed. In the kitchen, he wetted a paper towel, wiped at the cut on his cheekbone and the blood dried in his beard.

Lauren followed him. "That's a nasty cut. It needs to be cleaned. Got any peroxide or alcohol?" The towel he was held turned pink.

"Check in there." He nodded to the bathroom. "There's nothing upstairs." Lauren returned with a first-aid box containing a pair of snub-nosed scissors and a roll of white adhesive tape, but no astringent pads or alcohol. Pulling out a stool by the breakfast bar and pointed. "Sit. Let me look." Since she was the cause of the wound, the least she could do was help clean it up.

Blood continued to seep. She blotted it with a dry paper towel. "Hold this. Press hard. I'll wash it with soap and water, then butterfly tape it. That should hold it until you get to a doctor. Peroxide would be better."

Sam sat down. "It's okay. I've had worse and in worse conditions."

She grinned, held up a finger. "Wait, a minute…"

Along the bottom of the adobe wall, Lauren counted six blocks. She kicked hard with her heel.

Sam watched with a puzzled frown.

Lauren ran her hand over the upper blocks and pushed lightly. The lower block sprung open.

"Brilliant," Sam muttered.

Reaching in, she retrieved a dusty bottle. "AHA!" She turned back to Sam. "Nana loved secret hiding places, she used to put her jewelry in there. Jewelry and scotch. Never figured out why she hid the scotch." She held a clean towel below the wound. "Lean your head back." Tipping the bottle, she poured.

Sam jumped. "Holy shit, you are one sadistic woman."

"I'm okay. I've had worse," she mimicked and poured again.

He grabbed the bottle. "Johnnie Walker Blue! You're wasting very expensive scotch!"

"Hold on." Placing two glasses on the bar, she filled them with scotch and put them beyond his reach. "We'll have them when I'm done with you."

A hint of a smile played across his face. "You know you should wear gloves."

"Gloves?"

"Blood, diseases, HIV, hepatitis—you've got cuts on your hands."

"You have any of those?"

"No, my last blood test was good. No blood transfusions

or sex since, so I guess I'm clean."

She continued trimming tape. "Me, too."

"Me, too, what? No blood transfusions or no sex."

"Yeah. Head to the side." She pinched the edges of the cut together, taped, and then stood back to study her work. "You need stitches," she said, then handed him the glass of scotch.

Sam heated the leftover yellow chicken curry he'd made the night before. The pungent fragrance of spices and garlic filled the room. Jasmine rice and Naan bread completed the meal. He chuckled when Lauren's stomach growled in anticipation.

He spooned the curry over the rice and passed the bowl to her. She ate as if it were the first meal she'd had in a month. He waited for her to finish before asking questions. "Deke said he'd known you since you were a kid."

"Yeah, Deke's family moved here when I was four, and I got my first pony. His dad, Dan Farelle was a well-known riding instructor. He taught me most everything I know about horses and riding."

"Funny, Deke never mentioned him. Does he still train horses?"

"He passed away maybe twenty years ago. I was about nine. His horse spooked on the upper trail and Dan took a header into a boulder. It was strange that he wasn't wearing a helmet. The horse came back hours later. Dad formed a search party, but by the time they found him, it was too late; he never regained consciousness. Shortly afterward, Deke and his mom moved away."

"And you stayed in touch?"

"Not really." She soaked up the last bit of curry sauce with a piece of Naan bread. "I swear I could eat curry every night."

Sam wondered if there was more to the story about Deke's family, more than she'd shared.

"So, Lauren, where've you been for the past two years?"

"London." She lifted the blue teapot Sam had placed beside her, filled his cup and then hers. She'd learned to love living in London and after she worked through the roughest part of her grief she opened her shop. She took the Underground from her apartment to Sloane Square Station, then a brisk walk past Tiffany & Co., Cartier, and the flower shop.

Each morning she'd stop and admire her store—Grace Delaney Antique Linens. She'd renamed herself, Grace Delaney, after she bought the building, started the company, and pushed her past out of her future.

The brick building was tall and narrow with the store's name scripted in black and gold vintage letters on the front window, vintage like the goods inside. She'd longed for home, but she'd felt safe and successful being on her own.

Sam sipped the amber oolong tea. "You must have used an alias to get into Great Britain? And did you also get a work permit under an assumed name?"

She shrugged. The money Rand funneled to her had created opportunities unavailable to most people.

"All this time, you've been tucked away in London, while the world speculated whether you were alive or dead."

"What the world speculated is none of my business. And not as important as my need to stay alive."

"What made you disappear?"

"I'd taken a walk with my dog, Mr. Watson. We went from the Casa to the pear orchard. Someone shot at me. Killed my dog."

Sam listened, but she wasn't sure he believed her.

"My godfather, Rand Bainbridge heard me screaming." Rand had barreled down the driveway in his jeep, but by the time he reached the orchard, the shooter was gone.

"And he got you out of the country," Sam stated the obvious. Bainbridge's reputation was well known in Sam's line of work.

Lauren gave him a non-committal smile. She swirled the tea in her cup, watched the tiny dregs drift and settle to the bottom.

"Did you come back because of the book?"

"That disgusting Anna Brownlee book?"

"Yeah, *The Ghost of Lauren Sobrantes.* The author claimed you hired someone to kill your dad because he was upset over your deviant sex life. And afterward, you committed suicide because of your guilt," he recited what he'd heard on CNN.

"Obviously, I'm not dead. Brownlee has pontificated her psychic powers on radio and television talk shows for years. My family was her favorite target for prophesying doom and gloom." Lauren pounded the table with her fist. "I plan to sue her for every penny she's got or ever hopes to get."

"So the book brought you back?"

"That and another attempt to murder me."

"What happened?"

"I got off the Underground at Sloane Square Station and was walking toward my store when a jogger ran by and shoved me into traffic." It had been so quick and terrifying, falling in the path of an oncoming taxi. Horns blared. Tires squealed. "Someone grabbed me and pulled me back. The taxi swerved, missing me by inches."

"Could it have been an accident? Just a clumsy jogger?"

"You don't believe me?"

"I didn't say that."

"Isn't that how people get away with murder, Sam? Make it look as if it's an accident. Just an unfortunate death?"

"If the killer is skilled, that's exactly the way it happens."

Lauren gathered their dishes and carried them to the kitchen. She was tired of trying to convince people she'd been a target for murder. "Thank you for dinner. It was outstanding. I'll get my things and go over to the Casa, get ready for bed."

"You have to stay here tonight or go to a hotel. The Casa is empty."

"What!" The color drained from her face. "Where's the furniture? The antiques, the paintings, all my things?" She sat down in the chair opposite him.

"Bernie put them in storage. Too many attempted break-ins after you disappeared."

That made sense. People would vandalize the Casa if they could.

"You can use the guest room. You know where it is."

"I'll just get my suitcase and move my car."

"With the key that you lost in the brush—"

"Or with the keys I left in my purse on the front seat."
"You have something against that thing called truth?"
"Truth is highly overrated. Or is that patience?"
"Somehow, I doubt you'd recognize either one if they bit you on the ass. Stay here. I'll bring your car around."

A slice of the waning moon peered through hazy clouds. A barn owl called, a response echoed through the trees. Nocturnal creatures scuttled through the dry leaves.

Sam swept the beam from the woods to the meadow. Through the darkness, eyes reflected back. A skunk waddled along the edge of the meadow, but no coyotes were in sight.

The keys were where she'd said. He drove the Prius inside the compound, then closed and re-locked the gate, and parked her car in the garage next to his Land Rover. Opening the trunk, he pulled out a small, expensive suitcase and opened it. She'd packed light. The bag held a pair of black pants and blue jeans, a red sweater, jacket, silk robe and t-shirts, and a few cosmetics and personal items. He picked up her black Coach purse and did a quick check of the contents.

Puzzles had always intrigued Sam, the anticipation of searching for the minuscule pieces, discovering where each one fit, and putting them together for the whole picture. Usually, he couldn't leave them alone and rarely walked away before he finished.

There were too many missing pieces with this woman. Had there actually been attempts on her life? Or were they accidents? A hunter in the wrong place? A klutzy jogger who fell into her?

Was the Brownlee book factual? Was she involved with her father's murder?

He didn't plan on sticking around to put this puzzle together. Instead of schlepping her bags, he'd pack his own, catch a plane, and meet up with Flynn and Jon to find out what went wrong on their last mission. In the morning, he'd call them and tell them he was on his way, migraines or not.

Caretaking a rich woman with delusions of persecution wasn't a job he wanted. The last time he'd gotten involved with a wealthy woman, he'd spent six months in an Italian prison.

Chapter Nine
~~~~~

Water sang through the pipes of the upstairs bathroom. Sam visualized Lauren stepping into the shower, hot water sluicing, between her breasts, and flowing down her thighs. He imagined her slipping on that silky thingy in the suitcase he'd placed in the guest bedroom.

Good god-almighty, he had a boner coming on. She was one beautiful woman, wide-set gray eyes, and full lips that could make a man lose direction in a heartbeat. The shower turned off, and the cottage settled into quiet as if he were alone.

Sam scrubbed his face and worked to control his lust. Pieces of tape peeled off. She was right. He needed stitches. Scars were too identifiable in his line of work and increased the possibility of being recognized.

He picked up the house phone and tapped in a local number.

"Hello."

"Zach, it's Sam." A cold silence filled the line.

"Where are you?"

"La Lumbre, the Sobrantes estate."

"Really? You all right?"

It was harder than Sam expected. "I got cut, need stitches."

"You bleeding? In shock? Can you drive to my office?"

"I have to stay here. Will you come?"

"Give me twenty minutes."

Dr. Zachary Gallagher arrived fifteen minutes later, clean-shaven, horn-rimmed glasses, and dark hair like Sam's, but cut shorter and well styled. Of the four Gallagher brothers, they looked the most alike, both six-two with dark brown eyes. As teenagers, Sam was mistaken for Zach's brother's twin, rather than Gregory. They'd pranked people by trading places. Sam hadn't seen Zach since the family blow-up years ago.

They gave each other an awkward hug.

"You'd think with all your training, you'd learn to duck," Zach teased.

"Just bullets." Sam wasn't about to explain that a woman bested him in a hand-to-hand skirmish.

"Let's see what you got going here. I need a strong light."

Sam brought a lamp to the table while Zach washed his hands.

"How've you been?" Zach asked as he laid out a suture kit. He slipped on latex gloves, cleaned the cut, and injected lidocaine.

"Good," Sam said, relieved that Zach concentrated on the suturing rather than small talk.

"You'll want to keep it dry." Zach rattled off instructions when he finished. "You want something for pain? It can hurt like a bitch when the numbness wears off."

Sam's cheek felt icy and swollen. "I'm good."

"Still having those headaches?"

"Headaches?"

Zach continued packing up. He looked away and then turned back to his brother, chin raised in defiance. "Yeah, headaches—like the ones you had after your coma."

"You know about this...how?"

"We were there with you. In Germany."

"We? Who was there?" Sam didn't like where this is going.

"Your family, Sam. Remember your family—Mom, Dad, Greg and me, Flynn, and your sister, Brianna, who blew off her big interview for the job at CNN. She flew over from London to be with you."

"Flynn!" Flynn must have called in the whole family and never thought to mentioned it. He probably made everyone in the hospital promise they'd not tell him he'd had visitors.

"Yeah, Flynn. He called us because he didn't think a brother should die alone. We didn't know if you'd make it through the next hour, much less the next day. When you came around, we knew you wouldn't want us there. Dad refused to leave you. He stayed at a hotel nearby until you were discharged."

"Tell me, Zach, was Dad praying for me to live or die?"

Chapter Ten
~~~~~

Early morning in Silicon Valley.

"That Sobrantes woman is back."

"Yes, I heard," he said through clenched teeth. "I've had her under surveillance for weeks. One of my men flew back with her from London."

If the man had done his job in London, this would be over. And when he had a second chance, he'd let her slip by him at the airport.

"How do you want me to handle it?"

"Get rid of her. I don't care how you do it." The longer she remained alive, the more dangerous it was for him.

"It's going to cost you a few big ones."

"Just do it. Kill the bitch!"

Chapter Eleven

~~~~~

Sam leaped to his feet. Half asleep, he braced a hand against the wall. His bedroom was dark. The clock read 2:30.

He waited. There. There it was again, a tiny sound of metal against metal.

He slipped on black sweatpants and a green t-shirt, slid open the top drawer of the desk, removed a small Sig Sauer, and released the safety. Holding the gun at his side, he opened the bedroom door and moved along the dark hallway.

The guest room door was closed.

He paused. Listened.

Another ping. Adrenaline pumped his heart rate higher. He took a deep, controlled breath.

The house alarm was still on. No one could have by-passed the security system or broken into the cottage without it going off.

Tap. Chink. Scrape.

At the top of the stairs, still concealed in the darkness, he hesitated, then made his way slowly down the steps. The glow of a small light exposed the culprit in the kitchen. Soundlessly, he crossed the living room.

Lauren jumped. Squealed. Her hand flew to her heart. "For heaven's sake, stop sneaking up on me!" She stomped her foot and placed the bottle of milk on the counter with a thunk. "Did I wake you? I tried to be quiet." Her anger changed to alarm when she saw the gun.

"It's for burglars, not kitchen sneaks. What is this?" The kitchen he'd left immaculate after dinner was now a clutter of pots and pans scattered across the counter intermixed with eggs, milk, and a loaf of unsliced French bread.

"Breakfast. I'm still on London time, and I'm hungry." Her stomach growled as if to emphasize the point.

"You've got one noisy stomach." He turned and walked into the security room. She followed, poised in the doorway like a skittish animal ready to bolt until he put the weapon on safety, and stored it in the desk drawer.

He surveyed the monitors. Each displayed the status of areas around the estate, and the main entry off Congress Springs Road. Deke's man sat in his car at the first gate, the glow of his cigarette visible.

The second car parked by the compound gate was empty. Sam adjusted the view to find the other man, Freddie Upton walking back and forth, a high-powered rifle across his shoulder.

"The place is wired to the max," Lauren said from behind Sam.

Her soft fragrance of roses and musk filled his senses, the rustle of her silk robe made him want to turn around, take her in his arms, the way Deke had done. He wanted to run his hands over her, bury his face in her hair, and kiss her neck, her mouth. Take her upstairs and satisfy his hunger and hopefully hers.

Sam was not one to seduce a woman just for one night of sex, not like Flynn who had frequent and casual hookups. While Sam was usually cautious and protective of his emotions, all bets were off with this woman. He forced himself to think of football to override the images of her body, naked.

"Who installed the security?" she asked, bringing him back to reality.

Electronics and engineering—now there was a safe topic. Sam explained the efficiency of the technology and went into minute detail how the system was programmed.

Lauren chortled, "Way too much information, all I wanted to know was who did the installation."

"Right," he answered tersely "I did. And it's important that you know how it works, so you're confident you're safe."

"It's a conundrum, isn't it?" she said pensively, watching the screens flash with numerous pictures.

He turned to face her. "What? Being safe?"

"When you lock people out, you're locking yourself in. I'll be living in prison."

"A very nice prison. One that keeps you alive." Sam challenged. How could anyone complain about living on this estate?

"I wonder," she paused, looked into his eyes. "Is it the way I want to live my life?"

"When you consider the alternative is damn permanent, I'd say, yeah." Sam stood, took her by the elbow and led her to the kitchen. "Now, let's get you something to eat. It's too early for such deep-thinking."

"You don't have to bother. I can do it." She pulled her robe tighter, tying the belt in a knot which emphasized the outline of her breasts. She put a small saucepan on the stove and turned on the burner. Then, reached for the milk. "Do you have any vanilla?"

The empty pan heated. Sam removed it from the fire.

"Wait, I need that." She reached across the burner. Her sleeve hung over the open flame.

Sam grabbed her arm, swung it up, and clamped the sleeve in his hand. He turned off the burner. "You are a kitchen-disaster." He pointed to the other side of the counter. "Go. Sit."

"Hey, wait a minute." She rolled back the sleeve of her robe. The odor of scorched silk permeated the room.

Sam quirked an eyebrow.

"I'm not that bad," she grumbled, but she sat.

"Tell me what you were attempting to create?" He waved a hand over the chaos on the counter.

"French toast. But, I couldn't find any vanilla and cinnamon, and then I thought maybe hot chocolate, but didn't find the cocoa."

Sam quickly reorganized the ingredients and pans. "We'll start with French toast." His movements were efficient and decisive. He gathered cinnamon, ginger, cardamom, and vanilla and placed them next to a yellow mixing bowl. Taking a bottle of maple syrup from the refrigerator, he set in a bowl of hot water and put it aside. He pulled out a bamboo cutting board and sliced a thick loaf of French bread.

Lauren stood. "I can do that."

Pointing the knife in her direction, he said sharply, "Stay. This is a one-butt kitchen, and my butt is the only butt allowed in here. No knives, you'd slice off a finger."

Lauren laughed, shook her head. "Sam, I, uh..." She stared at his face.

Sam followed her gaze and raised his hand to his cheek. The bandage was gone leaving a row black knots along the cut.

"You got stitches?"

"Yes." He washed his hands, then placed a large skillet on the burner and added a small amount of oil.

"Don't tell me you did it yourself?"

"Not this time." He whisked the eggs and milk together, added unmeasured amounts of the spices and vanilla like the celebrity chefs on television.

"When did you go the clinic?"

"Didn't." He dipped the bread in the egg mixture.

"Are you going to tell me or is this going to be a twenty-questions game?"

"No." He slipped the egg-soaked slices of bread into the heated oil. Sweet fragrances of cinnamon filled the air. French toast had been the first recipe his mother had given him with the assignment of creating a new dish from standard ingredients of bread, milk, and eggs. He wouldn't want to tally up the number of failures he'd eaten.

Lauren gave up the questioning and sat silently, watching him cook. Within minutes, he plated the golden French toast, arranged two slices of orange on the side, and passed it across the counter to her, along with a small pitcher filled with the warm maple syrup. She took the first bite, closed her eyes, and gently rocked, emitting small mewing sounds.

"Oh, my god, Sam! This is like a taste explosion in my mouth. I've never eaten French toast like this before." She continued the tiny noises like a woman in the throes of passion, making him remember how soft she felt underneath him when they'd fought.

Sam possessed the remarkable ability to control his body,

to block out everything when sitting in a sniper hide for hours without moving, without reaction to biting bugs, slithering snakes, and unbearable heat or cold. But watching this beautiful woman lick the syrup off her bottom lip blew every inch of that control.

Lauren concentrated on her eating.

Sam concentrated on the 49ers, silently reciting the name of every player on the roster for the past three years.

Lauren pushed her plate away. "Sam, this was the best I've ever eaten. Curry for dinner, French toast for breakfast. Where in the world did you learn to create such great food?"

Sam shrugged off the question. "With my mom's cooking, it was every man for himself. My brothers and I learned to make our own food. I liked to experiment. Sometimes a dish worked, other times, not so much."

He saw no reason to mention he'd spent a few summers at the Culinary Arts Institute of San Francisco when he was younger. It would raise questions he didn't want to answer.

"I'll bet every woman you've ever cooked for proposed."

Who was last woman he cooked for before Lauren? Cosima? Ah, yes, Cosima on the yacht. Italian Rivera. Pasta Bolognese. She'd bet him he couldn't make the dish better than her mother's recipe passed down through generations of Italian women. If he did, the payoff was that she'd do anything he wanted in bed, and if he didn't, then he'd have to fulfill her whims. They had a roaring cook-off, and he'd won. It was a win-win situation that night and the following nights for several weeks.

"Not really," he said somberly, remembering how the relationship with Cosima ended. "No, no marriage proposals."

Lauren and Cosima had a lot in common. They were both beautiful women, strong-willed and wealthy. Both emanated sexuality and the promise of a good time. As much as he was attracted to Lauren, he couldn't, no, he wouldn't get involved. Not with another woman like Cosima.

Lauren watched Sam's demeanor change. Puzzling. She'd asked about women. Marriage. Maybe he played on the other team, as they say, and then quickly dismissed the thought. She could tell when a man was interested and there had been a zing between them when he'd taken her down yesterday, his body heavy on top of her. And she'd seen the look he'd given her in the security room, his eyes roaming over her breasts.

No, it had to be a woman. Someone he cared for, or perhaps, still cared for?

She passed her plate. Sam rinsed it under the hot water and placed it in the dishwasher. Selecting a clean saucepan, he filled it with milk. His movements choreographed like a dancer.

The man was an oxymoron. An excellent cook who made the best breakfast she'd had since, well, she couldn't remember when. But his muscular body, tats on his arms, and the cut on his cheek above his beard gave him a tough, bad-boy image. He was the ultimate *bad-boy* that every momma warns her daughter not to mess with; but even momma would have to admit Sam Gallagher was one sexy guy with his dark beard, long hair, and a row of tiny black stitches along his cheekbone, and a mouth—a mouth that was smiling as if he could read her thoughts.

Her breath caught, her nipples hardened. She was having a serious case of lust for a man she'd just met. Crossing her arms over her breasts, she struggled for composure. "What are you making now?"

"Hot chocolate. Isn't that what you wanted?" He grated a block of chocolate into the pan of milk.

"I'll make dinner for you when I get settled in the Casa. It has a multi-butt kitchen. I have a great pork loin recipe."

"I'll buy new batteries," he replied without looking up.

The *non sequitur* stumped her. "Batteries?"

He whisked the sugar and vanilla into the milky mixture, then added a dash of cayenne. "For the smoke alarm." The smile that played at the edges of his mouth made him even more inviting.

"Oh, of course, how else would I know when it's done?" she said drily, barely containing her grin at their repartee.

He poured hot cocoa into two mugs, passed one to her. "On a first name basis with the London fire department, were you?"

"Nice guys, they stopped by often as a matter of fact."

Sam laughed, raised his mug in a salute. Laughing changed his entire appearance. His face softened, dark eyes gleamed, and the grimness around his mouth momentarily softened. There was something vaguely familiar about Sam Gallagher— something that made her wonder if they'd crossed paths before.

Sam cleaned the kitchen and then stretched out on the sofa after Lauren went to bed. He stared unseeing into the fire, adrift in memories of the first time he saw her at that horse show years ago.

She was older now, but he refused to let anything get started with this woman. It was too dangerous to even think about.

He drifted off to sleep with dreams that lurched from Cosima to Lauren, hot cocoa, dead bodies, and missing clues.

Chapter Twelve

~~~~~

Sam's satellite phone rang early Saturday morning, pulling him out of a deep sleep.

"CNN is reporting that Sobrantes woman was found, and she's at the estate." Jon Malcolm never bothered with niceties, like hello. "Is she with you?"

Sam threw back the Afghan and sat up. He wasn't surprised that the news of her return had leaked so quickly.

"Morning, Jon."

"True?" Jon's voice was brusque.

"She dropped in last night." Sam ambled to the security room. He studied the monitors. Three network trucks were parked off Congress Springs by the first gate.

"So she's alive?" Jon brought Sam back to the conversation.

"Very much so, and alone." Sam didn't detail their confrontation.

"No security?" Jon asked, incredulously. That fact raised warning flags for Jon, who was all about security.

"None." Sam could hear Jon's questions churning through the line.

"So, a woman shows up alone, no security? You sure it's her?"

"Confirmed by a reliable source."

"What did you find out about those headaches?" Jon abruptly changed directions.

Sam hesitated. "Nothing yet." He was surprised that he'd not had another one.

"I'll send Flynn with the plane when he returns. You can get checked here or at the Mayo Clinic."

"When's he due back?"

"A few days."

"Did you talk to Senator Phillips?"

"His office is stonewalling me, but I'll get him. I know his favorite restaurant. I'll track him down tonight. Sam, be careful. Don't get pulled in and get caught up with this woman."

"Enough, Jon," Sam snapped.

"For God's sake, be careful. Keep your head down and your zipper up."

Sam knew the routine. Unwanted publicity put the entire company at risk. "Yeah, stealth and out of sight."

"Need I remind you of Italy? I can't bail you out this time." Jon abruptly hung up.

This situation was nothing like the thing in Italy when Jon broke him out of prison. Nothing like it! It was entirely different. Sure, Lauren was as beautiful and wealthy as Cosima, but that's where the similarities ended.

Cosima was loose and daring with a flashing temper and a throaty laugh. She was as earthy as her country. A fisherman's daughter, she'd married well, really well. Her disappearance was never solved, her whereabouts never revealed.

Not even Jon or Flynn knew what he'd done with her.

Chapter Thirteen

~~~~~

Kyle Montgomery woke precisely at 3:35 as he did every morning. He slipped into freshly laundered Weldon sweatpants and a t-shirt for his daily workout—treadmill, weights, and yoga stretches in his home gym. At 4:35, he shaved, showered, and blow-dried his blonde hair to perfection and gave it a light spray.

It was Saturday. He dressed casually in designer jeans, a pale blue button-down shirt, and a navy blue silk and wool sweater. He slipped his feet into handmade Italian loafers before going downstairs to his study.

Seated at his desk, he read his emails, and then pressed the remote to open the panel covering the flat screen television. He watched the business news first, followed by local traffic, and weather.

Angelica, his housekeeper, quietly entered the room with a breakfast tray—a carafe of black coffee, one freshly baked apple muffin, a small bowl of blackberries, and an egg white omelet, vegetables, no cheese. She placed the tray on the corner of the desk. He nodded but didn't look up.

Kyle poured his first cup of coffee and clicked on the national and international news on CNN.

BREAKING NEWS in bold red letters flashed across the screen followed by a photograph.

"What the devil!" Kyle leaped to his feet. Coffee splashed across his sweater. He hit the pause button and blotted the dampness with his napkin.

Lauren's face was frozen on the screen. Her luminous gray eyes stared at him, a slight smile on her lips as if she were watching.

He stared back. His emotions ran the gamut of shock, anger, and relief.

But was she alive or had they found her body?

He pressed the play button and waited.

"We have reports that last evening Lauren Sobrantes returned home. Daniel Cruz is outside the Sobrantes estate. Dan, what can you tell us?"

The reporter nodded. The camera panned a long shot of the Sobrantes gate at Congress Springs Road and the heavily armed security. "The sheriff answered a call around 4:00 last night and reported that a woman, who broke into the compound, is claiming to be the missing heiress, Lauren Sobrantes. We don't have official confirmation at this point."

The report continued with aerial shots of the Casa compound. A voiceover explained the Sobrantes history including the murder of Richard Sobrantes, a prominent leader in the electronics industry, and that the case remained unsolved.

Photos discreetly showed the murder scene in the remote area of the Santa Cruz Mountains, and video of Lauren walking from the family cemetery to the Casa, flanked by her godfather, Randolph Bainbridge, and her fiancé, Jeffery Davis. A blurry shot showed Kyle following beside Lauren's uncle, Bernard Anderson, and Richard's second wife, Fiona. The report concluded with speculations of how and why the heiress disappeared and what had made her return.

Kyle shuddered. He'd never get used to it, no matter how many times he saw the photos of his friend and business partner's body, or the funeral afterward, and then the search for Lauren. It always brought up fresh anger and sadness.

"Angelica!" Kyle yelled. "Clean this." He stripped off his sweater, thrusting it at her on his way upstairs.

So, Lauren was back, he mused as he changed into a white shirt and a black sweater. He re-combed his hair and stared into the mirror.

Where had she been?

Her return could cause trouble, big trouble for everyone. But first, he had to confirm that the woman in the Casa was

Lauren, and then he'd figure out the best way to deal with it.

Lauren ran down the cottage walk to where a metallic gold Lexus SUV was parked. The man waited by the driver's door.

"It is you!" Kyle cried, as Lauren came closer. He hugged her, lifted her in the air. "I saw the CNN report. I had to see for myself. Had to be sure."

"Oh, Uncle Kyle—"

"*Uncle Kyle.* I thought I'd never hear you say that again."

Kyle hadn't changed through all the years. Lean in body and face, Kyle was metro-sexual for years before it became an expression. He preferred expensive haircuts that guaranteed every blonde hair on his head lay with precision. His shirts were always handmade and tailored to fit. Lauren suspected even his Levi's were tailored.

"Where's Marisa? Didn't she come with you? I can't wait to see her."

"She doesn't know you're back. I wanted to make sure the rumor was true. Marisa hasn't been well. She can't handle a lot of upsets. Your disappearance took a heavy toll on her, emotionally, and well, she broke down. She's never been strong like you and me, takes after her mother, you know."

What he said was true to an extent. Marisa had always been quiet and introspective, the artistic one, but Lauren knew she had more strength than people realized. Whatever her dearest friend was going through, Lauren believed their bond was strong enough to be restored. It would all fall into place if Marisa could forgive her for disappearing and not telling her where she'd gone, or that she was alive and safe.

"Well, we'll have plenty of time. I'll call her. We'll catch up. Do you know where Bernie is? I've called him several times and left messages."

Kyle hesitated as if deliberating how to respond. "Bernie is off on some wild goose chase trying to catch the broker who sold the counterfeit components to the company. I'm not sure why. It's not that serious of a problem anymore, and so far we've been able to sort them out before they get to the assembly floor."

Lauren flashed on her dad's engineer's lab book wondered if Bernie had found it. She'd follow up on that later, but for now, she led Kyle toward the cottage.

He stopped and studied the Casa across the drive. "You don't plan to live here, do you?"

"Absolutely."

"The damn thing's falling apart."

Lauren followed Kyle's gaze to her family home, seeing it through his eyes. The morning sun did nothing to soften the deterioration. In the daylight, the house looked sad, like a beautiful woman fallen on bad times, abandoned by those who'd loved her.

Paint on wooden columns was dull and peeling. Weeds grew through the fissures in the walkway. The windows with broken glass and sagging frames were in worse shape than the columns. Two years of neglect was obvious.

Three summers ago, when her life was in order, renovations had begun on the house and were to be finished before she and Jeffery were married. This was going to be their home, mostly on weekends as her family had always done. It was their quiet place to get away from the din of the valley.

Jeffery had said he thought it was a great idea. She wondered if he'd lied about that, too?

"It'll cost a fortune to make it livable." Kyle's tone was scornful.

He was right. It would take serious money to bring the Casa and the grounds back to its original glory.

"Well, I do have a fortune," she chided.

"Yes, but you don't want to spend it on an old relic like this, do you? You should just bulldoze the thing. If you insist on living up here, then build something modern and up-to-date. I can recommend a good architect."

"Thanks, but I love this old house. The Casa has noble bones. She's worth renovating. Besides, all my ancestor spirits are in this house and the cemetery. I can't just abandon them." Lauren nudged his arm. "If I remember right, you never liked it up here."

"It's too big. Too country. Too far away from everything.

I'd think you'd want a fresh start someplace else, someplace without the bad memories."

Lauren wasn't sure which bad memories Kyle had in mind. The good times with her family and friends, the holidays, parties, summer picnics worked as a balance, most of the time, to the grief of losing her mom and dad.

"I'm good for now." Her parents had loved this place with its history, its old world charm, peace, and living in harmony with the land. No, she'd never give up the Casa. She was determined to bring it back to its full splendor in honor of her family.

Kyle stopped, placed his hands on her shoulders. "I'm very relieved to know you're safe, but why did you leave? Why didn't you tell anyone where you were?"

Before she could answer a loud buzzing, like the hum of swarming bees circled overhead. "What is that?"

"Get inside!" Sam yelled as he ran toward them from the stables.

"What?"

"Get in the house!"

"Why?" She continued to look for the source of the buzzing that grew louder.

Sam leaned low, planted his shoulder in Lauren's stomach, and threw her over his back, fireman style. He jogged into the cottage.

Kyle followed, speechless.

Sam put her on her feet inside the door.

"What the hell, Sam?"

"When I say move, then MOVE!" They stood toe-to-toe.

"I don't take orders. I give them!" She struck his shoulder with her fist for emphasis.

He grabbed her hand, held it tight. "Do. Not. Hit me" His face was so close he could easily kiss her.

"Who is this man?" Kyle spoke loudly. They jumped apart. Lauren introduced him to Kyle before asking Sam, "What's going on? What was that noise?"

"Drone."

Kyle looked out the front window. "Here?"

"Yeah, here. Undoubtedly equipped with camera and audio." Sam slipped the Sig out of the holster. He'd alerted security at the gate to hunt for the drone's operator along the highway. "Stay inside."

Adrenalin pumping, he moved cautiously out the kitchen door. Stopped. Listened. The faint buzzing told him the drone, naked to the eye, was still above them taking surveillance videos.

He crisscrossed down the path under the canopy of the coastal oaks between the cottage and the stables. The buzzing grew louder as the drone dropped lower. Sam waited until he saw it through the branches. A square with four propellers, one on each corner and underneath a miniature video camera transmitting images back to a remote receiver. Someone was watching, listening, and recording. Seriously compromising Lauren's privacy and security.

He released the safety and had sighted the drone when a blur of red covered it. Sam blinked. Blinked again and then shut his eyes tight, praying the illusion would go away.

He heard the blast of a shotgun. Lauren stood to his left in the open driveway. She fired again, the recoil knocking her on her butt.

The drone shattered, pieces fell among the trees, dropping near them. Sam holstered his gun and walked to where she sat. Offering a hand, he jerked her to her feet.

"What part of STAY IN THE HOUSE, didn't you get!"

"Don't yell at me," she retorted, the gun pointing down at her side. "You're pissing off a woman with a shotgun."

Sam stared. She'd overlooked the semi-automatic holstered under his arm. "Your shoulder's going to be sore as hell tomorrow. And, your butt."

He walked away from Lauren to meet the security men rushing toward them. After assuring them everything was okay, he put them to work collecting the drone pieces and the camera. Hopefully, the recording device was dead and dysfunctional. He bagged the bits and pieces to send to Jon, who'd have the lab check for fingerprints, registration, and DNA.

Kyle came out of the cottage. "Are you all right?"

"Absolutely. Drone's gone. Would you like a cup of coffee?" Her heart pounded double time. She hated guns. And she had no idea what impulse made her grab the shotgun and take down the drone. The only time she'd used the shotgun was for skeet shooting, and she sucked at it. Now her shoulder burned from the gun's kickback, her butt hurt from getting knocked ass over teakettle, and her solar plexus ached from bouncing on Sam's shoulder when he carried her inside.

She refused to rub any of them.

Kyle declined coffee but kept watching Sam as he directed the other men. "Who is this Sam guy? Has he been vetted?"

"I'm sure Bernie checked him out before he agreed to hire him." Lauren and Kyle entered the cottage, and she unloaded the shotgun and returned it to the closet. She prayed she never had to use it again.

"Are you safe here with him?" A worried crease cut between Kyle's eyes.

She explained that Deke Farelle had assured her Sam was a good guy to have around.

"He seems a little...I don't know..."

"Bossy? Overbearing?"

"A little off?"

Lauren joined Kyle at the window. Sam with his scruffy beard, jeans, and the flannel shirt did have a drifter persona. Earlier, that morning, she'd received a call from Rand. When she told him about Sam, he assured her that Sam was the best person she could have with her and that she should hire him to be her bodyguard.

"Rand says he's reliable."

"There seems to be a tremendous amount of security around here. You must be worried about people breaking in."

"Not so much, Sam's a security expert. He's got the place covered. All the doors and windows have alarms. If one camera doesn't catch someone, there are a dozen more that will. There are four cameras at the gate, and at least three covering the Casa, inside and out, plus others hidden along the driveway. He's talking about adding more for inside the house. Every square foot of this place will soon be recorded on a DVD." She gave in and rubbed her throbbing shoulder.

"I'll take your word for it. But I think the best thing for you to do is to move to the valley."

"The valley's not for me."

Kyle checked his watch. "I'm glad you're back, safe and sound. I do want to hear all about why you left, where you've been, and why you stayed away, but it will have to wait until next time because I'm late for lunch in Willow Glen. Time flies when you're shooting down drones."

They chuckled at the absurdity of the morning.

"Please tell Marisa that I'll call her."

Kyle nodded, his expression sad. "Lauren, prepare yourself, she's not the same person you knew before. She rarely leaves the house or uses the phone. She became so depressed that I hired a live-in physician, Dr. Hansen to take care of her 24/7. Maybe when I tell her you've returned, it will be just what she needs to... to find herself again."

The woman Kyle described was not the Marisa that she'd known all her life. Was it really too much—the deaths, Lauren's disappearance, or was it something else? She'd wanted to let her friend know why she was hiding, but the risk that the killer might find out was too great for both of them.

Kyle paused before he got in the car. "I'm having a small *soirée* tomorrow afternoon to watch the football game. Why don't you join us? Some of your old friends will be there."

"Maybe, I'll let you know." She waved goodbye as the gates closed behind Kyle.

She'd ask Sam to go with her. Get her life back to normal. She snorted a laugh at the idea of the new normal—one with invading drones and Sam Gallagher, the caretaker.

Chapter Fourteen

~~~~~

By Saturday afternoon, Lauren had received calls from major networks and countless numbers of reporters from around the world. She unplugged the phone.

Deke Farelle called on Sam's satellite phone to say he was picking up pizza from Jake's in Saratoga. He took their order for toppings.

While they waited, Sam secured the estate for the night and checked with the men who guarded the entrance off Congress Springs. The Highway Patrol placed temporary No Parking signs on the sides of the road to control traffic congestion.

Lauren set the DVR to record the major networks for news and interviews with the psychic, Anna Brownlee. If Brownlee continued to spread the lies that Lauren was involved in sex clubs, and had killed her father, and committed suicide, then Tully would use them as evidence of slander.

"Pizza-man," Deke called as he entered the cottage. A wonderful aroma floated in with him. "Sausage, a mushroom, and a pepperoni." He placed the boxes on the kitchen counter and then gave Lauren a lengthy hug.

"I want one of each." Lauren passed out the plates and napkins. Sam opened three bottles of beer and Deke opened the pizza boxes.

"Watch out, Deke. She'll eat hers and yours, too," Sam warned.

"Gotta love a woman with a healthy appetite," Deke chortled. "I'm always willing to share."

Lauren bit into a slice with sausage and nodded her

approval. They chewed in silence for a few minutes.

"Does Bernie know you're back in town? Your step-mom?" Deke asked.

She reached for a slice of the pepperoni. "I haven't reached Bernie yet. Kyle said he's out of the country. I have no reason to call Fiona."

Deke took a long pull of his beer. "Your stepmother sure is a piece of work. I caught her breaking into the Casa after you left. She'd loaded her car with boxes and swore everything belonged to her."

"Nothing in the Casa was hers. I hope you arrested her."

"I knew she had no business being up here. I called Bernie. He said to throw her in jail, but I did a quick body search, then made her carry everything back inside." He guffawed at the memory. "Your stepmother's gonna shit bricks when she finds out you're alive. You know how badly she wants this place."

After dinner, Lauren moved to the sofa by the fire. The men stayed at the table chatting while they finished their beer.

"Oh, my god!" Lauren stared at the television. She pushed the pause button. Sam and Deke rushed from the table and studied the picture of a man on the screen. Lauren reversed it and pushed the play button.

The San Francisco police ask that anyone with information on the identity of this man, who was killed last night in the Tenderloin area, to contact the SFPD. The SFPD number was displayed in large letters.

"He sat next to me on the plane. I called him the Cheshire man." She explained how the man, with tufts of hair in his ears and a wide smile, had hit on her all the way from Heathrow and finally, to make him back off, she'd agreed to have drinks with him at the Mark Hopkins Hotel, but then she'd slipped by him at the airport after changing disguises in the bathroom.

"Now, he's dead."

"You're sure it's the same guy," Sam asked.

"Yes, I'm sure. This is so weird."

Deke took down the flight information and her seat number. "I'll call the SFPD from the station. They'll get an ID from the airline. I'll get back to you."

Chapter Fifteen

~~~~~

Ominous music on the television caught Lauren's attention as she and Sam put away the leftover pizza and cleaned the kitchen.

MISSING HEIRESS OR CLEVER IMPOSTER? Flashed on the television.

"What is this!" she said, turning to Sam. The voice-over continued as an assortment of photographs of Lauren—at horse shows, her engagement party, and her father's funeral glided across the screen.

"Here's what we know." The voice-over droned on as more photos of Lauren and Casa de la Lumbre floated forward from the background. "A woman shows up at the Sobrantes estate on Friday evening claiming she is the heir to the massive Sobrantes fortune.

"We have discovered that she may not be Lauren Sobrantes. In fact, she could be an imposter, named Grace Delaney, a look-alike who owns a shop in London."

Lauren turned to Sam. "How did they find out about my shop?"

He shrugged. "Not from me."

"Who else knew?" She turned back to the television.

"We invited our panel of experts who've been tracking her disappearance for two years. But first, we'll talk to our guest, author of the New York Times bestseller, *The Ghost of Lauren Sobrantes*—Psychic, Anna Brownlee."

The lights brightened for a wide, two-person shot. Anna Brownlee smiled into the camera, plump and serene, her blonde hair feathered around her face like a halo.

"This woman has obviously taken advantage of the information in my book." She held up the book like a prized trophy, pausing again for effect. "Her claim that she's the deceased heiress is absurd."

"But are you sure Sobrantes is dead? Her body has not been found."

"It will be recovered this week," Anna crooned with conviction. "Lauren's ghost came to me last night, tormented because her remains are disintegrating. She told me that her body lies between a cluster of three redwood trees and a large boulder that looks like a whaleback, half buried in the hillside." Anna's smile grew larger. "I promised that we'd find her and give her a proper burial."

Lauren paced the room. "Three redwoods? You can find three redwoods every two feet on this place."

The commentator continued, "Anna, some people wonder why it's so important to the ghost that her body is found?"

"She wants peace. Forgiveness. Her spirit is plagued with guilt over what she's done, and it won't rest until all is revealed about her father's death."

"So, you believe she is responsible for his murder?"

"I can only tell you what her ghost told me—her father was distraught over her deviant sexual lifestyle. He threatened to cut her off, and she'd be penniless. After he died, she was so overcome with remorse and shame she had no choice but to end her own life."

"This other life seems to have been a well-kept secret. But I understand you've found witnesses who can confirm what you've written in your book."

"Yes, they're here with us tonight."

"Because of the subject matter, they've asked their names not be revealed. They are in disguise to protect their privacy."

Shadowy images of people in hats, false beards, and fake noses filled the screen. Their voices were distorted, their sex undefined.

"She was sexually insatiable."

"Bondage was her favorite—whips, chains, handcuffs."

"I was Lauren's best friend, and after her father died, she seemed depressed. She couldn't live with what she'd done."

"She was the best *bleep* I ever had."

"My best friend? Who are these people?"

It was as if they were talking about a stranger with her name. The truth could never catch up with the lies on television. There would be people around the world who'd believe she killed her father because of the accusations on this show.

"Lauren." Sam moved closer.

"They're shredding my reputation with their lies." Her voice trembled. Her eyes shimmered with unshed tears.

"Brownlee is counting on you being dead. The question is—why? What does she gain by discrediting you? Who benefits if you are deceased?"

Chapter Sixteen

~~~~~

Lauren woke, her heart drubbing against her ribs. She struggled for breath as if she'd been running hard. The dream was the same recurring nightmare she'd had so often in London. Loud voices. Arguing.

But this time it included the Cheshire Man. He chased her through the woods, shooting at her, bullets flying over her head. She ran into a grove of redwoods and stumbled over her dead body buried under leaves while CNN broadcasted it live.

Lauren sat up, the echo of the voices resounding in her head. She wiped the tears from her face and turned on the bedside lamp. The show last night with Anna Brownlee was seen by millions of viewers who now believed she was a sex-crazed woman, who'd hook up with every man or woman she met.

Inevitably, other networks would carry the story. The boost of ratings for the talk shows would continue for weeks as they titillated their audiences with more rumors and innuendos. Lies would feed on lies, obscuring truth into non-existence.

Quietly she walked into the guest bathroom, stripped off her nightshirt, and stepped into the shower.

How do you fight for your reputation with the media? There'd always be people who believed the worst about you. *Well, you can't follow them all home and convince them of the truth, now can you?* One of her dad's favorite quips when she'd complained about interviews and articles that distorted the truth about the family.

She wiped water off her face, poured shampoo into her

hands, and lathered her long hair. *No, I can't follow them home. But I can tell my truth after I sue the hell out of Anna Brownlee and the network that ran the program.*

Lauren dressed in jeans, shirt, and a sweater and plaited her hair in a braid. She slipped downstairs, snagged a piece of leftover pizza, turned off the alarm, and walked out the back door.

Sunrise streaked the sky in reds and oranges. A sign of rain, she supposed. One of Deke's men followed her at a discreet distance as she strolled toward the sycamore trees beyond the stables.

Don't let others define you—another one of her father's sayings. Brownlee had defined her as a sex-crazed maniac, a killer, and a suicide victim.

Lauren sat on the stump by the woodpile, slowly eating the slice of sausage pizza. *How do I define myself?* She knew she wasn't a killer or sex fiend. But who was she? A victim? Survivor?

Who was she going to be in the next phase of her life? Swallowing the last bite, she wiped her hands on her pants and stood when she saw Sam walking toward her carrying two cups of coffee.

He had a predator's gait—moving easily with a sharp thread of tension, alert, and on guard. A powerful man and one you'd want as a friend, rather than an enemy.

"What are you doing sneaking out?" he grumbled, pushing a cup toward her.

"Sneaking?" She sipped the hot brew, pleased to find it precisely to her liking. "I took a walk. You have a problem with it?"

He looked around.

"What are you looking for?"

"Anything. Everything. This place is too remote to be totally secure. A sniper could be anywhere."

"So, I should just stay inside?"

"Great idea. Let's go."

"I am not hiding anymore. If someone wants me dead, then have at it. Kill me." She moved away, spread her arms wide, and turned in a slow circle. "Hey, Mr. Sniper Man. Take your best shot!"

Sam threw his arm around her and pulled her tight against his body. His coffee splattered. "Damn it. Stop tempting fate."

"You don't believe in fate. I know you don't."

He pushed her away. "You should live in town. Someplace with security."

She felt cold without him. "A smaller prison, you mean."

"I'm sure any prisoner crammed in a jail cell would gladly trade places with you."

"Sam, I just want my life back!"

"Well, you can't have it, Lauren. You'll never get your old life back."

Looking away, she fought the escalating emotions. "I know I have to make a new life for myself, but how can I even begin until I have answers? I either find out who and why my father was murdered or I'll be—"

"Dead." Sam threw the last of his coffee in the brush. Lauren stood and did the same, leaving her cup beside his on the stump.

"Then it won't matter, will it?"

"You keep taking senseless risks, and it won't matter sooner, than later."

"I don't take senseless risks, Sam."

"Really? What was that little callout a minute ago—take your best shot? Or the way you climbed over these damn trees to get into the compound? Why didn't you press the call button at the gate and come in as a normal person?"

"I thought the place was empty."

"So, you were going to break into the house and just make yourself at home?"

"May I remind you that this is my home!" Lauren challenged. "I was coming home, not breaking in, exactly."

She marched off. Conversation. Over.

At the first sycamore tree, she paused and rubbed her hand over the faint carving on the trunk, lost in her own thoughts.

"What the hell were you thinking, climbing over these trees?" Sam's harsh voice interrupted her musings.

"I was thinking it was a lot easier when I was fourteen and

captain of the vaulting team at Garrod's Farm. And how glad I am that I'm in such good shape and can still do acrobatics."

"What if you'd fallen? What if you'd knocked yourself out and there was no one here to find you?"

"But I didn't—"

"Well, you could have," his tone, reprimanding.

"Sam, I did not fall. I did not knock myself out," Lauren said, patiently.

"And you don't call that a crazy, senseless risk?" He searched her face. "Whoever's been trying to kill you could have followed you up here, and your body would've been found under some redwood tree."

Sam was right. She had taken a risk, but after the last attempt on her life in London, she wanted to be home. Home where people knew who she was. Common sense said to be cautious. But common sense hadn't factored into her need to be here.

"Have you ever wanted something so badly you're desperate?" she asked, softly. The estate was her Zen place, a quiet, healing place and like the swallows faithfully return to Capistrano, she had to return to the Casa where she'd known the most happiness.

"I should cut the tree down," Sam muttered under his breath.

"No! These are spirit trees, over a hundred years old. It's part of my childhood. Marisa and I had our first tea parties under these trees from the time we were old enough to hold a teacup."

"Marisa?"

"Kyle Montgomery's daughter."

"The guy who was here yesterday?"

"She is my best friend. We grew up together, and when we were eight, we decreed ourselves blood sisters in a ceremony under these trees." The trees had been a special place throughout her life. Jeffery had proposed to her under the sycamore trees and he'd carved their initials in a heart. But the man she'd vowed to love forever betrayed her.

Chapter Seventeen

~~~~~

Lauren led the way up the slight incline to the stables. Sam unlocked the barn doors and pushed them open. Dust particles floated in shafts of light from the upper windows. Four horse stalls separated by a wide aisle were empty, their gates open, feed bins grimy with moldy hay, and rat droppings.

The classic stable was cold and dreary as if waiting to be awakened and brought back to life. When Sam switched on the lights, the fans above the stalls turned slowly, stirring up more dust. Lauren wiped a cobweb off her face and out of her hair. "Needs a good cleanup."

"Where are your horses?"

"Rand took them to his place. He'll bring them back when I get the stable back in shape."

"You had a black horse, didn't you?" Sam asked.

"A black horse? How did you know?" Brishan was an Andalusia gelding, sixteen hands high, and black as a moonless night.

"I saw you ride in the Menlo Charity event. You were about sixteen. I worked the show that weekend."

"I remember that show. I was seventeen. You were there? I don't remember you."

"You were doing the fancy riding."

"Dressage?"

"You'd lost your hair thing."

"My hair bow. Yes. You helped me find it." She studied Sam's face, trying to visualize him without the beard and the row of black stitches across his cheekbone. "That was almost twelve years ago."

"At least," Sam agreed.

"Last night, I felt there was something familiar about you. You were there with your brother—Frank. Fred. No, Flynn. He had to do community work for something. Right? You were in the army."

"Navy. Yep, that was my brother."

Lauren picked up a pitchfork laying in the aisle. "Did you know every girl in the show was madly in lust with you?" She tossed the words over her shoulder as she walked away.

Sam chuckled. "No." He'd only had eyes for Lauren that day.

She turned back. "For the longest time, I had a photo of you and me that Marisa took when you helped me mount up." Sam had been looking up at her, and she was leaning down toward him as if to kiss him goodbye.

"I kept it for months. Used to look at it every night."

"Did you dream about me?"

"Oh, yeah, then I tore that picture up." She put the pitchfork away, closed the remaining gates, and then walked toward tack room and office. "And burned it."

Sam trailed behind her. "Burned it?"

"When I found out who you'd gone home with after the show."

"Oh, yeah."

"Her nickname around the barn was *Sin-Sin*-Cindy."

"Got it."

"She was a strong rider."

"I remember," he muttered.

"She loved night riding."

Sam groaned.

"What she really loved was sharing the intimate details with everyone at the next horse show."

Sam urgently wanted to change the subject. "I guess what happened with your dad sidetracked your equestrian career."

"Sidetracked?" Lauren turned on him, body rigid and eyes narrowed. "Sidetracked means you get back on the rails and start again. His death was a crash-and-burn-full-train-explosion.

75

Completely derailed. Destroyed. There are no tracks left."

Compassion washed across Sam's face. He reached for her.

"Don't." Lauren threw up her hands to ward him off. "I don't need consoling. I sure as hell don't need your pity. I need answers!"

Sam waited, silently.

Lauren marched in front of him. "I need to know why. Who? What was he doing in that isolated area? Why did someone kill him? Why do they want me dead?"

She stopped, looked up, contemplated the gabled ceiling. "Did he know the person he was meeting? What was so important that he'd agree to meet a stranger in an isolated place like that? He wasn't a stupid man."

"No, no one could say he was a stupid man." Sam wondered if she knew AZEN had been called in to help with the investigation?

"I'm going to find out who met him that day." She punched the air between them. "Starting with Kyle's 49er party this afternoon." Decision made, she continued walking toward the tack room.

Sam hustled to catch up. "Wait up. What do you mean starting with the party? What party?"

"Kyle invited me to his house to watch the football game. I'll ask questions. Lots of questions."

"Like, oh, excuse me, but did you by any chance murder my father? No? Well, would you happen to know who did?" Sam said, sarcastically.

"I don't know, Sam. I'll think of something when the time comes."

"Are you fucking crazy? Go on, wave a red flag, and see what happens." He drew in a long, deep breath. "Let the sheriff handle it."

"Detective Ed Schott's investigation was worthless. He's got nothing. Two years. NOTHING!" Her anger echoed in the emptiness. "No suspects. He's probably given up, but I haven't. I won't."

"This is crazy."

She shrugged. "Crazy? What have I got to lose?"

"Your life?"

"What kind of life do I have if I'm constantly hiding? Waiting for someone to kill me?" She stared at him. "I can't give up, Sam."

"You'll need a reliable bodyguard."

"You applying?" She gave him a tight-lipped smile. "Rand suggested that I hire you."

"Me? No, I'm leaving soon. What about Deke?"

"He has a job." Lauren walked away.

Sam's jaw tightened. He'd go with her. Protect her as much as he could before he took off. He caught up with her. "All right, I'll go with you this afternoon. But tomorrow, you'll have to hire a personal bodyguard and a security force if you plan to live out here."

"Thank you. I appreciate you being my protector today."

"What you need is a keeper." Sam reached into his sweatshirt pocket and pulled out an apple. He polished it against his sleeve and offered it to Lauren on the flat of his hand.

She looked at the apple and then at him, her eyes sparkled. She laughed and took the apple.

As they strolled back to the cottage, Sam teased, "Did you really lust for me after that show?"

She stopped. Her gray eyes intensely searched his face. She bit into the apple. The juice ran down her chin.

Sam held his breath as she wiped it off with the back of her hand.

She chewed for a minute, and then smiled, broadcasting sex and mischief. "Oh, yeah."

Chapter Eighteen

~~~~~

"Just a few people, eh?" Sam drove past dozens of cars parked on both sides of Upper Alex Lane in Woodside. Kyle Montgomery's home sat behind a high brick wall that looked like a prison fortification. Security at the entrance checked the guest list before allowing them to enter.

Sam parked in front of the house. Two young men in red vests stood beside the driveway. They ran forward and opened the car doors. One marked a ticket, tore it off, and handed it to Sam. "Just leave the keys, sir."

Sam locked the car, pocketed the keys, and gave the kid a look. The man's smile faded to confusion.

"We won't be long," Sam said and walked around the SUV to Lauren. "You can let go of her, now," he snapped to the other man, who, wide-eyed with awe, still clutched Lauren's hand. Not that Sam could blame him for gawking. Lauren was dynamite in black high-heeled leather boots and tight black jeans that accentuated her lean body and long legs. A red sweater hugged her breasts and torso.

"Aren't you all charm and finesse," she murmured as they walked up the path where lavender and azalea bushes co-mingled with abstract sculptures.

Kyle opened the tall entry doors. An aroma of spicy grilled meats drifted through the air. He waved away the valet who'd rushed forward to explain why he couldn't park their car.

"Welcome." Kyle hugged Lauren, shook hands with Sam, and then escorted them down the entry hall to the open concept living room with its high-beamed ceiling. The kitchen and dining room were to the left. Servers, dressed unobtrusively in white, moved quickly from kitchen to the patio with loaded trays of canapés.

Cheers rose from the group congregated around the oversized television on the patio. The 49ers scored against their adversaries, the Green Bay Packers.

"This is quite the crush." Lauren surveyed the crowd milling about the house and the large heated patio.

Kyle shrugged. "Well, apparently when word got out you were coming, the people who'd previously declined changed their minds. What could I do?"

"You could've let her know," Sam countered.

"Everyone—" Kyle ignored Sam and loudly clapped his hands for attention. The guests turned, elbowing each other when they saw Lauren. "Friends, may I present, Lauren Sobrantes."

Lauren beamed a friendly smile as she faced Silicon Valley's elite, the young founders of billion-dollar companies, old money investors, hedge fund managers, venture capitalists, and CEOs and their spouses. Phone cameras clicked. Tomorrow, photos of her would show up on the Internet with creative captions, the truth optional.

Sam surveyed the group. Was Richard's killer among them? He overheard a few lewd comments—evidence that at least some had seen last night's television show.

Lauren waded into the circle chatting with people, leaving Sam behind. Then, she turned, her eyes searching for him. He pushed people aside, reached her, and then followed her gaze. A man made his way toward her like a heat-seeking missile.

Sam put a hand on her waist, felt a shudder go through her body. He leaned forward. "We can leave," he said.

She shook her head, eyes still on the approaching man.

Sam slipped his hand inside his jacket, rested it on the Sig. He kept his eyes on the man, and his hand on the gun. A buzz of excitement rippled through the crowd.

Lauren rocked back against Sam.

"Lauren, what a surprise. Welcome home." He studied Sam for a moment and then dismissed him as insignificant. "Can we talk? Alone?" He reached for Lauren.

Sam grabbed the man's hand. "Don't touch." The warning was clear.

"Sam, it's fine." She looked around. They had an audience listening to every word. She introduced Sam to her former fiancé, Jeffery Davis.

"We have nothing to say to each other, Jeffery."

"For old times, Lauren. Right over there, by the Koi pond."

Sam stepped between them.

"Don't make a scene." Lauren clutched Sam's arm. "You can watch me from here."

Sam leaned against the rough-hewn column of the patio and snagged a bottle of water from a passing waiter as he watched Jeffery lead Lauren away.

"He's a piece of work, isn't he?" The woman standing beside him was blonde with a dreamlike delicacy and a soft voice that dripped venom. She stared straight ahead, intently watching the couple.

"He a friend of yours?"

"No." She twirled the white wine in her glass before quaffing it down. "My husband."

"What is it, Jeffery?" Lauren faced the man who was once her lover, her fiancé, her future.

"Did it never occur to you to let me know where you were? That you were alive?" Jeffery's voice was petulant.

"Never did." She turned to go back to Sam.

Jeffery blocked her.

"Let's go somewhere quiet without that Neanderthal hovering about. We need to talk about us."

"There is no us, Jeffery." When she'd first met him, he was charming and seemly unimpressed with her father's wealth and her social standing. He'd made her feel special. She'd once believed he was her soul mate.

They became engaged after a long courtship. The celebration merited a two-page spread in Town and Country. Save-the-date cards for their wedding were mailed months in advance, caterers and menu selected, cake ordered, and the tents and tables reserved. After Richard's death, the three hundred hand-addressed invitations were never mailed.

"There used to be an us before you disappeared."

She paused before answering. Several people strolled by for fresh air or to eavesdrop, or to take photos for their media pages.

Lauren lowered her voice, "I didn't come back to be with you." His betrayal, a betrayal he'd conveniently forgotten was enough to make him *persona non grata.*

"Have dinner with me. I bought a house in Aptos, right on the beach. We could grill a couple of steaks, open a bottle of wine, and talk about our future."

"There's nothing to talk about."

Jeffery's expression hardened. "When a man is killed, and his daughter disappears, the first person the sheriff suspects is her lover—or lovers. It sounds like you had several that I never knew about."

"Don't be crude. You know the book is a pack of lies."

Jeffery leaned in close, his voice thick with anger. "I was questioned. Followed. The sheriff leaked rumors that they had proof that I'd murdered you and your dad."

He stepped back, his body rigid with anger. "You have any idea what it's like to have people watch you and wonder—did he do it? Is he capable of murder?"

"No, I don't. I'm sorry you were a suspect." Again she turned to leave.

"I know why your dad was shot," he called after her.

Lauren spun back to face him. "You what?"

"Richard found out that someone wanted to destroy RKB. They put a hit out on him."

"Who? Where did you get this information? Did you tell the sheriff?"

Jeffery hawked a menacing laugh. "Come away with me, and I'll tell you everything."

"Tell me now."

"What would that get me?" He blocked her path

"You're lying." She pressed by him. "I'm going to say hello

to Marisa, and then we're leaving."

"Marisa won't come downstairs."

Lauren hesitated, stared at this man she'd once trusted. "What?"

"She's crazy as a loon. Paranoid. Schizoid, the doctor says. Hides in her room all the time, afraid someone's out to get her."

"I don't believe you." Marisa was as sane as she.

"We were good together." He cupped her cheek with his hand, leaned in, his mouth close to hers.

She pushed at him and saw Sam approaching like a quiet piece of thunder. "If you value your life, Jeffery, you'll take your hands off me."

"You'll regret this, Lauren. You've no idea what's going on," Jeffery taunted as she walked away.

Sam met her halfway down the path.

"Don't." She braced her hands on his hard chest aware of the people watching. "Smile, like we're having a great time."

"I warned him not to touch you." His smile was mercenary.

"I took care of it."

"What did he want?"

"For me to go away with him; said he knew why my Dad died. We'll talk later, too many ears and cameras around. I'm going to find Marisa."

Sam watched Jeffery over Lauren's shoulder. He pulled her closer. His beard tickled her cheek. She turned her head as he leaned down. She kissed him, his lips as firm as she'd imagined. She felt his shock, and then his arms tighten around her, and he deepened the kiss.

A kiss that left her tingling and wanting more, but she turned away, leaving them both a little breathless at her impulsive action.

Marisa hid behind the patio post where she felt invisible. She watched Lauren kissing that man.

Lauren had always been in the spotlight. She was beautiful, charming, and charismatic. That's how the writers described her in those gushing magazine articles.

Marisa never cared about Lauren's fame when they were younger. It took the pressure off her and left her free to do her art. Besides, she and Lauren had a special bond—they were blood sisters.

Risa and Lulu. Marisa stifled a laugh. Sisters forever. Look how long that lasted. Lauren disappeared without a word to her. Marisa stared at her wine glass and wondered why it was empty.

Across the patio, Kyle smiled as he chatted with a group, but his eyes skimmed the crowd. She knew he was looking for her. If he found her, she'd have to go upstairs. *Can't have the crazy one at the party, no telling what she'll do.*

I'm not crazy. She checked her clothes—brown cords, brown sweater, things that were laid out for her on the chaise in her bedroom. She'd even worn shoes this time.

Silence. Marisa raised her head. And there was Lauren, beaming at her; a semi-circle of people watched them. Panic rose from Marisa's gut, squeezing so tight she couldn't breathe. She opened her mouth, but the words ricocheted inside her head, colliding in nonsense.

Lauren held out her hand. "Come on, Risa. Let's go inside."

Marisa let herself be led away by the woman she'd thought she'd never see again.

Lauren gripped Marisa's cold, bird-like hand and led her into Kyle's study off the living room and closed the door. Sam remained outside the door to ensure their privacy.

Marisa looked like a well-dressed street waif, large-eyed, with thin blonde hair, emaciated body, and frenetic movements.

"Are you real?" Marisa's voice was whispery. Her eyes searched the room.

"I'm real, Risa." What had happened to Marisa in the two years since she'd been gone? Where was the confident, strong woman?

"You were away a long time. They told me you were dead. I thought I'd killed you, too." Marisa pulled away and paced the well-ordered room, her footsteps muted on the thick Persian rug. The room, like Kyle, was precise and austere.

Tentatively, Marisa touched the antique globe on the credenza and quickly withdrew her hand. "Dad, I mean, Kyle, doesn't allow anyone in here."

Lauren studied her friend. She seemed nervous, scared. Lauren couldn't believe this was the same self-assured woman who'd taken care of her when Richard died.

"Marisa, you said you thought you'd killed me." *Too, thought you'd killed me, too.* There was no way she'd have killed Richard. She loved him. Marisa didn't have it in her to be violent.

She stared at Lauren as if seeing her for the first time. "Kill you? You're alive, aren't you? I saw you talking to Jeffery. At the Koi pond. Expensive fish. Don't play with them."

Lauren didn't follow Marisa's logic. "I talked to Jeffery."

"What do you want from me? Why did you bring me in here?" The words were spiked with bitterness.

"I wanted to see you, talk to you. Why don't you come over to the Casa? We'll take a walk by the creek like we used to do. I'll make lunch." Lauren leaned against the desk feigning calmness. As friends, they'd told each other anything and everything. Spent hours walking and talking about spirituality, boys, clothes, and fantasizing their futures.

"Jeffery has a place in Aptos. Takes all his bimbos there."

"He mentioned it. Listen, can we—"

"Just tell me. Are you screwing my husband, or not?"

Husband? Jeffery? Was Marisa delusional, thinking she married Jeffery?

"I'm not going anywhere with him."

Marisa wandered about the room, mumbling to herself. "You dumped him. I had to marry him." She stopped at the window.

Lauren joined her. Outside a tranquil garden with lanterns and water fountains was tucked between massive ferns. "You never liked Jeffery."

"Like him? I hate him. Kyle forced me to marry him." She looked Lauren up and down. "You look great. Glad you're back. I missed you. We should get together for lunch sometime."

Lauren laughed. Keeping up with this conversation was

challenging. Was this what Jeffery meant when he said Marisa was crazy?

"Do you remember when we were girls, and we created our alter egos, Risa and Lulu?" Lauren asked, tentatively.

"*The Adventures of Risa and Lulu—Girl Wonders of Casa de la Lumbre.* There was a book, wasn't there? We wrote about our adventures and how we saved the world?"

"Yes, you drew illustrations, and I wrote the story. I believe I still have my copy; do you have yours?"

Marisa looked bewildered as if holding the sequence of multiple thoughts was too much.

"Here you are!" Kyle called out as he entered the room. He introduced the man with him as Dr. Hadley, Marisa's personal physician. Hadley, a small man with an abundance of unruly gray hair, offered his hand to Lauren. It was as limp and emotionless as the rest of him. He smiled but didn't speak. Sam slipped into the room behind them and waited by the door.

"Sweetie, we've been searching all over for you. It's time for you to go upstairs and rest now." Kyle's smile was warm, his tone stern.

Marisa stepped behind Lauren as if trying to hide. Her fingers gripped Lauren's shoulder. Lauren wanted to grab her and run.

Marisa buried her face in Lauren's long hair. "Secrets. Risa has secrets," she whispered.

Chapter Nineteen

~~~~~

"I'm sorry, Lauren. I did tell you that Marisa hasn't been well. The smallest change in routine upsets her. We thought it best for her to stay upstairs during the party, but she slipped by us. I hope it wasn't too unpleasant for you. She didn't say anything, well, outrageous, did she?"

Like she'd thought she'd killed me and she had secrets. "She said was married to Jeffery Davis."

Kyle laughed ruefully. "It's true." He gestured for her to sit.

"Seriously? She said you made her do it."

"I tried my best to talk her out of it, but Marisa was determined. I think everything piled up on her. With her mother abandoning her and your mom and your dad gone, Dr. Hadley believes your disappearance was the final push. And she turned to Jeffery because he symbolized you and your family."

Kyle walked around the room as Marisa had done earlier. He straightened the globe on the credenza and then turned back to Lauren. "Hopefully, your return will bring her back to her old self."

"Hopefully," Lauren agreed. She fully intended to ferret out Marisa's secrets, even if it meant she had to maneuver around Kyle and Jeffery.

"Lauren." Kyle sat down beside her. "I have a favor to ask. This year, I'm chairman of Heavens Child fundraiser."

Heavens Child was the charity that her parents started after Lauren's brothers died at birth. She'd forgotten about the annual gala, held every year in November before Thanksgiving.

"Would you be the keynote speaker? Ticket sales and donations have been slow this year."

"And people are curious."

"Yes, but it's for your mom's charity." He chuckled. "If it means more donations for the hospital, then I'm not ashamed to use coercion. Only if you want, I'd understand if you don't."

Her presence would be a draw for inquisitive people who'd pay big bucks to dine and gawk and say they'd met her. She was now a public attraction, like a freak in a carny sideshow. But she remembered the previous fundraisers and how the donations provided additional funding for the neonatology department at the Lucile Packard Children's Hospital.

"I'd be happy to do it, Kyle."

"Perfect," he beamed his gratitude.

"Kyle, how is the corporation doing? What's the latest on the counterfeit components? You said Bernie is searching for the supplier. Do you think that will tell us who or why dad died?"

"Honestly, I haven't found any connection between the counterfeits and what happened to your dad. It's still a constant threat to the industry. Customs caught a shipment last month. The men who did the manufacturing were arrested, but the truth is we must remain vigilant."

"Rand said he's investigating a few leads, too."

"Really? Well, that's good news, I suppose. Finding the source could control the inflow. In the meantime, the new security controls at RKB have been successful in catching most of the infiltration."

Lauren wanted to know more, but Sam entered with two plates of food. Kyle excused himself and went back to his other guests. Sam and Lauren sat down in the living room to eat.

"Kyle invited us to a gala next weekend." Lauren explained that she was to be the guest of honor at the event. She kept the conversation light; too many people around to discuss Jeffery and Marisa, or Kyle's reaction to Rand's investigation.

"A what?"

"A gala with dinner, dancing, raffle—it's to raise money for the charity that my parents founded. Will you be my date?"

"Fancy?"

"If you mean do you have to wear a tux? Yes, it's a black tie affair."

"Sounds like a freaking prom." He grimaced.

"I'll buy the tux. You won't have any expense."

"If I'm still in town, I'll get my own tux. I'll be damned if I'll wear a cummerbund to match your dress."

"Thanks, Sam. You don't have to bring a corsage either." She refused to think about him leaving.

"You want to tell me what Jeffery had to say?"

"Later." She put her plate aside and then nudged Sam with her shoulder. "See the redheaded woman in the kitchen, smiling and waggling her fingers at us?"

"Yeah."

"She propositioned me earlier. Wanted to know if I'd like to do a three-way with her and her girlfriend."

Sam hooted with laughter. "Did you say sure?"

"I declined." She giggled, mischievously. "But I told her you'd love to, that's why she's coming this way."

Chapter Twenty

~~~~~

"It's blackmail. Sex for information." Sam skillfully maneuvered the Land Rover through the Sunday drivers as they drove to the Casa. They'd left the party after Sam graciously declined the *ménage à trois*, said goodbye to Kyle, and generously tipped the valets for not parking his car.

"Jeffery claims he knows why it happened." Lauren had shared the conversation she'd had with Jeffery—emphasizing his claim that Richard had proof, someone wanted to destroy the company.

"The whole thing sounds like a set-up. Did he tell the investigators?" In Sam's opinion, Jeffery lacked integrity, propositioning Lauren when he was married.

"Perhaps he did tell them. Maybe they didn't think it was significant."

"How does Jeffery know Richard had proof? What proof? Where is it now?"

"He didn't give any details. I didn't ask." Lauren sighed. "I should've just gone to Aptos with him and screwed his brains out until he told me what he knows."

The image of her naked and rolling in the sheets with Jeffery made Sam want to grab his gun. "Oh, yeah, that would work. I'm sure he'd tell you everything. The moment he could catch his breath, he'd spill it all! He's an extortionist, Lauren!" Sam hit the steering wheel with his fist. "They don't give you what you want until they've drained you dry or killed you."

"I know he's an opportunist, but what if he's telling the truth?" she yelled. "The sheriff has nothing. Sex would be a small price to pay for information. You have no idea what it's like to lose someone you love to violence."

Oh, I know, Lauren—to be with a friend one minute and the next watch their life drain out of them because your puny attempt to save them failed. The emptiness. Being alone with your guilt and the thousand what-ifs that devour your waking moments and the nightmares that steal your sleep.

"You'll not get Jeffery to admit anything by fucking him," Sam said calmly. "I could interrogate him."

"Know any torture techniques?" Lauren stared straight ahead, her voice flat.

"A few."

"Are they legal?"

"Not really."

"Go for it."

Sam knew she didn't mean it, but messing with Jeffery's head was appealing. "Let's go over it all again. What did Jeffery say?"

"That Dad found out RKB was being sabotaged. And that was why he was killed."

"The company is sound and the stock still solid, so there's been no damage, right?"

"Well, yes and no. Kyle said the U.S. Customs recently intercepted shipments of the counterfeit parts. He believes the situation is under control. Rand is still investigating and is adamant he can find whoever is behind the manufacturing. He's sure there's a connection to dad's death."

"The problem is happening all over the electronics industry, isn't it?"

"I believe so."

"Jeffery said your dad knew what was going on. Would he have confided in anyone?"

"Kyle and Bernie, I suppose."

"They've said nothing to you?"

"No, I'd think they'd tell me, but I never asked."

Television vans were parked along the road, defying the No Parking signs. Deke's men waved Sam through the Casa's entrance on Congress Springs.

"Would there be anything on your dad's computer? What

happened to his things?"

"I don't know." She'd left before the sheriff released the car. "They could be packed away with the household furnishings. Bernie was looking for Dad's lab book, but I don't know if he found it or not."

"What's a lab book?"

"It's like a journal. Bernie said Dad wrote down everything from meetings, sketches of things to patent, and phone conversations, that sort of thing. There was a book for every year, and the last one is missing."

Sam parked by the cottage. "Where would he have kept it?"

Lauren slipped out of the car and stopped to stare at the Casa. "We never checked the safe. It could be in there."

"Would Bernie have cleaned it out along with the other things?"

"He cleaned out the desk at the office. But Dad told me that he and I were the only ones who had the combination to the safe."

A cold wind blew across the trees carrying a promise of badly needed rain. Lauren led the way across the lawn, up the wide steps to the portico. Sam unlocked the door. Inside the air was stale. She waited in the dark foyer while he switched on the lights and turned off the alarm system. They walked down the shadowy hall to the study, their footsteps resounding in the emptiness.

The study was the only room in the Casa that hadn't been severely remodeled over the past decades. It maintained the rich paneled walnut of the 1900s. Lauren ran her hand over her father's massive mahogany desk. Too heavy to move, it had been pushed aside.

Sam looked around. "Where's the safe?"

On the opposite wall, Lauren pushed a concealed button. The four-foot carved panel squeaked open to reveal the safe. She tapped in a combination of numbers, but the safe remained shut. She tried again, still nothing.

"You're sure you're the only one with the combination?

What about Bernie or your stepmother?"

"It's a possibility, but I don't think Dad gave it to anyone else." She tried the combination slower, and this time the door opened.

The safe was empty.

"Strange, there should be some papers here. Family stuff, at least." The day she'd fled, she'd rushed to the house to get her passport and remembered the safe being full of boxes. Where were they now and who had them?

"Help me move this." With Sam's help, they pushed the desk away from the wall. She opened the drawers, but they were empty.

The desk had been her favorite place to play as a child. Richard had created a hidey-hole underneath where the wood was split. He'd hidden treasure maps, coins, and chocolates for her to discover.

"I need more light." Sam turned on his cell phone light, and she crawled underneath hoping to find a note or a key.

Instead, her vision narrowed like a long tunnel. Everything moved far away.

The rapid beating of her heart obscured any sound.

She knew Sam was talking, but other voices, angry voices filled her head and shut him out.

Swallowing against rising nausea, she gasped for breath, fought to get out from under the desk and out of the room.

She stumbled. Sam caught her, carried her outside. He sat on the steps and held her in his lap.

Cold, damp air filled her lungs. Sam's soothing tone filtered out the cacophony of loud voices. The voices finally faded just as they'd done in her nightmares.

"You going to faint or hurl? You can't be weak from lack of food cause you ate your plate and half of mine."

"Did not," she said and promptly fainted.

Lauren lay on the sofa in the cottage. A man stood over her, holding her wrist in one hand, a watch in the other.

"Who are you?" He looked like Sam but without the beard and long hair.

The man laughed, his expression softer than Sam's. He nodded over his shoulder and Sam appeared beside him.

"Are you twins?"

"Sam's brother. I have a twin, but his name's Greg."

"This is Dr. Zach Gallagher," Sam clarified. "You were unconscious a long time. I asked him to come over, make sure you were okay." Sam stepped away to give her privacy while Zach checked her vitals signs and pronounced her healthy.

"Ever had panic attacks?"

"Panic? I don't think so."

"Tell me what happened."

Sam handed her a glass of water. She sat up, and he slipped a pillow behind her back. The men sat beside the sofa.

"I was dizzy. Voices. I heard loud voices like you'd hear in the Underground. Then, I couldn't see or breathe."

"She hyperventilated," Sam interjected.

"So, what are these voices saying?" Zach asked carefully.

Lauren sipped the water. "I have no idea." She explained about the dreams, waking up in a fright, still hearing the shouting, but unable to make out the words, or determine why the dreams terrified her.

"I can leave something for the anxiety if you like. It'll work short term. When you have something buried in your subconscious it keeps coming up in various ways to make you pay attention. Sometimes, if you can just relax, then the recall will happen naturally. If it doesn't, then seeing a therapist would help."

Lauren thanked Zach and declined the drugs. Sam saw his brother out. She waited as he locked up, securing the cameras and alarms.

"You ready for bed?" he asked when he returned.

He helped her up and then protectively wrapped his arms around her as they walked up the stairs.

Voices. Panic Attacks. Passing out.

Was she cracking up like Marisa?

Chapter Twenty-One

~~~~~

Every inch of Marisa's skin tingled like a thousand spiders had inundated her body and were crawling to get out. She paced from the bedroom to the sitting room, not that she could sit for very long. The chairs and sofa were rigid and uncomfortable.

While she and Jeffery honeymooned in Europe, Kyle hired a designer to redo the rooms. Gone were her childhood mementos, like her satin rabbit, dirty and worn, photos of her and her mother, snapshots with Lauren's family, and the book she and Lauren created. Kyle had assured her they were safely packed away in her closet.

Jeffery thought the room was the perfect man cave with the austere gray sectional and chairs in black leather and cold steel. She'd despised the new decor as much as she'd despised her new husband.

She'd wanted a divorce, but Kyle said no, what would people think of you divorcing after six weeks of marriage? He'd convinced her to wait.

Now she no longer had the strength or courage to go against them both.

A knock at the door interrupted her. Angelica, a thin woman with black hair and black Peruvian eyes, entered with a tray with grilled chicken, potato salad, and fruit left over from the party. Placing it on the table, she beamed at Marisa. "Clean. Plate," she said haltingly in English.

Marisa nodded her thanks and Angelica slipped away as softly as she entered. *Clean your plate.* There was nothing on the tray she'd eat.

Stripping off her clothes, she turned on the shower with the water as hot as she could tolerate. Closing her eyes, she visualized a waterfall on an exotic island where no one could find her. What would it take for her to disappear and begin her life all over again as Lauren had done?

Lauren—*Lulu* was back, wasn't she? She hadn't imagined it like before, had she?

The lines between reality and hallucinations were often blurred. She remembered the little book they'd created. She had done the drawings. She'd been good at art and on her way to being a recognized artist, but now, that too, was gone.

Marisa dried off, avoiding the mirror and the reflection of the hollow-cheeked woman with sad blue eyes. Slipping into pajamas, she searched the large walk-in closet for her copy of their book.

Adventures of Risa and Lulu—two girls, brave and true, fearing nothing, well, maybe snakes, and fat salamanders. Courageously, they saved the world from evil. They'd lived in cheerier times when Risa was brave and happy.

Marisa pulled a heavy plastic tote from the closet and emptied the contents on the floor and sorted through the smaller boxes of jewelry, old school report cards, and childhood sketchbooks. She recited what she remembered of their story, *"Once upon a time, two brave girls named Risa and Lulu, lived in the woods..."*

"What the fuck's going on?" Jeffery loomed over her.

"Nothing." She turned her back to him.

"Talking to yourself in the third person?" He walked around the jumbled mess on the floor. "You've got to stop this craziness, Marisa."

"I saw you with Lauren."

"Nothing gets by you, does it, cutie?" He stepped into his closet and pulled a fresh shirt from the drawer.

"You're going out?" She got to her feet, followed him, but even standing he towered over her.

Jeffery tucked in his shirt before answering. "Got a hot date."

"Lauren?" She couldn't stop herself from asking.

"Of course." He pushed her against the closet wall. "Lauren knows how to give a man a good ride." He slipped his hand between her legs, gripped her hard. "At least her pussy's hot, not frozen like yours."

Marisa refused to cry out. She struggled and slapped at him. "You're disgusting."

Jeffery laughed at her puny attempts to fight him.

"I'm getting a divorce," she declared.

"Daddy won't let you do that," he taunted. "The only way you'll get rid of me is if I'm dead."

"That can be arranged."

She pushed by him, tripping over the clutter.

"How? You think you can hire someone? On what? Your allowance? All one hundred dollars a week?"

Screaming, she jumped up and attacked, arms flailing, hitting, and scratching.

He held her at arm's length and then pulled her tightly to his chest. "Go ahead, fight me. You want to be punished, don't you?"

The bedroom door crashed open.

"What the hell's going on in here?" Kyle's face was red, his body stiff with rage. "I can hear you all over the house."

"She's lost it again, Kyle." Jeffery words sounded contrite, even to Marisa.

Dr. Hadley watched from the hallway, then went to his room next to theirs.

"I tried to calm her down, doctor, but she escalated," Jeffery explained when the doctor returned.

Marisa's screams dissolved into sobs, tears streaming. She wiped her runny nose and backed away. "Please, daddy, don't. I'm calm. See. I'm calm."

The revulsion on Kyle's face stopped her begging. The three things her father hated—disorder, a weak, sniveling woman, and to be called daddy.

"Kyle," she said as serenely as she could manage. But it was too late for leniency. Dr. Hadley walked toward her, a hypodermic needle in his hand. Kyle imprisoned her hands. Jeffery lifted her off her feet. They threw her face down on the bed. She screeched like a trapped animal and twisted to get free.

Cool air hit her bare skin as Dr. Hadley pulled down the bottoms of her pajamas. His fingers slowly rubbed across her bare butt cheek, then the sharp jab of the needle.

Marisa fought to stay awake. She had only a few minutes of consciousness before the strong tranquilizer took control of her mind and body.

Kyle turned her over, laid her head on the pillow. "I can't allow you to continue hurting yourself. You understand, don't you?" Her eyes were dulling as he pulled the duvet over her and tucked her in.

"She's all yours, doc," Jeffery said to Hadley.

"Angelica!" Kyle called downstairs. "Clean up this mess," he instructed when she entered.

Marisa couldn't combat the power of the drugs. As her eyes closed, she swore that this was the last time.

The bedroom was in chaos with jewelry, clothes, and books strewn about the floor. Angelica began refolding the clothes.

Dr. Hadley stood by the bed staring at the prone woman who was too drugged to move. "Leave now. Do that later." Hadley ordered without looking at Angelica.

"*Si.*" She kept working as if she didn't understand English.

"I said—out. Understand? Out! Vamoose!"

She nodded and prayed her hatred for the man didn't show. "I clean." She held up a sweater and continued folding like an idiot.

Angelica Olivia Maria Porter was anything but an idiot. Born to a Peruvian mother and an American father, Angelica was fluent in five languages, including native *Quechua*, the language of her mother's family, plus French, Portuguese, Spanish, and English. She knew what Hadley was saying, and she knew why he wanted her out.

Frustrated, he gave up, and muttering obscenities left the bedroom. Angelica followed and locked the door. He'd be back when he thought she'd gone. Dimming the lights, she examined Marisa, who had a weak pulse, clammy skin, and shallow breathing.

In the bathroom, Angelica ran warm water over a washcloth and returned to the bedside. She gently cleansed the young woman's face, softly blotted the tears that seeped from Marisa's eyes.

"I know you can't hear me, *suma sipas*, beautiful girl, but we'll get through this." Reaching into the pocket of her smock, she removed a small vial, and gently placed three drops of tincture under Marisa's tongue. "This will help counter-act that drug," she promised the unconscious woman.

Angelica descended from a long lineage of healers. Her maternal grandfather was a member of the *Kallawayas*, men who originated from the ancient Aztecs and used plants as medicine.

She'd spent summers with the family walking the Andes gathering plants. Winters she'd spent in Connecticut with her father, a corporate attorney.

Ignoring the intermittent rattling of the doorknob, she finished putting the room in order. It was unlikely Jeffery would return before morning, so she had plenty of time.

She'd gotten this job through her cousin, a software engineer in San Francisco. He'd warned her that Kyle, super vigilant about his family's privacy, hired only non-English speaking help because if they didn't understand English, they couldn't repeat what went on in the household. If they learned English, he'd fired them, and they'd get a surprise visit from ICE and be deported.

Angelica administered three drops of the tincture every hour. She was relieved when she saw color return to the young woman's cheeks, and her breathing deepened.

By four in the morning, Marisa was covered in sweat. Angelica drew a bath, added oils, and a bag of relaxing herbs. She walked the barely conscious woman to the bathroom where she stripped away the damp pajamas and helped her into the tub.

Marisa lay in the water, staring with unfocused eyes, like a newborn baby. Angelica sponged water over her shoulders, and back, cringing at the sight of her knobby spine, sharp hipbones, and visible ribs. Another month and this woman would have been beyond saving.

When it seemed safe to leave her, Angelica stripped the bed of the damp sheets and cautiously stepped out to the hall closet for fresh linens.

Dr. Hadley stood in the doorway of his bedroom, hair mussed and standing on end. He wore a short robe. His scrawny legs, covered in thick hair reminded her of the Wandering Spiders of Peru that came out at night searching for prey.

"What are you doing?" he asked, moving toward Marisa's bedroom.

Angelica pantomimed vomit and diarrhea in such detail he looked bilious. He hesitated but went back to his room. With a satisfied smile and fresh sheets, she stepped back into the bedroom and re-locked the door. She checked on Marisa and then remade the bed.

Helping Marisa out of the tub, Angelica dried her with a thick white towel, redressed her in fresh pajamas, and tucked her in bed, where she curled on her side, a hand tucked under her cheek.

With an intuitive eye, Angelica studied the sleeping woman. Her aura glow was stronger—the colors were still weak and small, but no longer the dark gray of fear. Her spirit energy was coming back into her physical body.

"When your spirit is stronger and your *Ajayu*, your soul, returns to you—then I will tell you the truth about what happened to your Mama."

Chapter Twenty-Two

~~~~~

Early morning ~
The phone rang twice.

"Yeah." Sam was instantly alert.

"I hear you're a professional. I hear you hire out." The voice undulated between Darth Vader and Mickey Mouse.

"You hear a lot."

"I have a job for you."

"How much?"

"How much?" the voice squeaked.

"What are you paying?" Sam listened for background sounds.

"500K."

"Who?" Like he didn't know.

"Lauren Sobrantes."

"Ha!" Sam snorted, "Can't do it for less than a million—half up front, in used bills."

Darth Vader breathed heavily. "I'll get back to you."

Chapter Twenty-Three

~~~~~

The outbuildings slowly vanished in swirls of damp fog, making the compound look like a background for a horror flick. Sam walked to the tool shed by the stables. The weathered gray boards were reminiscent of his grandmother's potting barn at the herb farm, where he and his friend, Andy hid to smoke a joint and got mind-blowing stoned when they were thirteen.

Inside the shed, he turned on the flashlight and unlocked the gun case hidden behind a storage cabinet. An M40 rifle, two handguns, and a gun holster lay between foam blocks. He ran his hand over the rifle he'd not picked up since he was injured.

Did he still have his uncanny skill? Or had his headaches affected his accuracy? One of these days, he promised himself, he would test it.

Unzipping and removing his sweatshirt, he slipped an underarm holster in place. Taking a Glock from the case, Sam let the metal warm in his hand as he weighted the gun's heft and familiar balance. He slipped the smaller Sig between the foam. Holstering the Glock, he stuck an extra clip in the pocket of his sweatshirt before turning out the light.

He'd wait for the next phone call and assurance the money had been delivered before he took action.

Chapter Twenty-Four

~~~~~

Detective Edwin Schott, a veteran of the La Lumbre Sheriff's Department drove over the rough gravel driveway to the Sobrantes compound. Not a day had passed in the last two years that Ed hadn't thought about Richard's murder.

Schott had remained the lead detective, refusing to let it go into a cold case file. He'd spent hours going over the information in the thick blue folder that lay on the seat beside him.

He firmly believed that a perfect murder was impossible. But this was as close to perfect as one could get. Sobrantes was shot execution style, two-tap to head and chest. The crime scene was clean, no spent shell casings found, and the storm destroyed any footprints or tire prints.

The keys to Richard's BMW were taken along with his cell phone, an antique Patek Phillipe watch, a gold signet ring, and his wallet full of credit cards. Pawnshops, Craig's list, and eBay were monitored, but the watch and ring never turned up. Credit cards were never used.

He speculated that the shooter planned to return to get the car, but the sheriff got there first.

Ed had been one week shy of handing in his retirement papers. A long vacation was booked, including a cruise to Alaska. The trip was to have been a combination of celebrations with his wife, Beatrice—the honeymoon they'd never taken, their 30th wedding anniversary, and his retirement.

Then, came the call that changed it all.

He felt he had to postpone the trip and the retirement

ed to send a stale investigation in a new direction that led to
rrest.

But he had trouble believing the hyperbole that Brownlee
ved about Lauren, the sex clubs, and murdering her father
ause he found out. Still, he had to factor in the statics. Eighty
cent of all the murders were committed by someone the
im knew, and thirty percent of those were by family
nbers.

The Casa lay to the left of the circular driveway, the
etaker's cottage to the right. Ed parked and picked up the
ler from the passenger seat. He stepped out of the car and
used. The estate was a peaceful place, and yet it held such
believable tragedy for the Sobrantes family who had it all until
deaths started. First, Elizabeth died from an unknown
ergic reaction, then Richard's murder, followed by Lauren's
appearance. It was as if they were being systemically purged.

A tall, lean, and vaguely familiar man walked toward him.
e no-nonsense military posture was incongruent with the
orn jeans, long hair, and beard. He reminded Ed of the hippies
no used to hang around La Lumbre's town square when he
s a kid, selling their candles, incense, and jewelry.

"Good morning, I'm Detective Schott."

"Morning, Ed."

He had a firm handshake. Schott took off his sunglasses,
uinted at the man's face. The voice was familiar. Names ran
rough his mind like a computer search.

"Sam Gallagher!" The handshake deepened. "Good
acious, man, how long has it been?"

Years ago, Ed got a call that two boys hiking around the
ld Berry Falls quarry were in trouble. They arrived too late to
ve Andy. Sam had done his best to hold his friend who'd
ipped over the side, but he wasn't strong enough.

Guilt had consumed Sam. He'd believed he should have
one more. If he'd just held on longer or had been stronger, or
e'd convinced Andy to leave the drugs home. Ed had worked
ard to make Sam understand the fall was not his fault. But he
vatched as Sam withdrew from his friends and family. He'd lost
rack of him when he joined the military. Rumors spread that his

plans until the case was solved. Beatrice had
betrayed. She told him that he'd chosen his
She'd taken their daughter on the cruise and
she moved into an apartment in downto
promised to come back when he retired.

Schott had never given up on a case. He'
arrested Richard's killer. Maybe it was his
maybe his bulldog persona, or maybe he just
best man for the job. But he also knew he l
soon because he wanted his wife back.

He'd gone over every detail of the evider
multiple theories. It appeared the murder had l
planned.

What was he missing?

Who had the most to gain?

Usually, you follow the money. Then facto
opportunity.

The estranged widow, Fiona Sobrantes-Wi
nup agreement that gave her a small portio
wealth. If you could call a hundred million
Richard had filed for a divorce, but it wasn't fina
died. Ed wasn't sure how much she'd receive (
was settled.

Lauren didn't need more money. She'd inh
from her mother and grandmother.

The business partners, Bernard Anderso
Montgomery certainly didn't need money. Schott
any animosity between the men. In fact, there did
anyone who had a vendetta against Sobrantes.

The counterfeit component issue had to
Richard's murder, but for the life of him, Schott c
out how it was connected.

He decided to start over. Question everyone a
with Lauren, who'd skipped town the day after
funeral. What made her leave so abruptly? Guilt? Rer

Ed had watched Anna Brownlee on CNN.
experiences with psychics through the years. Those
saw and knew things that most people didn't. Th

plans until the case was solved. Beatrice hadn't agreed. She'd felt betrayed. She told him that he'd chosen his job over her, again. She'd taken their daughter on the cruise and when they returned she moved into an apartment in downtown San Jose. She promised to come back when he retired.

Schott had never given up on a case. He'd resign the day he arrested Richard's killer. Maybe it was his over-inflated ego, maybe his bulldog persona, or maybe he just knew he was the best man for the job. But he also knew he had to wrap it up soon because he wanted his wife back.

He'd gone over every detail of the evidence and examined multiple theories. It appeared the murder had been meticulously planned.

What was he missing?

Who had the most to gain?

Usually, you follow the money. Then factor in motive and opportunity.

The estranged widow, Fiona Sobrantes-Wilson had a pre-nup agreement that gave her a small portion of Sobrantes wealth. If you could call a hundred million dollars, small. Richard had filed for a divorce, but it wasn't finalized before he died. Ed wasn't sure how much she'd receive once the estate was settled.

Lauren didn't need more money. She'd inherited millions from her mother and grandmother.

The business partners, Bernard Anderson and Kyle Montgomery certainly didn't need money. Schott couldn't find any animosity between the men. In fact, there didn't seem to be anyone who had a vendetta against Sobrantes.

The counterfeit component issue had to factor into Richard's murder, but for the life of him, Schott couldn't figure out how it was connected.

He decided to start over. Question everyone again, starting with Lauren, who'd skipped town the day after her father's funeral. What made her leave so abruptly? Guilt? Remorse?

Ed had watched Anna Brownlee on CNN. He'd had experiences with psychics through the years. Those people who saw and knew things that most people didn't. They'd often helped to send a stale investigation in a new direction that led to an arrest.

But he had trouble believing the hyperbole that Brownlee spewed about Lauren, the sex clubs, and murdering her father because he found out. Still, he had to factor in the statics. Eighty percent of all the murders were committed by someone the victim knew, and thirty percent of those were by family members.

The Casa lay to the left of the circular driveway, the caretaker's cottage to the right. Ed parked and picked up the folder from the passenger seat. He stepped out of the car and paused. The estate was a peaceful place, and yet it held such unbelievable tragedy for the Sobrantes family who had it all until the deaths started. First, Elizabeth died from an unknown allergic reaction, then Richard's murder, followed by Lauren's disappearance. It was as if they were being systemically purged.

A tall, lean, and vaguely familiar man walked toward him. The no-nonsense military posture was incongruent with the worn jeans, long hair, and beard. He reminded Ed of the hippies who used to hang around La Lumbre's town square when he was a kid, selling their candles, incense, and jewelry.

"Good morning, I'm Detective Schott."

"Morning, Ed."

He had a firm handshake. Schott took off his sunglasses, squinted at the man's face. The voice was familiar. Names ran through his mind like a computer search.

"Sam Gallagher!" The handshake deepened. "Good gracious, man, how long has it been?"

Years ago, Ed got a call that two boys hiking around the old Berry Falls quarry were in trouble. They arrived too late to save Andy. Sam had done his best to hold his friend who'd slipped over the side, but he wasn't strong enough.

Guilt had consumed Sam. He'd believed he should have done more. If he'd just held on longer or had been stronger, or he'd convinced Andy to leave the drugs home. Ed had worked hard to make Sam understand the fall was not his fault. But he watched as Sam withdrew from his friends and family. He'd lost track of him when he joined the military. Rumors spread that his dad disowned him and that was why he never returned La Lumbre.

"You moved back?" Schott asked.

"Living here, for now, I'm leaving soon."

"How are you connected to her and all this?" Ed swept a hand toward the house and cottage.

Sam explained his injury and his work as the caretaker on the estate. He led the detective to the cottage, lightly rapped, and then opened the door.

Standing next to Sam at the front door of the cottage, Detective Schott looked like a small gnome with his thick mustache, receding hairline, and penetrating hazel eyes.

Lauren smiled and invited him inside. The detective had been kind to her when her father died. He'd called daily in the days before the funeral to keep her informed of the investigation's progress, or lack of progress.

But now, they played at the social pleasantries, each knowing this was not a social visit. She offered coffee. He accepted. He sat down at the table, opened the blue folder. Then he took out a notebook and removed the cap from his silver pen.

"I understand that you flew in on Friday night."

"I did." Lauren looked up from pouring coffee.

"I got a call from the San Francisco Police about the man who sat next to you on a flight from London. He turned up dead the next day. What do you know about it?"

"Only that he kept hitting on me during the flight."

"I see. The SFPD is investigating. Did you know him from before?

"No. He was a stranger." Lauren placed the cup before him. He declined cream and sugar. "Do you have anything new on my father's case?"

"Not yet."

"Nothing? Two years and nothing?" The silent accusation of ineptitude hung in the air between them. She sat in a chair on the opposite side of the table.

Schott sipped his coffee and watched her over the rim of

his cup. "I'm starting from the beginning, re-interviewing everyone. You left rather abruptly," he said, thoughtfully.

"Yes. And apparently your investigation stopped the day I left."

Schott leaned back in the chair, the cup casually resting in his hands. "You disappeared and we—"

"I went away. I did not disappear."

"Where did you go?"

"Here and there. I settled in London."

"You were missing; everyone thought you were dead. The search was extensive. You cost the department a great deal of money."

"I wasn't missing."

"But you told no one you were leaving or where you were." Schott challenged.

"People knew. They chose not to tell. I believe someone did let you know I was safe, and you took it as an unsubstantiated rumor."

Schott tapped his silver pen against his notepad. "So when you suddenly disappeared—"

"Left—"

"Because—?"

"Because someone tried to kill me."

Schott leafed through the papers in the file. "Did you report it?"

"No." The gunshot that killed her dog left no doubt that someone was trying to kill her, too.

Schott studied her for a moment. His eyes searched her face before he asked, "How long have you known Sam Gallagher?"

"I met him Friday evening."

"Friday? Was he the man you were kissing him on Sunday?"

Lauren grimaced. That kiss was impulsive. Someone had posted a photo of it on Facebook, and it went viral.

"Did he help you?"

"Help me what?"

"Disappear."

"I met the man on Friday evening."

"He's military. Quite the marksman from what I hear."

"What are you implying?"

"How long did you say you've known him?"

"Since Friday."

"Friendly with someone you'd just met. Are you sure, you didn't know him before?"

"Years ago, he was a volunteer at a horse show I was in, but—"

"So, you did know him."

"He was one among hundreds of people there, and he helped me mount up before I went in the ring."

"Do you still believe someone wants to kill you?"

"I hope not." She didn't bother to tell him about the incident in London. She hadn't filed a police report there either. She'd packed up and fled to California.

"Where were you when your dad died?"

She'd held those memories at bay. And now she would have to relive the trauma as if it just happened.

"I was with Jeffery Davis, my fiancé. We'd been out to dinner the night before, and I'd gotten sick at the restaurant. He brought me home to the Casa and came back the next day before noon as I remember. Our housekeeper, Etta was with us."

"I'll get his statement again. You said fiancé at the time—are you still in touch with him?"

"No, we called it off before I left. You probably already know that. I saw him yesterday at the get-together at Kyle Montgomery's home. I'm sure Jeffery will corroborate everything I've told you."

"Thank you, Ms. Sobrantes," Schott smiled reassuringly. "I'm going over all the evidence and everyone's statements again."

"Did Jeffery tell you that he'd found out why Dad was killed?"

"There were many theories and fabrications bouncing around after you left. We checked out all of them and found they were baseless."

"He claims he has a name." Schott looked up from his notes.

"Who?"

"He wouldn't tell me. He said there was a plot to destroy the company, and they went after my dad."

Schott paused a few moments as if in deep thought, then closed the blue folder, put away his pen, and stood. His worn tweed jacket hung from his rounded shoulders, the pockets bulging.

"I'll check with Mr. Davis this evening. I'm reviewing everything. Ms. Sobrantes, I must warn you not to leave the country, the state, not even the county."

"Unless you're charging me, I believe I'm free to go wherever I want."

"I can always have a judge declare you a flight risk, impound your passport, and freeze all your assets."

"On what basis? What would you tell the judge? Maybe the word of that incompetent psychic who claims she talked to my ghost and my ghost confessed that I killed my dad and then I committed suicide out of guilt? I'm still alive, so that blows her credibility, doesn't it? Detective, you'd be laughed out of the judge's chambers."

Chapter Twenty-Five

~~~~~

Lauren hopped out of the passenger seat after Sam parked the Land Rover in front of one of the oldest houses in the historic district of La Lumbre Village.

Tully Jones, Attorney at Law, was painted in large gold letters across the picture window.

Tully had lived in the house since he was a young man of twenty, over sixty years ago. Once the elected mayor of the town, Tully was now the unofficial mayor and probably would be until he passed away. If you had a question, Tully Jones was your go-to man. He'd been the Sobrantes family attorney for generations.

The first floor was a combination of modern and cottage chic, with some items so old they were new again. At the desk by the window, a man with dark hair and dark eyes glared at Sam as they walked toward him.

"We're here to see Tully," Lauren said, looking back and forth between the two men.

"Sam." The man stared at Sam.

"Another brother?" she asked. The family resemblance was strong.

Sam nodded. "Lauren, my brother, Gregory Gallagher, Zach's twin. Gregory, Lauren Sobrantes."

Lauren extended her hand. Greg's handshake was cordial. He buzzed for Tully.

"Zach told me you were back." Greg's tone was hostile. He turned his back and walked away without waiting for a reply.

Tully Jones came along the hallway moving as rapidly at

eighty as he'd done at eighteen. He was a slight, dapperly dressed man and was wearing, as he'd always done, a snappy bow tie, blue suspenders and a belt—evidence of a cautious man, he claimed.

"Lauren, look at you, lovelier than ever. Beautiful. Welcome home." He wrapped her in a hug.

"Tully, you're as big a flirt as always." She knew Rand had assured him and Bernie that she was safe, without telling them where she was living.

"Sam, how are you? Good to have you back in town." He threw a quick glance to Greg, who busily examined files and ignored them.

Tully led them into the conference room. "I believe I know why you're here, Lauren. Tell me what you need, besides just saying hello after all this time."

"That *Ghost* book, I want it stopped. Sue the TV station, the author, her publisher, and the people who gave statements that they were my so-called sex partners. I want a hefty settlement, and it's to be paid to the Heavens Child Foundation."

"We've already started on it, my dear. When I heard you'd returned, I had Greg draft a lawsuit against all parties.

"He's going to be taking over for me. I'm going to Greece for the holidays and won't back until the weather here warms up."

Lauren wished him the best when he walked them to the door. Tully tugged her in for a goodbye hug. Then, he turned to Sam. "Your brother's a fine lawyer."

Sam smiled at Tully's compliment. "I'm sure he is. Greg's been arguing from the time he learned to talk."

It was late afternoon by the time they finished at the law office and returned to the Casa. The painting contractors arrived to discuss projects and work schedules. Tully had recommended the company, so Lauren felt assured the men were reliable and trustworthy.

Lauren pulled up the hood of her sweatshirt against the chilly afternoon air and pointed out what she wanted to be done on the portico. "I want the outside painted a warm white, not a cool white," she explained.

"What? Not pink and purple?" said a voice behind her.

She froze. Uncle Bernie was the only person who'd remember her purple and pink phase when she was four and determined the Casa would look much better if painted her favorite colors. No one else had agreed, so she took her paints and made wide swaths of purple as far up as she could reach.

Lauren turned slowly. Bernie's arms were open wide, just as they'd been so many times in her life. She stepped into his embrace, felt his chest heave. She tried to hold back, but gave up and cried with him.

Sam tactfully led the men around the back of the Casa to assess the work and to give Lauren privacy.

Bernie released her and wiped the tears from her cheeks and then wiped his own eyes. They walked arm-in-arm to the caretaker's cottage.

"Here you are, looking just like you did before you disappeared. You have a lot to explain, Lauren. All this time and not one word," Bernie said, once they stepped inside. He sat in the wing-backed chair next to the fireplace.

Lauren sat on the sofa, kicked off her shoes, and tucked her feet up. "I kept thinking I'd return when they arrested Dad's killer. At first, I was looking over my shoulder all the time. I went from place to place, afraid that if I relaxed someone would find me, kill me. I tried Belize and then ended up in London." Lauren told him about her shop—Grace Delaney Antique Linens.

"What made you come back?" She hesitated to tell him about being pushed off the sidewalk into traffic. "Well, there was that book."

"The one about the ghost?"

"Yeah, remember that psychic Anna Brownlee? She claimed my ghost dictated the information to her. That I was into those sex clubs, and Dad planned to cut me out of the will, so I had him killed."

"Well, hell, if I'd known a book was all it took to bring you home, I'd have written it myself, a long time ago."

He stood and paced the room. "Two years, and it never occurred to you to call, text, or email? Send a goddamn postcard, with something like, hey, Uncle Bernie, I'm alive. You can stop searching for my body now?"

"I called—"

"What were you thinking?" He stopped, breathing heavily, his silence as intense as his anger. "You were gone. We searched the house and grounds, brought in the dogs, checked out thousands of rumors, followed up every lead, weeded out the crackpots who claimed to be you and please send a million to buy a ticket home."

What could she say? She'd been too busy running, trying to stay alive. Rand kept assuring her that he'd let Bernie know she was okay. Obviously, her uncle hadn't believed him.

"I'll never forget the day the sheriff told me they were changing your case from search to recovery. Every time a body, a skull, or a bone was found, I'd send photos and dental records. Scared it was you. Elated when it wasn't. Frustrated because I knew there'd be another body, another set of dental records, and I'd have to go through it all over again."

He leaned over her, his voice ringing with anger. "Why the hell didn't you call me?"

"I did call you."

"Whatever was going on I could have helped you."

"Help me?" She jumped up. They circled like boxers, waiting for the right moment to throw a lethal punch. Lauren got in close. "Like when I called you from Belize to tell you where I was, and you sent two goons after me?"

"I don't know what you're talking about. I never got a call from you. And I certainly didn't send any goons."

"So how did they find out? Were your phones tapped?"

Bernie gaped at her. "What?"

"Either that or you gave out information."

"I would never. Is that what you think?"

"Someone told those men where to find me. They showed up within an hours after I called you. They weren't dropping by for tea. Where else would they get the information?"

"Lauren, why would I do that? I love you. You're all I have

left of my family. Why would I send someone to hurt you? I thought like everyone else that you were gone." Bernie rubbed his eyes with the heel of his hands.

The anger and fear spent, Bernie's shoulders slumped, the fight deflated out of him.

Sam entered the cottage, hung his coat on the rack.

"Sam, do you think there's a possibility the person who killed Richard is still after Lauren?" Bernie asked.

"She's obviously a threat to someone. Fear's a great motivator for murder."

Bernie nodded. "Lauren, you'll move in with me. I'll send someone this afternoon for your things and—"

"I'm staying at the Casa."

"This place is too hard to protect. Right, Sam?" Bernie looked to him for backup.

"It is difficult," Sam agreed.

Lauren gave Sam a severe look. "What about the security guards and those cameras you put up all over? How can a place be any more secure than this?"

Sam grimaced and threw up his hands. "Leave me out of this." He went into the security room and closed the door.

Lauren turned to Bernie, "I feel safer here."

Bernie continued to pace as if sitting still was impossible. He lingered at the old redwood dining table and ran a hand across the surface, deep in thought.

"Fiona tried to take things out of the Casa, didn't she?" Lauren asked.

"Deke said he made her return everything."

"Right, he told me."

"After her break-in, I put everything in storage. I took your personal things to my house. I'll bring them back tomorrow."

"Would you call the storage company and set up a delivery time as soon as possible? I want to get settled over there rather than staying here with Sam."

"First thing tomorrow morning."

"Jeffery told me someone was hired to kill my dad. Did he tell you?" She filled him in on what Jeffery told her. "Schott dismissed it as a speculation."

"Those rumors started the day you disappeared. Conspiracy theorists had many scenarios that they touted for weeks. It was mafia hit because Richard knew too much. Russian spies did it because he had a secret formula for some device and the CIA found out. You were murdered because Richard told you what he knew before he died. It was all as outrageous as Brownlee's claim you paid someone to murder your dad and then committed suicide."

"The theories were investigated, right? Schott told me they were baseless."

"Everyone knew it was an exaggeration. ABC, Fox News, and CNN had their panels of experts with their lofty opinions and theories of exactly what happened to Richard and you."

He snorted in disgust. "Sometimes it's just a random act of violence happening to good people. Richard's death might never be solved. We may never know who, what, or why."

"I can't live with that," she said, brusquely.

"Sometimes we have to live with a lot of stuff we never thought we could," he replied, gloomily.

"I had an odd meeting with Marisa yesterday."

"How so?"

Lauren wasn't sure what to tell him. "She seemed agitated, almost crazy talking. She has a personal doctor, a Dr. Hadley."

"Weird guy, isn't he? Jeffery says he's done a good job of keeping Marisa from hurting herself."

"Do they think she's crazy? Suicidal?"

Bernie shrugged. "No idea. Haven't seen her but once and it was at her wedding. She seemed okay then."

Lauren sighed. "So, what Jeffery told me about Dad's death is fabricated, right? And RKB is solid?"

He hesitated, checked his watch before answering. "We're still having trouble with the counterfeits, but overall things are good. Rand and I are working on finding the manufacturers so we can put a stop to it at that end."

"Kyle told me it was under control."

"Well, Kyle and I have different views on what under control means. It's still an issue; the counterfeits continue to show up in the supply line. And I don't plan to stop investigating until I find the people behind it. I have to get going. I have a meeting in the city."

Rain spritzed in a fine mist as they walked to his car.

"Did you ever find Dad's engineering lab book?

"No. I never did." Bernie slid behind the wheel and started the car.

She leaned in the driver's window. "Oh, one more thing, do you know the combination to the safe in Dad's study?"

"Of course."

Chapter Twenty-Six

~~~~~

The morning forecast for sunshine looked promising. The horizon was clear as Sam drove to the village to meet Deke at Nick's. The diner was the place for the locals to catch up on the town news and gossip over their bacon and eggs.

Opened in the 40s, owners had changed through the years, but the place maintained the quintessential coffee shop facade with an ancient neon sign, red bar stools, padded booths, and a snarly cook behind the grill.

Deke waved to Sam from a stool at the far end of the counter across from a large flat screen television high on the wall where a reporter soundlessly aped the news of Lauren's return.

"What's up?" Sam asked. Deke had called and said he had information he wanted to share before Lauren was told.

"I told Schott about Lauren and the man who was killed in San Francisco."

"The Cheshire Man." Sam smiled, remembering Lauren's nickname. He wondered if she'd felt like Alice, falling through the rabbit hole?

"Hey, Mr. Deke, how's it going?" A.J., the cook, called to them through the window of the grill. "Ham and eggs?" he asked pointlessly. Deke never ordered differently. "What about your friend?"

Sam ordered the same and black coffee.

"Forty-niners kicked ass Sunday," Deke teased as the cook filled their cups. "Yeah, A.J., you know that Green *Bagger* team of yours never had a snowball's chance in hell."

116

Begrudgingly, A.J. slapped a fifty down by Deke's coffee cup. "You just wait, Deke," he growled. "Remember, those sun-shiner-niner boys have to play in Wisconsin next on the frozen tundra, minus twenty. Then, we'll see who's got a snowball chance of kicking ass."

He returned to the kitchen, flipped a couple of slices of ham, and broke four eggs over the sizzling grill.

Deke pushed a folder to Sam and keeping his voice low, said, "SFPD checked out the information Lauren gave us and located the man's hotel room. Look what they found." Deke gestured to the folder.

Lauren's photo was on top. A large X marked with red ink on her forehead, right between her eyes. Over-dramatic, Sam thought, but chilling just the same.

"The police recognized Lauren immediately."

"And they'll ask questions."

"Right," Deke agreed. "I'm guessing the Cheshire was a professional. They're checking fingerprints, dental records, and DNA to see what pops." He stirred sugar and cream into his coffee.

"You think this guy did Sobrantes, too?"

Deke nodded thoughtfully. "Could be."

The same unanswered questions hung between them. Why was Richard killed? And why come after Lauren? What was the connection?

Sam leafed through the rest of the photos—Lauren in the park, the underground, and walking to her work. The man must have tracked her for months, waiting for his opportunity. Was he the one who pushed her into oncoming traffic?

If that was the case why was he killed in San Francisco? Random robbery? That was doubtful, very doubtful.

"Someone is paying big bucks, and I mean big bucks," Deke said.

Sam agreed, remembering what he'd been offered.

Deke continued, "If she'd met him at the hotel for drinks as he wanted, she'd never have made it home."

Sam closed the folder and set it aside. He'd wait to ask what Deke knew about Jeffery's claim that he not only had information but he knew the reason Richard was murdered.

A.J. slid the plates across the counter. The aroma of ham, thick and greasy, filled the air. Next to the slices of ham and potatoes were two eggs, lacy brown on the edges, the whites half cooked and runny.

Deke dove into his breakfast, cutting the ham, eggs, and potatoes into one heaping mess, and then covered it with ketchup. Leaning over his plate, he ate like a hungry dog expecting the food to be snatched away before he finished.

Some people possessed a special talent for crucifying eggs, and A.J., evidently, was a leader extraordinaire. Sam separated the cooked from the uncooked part of the eggs. Years ago, in Pakistan, he'd stolen eggs from under noisy hens and sucked them down raw before the farmer chased him off.

That was survival. This was a choice.

Deke spread honey over his last piece of toast, carefully covering the bread to the edges. Then, he and A.J. continued to discuss football.

"Double or nothing," Deke said, challenging the cook.

A.J. agreed with a grin. "So easy to take this dude's money." He refilled their coffee and then leaned forward, his tone conspiratorial. "Is it true? Is it that Sobrantes woman? Think there's anything to that book the psychic lady wrote about the sex, drugs, and murdering her dad?"

Deke cut him off. "Brownlee's book is full of lies and sensationalism to sell books. Those weird sex clubs Lauren supposedly took part in are so far-fetched, it's laughable."

A.J. wasn't buying it. "I need to hook up with that kinda woman."

"You couldn't handle that kinda woman," Deke countered.

Sam laughed at the thought.

They left the Grill and stood in the parking lot to talk privately. Deke tapped the file in Sam's hand. "This gives credibility to Lauren's claim someone wants to kill her."

Sam tossed the folder in the back seat of his car. "Evidently, they still do. If they've hired one hit man, they'll hire another."

Deke nodded. "Between Schott and the SFPD, they'll sort

it out."

Sam had his doubts about the *sorting out.* "What's with Jeffery Davis?"

"Jeffery, the letch?"

Sam grinned to hear Jeffery called a letch.

"You could call him an opportunist, I suppose. The truth is he's more of a con man who worked his way up."

Sam leaned against the Land Rover. "How so?"

"Scuttlebutt is that Davis started out in high school working for this pool maintenance company in San Jose. They had clients from Atherton to Almaden Valley. Jeffery serviced the pools and the lonely wives of the elite while the hubbies were off making big money.

"In exchange for the extra service, they gifted him with hot stock tips, new clothes, and new cars. Jeffery videotaped his little games of hide the sausage with these women and swore he'd never show them to anyone. But if a woman refused to cooperate or didn't pay enough, she'd find herself the subject of a damaging tell-all article. I heard he had more than a dozen women supporting him in the good life and they all kept their mouths shut while he climbed higher up the social ladder."

"Then, he met Lauren."

"And then he met Lauren. The guy is a computer whiz. He interned for her dad one summer, and Richard introduced them."

"Did he have anything on Richard?"

Deke shook his head. "Not as far as I know. I think I'd have heard the chatter."

"Jeffery told Lauren that he knew the reason her dad was killed."

Deke snorted. "That thing about someone wanted to destroy him and his company?"

"Yeah, something like that."

"Well, that rumor went around after she left town. The investigators couldn't find anything to substantiate the claim. It was Jeffery's last hurrah. Lauren had dumped his ass the night of Richard's funeral. The guy was nothing without the Sobrantes, so he made up things to be the big guy and hold on to his image of the grieving fiancé."

"Why'd she dump him?"

"Not sure. I know we got a call asking for help to remove two people from the estate, Jeffery Davis and her stepmother, Fiona Sobrantes-Wilson."

"You think they had anything to do with this Cheshire Man?"

Deke shrugged. "Who knows? But this means we have to keep a closer watch on her."

"She's going to interview for a new security and a personal bodyguard this week."

"I thought you had the job?"

"I'm leaving. Taking off on Sunday. Monday at the latest."

"Huh, personal bodyguard, eh? I should apply." Deke beamed like a gleeful kid who'd been promised the Christmas gift he'd always wanted. "Man, travel all over the world with a beautiful woman, private jets, first-class hotels, and make more money than I'd ever make here."

Sam bristled at the idea. If Deke were her bodyguard, it would only be a matter of time before he'd try to worm his way into her bed. Sam wanted to grab him by the throat and tell him to leave Lauren the fuck alone.

Chapter Twenty-Seven

~~~~~

It was just as well that Sam had gone to town, Lauren decided. He'd insist on body searching every worker for weapons and confiscate their cell phones before allowing them on the place.

The relentless ringing of the doorbell interrupted her again. How many times did she have to tell Freddie just to come in and find her rather than ring the bell?

She swung open the door. Standing in front of her was the last person she expected to see.

"What is it, Jeffery?"

He was casually dressed in monotone—dark maroon slacks, a light maroon cashmere sweater with a pale maroon shirt underneath. He'd always been clothes-conscious, but it appeared he'd taken it a level higher, following the style of his father-in-law, Kyle. Head bowed, he managed to look both chagrined and apologetic as he held out a perfect red rose, the symbol of true love.

"How did you slip past security?" she demanded, her voice emotionless. She looked at the rose but didn't take it.

"He said you were expecting him." Freddie stepped forward, watching, waiting for a signal from her to throw the man out.

Jeffery smiled, flashing teeth too brilliant to be natural. "I wanted to apologize for my disrespect on Sunday. I'm so sorry." He held the rose out to her again.

"Thank you." She took the offering but didn't invite him inside.

"I brought your things." He pointed to moving boxes at

his feet.

"My things?"

"Stuff you left behind in our apartment—clothes, books, and jewelry. I moved out when you, uh, didn't come back."

Lauren couldn't recall what she'd left behind at the apartment they'd shared in downtown San Jose. It was like remembering someone she'd known once but no longer recognized. She'd stayed there when working late at RKB.

Holding the door open, she gestured for him to bring the boxes inside. Freddie carried them upstairs to her bedroom. When she told Freddie she didn't need him, he reluctantly went back outside. Lauren took the rose to the kitchen, put it in a paper cup, and filled it with water.

Jeffery followed her. "Where's your bodyguard? That thug you had with you on Sunday?"

"He's around," she lied.

Jeffery wandered into the cavernous living room. "It's like an echo chamber in here. It's weird without furniture."

"Everything's in storage. They'll deliver on Thursday."

"Money sure talks fast."

"I'm not following you."

"You come back, and within days you've got workers buzzing around and storage companies busting their butts to get things done for you. Big money must've greased numerous palms to get all this instant service."

Freddie opened the door for the floor cleaners with their heavy machines. They'd polish the hardwood floors on the first floor. Carpet cleaners were already upstairs working in the six bedrooms.

Lauren and Jeffery moved to the hallway, but instead of leaving, Jeffery turned back to the French doors leading to the terrace. She trailed behind him and wished that Sam were back from town. Trance music with a deep bass pounded out the beat from a worker's radio over the roar of lawnmowers, hedge trimmers, and leaf blowers. When the men were finished, the formal garden between the tennis court and swimming pool would once again be elegant and refined.

"Our wedding..." Jeffery's eyes shone.

They'd planned a garden wedding. She'd dreamed of walking on her father's arm behind two flower girls sprinkling rose petals along the path to the gazebo. Hundreds of their guests would've lined the path.

"We'd have celebrated our second anniversary and maybe even been expecting a baby by now. We were going to have at least four children." His voice trailed off.

Lauren waited, giving him time to compose himself.

"All our plans, gone." He snapped his fingers. "Just like that. Gone." Anger flashed in his eyes. "Did it ever mean anything to you? Us? Our future?"

"Of course, it did," she replied. She remembered when her dad had introduced them at the company picnic four years ago. Jeffery had just started working at RKB as an IT intern for the summer. When Richard left them alone, Jeffery joked, "So, you're the boss's daughter. Are you still as spoiled and obnoxious as people say?" There'd been a sparkle in his eye.

She'd shrugged at the impossible question. "Are you still the genius asshole like everyone claims?" He'd laughed loud and long and offered to buy her a beer.

Jeffery had made her laugh and brought her flowers for no reason. He never took advantage of her wealth, always insisting he pay his share. When she was sick, he made tea, brought her soup and crackers to ease her churning stomach. Every time she'd needed him, he was there until the one time she'd needed him the most, the evening of her father's funeral.

He took her by the shoulders. "Lauren, I loved you. I still love you."

"Time to go, Jeffery." She motioned to the door.

"You dumped me. How could you do that to us?"

"You betrayed me." She twisted out of his hands.

"You never gave me the chance to explain."

"There was nothing to explain." She knew what she'd seen that night in her father's study.

"No one will ever love you as I do." He declared as she walked him toward the door.

"How long have you and Marisa been married?"

"Why?"

"Curious."

"A little while—"

"A year?"

"Hmmm—"

"Maybe two years?"

"Does it matter?"

"You married Marisa within a month after I left, didn't you?"

"I thought you were never coming back—"

"And you needed money," she retorted. "Thanks for bringing my things."

"All right, I married Marisa after you disappeared. I was heartbroken, on the rebound. Marisa and I consoled each other and then Kyle, well, he pressured me to marry her."

What he was telling her made sense, except Marisa told her that Kyle pressured her to marry Jeffery and Kyle said that Marisa had insisted on marrying him. Where was the truth, she wondered?

"Marriage to you doesn't appear to be working. Marisa is in bad shape. What have you done to her?"

"Me? I've done nothing. She's crazy."

"She wasn't crazy before she married you."

"Schizophrenia is hard to detect until it gets full blown."

"You are not claiming Marisa is schizophrenic, are you?" Lauren was outraged at his allegation.

"Crazy, bonkers, and as schizoid as her mother. That's why Kyle had her mother committed."

"Sandra walked out years ago, abandoning them." Marisa, who was ten, had gone into a deep depression and Kyle had put her in therapy because of her mother's desertion. There was never talk of mental illness. "How do you know this?"

Jeffery smirked, making Lauren uncomfortable. "I know a lot of things about many people, sweetie. Trust me."

She wasn't sure if he was bragging or threatening. "I don't believe you." Her voice rose over the noise of the floor polisher.

Jeffery grabbed her shoulders again. "Well, believe this," he hissed, spittle flew in her face. "Schott called me yesterday about your alibi the night your dad died. Funny, I can't remember that day very well."

That was absurd; people always remembered where they were when tragedy struck—9/11, the shuttle explosion, Princess Diana's death. The emotional imprints stayed with you.

"We were at the restaurant in Saratoga." Her memory was as fresh as if it were last night. "I got sick, and you dropped me off at the Casa because it was the closest. The next day you came over around mid-morning." She repeated what she'd told Detective Schott.

"Hey, if that's how you remember it, then that's how I remember it."

He grinned, tilted his head, a shock of brown hair fell over his forehead. The things she had once loved—his smile, the hunger in his eyes—now disgusted her.

"Just tell Schott the truth."

"You're willing to take a chance my story might contradict yours?"

"Only if you lie, Jeffery."

"You owe me, Lauren!" His grip tightened, his fingers dug into her skin.

She twisted away. "I owe you nothing, Jeffery. Nothing. Get out."

He dropped his hands to his side. "Listen, I'll back you up, honey, whatever you want. Come with me. We'll work on our story at the beach house. You love the ocean."

"You tell Schott whatever lies you want. I'll not be blackmailed."

"Careful, you don't want to do anything you'll regret, now do you?" His smile was predatory.

"Do I have to call Freddie and have you thrown out?"

Jeffery threw up his hands in surrender. "Look, I'm sorry. I get carried away, forget to take things easy." His voice was contrite. "I want us to be friends. I want you to forgive me and for us to get back together. Marisa wanted to divorce me before the honeymoon was over. She'd be glad to get rid of me."

"Just leave."

"I can't leave it like this. There must be a way for us. I won't give up."

"I'll get a restraining order if I must." Lauren opened the door searching for one of the security detail, but none was in sight. Luckily, Jeffery got in his car.

Lauren felt serene even with the chaotic noise going on around her. *Change always follows chaos.* Her mom's favorite saying when things got rough.

Lauren was ready for a quiet change.

No more running.

No more hiding.

She stood in her empty bedroom with its soft cream walls, the gas fireplace in the corner, and French doors that opened to the balcony overlooking the circular drive, the cottage beyond, and what used to be her grandmother's bedroom, now Sam's. She and Nana had a ritual of waving and throwing kisses to each other before bedtime.

Lauren punched in Sam's number and was deep in thought of paint colors, and new decorating ideas as she listened to it ring. Maybe she'd ask Marisa to help redesign the room.

She didn't hear the door open.

A hand slapped over her mouth.

Fingers pinched her nose shut.

She dug her nails into his hand, but he gripped tighter.

Fighting for breath, heart pounding, she fought—hitting, scratching, struggling to punch him.

Black spots danced in her eyes. Consciousness faded, but she had to keep fighting or die.

"You fucking, cunt," Jeffery hissed, his breath hot on her neck. "Who'll kick me out now?"

He let go of her face and gripped her breast. "You are mine, Lauren. MINE."

She labored to get a deep breath, clear the blackness from her head. Taking a deep breath, she screamed. And elbowed him in the ribs.

Jeffery flung her down. Her head slammed against the wall.

Stunned, she crumpled on the floor.

He pushed her over and dragged her sweatpants down; harsh fingers probing her vagina.

Then he was gone.

She heard him shriek—high-pitched and painful, followed by loud curses.

Sam held him in a hammerlock, twisting Jeffery's arm behind him, and rammed his head into the wall for good measure.

Deke sprinted into the room. "Sam, let him go."

Jeffery slumped to the floor. "Arrest him," he bellowed, holding his bleeding nose with one hand, the other pointing at Sam. "He tried to kill me. Bastard broke my nose. Arrest him!"

Deke called for backup and led Jeffery away.

Sam knelt beside Lauren, who lay in a fetal curl, her eyes closed. He tugged her sweatpants up as best he could before checking her pulse that was rapid and erratic. Cradling her in his arms, he made his breathing deep and even until she began to breathe with him in the same quiet rhythm.

"Open your eyes for me." Smoothing back her hair, he felt her jump when his fingers touched the lump on her head. He cursed under his breath at the red marks around her mouth and nostrils. Using tremendous self-control, Sam stayed calm and curbed his temper. He'd beat the shit out Jeffery if he ever got close to her again.

Lauren stared at him with dazed eyes that slowly focused as she tracked the index finger he moved from side-to-side in front of her.

"Where is he?" she mumbled into his chest.

"Deke has him."

"How did you know?"

"Your cell phone. I was almost to the gate when you called. I heard you fighting, and then you screamed." It was the most terrifying drive of Sam's life as he raced inside the Casa.

In the cottage that evening, Lauren recounted the details of Jeffery's attack. "I thought he was going to kill me."

During other attempts on her life, she'd been terrified, but those were over in seconds. Today's attack felt like it lasted for hours. When Jeffery cut off her air supply, she'd panicked, certain she was going to die.

"Freddie is off the security detail," Deke said.

"No, he's not." Lauren protested.

"It was Freddie's job to make sure you were safe," Sam added.

"Freddie stays. It wasn't his fault. I waved him away and invited Jeffery in." She lay back on the sofa with the yellow Afghan tucked around her legs. "I just never thought Jeffery, of all people, would attack me."

Sam leaned forward, bracing his forearms on his knees. "Do you think there's a possibility that Jeffery is responsible for Richard's—"

"What was his motive? Opportunity?" Deke shook his head. "He was going to marry Lauren. The guy had it all."

Lauren agreed with Deke. "He'd signed a prenup that would have set him up for life, even if we'd divorced, he'd still have been quite wealthy. Besides, he was here with me most of that day."

"If you'd just press charges, I could throw him behind bars." Deke rubbed his hands together and grinned at Lauren.

She liked the vision of Jeffery behind bars but shook her head. "Sam took care of him."

The doctor, who'd attended Jeffery at the hospital, had diagnosed a bruised and bloody, but unbroken nose. Deke talked Davis out of filing charges against Sam, explaining that if he did, then Lauren would be forced to press attempted rape and assault charges against him, and he'd be the one behind bars. Jeffery backed off with sputters and threats.

Deke paced in front of the fireplace before turning to Lauren. "There's new information about the Cheshire Man that you need to know." He hesitated and looked at Sam who gave a small nod to keep going.

"I gave the SFPD your flight information. They traced the man to Mark Hopkins hotel, just like you said." Deke stopped, scratched the back of his head before continuing. "The thing is they found a stash of cash, an arsenal of weapons and ammo, and photos of you in London. The detectives figure he met up with someone here in San Francisco who supplied the guns and money and hired him to kill you." Deke sat down abruptly.

Lauren's hands trembled as she lowered the cup to her lap. Was he the man who tried to kill her in London and failed?

"He's dead, right?"

Sam leaned back in his chair. "If you'd met him for drinks

that night, you'd most likely be dead, too."

Deke nodded his agreement. "The police believe he was targeted. It wasn't just a robbery gone wrong."

"Why?"

"He failed to do his job," said Sam, "which means you're still not safe."

Deke leaned toward her. "Until we know who hired him, you'll need to be more cautious. No more risks like today."

"Which includes canceling that party thing on Saturday night," Sam added and looked to Deke for backup.

"What party thing?" Deke asked.

"The fundraiser for Heavens Child. It's at the Fairmont Hotel in San Jose. I'm the guest of honor." Lauren placed her cup on the end table, pushed the Afghan aside, and swung her feet to the floor. "I plan to be there."

Deke stood up. "That hotel is too big to secure."

"Deke's right," added Sam.

"Thank you both for your opinions, but the gala is the biggest fundraiser for Mom's charity. I'll hire extra security if I must, but I *will* be there. Right now, I hurt all over. I'm going to go soak in the tub and then go to bed." She hugged Deke and thanked Sam again.

They watched her go upstairs.

"One stubborn woman, that gal. You have to talk to her, Sam," Deke said. "You gotta make her understand the danger she'll be in if she goes to that thing."

Sam knew she was aware of the threat hanging over her. "Like there's a man alive who can make her change her mind?"

Deke laughed. The afternoon sun cast a long shadow over the driveway as they walked to Deke's truck. "Maybe I should stay."

"We'll be fine with your men and the alarm system."

Jon called after 11:00.

"Flynn's not having any luck in Marrakech. I caught up with Senator Phillips at the Oval Room restaurant. He didn't want to talk. When I pressed the issue and asked him to explain who asked him to hire us for the rescue, he warned me off. Said if we continue to investigate, we'd all be killed. I need you over there with Flynn, headaches or not. When can you leave?"

"Tuesday."

"Tuesday! That's a week from now!"

"It's the best I can do."

"I'm sending the plane," Jon was firm. "Now. Tonight. CNN is already speculating about who the man is with Lauren. That's what you get for kissing her in public. It won't take long to dig up everything about you. About us."

Sam knew Jon was right. "Let me secure things here. I'll leave Sunday morning. Can you find someone to take over here?"

"Rubio—"

"Oh, hell no!"

"What? He's a good man."

"The man can't keep his hands off his junk. He's always scratching and jiggling his balls. No. I won't have a man like him around Lauren. Get somebody else."

Chapter Twenty-Eight

~~~~~

The woman marched through the gate straight toward Sam. Her black raincoat flapped about her legs. Her hair was tightly pulled into a bun, a resolute look on her face, and a black umbrella in her hand.

"Who are you?" she demanded. Penetrating green eyes inspected his face.

"Sam," he responded, puzzled. "And you are?" His tone, respectful to the older woman.

"Miss Etta. Where is Lauren?"

Sam had heard stories about the housekeeper. He pointed to the cottage. She hung her umbrella on his outstretched arm and charged up the walk. He caught up and held open the door. She slid out of her raincoat and handed it to him as if she were the queen, and he, the butler. Sam choked back a laugh, but took her coat and hung it up.

"Lauren," she commanded loudly. "I want to see Lauren."

A shriek came from the bedroom. "Did I hear—" Lauren raced down the stairs and engulfed the older woman in a hug.

"You're back," Miss Etta said without judgment.

"Yes, I'm sorry if I worried you."

"No worry. Mr. Rand tell me you are safe, so I know."

Sam made tea and sliced the fresh pumpkin bread he'd baked that morning. He placed the teapot and cups on the coffee table.

Etta watched him suspiciously. "What does this man do?"

Lauren grinned and introduced the two of them. "Sam is my bodyguard. He takes care of me."

Etta nodded, knowingly. "I take care of her, too."

"She's a handful, isn't she?" he quipped and offered her a cup of tea and a slice of the bread.

"Sam made the pumpkin bread," Lauren boasted.

Etta chewed slowly, watching Sam. Her face relaxed, "Keep this one," she said to Lauren. "He's good. Not like that other one."

Sam felt as if he'd been given a seal of approval. He bet the *other one* was Jeffery.

"I make my raspberry scones for you." She sipped her tea.

Lauren beamed. Sam wondered if he'd been handed the Holy Grail.

"Does this mean you'll come back to the Casa?"

"I have to stay at Mr. Rand's house until he comes home. Then, I move back here, if you stay."

Lauren laughed. It was the first unaffected laughter Sam had heard from her. "Yes! Yes, I'm staying."

"Where is Arlo?" Lauren asked as they walked to Etta's car beyond the gates.

"He went home to Poland to be with his mother. She says she's dying, but she's just old. Have old lady pain."

Etta opened the back door of the car. "For you."

Lauren gasped.

Impossible.

Watson sat up. Stretched. He saw Lauren and jumped out, his body wagging from tail to nose as he whined in doggy ecstasy. She fell to her knees, buried her face in his white fur, and sobbed.

"I thought he was dead." Watson licked her tears.

"Mr. Rand rush you away. We take Watson to dog doctor. He sick for a long time, so we not say anything until we know he would live. Then, didn't know where you were. We keep him for you until you come home."

Chapter Twenty-Nine

~~~~~

Miss Etta returned to Rand's house to pack and wait for him to return. She promised Lauren she'd move back to the cottage when the place was available, which meant that Sam would be gone.

Lauren kept herself busy unpacking the boxes that Bernie brought over to avoid thinking about Sam leaving. But it wasn't enough to distract her from acknowledging that her attraction to him was strong and getting stronger.

The weather had turned colder, and rain showers were forecasted for the afternoon. By mid-morning, the rain, and the movers arrived. They unloaded the first truck and assembled the sleigh bed in Lauren's bedroom. While she made up the bed, Sam, and Deke, who'd stopped by for a few hours, brought up more boxes, stacking them to one side of the bedroom.

They settled into a routine. The men cut the boxes open, and Lauren sorted out the contents. She set aside clothes to be hung in the walk-in closet, linens to the hall closet and tucked personal items in the dresser.

When Deke loaded the last box on top of the others, the stack tumbled over. One carton broke open, spilling the contents across the carpet and under the bed.

Lauren yelped in surprise. Watson jumped up from the hearth where he'd been sleeping and pushed against her. She flopped on the floor, laughing, with the dog in her lap. "I think we're getting punchy. Let's clean up and have lunch."

Deke straightened the stack. Sam retrieved a small-carved wooden box from under the bed. He passed it to Lauren. She turned it over in her hands. "I've never seen this before."

Opening the lid, she folded back the crisp, white paper. And screamed. A sound of terror Sam had heard in battle.

Deke reached for the box.

Sam reached for Lauren. "What is it, Deke?"

"I think it's Richard's watch."

Leaving it in the paper, Deke held it out to Sam. Lauren nodded, confirming it was Richard's Patek Philippe watch; the one he was wearing when he was killed. Flakes of dried blood clung to the crystal and the black crocodile band.

"Blood." Lauren shuddered. "It's... it's his blood."

Watson paced, whined, and then nudged Lauren's arm.

The men stared at each other, acutely aware of the implications.

Could the Brownlee woman be right? Was Lauren involved with Richard's death?

Deke rewrapped the watch and put it back in the wooden box.

"We have to give that to the police." Lauren pushed away from Sam.

"Your fingerprints are on the box, Lauren," said Sam. "It was found in your possession.

"You'll be under suspicion once it's turned over." Deke cautioned.

"Like I'm not already under suspicion?" She got to her feet, braced herself against the footboard of the bed. "I have no idea who put it in my things, or why, or how, but it has to be reported."

Schott stood in front of the sofa where Lauren sat stone-faced. Deke held her hand. Sam stood by the windows. Watson lay at his feet.

"So, you say you found this while unpacking? And that you didn't put it there?"

"No! I didn't put it there! Everything has been in storage for almost two years. Many people had access—the movers, Bernie, Fiona, and obviously, the killer."

"And you..."

Upstairs his men photographed her bedroom and the stack of boxes. The watch and the wooden box were placed in an evidence bag to be taken to the lab.

"I never saw it until an hour ago when I opened that box."

"Ms. Sobrantes," Schott's voice was stern. "How much would you say this watch is worth?"

"I've no idea. Fifteen, maybe twenty, twenty-five thousand; I don't keep up with antique watch prices."

"How about ninety-five thousand?" He'd had it evaluated when it was listed on the missing items file.

"Could be, why?"

"If Richard's death was part of a robbery gone bad, don't you think the perpetrator would've tried selling it if he, or she, could get, say, forty or fifty-thousand?"

Schott's implication was clear. If a person didn't need the money, then the item could be tucked it away and forgotten.

"The lab will check it for finger prints." Schott gathered his blue file folder and briefcase. "By the way, Ms. Sobrantes, I spoke to Jeffery Davis yesterday. He doesn't remember if you were with him the day before or the day your dad died."

"He's lying."

"Why would he lie?"

"He said he'd tell you the truth if I had sex with him. I refused. So, he lied."

Schott nodded. "I'll contact him again. Until the lab report comes back, none of you are to leave town."

"I'm shipping out on Sunday," Sam turned from the window.

"No, Mr. Gallagher. You're now a person of interest. I can get a court order and seize your passport if I must. In the meantime, all of you stay put until we find out how this watch made its way into Ms. Sobrantes' possession."

Lauren was ten yards down the wooded trail by the creek when Sam spotted her. Why she was allowed to leave, unprotected was something he'd discuss with security when he got back. He sprinted to catch up.

"You're not to leave without a guard." He fell into step

beside her.

"Whatever." She kept walking. The redwood trees shifted in the wind. Water shook from the branches, remnants of the earlier rain.

Sam wiped his face. His jacket kept the Glock dry in the holster under his arm.

Lauren pulled up the hood of her sweatshirt. "Do you believe in God, Sam?" she asked, without slowing her pace.

Any man who has been to war believes in God to some extent. God was the first name they cursed or cried out to in battle.

"I suppose," he answered vaguely. God had never listened, much less answered any of his prayers.

"When I was a little girl, my Sunday school teacher told us we had to pray every night before we went to sleep—*Now, I lay me down to sleep, I pray the Lord, my soul to keep, if I should die before I wake, I pray the Lord, my soul to take.*

"For years, I was afraid to sleep. I'd lie in the dark, forcing my eyes to stay wide open, afraid if I went to sleep that I'd die, and in the morning I'd wake up and be missing a soul. Not that I had any idea what dying or what a soul was at that age."

They paused at the end of the path where the woods opened to the meadow and the family cemetery. The grave markers, a mixture of wooden crosses, marble angels, and classic tombstones were spaced among the long grass.

"Let's go," Sam urged.

She didn't answer. Instead, she crossed to the newer row of tombstones. Sam followed. The more visible and vulnerable they were the more his unease increased. Someone hiding on the ridge with a high-powered rifle could easily pick them off.

Lauren stood by her father's gravestone; the letters deeply carved into the granite were filled with gold.

> *Richard Sobrantes*
> *He dared to dream*
> *Beloved Son * Loving Husband * Caring Father*

Tears and mist glistened on her cheeks. Sam stood guard as

Lauren knelt in the wet grass and laid her head on the cold marble and wept.

"Let's go." He touched her shoulder. She pulled away, keeping a grip on the headstone.

He crouched down beside her. "You're wet, and you're cold—"

"Have you ever been shot?"

He hesitated.

"What's it like?"

"Lauren—"

"You must have taken a bullet sometime or another in your line of work," she insisted.

"An in-and-out in the right leg."

"I have nightmares about someone pointing a gun at me and shooting." She shuddered. "Tell me what it's like."

"At first, it's hard to process you've taken a hit. Then it burns, then hurts like hell." After that, you stitch it up yourself and trust it doesn't get infected before you can find a doctor.

"Do you think that's the way it was with my dad? Did he suffer? Was he in pain?" She continued to hold tightly to the tombstone.

"No, I don't believe he suffered, Lauren." According to the police report, Richard was dead before he hit the ground.

Sam lifted her to her feet. She leaned against him for support. "Meet my family, Sam." She swept an arm toward the row of graves. The tombstone next to Richard's read—

Elizabeth Eleanor Sobrantes
Loving Wife & Mother

Lauren pointed to the grave to the left of Elizabeth's marker. Two small cherubs on each side of a narrow white marble edifice.

"My brothers," she explained. "God didn't answer those prayers either. They died hours after they were born. My grandparents are on the other side of Dad. All my relations."

Sam couldn't imagine what his life would've been like without his siblings—his brothers and his sister, Brianna. He turned Lauren toward the path to the house, but she pulled away and moved quickly to the other side of the cemetery and stopped at a large stone formation.

"My altar to Dama de la Lumbre. I created it after Marisa and I were lost in the woods, and the Dama guided us home. She's the town deity, the spirit woman of fire. The Casa was named in her honor."

Lauren brushed leaves and sticks off the top of the rock. Underneath were two small candles, once red, now discolored from the elements.

"Every day after riding, I'd come here and bring flowers, candy, and fruits—light a candle. When I heard that my mother had been rushed to the hospital, I came here. I prayed. I begged. I made promises. I bargained with the Dama and with God to let my mother live, and I'd give up everything. I'd never get on another horse. If that wasn't enough, then take me, instead."

She pitched the candles into the brush. "Uncle Bernie brought me home from the hospital after she died. That was the last time I prayed." Lauren pushed by Sam. She moved fast, almost running to the road.

Sam caught up with her. "You've got to stop taking risks, Lauren." He slung his arm around her waist and maneuvered her behind a large pepper tree, shielding her from any potential threats of snipers on the ridge, and the increasing rain.

"I needed to come home, find out who killed my dad and now, Schott believes I did it." Rainwater dripped from her hair. She shivered as Sam tugged the hood of her sweatshirt over her head.

"First of all, we're going back to the house and get you warmed up. Then, we'll deal with the watch and everything else."

Lauren sat on the sofa in front of the fire. A hot shower had warmed her body and cleared her mind. "I know that I didn't put the watch in the box. Obviously, someone is trying to frame me."

"Someone with opportunity and motive." Sam threw a log in the fireplace. He stood with his back to the heat. "Start at the beginning. Who was here at the Casa before you left town?"

"Jeffery came mid-morning. Marisa and Bernie and Kyle came in the late afternoon because no one had heard from my dad. We knew something was wrong. Everyone was still here when Detective Schott came and told us that he had been found."

She remembered vividly when Schott had arrived that night. She'd wanted to lock him out because she knew something terrible had happened to her father and she didn't want to hear it.

"Numerous people helped with the investigation and the funeral. Do you think that was when his watch was stashed here?" Lauren sat up. "A lot of people came to offer condolences I suppose any one of them could've slipped the box in my things."

She'd been dull with grief and allowed others to help organize the funeral—dozens of people were in and out of the house, even Deke and Schott, not to mention dozens of workers, cleaners, florists, caterers, gardeners, and security guards. The place was full of mourners the day of the funeral.

Had the killer been among them?

"You left the day after the graveside service, right?"

"I was on Rand's plane the next morning." She watched Sam pace. "But the Casa was locked up. Miss Etta and Arlo were still here."

"Bernie said there were break-ins after they left. That's when he had everything sent to storage."

Unable to sit still, Lauren joined Sam in his pacing. Watson raised his head to make sure all was well, then laid down again with a heavy dog sigh.

"You're saying someone broke in and put that box in my things. Then Bernie packed it up where it stayed until this afternoon."

"That's one theory."

"And the other theory?" she asked.

Sam stood close behind her. She wanted to lean against him as she had done in the cemetery and soak up his strength.

"Deke said he caught Fiona putting things in her car and

made her return them. Could she have been trying to hide or recover the little box?"

"You think Fiona could have killed him?"

"She had the opportunity. Does she have a motive?"

Lauren shivered as Sam's eyes paused at her mouth. She inhaled deeply to control her urge to step closer and accept what he was offering, a haven of safety and sex.

"Fiona is a bitch, but in her peculiar way, I guess she loved my dad. She wouldn't gain anything through his death or divorce, just the opposite. The others all had an opportunity, but what would be their motive? Besides, everyone had solid alibis."

Sam opened a bottle of wine, poured two glasses, and brought one to Lauren.

"I wonder if Jeffery or Marisa know anything about the watch?" Lauren mused. Marisa had secrets. Secrets Lauren wanted to uncover now more than ever.

Sam studied her as he sipped the wine. "The bigger question is—what else is hidden inside the house?"

"You think his wallet and car keys—" Lauren broke off, realizing that finding the rest of the missing items would reinforce her involvement and the appearance of her guilt. She could even be arrested for murder.

"If killing me doesn't work, they'll frame me for murder."

Chapter Thirty

~~~~~

Marisa's life had radically changed since the football party. She'd discovered Angelica spoke English, was a healer, and had herbs to counteract the drugs in her system. Each day she felt healthier as she gained strength and energy. With Angelica as an ally, she had a new sense of resolve to take charge of her life.

She called downstairs. "Angelica, would you come up for a moment, please?"

There was a light tap on the door, but it wasn't Angelica. Dr. Hadley stood in the doorway, a fawning smile on his face. "I've noticed you've grown quite excitable lately. You need your medication."

"Leave. Now!" Marisa said in a strong voice that she'd not used in a long time. "Your services are no longer needed. Pack your things and get out."

"That would be a mistake." His threat was softly worded, but there was a gleam of cruelty in his eyes. He held a hypodermic needle at his side as if she wouldn't notice. And before in the drugged condition that he'd kept her in, she probably wouldn't have.

"I'm terminating our doctor-patient relationship."

He scoffed and moved toward her. "You don't have the authority."

"Yes, I do."

He hesitated. "No one will believe you because you're unstable; it's my word against yours."

"And mine—" Angelica said in halting English from behind him.

He spun around, not bothering to hide his annoyance at the intrusion. "Get out!"

"Dr. Hadley. You. Are. Dismissed. Fired. Finished. Leave, or I'll call the police."

"Your father hired me, not you." He pointed his finger at Angelica before he stomped out. "You—you'll regret this."

Marisa and Angelica stared at each other for a moment.

"Way to go, Marisa! Now, what can I do for you?"

"I'm going to the Heavens Child fundraiser tonight." Her eyes were glittery with anticipation. It was her first public event since she'd returned from her honeymoon. "Will you help me select something to wear?"

Angelica beamed. "Of course," she said and entered the walk-in closet. "Does your father know you're going?"

"No."

Angelica unzipped the bag of evening dresses. "Does Jeffery know?"

Marisa chewed her bottom lip. "Maybe this isn't such a great idea."

"It's a wonderful idea. Like Cinderella, you'll show up unannounced and surprise everyone. Remember to keep your shoes on. Now, long or short?"

"Long, I think. Or, short. Or whatever fits."

They settled on a full-length gown of pale blue embroidered silk organza with long sleeves to hide her thin arms. Next, she luxuriated in a scented bath and drank a cup of herbal tea that Angelica prepared.

There would be repercussions to her daring decision. Kyle would be shocked. He expected her to stay home. Jeffery, who was living a free, unencumbered life, would be polite in public and abusive later.

It was imperative that she attended the gala. She couldn't wait any longer to tell Lauren her suspicions. After her bath, she treated herself to her favorite body lotion, and then selected a set of lacy undergarments that she'd bought before her wedding, but never worn. Angelica styled her hair in loose curls, and Marisa applied a touch of eye makeup that emphasized her blue eyes and finished with a soft rose blush over her delicate cheekbones.

She studied herself in the full-length mirror and saw the reflection of a spirited woman that she'd not seen in years. She beamed at the image and decided she liked what she saw, but the bravado faded quickly.

"I'm nervous," she admitted, holding out shaky hands to Angelica. "Maybe I should just wait."

Angelica gave Marisa's hands a squeeze. "You'll be fine. Remember why you're going. You want to talk to Lauren. And have fun. You deserve to have fun." She gave her a tight hug, careful not to muss up Marisa's hair and makeup.

"You have my cell phone number. Call if you need me. I'll come and get you. Now, let's select your jewelry and find a pair of shoes to wear with this beautiful gown."

Marisa's stomach churned as she went downstairs to the hired Town Car. The driver opened the back door, and she slid inside. As they drove away, she practiced the breathing exercises and the visualization that Angelica had taught her—breathing in and out, visualizing peaceful colors. She imagined gold as the color of courage.

Then, added pink for freedom.

Freedom from her father and Jeffery.

Freedom from the burden of her secrets.

Bernie Anderson hated these damn fund-raisers and usually sent an over-sized donation to ease his conscience. But this was Lauren's first big plunge into the public arena. He would be there to support her. There was enough blather about his family already. No need for mass speculation as to why the remaining member of the family had spurned the event.

Dressed in tuxedo pants and a white shirt, he padded barefoot to the safe in his study and punched in the code to unlock it. A small Sig Sauer lay in the front. Bernie placed it on the table and then took out a black box that held a set of antique gold cufflinks that his sister had given him when he graduated from Stanford. He sat in the leather chair and slipped the links into the French cuffs.

Many a night he'd sat by the fire with the gun in his lap.

Elizabeth dead, Richard murdered, and Lauren— whereabouts unknown. At his lowest points, he, too, believed she was dead; even though Rand had kept assuring him, she was safe but refused to tell him how he knew.

On those nights after work and too much bourbon, he'd driven to the Casa's graveyard with the loaded gun on the seat beside him. It wouldn't have taken much for him to join the others, but something always stopped him.

Maybe it was his dead sister's voice he'd heard crying for him to live. Begging him to find out who had destroyed her family.

He and Elizabeth had grown up in Willow Glen when it was still a relatively small town. She'd always been full of life. As the older brother, he'd taken pride in her accomplishments, mourned the loss of her babies, and supported her foundation.

Elizabeth had remained loving and steady. She'd never let wealth or fame or tragedies bring her low. He was stunned when she died. Allergy. She'd never been allergic to anything in her life. Still, she was gone. Never regained consciousness. She'd picked up Marisa that morning. They'd gone shopping, had lunch, and an hour later she went into anaphylactic shock. By the time the ambulance arrived, she was in full cardiac arrest.

The paramedics stabilized her, rushed her to the hospital, but her heart stopped, and she'd died that night with the family gathered around her.

Bernie was skeptical, but Marisa confirmed that she'd asked Elizabeth to go shopping with her for Lauren's birthday present. He knew in his gut there had to be something else, but never found the missing link. Now, all he had were memories and a shit-load of fear and regret.

Until he found the proof to confirm what he and Richard had suspected, he would protect his niece with his silence. The investigations he'd done with Rand were dead-ends so far, but that wouldn't stop him. He'd keep going, searching, even if he had to accept that he might never know why Richard was murdered. Or who killed him.

He worried about Lauren's safety. She'd be better off living in town, either at his house or a condo anywhere but the Casa.

At least, Sam was with her. He'd protect her until she understood it was best for her to move to a safer place.

Bernie slipped on his shoes, adjusted his cuffs, put the Sig in the safe. He carried a smaller one in his Mercedes, just like the one Richard had carried in his glove compartment. He wondered where that gun was now.

Fiona Sobrantes-Wilson studied her reflection in the mirrored closet doors. The bronze silk dress she'd chosen to wear to the gala hugged her generous curves and dipped between her breasts displaying provocative cleavage.

Assured that the sporadic sessions of yoga, karate, and Pilates had done their job, she smoothed the fabric over her hips. Gold strappy shoes with four-inch heels took her height to almost 5'11"—tall enough to hold her own with the men of power at tonight's event.

From the jewelry box, she selected a 50 CT chocolate teardrop diamond necklace, a cocktail ring in a floral motif, and matching drop earrings. The dress and diamonds set off her auburn hair and tan shoulders. She dabbed a drop of perfume in between her breasts and behind her ears.

Fiona sighed. Her life had disintegrated the day Richard died. She'd been in Palm Springs on a spa vacation with friends when Bernie called to ask if she knew where Richard was. Then the next morning he'd called with the terrible news that Richard was gone.

A full investigation was underway when she returned. Lauren was unresponsive, numb with grief. Not that Fiona had ever expected Lauren to support her. She'd resented their marriage, the fact that Fiona was only twelve years older than her, and that Richard loved her.

Fiona had longed to be part of the Sobrantes family. She'd worked for the Heavens Child Foundation and thought the world of Lauren's mother, Elizabeth.

When Richard had asked her out, she was beyond elated. She'd wanted a family and babies, but those dreams never panned out. She could be a bitch with the sharpest tongue this side of Texas, and she'd used it repeatedly in self-defense, which alienated Lauren further. Finally, Richard had had enough, and they separated, but she'd believed it was only a matter of time before they reconciled.

Lauren had viewed her as a threat, a gold digger, and a wannabe, a poser. Oh, she'd heard all the names her stepdaughter called her. The truth was she'd loved Richard and would have even without his wealth. He was an exciting man, full of life. After he died, she'd hoped the commonality of grief might bring them closer.

Tonight, she would have to face them for the first time since the funeral and the regrettable incident after the funeral. She didn't have to attend. She could stay home, eat popcorn, and watch a movie. But taking the coward's way out had never worked for her.

No, she'd show up with a smile. And to hell with them all. She vowed to have only one glass of wine. One glass. Well, maybe two.

Lauren stepped out of the shower, wrapped a cream-colored bath sheet around her, and strolled into her dressing room.

Sam and Deke were against her going to the gala. They'd tried to convince her to stay home where it was safe. She'd given her word to Kyle. After he'd announced she was to be the guest of honor, the ticket sales skyrocketed, and the event sold out.

Of course, she'd be safe. Who in their right mind would attempt to attack her at such a public gathering?

She exhaled a laugh. Who'd have imagined that she'd be accused of murder, branded a sex fiend by Anna Brownlee, and then sexually assaulted by her ex-fiancé? Plus, find the watch and be interrogated by Schott, who now questioned if Anna Brownlee's book was factual.

The doubt in Detective Schott's eyes was obvious when he questioned her. Doubt that she just *found* the watch in the boxes. Doubt that someone had tried to kill her.

An array of evening gowns hung in her closet. She selected a classic Givenchy red silk that had been her mother's. Opening the lingerie drawer, she chose silky red underwear and a matching strapless bra. Sitting at the dressing table, she created an up sweep hairstyle, pinning the sides up with diamond-studded clips and letting the rest cascade down her back in long curls. She applied a touch of makeup, a quick gloss of red on her lips, and she was done.

Lauren stepped into the gown, slipped her arms through the narrow straps, and smoothed the dress over her body. Soft layers of chiffon hugged her torso from her breasts to below the hips where the skirt flared out in layers.

She studied her reflection in the mirror. The red dress made an undeniable statement—*Go big or go home.* Opening a long flat box that was couriered over from the jeweler, she took out a large pear-shaped ruby pendant scrolled in a gold Art Déco design, surrounded by European-cut diamonds. The pendant hung just above her breasts and sparkled in the light. Matching earrings lay tucked in a small bag. She added a ruby ring and a red clutch bag.

She was ready, but where was her date?

Sam left that morning to run errands, leaving Freddie in charge as the bodyguard. After the incident with Jeffery, the man was excessively cautious, hovering around her until she finally told him to wait in the kitchen.

Etta kept him busy chopping vegetables, but he still managed to check the locks and the alarm every few minutes.

Jeffery's attack was unnerving. But his intent was sex, not murder. Not that being raped or brutalized was better, but it wasn't as final as being dead. Anyway, she refused to cut off communication until he told her everything he knew.

She called the cottage. Sam didn't answer. He'd refused to allow her to buy him a new tux. He said he had it covered, but she wondered if he was having trouble getting dressed.

She imagined him in an ill-fitting rental with his scruffy beard, and black stitches across his cheekbone.

Neanderthal, Jeffery had called him. She remembered how Sam had pulled Jeffery off her. How he'd held her until she stopped trembling. And at the cemetery, how he'd brought her home and gave her the incentive to keep going.

Sam might be a Neanderthal, but he was her Neanderthal, at least for tonight. Tomorrow he might be leaving. The doorbell interrupted her musing.

Freddie motioned for her to stand back.

Lauren waited in the foyer. Etta joined her.

"Oh, my goodness," Lauren whispered.

Miss Etta moaned.

Watson wagged his tail as Sam entered.

There was no sign of the bearded flannel-shirted-mountain-man. The new version of Sam Gallagher was handsome and polished, straight off a GQ Magazine cover.

He looked sexy as the devil in a black tux that fit as if it were hand-tailored for him. His hair was precision cut. The stitches were gone leaving a minuscule red line across his cheekbone, his nails manicured and buffed.

His clean-shaven square jaw shouted stubbornness, while his sculpted lips murmured sin.

A dimple in his left cheek deepened when he smiled, promising trouble.

Lauren realized this was going to be a long night.

Chapter Thirty-One
~~~~~

Spotlights in the Plaza de Cesar Chavez Park crisscrossed, illuminating the night sky. Network trucks lined the streets around the park. Satellites rose like supplicants to the electronic heavens.

Spectators lunged against the restrictive ropes in front of the Fairmont Hotel. People hung over the barricades, screaming and whistling to celebrities. Voices shouted above the scrum of reporters, photographers, and television crews, all fighting for space on either side of the hotel's portico.

"*Ms. Sobrantes—Lauren, look this way—*"

"*Who d'you hire to kill your dad?*"

"*Hey baby, I got it, right here. Call me, sugar—*"

A twitter rippled through the crowd.

Lauren kept a brave face and waved to the people amid the flashes of cameras and television lights. Sam ducked his head to avoid the cameras.

A uniformed woman from the hotel, flanked by security, greeted them, verified their invitation, and directed them to the escalators and the Imperial Ballroom on the second level. A string quartet played in the vestibule where men in tuxedo black gathered in small power groups to talk business.

Deke met them by the escalator. He tugged at the jacket of his rental tux. "Hey, brat. Look at you. You clean up nice, don't you?" He gave Lauren a quick peck on the cheek.

"Who is this guy with you?" he joked, shaking hands with Sam. "Have you ever seen so much bling in your life?" He kept his voice low.

149

Sam smiled. The last party he'd attended in Monaco made this event dull in comparison.

"One of us will be with you at all times," Sam stressed to Lauren.

"You are so over-reacting. No one here is going to shoot me."

"You agreed to let us protect you, so behave, or I swear to God, I will pick you up and carry you out." Sam glowered in her direction.

"I'll run interference," Deke added, his smile not reaching his eyes. "We're unified protection—oh, shit, here comes trouble." He nodded toward an approaching woman before he rapidly scurried away.

"So much for *unified*," Lauren muttered as Fiona joined them.

Fiona looked Lauren up and down. "Well, I see you're not dead like that psychic said."

"Quite alive, actually."

"Pity."

"Sam, my father's wife, Fiona Sobrantes-Wilson. Fiona, Sam Gallagher."

"Well, isn't he nice and big? You look like you'd be a great dancer, Mr. Gallagher." Fiona all but purred before she turned to Lauren. "Will you be staying, this time, Lauren, or do you plan to vanish again when the mood strikes you?"

"I'm staying."

"Well, should you decide to leave, please notify the authorities before you take off. Being called in for questioning is so tedious. You know how that is, don't you, since Richard's watch turned up in your possession?"

Lauren wondered how she found out.

Before she could ask, Fiona turned, and smiled at Sam. "I'll be at the bar having a *real* drink. Join me if you desire something stronger, Mr. Gallagher." Hips swaying, she strolled away.

"Wow." Sam released the breath he was holding.

"Yeah. She's a piece of work." Fiona could be a viper, obnoxious, and inappropriate, but was she a murderer?

Waiters in silvery blue vests served champagne in crystal

goblets. Sam handed a glass to Lauren. She sipped and smiled to people as they passed by.

"Does it feel like old home-week?" Sam asked.

"More like a bug under a microscope."

"Promise me you won't ask any of them about your dad."

"We'll see."

They drifted into the ballroom. Round tables draped in silver with centerpieces of roses, carnations, and ferns; each had a 25th Anniversary flag. The program's cover, designed by Marisa years ago was a silvery blue cloud with two cherubs playfully peeking out.

Large flat-screen monitors on each wall narrated the charity's history. Lauren held Sam's arm as she watched her family's progress through time, unshed tears glistened in her eyes. The presentation paused on a photo of her parents, heads together laughing. Two months later, Lauren's mother was dead.

"Here she is," Bernie called out as Sam and Lauren approached their table at the front of the room. Sam left Lauren with Bernie and he went to find Deke.

Jeffery joined them, a fresh drink in hand.

"I understand you told Detective Schott that you couldn't remember being with me the day my dad died."

Jeffery lifted his glass. "Memory is a funny thing, isn't it?"

"I suggest that you start sharpening your recall because lying to the authorities is a bad idea."

Jeffery smirked and sauntered off before Sam returned. Lauren chatted with Kyle until he suddenly frowned. Following his gaze, she saw Marisa enter the ballroom; her blue gown shimmering in the bright lights.

Lauren worked her way through the crowd to meet her. "I'm so glad you're here, Risa." She slipped an arm around Marisa's waist as they walked toward their table. "You look lovely."

"Thanks. Listen, we have to talk—" she stopped abruptly when Kyle joined them.

"Well, this is a surprise."

"Last-minute decision," Marisa replied, lightly.

Lauren knew that whatever Marisa had to tell her would

have to wait until they were alone.

Sam escorted Lauren to the microphone when Kyle introduced her. He waited in the shadows and scrutinized the crowd, trying to envision the one person in the room who hated Lauren so much that they wanted her dead.

"Good evening, thank you, Kyle, for your kind words," she paused; the room hushed in anticipation.

"I am...Lauren Elizabeth Graciana Sobrantes." Her voice was firm and musical. I am here tonight to declare that the news of my death was greatly exaggerated."

The audience burst into boisterous laughter.

She paused a tad longer. "And I want to assure you that my *ghost...*" she laughed. "My ghost—she is such a liar."

They rose to their feet, clapping, whistling, and laughing with her. She grew serious as they sat down. "I also want to say how much I appreciate your support in carrying forth the wonderful work of my mother, Elizabeth Sobrantes, who instead of losing herself in grief with the death of her sons, created the Heavens Child Foundation."

The crowd watched her with a look of joy for this woman, one of their own, who had returned to them alive and unharmed. Some discreetly wiped away tears, others obviously lusted, and a few stared with disgust.

Lauren concluded her talk by generously praising Kyle and the organizers and asked everyone to dig a little deeper to make this the biggest fundraising ever.

She accepted as many congratulations and promises of donations as she could handle before she needed to visit the ladies' room. Sam ducked into the men's room, leaving Deke in charge of guarding Lauren.

Washing her hands, Lauren looked up in the mirror. Fiona stood behind her, lips twisted in a fury.

"You're quite a little comedian aren't you? They all love you. I know it's just an act. They don't know the real you, not like I do."

"Fiona, perhaps—"

"You bitch," Fiona spit the words, her face contorted with

indignation. "I was questioned like a criminal when you disappeared. And again, after they caught you with Richard's watch."

"I have no control over what the police do or whom they question. I told Schott the truth. Deke said you had taken boxes out of the Casa after I left and that he made you put them back. That's all."

"Those things were mine. Everything I packed up was mine. You had—you have no right to keep them."

The alcohol on Fiona's breath was overpowering. She obviously had several of those *real* drinks.

Lauren stepped back. "I'm sorry that you..." But she wasn't sorry. She hadn't cared about her stepmother after Richard's funeral. "Honestly, I'm not sorry. Not at all." Lauren turned and walked away.

Fiona followed. "You damn well will be sorry and soon."

"What do you mean?"

Fiona stepped closer, jabbed a finger at Lauren's face. "I'm suing you for half of the estate, which is rightfully mine. Richard left the Casa and surrounding property to me."

Lauren chuckled. "Go right ahead, Fiona. Do what you need to do and see how far it gets you."

Fiona turned on her heel. Deke stepped forward and escorted her away from Lauren.

Jeffery came out of nowhere. He grabbed Lauren, held her close, tried for a slobbery kiss, but missed her mouth. His breath, like Fiona's, was thick with booze. She had to fight her rising panic and the rush of adrenaline.

"Let me go, Jeffery."

Jeffery rocked back and then gripped her arms tighter, using her for balance. "You're doing that guy, aren't you? Of course, you are, you slut."

"Who I *do* is none of your business."

"You have to take me back. My life is ruined because of you," Jeffery whined, leaned into her and nuzzled his face into her neck. He ran his tongue across her skin.

She shuddered with revulsion. "Get away from me. Or this time I *will* have you arrested." Had he forgotten he tried to rape her on Tuesday?

He reared back, lips twisted in fury. "You owe me! I wouldn't be married to that skank if you hadn't run out on me."

"I owe you nothing."

"If you'd just give me a chance to explain."

"There is nothing to explain." Where were Sam and Deke when she needed them?

"Oh, yeah, there is—it wasn't what you thought."

"You're right. It wasn't what I thought. It was what I saw. You. Banging my stepmother in my father's study." Old rage infused the memory of that night. She stomped a stiletto heel on the toe of Jeffery's patent-leather shoe, but he was too drunk to notice.

"You'll regret this, sweetie." Jeffery's voice was harsh. "I have a name. I have the name of the man who killed your dad."

Sam rushed from the men's room, pulled Jeffery away from Lauren and held him by his throat. "I told you to leave her alone."

"Whadda you gonna do? Beat me up, again?" Jeffery challenged, breaking the hold. He swayed toward Sam. "Or, kill me?" he shouted.

"That can be arranged, so don't push me," Sam retorted.

"Wait." Lauren grabbed Sam's arm.

"Too late, baby." Jeffery twisted around Sam, smirking. "Too fucking late."

"Time to go home, Jeffery." Marisa stood behind them with Deke and a security guard at her side. "Please, escort him to the lobby and call a taxi to take him home."

The men took Jeffery down the hallway to the back escalator. The information Lauren needed went with him.

Lauren turned to Marisa. 'I want you to know I haven't encouraged Jeffery. I don't want him."

"Neither do I." Marisa continued to stare down the hallway. "Kyle won't be pleased about this. He hates it when Jeffery makes a scene."

"Mom would be so happy that you're here tonight," Lauren said, remembering past galas they'd shared.

Marisa sighed. "I miss your mom."

"Me, too. Marisa, you said you had something tell me."

"Not now," Marisa whispered. "Not here. Can we meet tomorrow? In the afternoon, maybe"

"Come over. We'll have lunch."

"I'll call you."

"Risa, I want us to be friends again, like when we were kids. Risa and Lulu. We'll create some new adventures."

Sadness filled Marisa's eyes. "Too much has happened for us to ever be friends again."

Media diehards hung around the exit hoping for one last photo of someone famous but were silent when Sam and Lauren walked out.

"That's not our driver," Lauren protested, as they got closer to the limo parked under the portico. Sam nodded to the man holding the passenger door open.

"I know him. He's okay." Sam assured her. Lauren slipped inside. Then he walked around to the driver's side of the limo.

Sam shook hands with Flynn. "That's some disguise you have; you look good with a mustache. You're the last person I expected to see. What are you doing here?"

"Heard you were hanging out with an ultra-hot woman. Thought I better check her out."

Flynn looked Sam over from head to toe. "I'm glad you're back to your old style, except that new scar on your cheek. What the hell are you doing at a public gig like this? Media's all over the place."

"What's going on?" Sam knew Flynn wasn't here to check out a woman, especially one he couldn't have.

Flynn's demeanor changed. "We need you to get back on the job."

"I told Jon I'd leave tomorrow."

"Damn straight. I'm the one flying you out in the morning. Early." Flynn jerked open the driver's door. "And you better be ready!"

Sam got in the back seat with Lauren. The limo pulled smoothly into the flow of traffic.

"The evening went well, I'd say," Lauren commented. It

had almost felt normal.

"Except for Jeffery and Fiona, and Marisa showing up."

She laughed. "Yes, except for them. Sam, thank you for coming tonight." She placed her hand on his thigh. "Did I see women slipping their phone numbers in your pocket?"

If they had, he didn't notice. Lauren was the only woman he'd seen tonight. He lifted her hand to his lips and kissed her palm.

She shifted toward him. Reaching for her, he cupped her head, drew her closer. His mouth settled on hers, gently at first, the kiss deepening when she hungrily responded. She moved closer, pressing against him. He trailed kisses down the side of her neck, across the top of her breasts—she sighed and slipped her hand over his erection.

Sam heard Flynn whisper, *mercy* before the privacy window closed.

At the estate, Flynn parked at the cottage as Sam had directed. He kept the limo idling while they composed themselves. After a few moments, Sam ushered Lauren inside and deactivated the alarm.

"Look at you Sammy-Sam," Flynn chided when Sam came out again. His tie off, shirt pulled out, and his hair messy.

"No wonder my windshield got so goddamned steamed. I could barely see where I was going." Flynn pulled out a handful of foil packets from his coat pocket and passed them to Sam. "Here, I'll share with you. Have a good time while you can, brother."

"Condoms?"

"Shit man, I figure yours are so old they're rubber bands by now." Flynn pulled more from another pocket.

Sam's hands were filled. "How many you got—a dozen?"

"Two..." Flynn's laugh was deep. "I gave you half. Now, go, make your family proud. Just be at the airport and ready to go by 6:00.

Flynn drove away. Sam stuffed the condoms into his coat pockets before he went inside where Lauren waited, curled on the sofa, feet tucked under her. She closed her cell phone, looked at him, and smiled an invitation to carry on.

An invitation he gladly accepted. He hurried to the control room, checked the perimeter alarm systems, and then reset the alarms for the main house and cottage. He took off his jacket, removed the Glock and holster, and set the safety before locking the weapon in the drawer. He took a few condoms, and then a few more, and tucked them into his pants pocket before he took Lauren upstairs to his room.

In the moonlight, she slipped out of her dress and let it pool on the floor. Sam kissed her soft, exposed skin and unfastened her strapless bra leaving the ruby nestled above her breasts, and the tiny, mind-blowing scrap of red silk covering her bottom.

She removed the studs from his shirt and pushed it off his shoulders, caressing the hardness of his chest.

"Lauren, I'm leaving tomorrow morning."

She unbuckled his belt. "Then we'll make this the best one-night-stand ever."

"Count me in," he said, voice husky with desire. "But, are you sure?"

"You started this, Gallagher. I want you out of the pretty-and-polished and down to the skin." Her nipples pebbled against his bare chest. She ran her fingernails through his hair and kissed him greedily.

Coming up for air, he held her tight, savoring the essence of this gorgeous woman naked in his arms.

The moon highlighted her hair, glowing like liquid gold.

A red dot danced past her temple.

Sam pulled her to him.

Held her tight.

Threw her on the bed.

And rolled to the floor, shielding her with his body.

The window exploded.

Glass shattered across the floor.

Two bullets embedded in the wall above them.

Chapter Thirty-Two

~~~~~

The security alarm screeched. Sam rolled off Lauren and ran his hands over her shaking body, but felt no cuts or blood. Crouching low, he dragged the comforter off the bed and threw it over the broken glass on the floor.

He yanked t-shirts from the dresser drawer and helped Lauren into one. Then, he grabbed the pair of jeans he'd left hanging over the chair and pulled them on and a sweatshirt. They crawled over the comforter and ran downstairs in the dark.

In the control room, Sam turned off the alarm. The system was programmed to the sheriff's department. When Sam's phone rang, he confirmed a break-in.

"They're on their way," he told Lauren.

In the closet of the computer room, he took a pair of night goggles. He checked the Glock and slid an extra clip in his pocket.

Lauren pulled Sam's tux jacket over the t-shirt that hung to her knees. Adrenaline pumped erratically through her body.

"Stay here. Lock the door. Watch the monitors. Security will be here any moment. Do not let anyone in unless you've got a positive ID."

Sam was out the back door before she could protest. Two shots through the window—a professional or just a lucky hit? Had the killer hired someone else to murder Lauren? Or, were the shots meant for him?

He paused, listened, watched. No movement, just the thrum of a motorcycle in the distance, but difficult to discern if the sound came from the highway or the woods. He quickly searched the area behind the cottage and house. All clear. Then he started back toward the Casa, staying in the shadows of the trees.

Suddenly, bright lights and shadowy figures blocked the path.

"Drop your weapon!"

Sam took off his goggles, raised his hands, and very slowly bent to lay the gun on the ground. Rising cautiously, he clasped his hands behind his head before an officer forced them behind his back and handcuffed him.

Lauren burst out the door, barefoot, clutching Sam's tuxedo jacket closed. "He's not the one—" she yelled.

Guns spun in her direction. Sam roared, "STOP. Lauren. For god's sake, stop."

She froze in place. "I'm Lauren Sobrantes, owner of this place and that man is Sam Gallagher, the caretaker. He takes care of the place," she announced in a shaky voice.

"Oh baby," said the officer next to Sam. "I could take care of ya."

"Watch it," Sam warned.

"Shut up." He whacked the back of Sam's head with his hand.

Four men led Sam inside and pushed him down in a chair at the table. A heavy-set, bald-headed man who appeared to be in charge, pointed to the sofa and commanded Lauren to sit. "What happened?" he asked.

"Someone shot at us through the window." She explained as best she could without going into the details of what they were doing at the time.

"You say you were both *sleeping* upstairs. The shots shattered your bedroom window. Or, maybe your boyfriend here took a couple of shots at you, and you won't tell us because you're afraid of him."

"That's ridiculous." Lauren bristled at man's suggestion. "What gave you that idea? He was with me. Where's Detective Schott?"

"You'll talk to me first. Schott is on his way. Take her upstairs."

Lauren cried out when the officer pulled her up.

"Let go of her!" Sam shot up from the chair but was pushed back, his head slammed on the table. Blood spurted from his nose.

"What the devil is going on here?" Detective Schott shouted from the doorway. Deke stepped in behind him.

Schott cleared the room and ordered the cuffs removed from Sam. He sent his investigators upstairs to inspect the crime scene. Sam told him the guards were missing. Deke went to search for them.

Sam stanched the blood flowing from his nose with a kitchen towel while Lauren explained what happened. "Someone tried to... kill us."

Deke's cell phone rang as he walked back inside. He listened. Hung up. "They found your men, unconscious, but alive. We've called for an ambulance."

Schott went out to see them. When Sam stood to go with him, Deke stopped him. "We'll check it out. In the meantime, you stay inside. I don't want to have to arrest you for assaulting someone."

"If you think I'm cowering in here when there's a killer after us, think again."

"Don't make me handcuff you to that chair."

Sam sat.

"I'm sorry you got hurt."

"Forget it." The head-slam was kid's play compared to the interrogation from the Italian Police.

Deputies were posted to the estate, which was now a crime scene. They waited for Lauren to retrieve her clothes before they escorted her and Sam across the drive to the Casa.

Lauren put her jewelry in the safe, set the alarm, and looked for Sam, but he was gone.

A groan came from the kitchen. Sam was curled in a fetal position on the floor by the refrigerator.

"Where is he?" Zach asked as he entered the Casa.

Lauren led him to Sam. Zach crouched beside him. "Sammy, it's Zach. Hang on, buddy." Zach shined a small light back and forth in Sam's eyes.

He turned to Lauren. "What happened?"

"An officer slammed Sam's head on the table."

"We'll do an MRI. Make sure there's no new injury."

Lauren ran upstairs and dressed in jeans, shirt, and a knit sweater and raced back downstairs.

Zach had Sam on his feet when she returned. She braced her shoulder under Sam's other arm and helped walk him to Zach's car. Then, she slid into the back seat and held him while Zach sped to the hospital. They disappeared behind the restricted doors of the emergency room. She waited, wandered around the room, picked up, and discarded outdated magazines.

People died from head injuries. Was the head-slam to the table hard enough that Sam could die? She walked the length of the waiting room.

A tall, gray-haired man in worn chinos and a green Carhartt jacket rushed through the doors. At the desk, he asked for Zach and was told to wait.

The man paced. Nodding as he passed by her. He sat down, jumped up, and walked in circles. He sat down again and dropped his head in his hands as if he couldn't go on any longer.

Lauren couldn't abide seeing the man in such anguish. She moved to sit beside him. "Are you all right?" she asked.

He looked up. "My son was brought in with a head injury."

She studied his face and saw the resemblance to Sam, and of course, to Zach. "Sam Gallagher?"

The man looked at her with surprise. "Yes, you know him?"

"I was with him tonight."

"Then you must be—" His eyes widened, and his body relaxed a little.

"Shush," Lauren whispered, looking around to see if they'd been overheard. "I am."

"I'm Sam's father, Emmett. I... I worry about Sam."

"Zach told me that he'd be fine." She prayed he was right and not just placating her to keep her calm.

"Sam takes chances, so many chances. I never know." His voice choked. He cleared his throat before continuing. "We don't talk, but you probably know that. He refuses to meet me, returns my letters unopened, ignores my phone calls, so there's no way I can tell him how sorry I am." Emmett abruptly stood and began pacing again.

After a long wait, a nurse pushed Sam out in a wheelchair. Zach spoke loudly enough for his father to hear. "Sam's got a bad headache. No concussion or further injury."

Lauren choked back a sob. Sam sat slumped, eyes closed. Emmett gave a wobbly grin when he heard Zach say that Sam was okay, but he didn't join them.

Zach nodded to his dad. "He's high on pain meds right now."

While Zach went for the car, Lauren walked out with the nurse and waited beside the wheelchair. The nurse and Zach loaded Sam into the back seat.

"I'm fine." Sam protested laconically to no one in particular. He gave Lauren a loopy smile when she got in and buckled the seat belt around him. "Just fine."

He stared at her for several moments. "Zach, I found her. Did ya know that? She was lost. I found this beautiful woman falling out of a tree. I caught her and took her home."

Lauren tried hard not to laugh.

"Isn't that right, honey?"

"Yes, Sam, you found me." Difficult to believe it was just a little over a week ago.

"Finders keepers…" Sam closed his eyes and collapsed against her.

Zach and Lauren burst out laughing.

"This is certainly a different side of him," Lauren said.

"He was funny like that as a kid until a friend of his died. Then he changed."

"What happened?"

Zach was silent. Lauren wondered if he'd heard her.

"No one knows for sure. You'll have to ask Sam."

Chapter Thirty-Three

~~~~~

The sky had lightened to a deep blue when Lauren and Zach returned to the Casa. Yellow tape fluttered around the cottage, a grim reminder of how close she and Sam had come to dying. The sheriff posted a new man as guard and Deke replaced others for the men who were injured.

She and Zach struggled to move a very relaxed Sam upstairs to the guest room. Zach helped him undress and get into the bed. Lauren reassured Zach she'd be safe with the new security and she promised to call immediately if there were the slightest change in Sam's condition.

Lauren showered and slipped on a white silk nightshirt, turned back the covers, and spooned against Sam's back. What a mysterious man, so full of secrets—the injury in Afghanistan, his estrangement with his father, and his friend dying when they were young. She wondered what else he was hiding.

Lauren dozed sporadically and woke mid-morning. Last night's festivities seemed so long ago that they felt almost dreamlike—the gala, Jeffery's confrontation, bullets flying, inches from death, Sam protecting her, and then him being injured.

He lay on his side with his arm folded under the pillow, the stubble of whiskers dark against his pale, bruised face. She watched him sleep, his breathing deep and even. She wanted to stay snuggled beside him, but nature called, and along with the need for coffee.

Downstairs, Lauren turned on the coffee pot that Miss Etta had prepared before leaving for Rand's house. Was that just

163

yesterday? Had Etta suspected that Sam would end up in Lauren's bed? Was that why she took Mr. Watson with her; to give them privacy?

She returned to the bedroom with two cups of coffee and a plate of the coveted raspberry scones. Sam sat up in bed as she entered.

"Nice nightshirt," he smiled, his eyes roaming over her body.

She slipped in beside him. "How's your headache?"

"My head feels dull."

"I like your brother." Lauren felt him tense. "Zach was worried, but he said the MRI looked good." She didn't mention the talk she'd had with his father or that she'd invited him to visit.

"Zach took me to the hospital?"

"You were in bad shape. He checked you out to make sure you didn't have a concussion."

Sam drank his coffee before answering. "He's a good brother. My family is rather, well, it's hard to explain."

They'd save the storytelling for later, Lauren decided. Placing her cup on the nightstand, she sat up on her knees, facing him. "You slept well."

"I did? Was I alone?"

"Hmm." She unbuttoned the top button of her shirt.

He smiled, placed his cup beside hers on the nightstand, and reached for her. "Was I compromised?"

"Don't you remember?" she teased and held his gaze as she undid two more buttons, exposing a wedge of breast and taut belly.

"Maybe you could remind me." Sam ran his hands up her sides and cupped her breasts in the palms of his hands.

"Is your headache really gone?"

"Yep."

"Good, cause I'm about to have my way with you." Slipping off the shirt, she straddled Sam's hips and lowered her mouth to his.

Sam drew her closer, caressing her nipple with thumb and finger.

She gasped. "Do we, ah, have protection?"

"Do I have protection? Honey, if you only knew."

Sam cursed when his satellite phone rang. Lauren sighed, repositioned herself to nestle beside him, his arm around her, and the warmth of her breasts against his chest.

"Yeah, what do you want," Sam snapped at Flynn. He caressed Lauren's shoulder as he listened.

"Heard you had another rough headache." Flynn's voice boomed over the phone, ignoring Sam's testiness.

"It was nothing."

"Emergency room, MRI, Vicodin—that adds up to something in my book."

"What happened to that doctor-patient-privilege concept?"

"It's superseded by brotherly intimidation."

"I thought Zach could keep a secret."

"Not like you. So, what happened? I drop you off with a beautiful woman hot for your body, and you end up getting shot at, head thumped, and hospitalized. Do I have to watch you all the time?" Flynn chuckled before turning serious. "That was too damn close. You have any idea what's going on?"

"They're investigating. I'm not sure if the target was Lauren or me."

"Sam, don't stick around for this one. It won't end well. Get out before it's too late."

Sam looked at Lauren curled against him. *It already was too late.* Flynn was right. Of course, he was right. It was dangerous for him to stay. But how could he go back to work with Flynn and Jon? Not now. Not until Lauren was safe and not until he was a hundred percent—over the headaches and hallucinations.

Flynn interrupted Sam's thoughts. "Listen, if you need to get out quick, call me. Just don't get trapped again, Sam. Please, for God's sake, don't let yourself get trapped again."

Chapter Thirty-Four

~~~~~

Morning sunlight danced through the canopy of trees along the two-lane road as Detective Schott drove toward Woodside to talk with Jeffery Davis. Just another sunrise in paradise, he mused. But this wasn't paradise.

Paradise—*ultimate abode of the just.*

What was *just* about the fact that Richard Sobrantes' killer was still at large after more than two years and that someone tried to murder the man's daughter?

It was not paradise if you found yourself awake in the middle of the night so starved for the sound of another person's voice that you turned on the emergency scanner for company. Which was how he'd learned that shots were fired at the Sobrantes estate.

The attempted murder of Lauren and Sam created more questions than answers.

Why was Lauren a target? She had to be a threat, but to whom? And, why? Deke told him about the confrontation between Sam and Jeffery at the gala, but was it enough to provoke Jeffery to shoot at them?

Ed pulled up to the Montgomery gates, pushed the intercom, and identified himself. The gates slowly opened.

A dark-haired woman greeted Ed and escorted him inside, her shoes soundless across the gray terrazzo floors. She led the way to the breakfast room where Kyle sat at a round glass-top table, eating breakfast. He rose from his chair and greeted Ed with a friendly smile and outstretched hand.

Schott showed his credentials and shook hands. Kyle

166

nodded, "Yes, of course. I remember you from the investigation of Richard's death." He gestured to a chair. "Please, join me. Would you like breakfast?"

"Just coffee, thanks." He encouraged Kyle to finish eating. In his experience, people were more relaxed while eating, which made it easier to gather information. The dark-haired woman brought his coffee and placed a basket of muffins beside him.

Kyle resumed eating. "What brings you out so early on Sunday morning?"

Ed sipped his coffee, leaned back in his chair as if he had all the time in the world. "I'd like to speak with your son-in-law, Jeffery Davis."

"Christ, what's he done, now?"

"He may have done nothing, that's why I need to see him."

"Angelica, get Mr. Jeffery." Kyle ordered the woman in English, gesturing upstairs. She left the room in a controlled graceful rush.

Ed broke open a warm blueberry muffin. It smelled freshly baked and homemade. It reminded him of the muffins his wife used to make for their Sunday brunches.

"Lauren mentioned that you're re-investigating Richard's murder."

"We're taking another look at everything—in case someone remembers details that we didn't have before."

They waited in silence until Angelica returned, followed by Marisa, who floated across the tile floor wearing a silk kimono of brown and gold chrysanthemums. Her blonde hair was pulled back and tied with a simple ribbon. Her face, without makeup, was as pale as porcelain.

Ed stood as she entered.

Following her was a dapper dressed man in gray slacks and a starched white shirt. He had a thin face, bushy gray hair, and an air of supremacy.

"You remember my daughter, Marisa." Kyle re-introduced her to Schott. "And, Dr. Hadley, her physician."

"Good morning," she said, placing her small hand in his large, warm one. "You wanted Jeffery?" She positioned herself away from the doctor.

Ed waited until she was settled before replying, "Yes."

"He's not here." Marisa nodded thanks to Angelica for the coffee. There was a delicate trembling of her hand as she lifted the cup to drink.

"Any idea where he might be?"

"Did you check his place at the beach in Aptos?" She put the cup aside and broke open a muffin.

Schott took out his notebook and silver pen. "When did you see him last, Ms. Davis?"

"Montgomery. I kept my family name when I married."

"Sorry. *Ms. Montgomery*. When did you last see your husband?"

She tensed at the word husband, piquing Schott's curiosity about their relationship.

"Between one and two o'clock this morning. He came into the bedroom to change clothes, answered a couple of phone calls, and went out again."

Around the table, everyone watched Schott tensely as if they were holding a collective breath and waiting for—for what?

"Do you know who called?"

Marisa hesitated, glancing at her father and the doctor.

Schott changed directions. "I understand there was an argument between Jeffery and Lauren Sobrantes at the event you attended."

"I wasn't there," Dr. Hadley declared without being asked. He snapped his fingers for more coffee. Angelica, who stood nearby brought the carafe. Her dislike of the man was palpable.

"Well, I was there, and there was no argument." Kyle threw a sharp look at his daughter.

Marisa ignored him. Her blue eyes locked to Ed's. "Jeffery was drunk. He started bullying Lauren. Sam intervened, and Jeffery was taken away by hotel security. I asked the man to call a taxi." Her voice was clear and unwavering; the muffin mushed between her fingers.

"Marisa, honey." Kyle's voice had a warning tone. "Why don't we let Dr. Hadley take you back upstairs? This seems to be upsetting you."

"I'm fine, Kyle," she replied tersely.

The doctor pushed back from his chair. "You missed your medications last night and again this morning."

Marisa wiped her hand on the napkin before she looked at the doctor. "Perhaps you've forgotten that I fired you. Touch me, and I'll have Detective Schott arrest you."

Kyle looked as if he was ready to say more, but he remained silent. Schott was impressed by the young woman's grit. The undercurrent between her and the two men was obvious. It looked as if it took every ounce of courage this woman had to safeguard herself from them both.

"Ms. Montgomery, perhaps we could talk in private."

"I can't allow you to question her," Kyle protested. "She's not been well. That's why we have a personal physician living here." He stood as if to escort Schott out.

"This isn't an interrogation, sir. Marisa is of legal age, and as such can choose whether she wishes to speak to me in private."

"I'll call my attorney."

Schott sighed. "Your choice. We can talk here, or I can take her to the station." His voice was calm; the intent of his message clear.

"Why do you want to talk to her?"

"As I said, I'm reevaluating the Sobrantes murder." He'd tell them about the shooting later, if necessary.

Marisa watched the men and finally, she stood. "Let's go into the study. My father won't object, will you, Kyle?"

Schott closed the door behind them. Marisa walked to the window and looked at the garden and the bubbling water in the stone fountain, all designed to promote tranquility inside as well as outside. It was an elaborate façade. Her constant struggle for perfection in this house had destroyed any peace she might have ever possessed.

Heat flashed through her body; her palms sweated, heart pounded. She knew it was her body's process to rid itself of the drugs, to clean out the toxins built up over the months of Hadley's treatments.

How much should she tell this detective? Telling the truth

might cleanse her guilt, but who'd be destroyed in the process?

"Ms. Montgomery?"

She heard him talking. She forced herself to concentrate. No screaming, no crying, or Kyle would be on her, letting the doctor inject his drugs to keep her docile.

"Sorry," she mumbled. "What did you say?" If only her heart would stop racing.

"I asked if you're all right?" Schott spoke quietly.

She nodded. "You can do this," she said to herself.

"Pardon?"

Marisa took deep breaths. "Give me a moment."

"Of course." Schott began to talk about the garden, his wife, and how much he missed her. He told Marisa about their plans for the cruise and the long list of places they planned to visit after he retired. She couldn't concentrate on the details but his soothing voice put her at ease.

"Thank you," she said turning to look into his sympathetic face. Her heart rate slowed to normal, and the buzzing in her head dissipated a little. She could tell from his smile he'd been aware of what she was going through.

"Shall we sit?" She led him to the sofa. "My husband is often gone," she volunteered when they settled. "I told you about the beach house in Aptos. That's undoubtedly where you'll find him."

"You said there was a confrontation between Lauren and Jeffery. Do you know what it was about?"

Photos of Jeffery and Lauren had made the rounds on multiple social media sites that she read last night when she couldn't sleep. And there was a blurry photo of Sam with his hand on Jeffery's throat.

"I wasn't there when it started." She gave the details of what she'd witnessed of the argument with Lauren, including Jeffery's taunt to Sam about beating him up again or killing him.

"What did he mean?"

Marisa shrugged and gave a ragged sigh. "I just know Sam told Jeffery that killing him could be arranged."

"Someone called after you got home, right?"

Nausea pushed up into her throat. Unable to sit still, she

stood, stepped away from Schott, and wiped her sweaty palms on her kimono.

"Marisa, who called Jeffery?" Schott got to his feet but didn't approach her.

She shook her head.

Ed pushed. "You know, don't you?"

She turned away. Refused to answer.

"If I find out you're withholding information, you could be charged with obstructing an investigation."

She nodded that she understood and raised a trembling hand to her mouth as if to keep the words inside.

"I'm asking again. Who was it?"

Marisa still hesitated, but the name rushed out. "Lauren. Lauren Sobrantes. Jeffery said she asked him to meet her."

Kyle and Dr. Hadley were standing outside the study door when Schott and Marisa walked out. The concern on Kyle's face was obvious.

"Thank you, Ms. Montgomery, you've been most helpful," Schott said softly, offering solace in his voice and in the steadiness of his handshake.

Kyle nodded to Angelica. She moved to Marisa's side. He turned to Schott. "I'm curious as to why you've come so early on a Sunday morning. If you are re-investigating Richard's case, why didn't you wait until tomorrow during regular hours?"

The news of the shooting had to be public by now. There was no reason for them not to know. "Someone tried to murder Lauren Sobrantes early this morning."

Marisa screamed and crumpled to the floor. Dr. Hadley rushed to her, but she pushed him away.

"Leave her be," Schott commanded. He lifted her up, supporting her as she wheezed for breath. "Lauren is fine. The shooter missed," he assured her.

"I'll take her." Hadley reached for her again. She batted his hands away.

"I will charge you with assault if you touch or treat her without her permission."

A look of relief flashed over Angelica's face, and Schott

realized the woman understood more English than she'd let on.

Kyle took charge. "Take her upstairs, Angelica." He gestured to Hadley to stay.

"I'll see you out," he said to Schott. "I'm glad to know Lauren wasn't injured or, God forbid, killed."

He opened the front doors and walked Schott to his car. "You know, Detective, Marisa is emotionally unstable. Whatever she's told you mustn't be taken as an absolute fact. Unfortunately, she's been known to fantasize, believing that someone is out to harm her. That's why we hired a physician to live with us. Her breakdown became too much for me to handle."

"Have you had her evaluated by a therapist?"

"Dr. Hadley has been monitoring her progress."

"It's obvious she doesn't like the doctor. He can't treat her without her consent. I suggest you take her to a hospital if she's in such a problematic state of mind." Personally, he didn't see the issue the same as her father.

Chapter Thirty-Five

~~~~~

Police checked Jeffery's beach house in Aptos and reported the place empty, no sign of recent activity. Schott put out a statewide BOLO for Davis and his car. Of course, if he had been the shooter, chances were slim that he'd still be hanging around unless he had a solid alibi. Most likely, he was out of the area, or someone was hiding him.

Ed's thoughts were full of various scenarios as he drove to Casa de la Lumbre. Lauren had failed to mention her phone call to Jeffery after the Gala. Why? Had she made a bootie call? Had Jeffery come after her? And then, he shot at Sam, or had Sam shot at the two of them?

Schott drove slowly through the enlarged crowd of media trucks outside the gate on Congress Springs. At the compound, he checked with the forensics team inside the cottage, and with the investigators who were combing the grounds outside.

He found Lauren in the living room by a roaring fire. Dressed in jeans and a sweatshirt, she looked like a teenager on a lazy Sunday morning, rather than a woman who'd come close to dying a few hours ago.

She greeted him with a smile. "Sam's checking security. Trying to figure out how someone got so close without setting off the alarms. Did you want him?"

"Let's talk first. I understand you called Jeffery after you got home." He lowered himself into a chair opposite her. "Strange that you'd be calling your former fiancé, especially after you argued with him hours before at the gala."

"Well, yes, I guess it might seem odd, but I was upset over

the conversation we'd had at the fundraiser. Why? What did he say?"

"I haven't talked to him yet. Marisa said that he left around two this morning and hasn't returned."

"I don't understand."

"His wife said you invited him over for a night of *hot sex*. Perhaps you turned off the alarm so he could slip in."

"Sex! With Jeffery? That's total dreaming on his part. Turn off the alarm, absolutely not! He didn't answer when I called, so I left a voicemail. Call him. He'll confirm I left a message." At least she hoped he'd confirm that she'd called.

"Why did you want to talk to him?"

"He said he had information about my dad's death; he said he had a name. He was drunk, got pissed off, and refused to say anything more. When I got home, I called."

"At two in the morning?"

"Whenever I got home. I have no idea what time it was. I left a message, asked if we could get together today. I haven't heard from him. Call him."

"We've tried. It goes to voicemail."

"Did you try his beach house?"

"You know about the place in Aptos?"

"Marisa said he takes his women there. Did you check?"

"Empty. What did you do after you called him?"

Lauren hesitated and then smiled. "Well, I went upstairs with Sam Gallagher."

She stopped talking when she saw Deke standing in the hallway in full uniform, his hand resting on his gun. Blushing, she wondered how much he'd heard her say and then, wondered why it mattered.

"Good morning, Deke."

He walked over and gave her a brief hug, "How are you doing?"

"I'll feel better when you catch whoever tried to kill me."

Schott interrupted. "What do you have?"

Deke stepped away from Lauren. "We got information on Jeffery's cell phone. It pinged off a tower near here at the time of the shooting. GPS on his car is apparently turned off.

Nothing on his location."

There were numerous ways to disappear after leaving the estate—down the mountain through Saratoga, or up and over to Boulder Creek and Santa Cruz. From Skyline, he could have gone north to San Francisco and Half Moon Bay, or south on Highway 1 to Watsonville and beyond. The combinations were numerous.

"So, he could have driven by here, taken a couple of shots, and then disabled his GPS so he wouldn't be tracked. Any pings or calls after that?"

"They're still tracking. We're working with the cell phone server to obtain a list of his calls and messages."

"Check the roads, all of them. See if any cameras, especially on the bridges picked up his car, a black Lexus 350."

Chapter Thirty-Six

~~~~~

"What the devil are you doing here?" Lauren stood in the foyer, hands fisted on her hips.

Fiona looked as if she'd dressed in the dark, throwing on whatever was handy—black yoga pants and a pink sweater that hadn't seen daylight since the '90s. She wore no makeup or concealer for the dark circles under her eyes. Even her hair hung lifeless as if she'd not taken time to brush it.

Lauren could count on two fingers the number of times she'd seen her stepmother without makeup, and never as disheveled as now.

Fiona hesitated. A nervous Freddie, who was fresh out of the hospital, stood behind her. "You want she should go?" he asked Lauren.

"No, it's okay." Reluctantly, he went outside.

"Fiona, what's going on?"

"I heard there was a shooting and just wanted to...to see you." Her voice quavered.

"To dance over my cold body?"

Fiona held up her hands in surrender. "I never wanted you hurt, much less dead. I, uh... should go." She spun around, and stopped, braced a hand on the wall, and bent at the waist, breathing hard.

"It is amazing how you feel you can walk in here..." Lauren who was always a sucker for the suffering, reached out to support her. "You sick or hung over?"

Fiona nodded yes.

"Come on. Can't have you passing out on the drive down

the mountain." Lauren led her to the breakfast bar. "You look like hell," she said, helping her sit down. Then she poured a glass of orange juice and passed it to her.

Fiona bobbed her thanks. "Blood sugar is low." She held the glass in both hands, slowly raising it to her lips.

Lauren placed bagels in the toaster and poured coffee into two cups. She'd never have dreamt she'd be having breakfast with this woman, of all people. What a crazy, crazy morning.

Color slowly returned to Fiona's face. "Lauren, I..." She dissolved into tears and buried her face in her hands.

Lauren passed a napkin. "You crying because they missed?"

Fiona's head snapped up, eyes large with shock. "No."

"Last night you threatened me, and now I'm supposed to believe you're concerned about my well-being?"

Fiona appeared confused. "I threatened you?"

Lauren set the plate of toasted bagels and a container of cream cheese between them. "Last night at the gala. You do remember being at the Fairmont Hotel, don't you?"

"Sort of, I was drinking a lot. It's fuzzy. What did I say, exactly?"

"Something about suing me for the estate that was rightfully yours. You said Dad told you he'd willed it to you." Lauren studied her. *Did she not remember what she'd said or done or was this just another Fiona scam?*

"I shouldn't drink," she mumbled, and then as if lost in deep thought, she stared through the French doors to the garden beyond. "I always liked it here. So peaceful. Or it used to be peaceful. Richard told me that if anything ever happened to him, this would always be my home." Her voice trailed off, her eyes again filled with tears.

"We both know that's not going to happen, don't we? Just as an FYI, Fiona, my dad never owned Casa de la Lumbre. His mother did. After the twins died, and they knew there'd be no more children, she sold it to me. This place has belonged to me, and only me, for decades."

Fiona looked surprised, but nodded she understood.

Silence steadied between them as if an understanding

beyond words had been agreed upon. Each woman was lost in memories.

Lauren broke the quiet. "Now, tell me the real reason you came up here today."

Fiona wiped her eyes, blew her nose on the napkin, and set it aside. "I came because the news said someone had shot at you, but they had no report of injury or…" She reached for a new napkin.

Lauren watched Fiona in stunned disbelief. Who was this woman sobbing as if she truly cared? This woman who'd become her enemy before the honeymoon was over. This woman who held the prize for the sharpest tongue in the west, the one who could throw barbs at twenty paces, nailing her target every time.

"What happened?"

Lauren hesitated. "We were getting ready for bed."

"You and Sam?"

"Yes." Her tone challenged Fiona to make a judgment.

"Good for you," she chuckled. "I *do* remember what a hunk Sam was in that tux."

Lauren shared how Sam had protected her from getting shot. And how afterward he was injured and ended up in the emergency room.

"Terrifying. Any idea who?"

"No, but I imagine the police will question the family as they did before."

"That means me, of course, and Bernie, and Jeffery.

"Jeffery seems to be missing."

"What do you mean, missing?"

"He left home in the early hours and hasn't been seen since."

Fiona seemed deep in thought as she mixed cream in her coffee, stirring continuously. "Your father didn't like Jeffery."

"What? Dad liked Jeffery. He was proud of him and his work at RKB."

"I don't know what changed his mind, but he mentioned that he had found out something on Jeffery and said he'd give him a choice of resigning or being fired."

Lauren sat back, stunned at this revelation. "He never told me."

"I think he was waiting for some documents before he talked to you about canceling the wedding."

"Why would he do that? The invitations were ready to mail. The second photo shoot for *Town & Country* was set for publication. It would've had to have been something extreme if he wanted to cancel everything."

"I have no idea what he had on Jeffery, but I got the idea whatever Richard found out would have destroyed him and his plans to marry you. I just know Richard was livid and intended to stop Jeffery before he ruined your life."

"Did you tell Detective Schott?"

Fiona looked away, unable to meet Lauren's eyes. "No."

"You never thought to tell him?" This was incredible. The information could've had an impact on the investigation.

"Everything got pushed aside after they found Richard. You remember how we were in shock, none of us coherent enough to talk about other things."

"But you told Detective Schott eventually, right?"

"No." Fiona turned away.

"Why not?"

Fiona took her cup to the sink, rinsed it, and then held on to the edge of the counter.

"Does Jeffery have something on you?" Lauren asked.

"He has photographs."

"Is he blackmailing you?"

"He threatened to publish them along with some sordid story. He twists things, even when they're untrue; he twists them, and it makes you look guilty."

"But you have to tell Schott. What if he's the one who killed Dad?" This put a new perspective on things. Was Jeffery the killer? Did he think she knew, and that was why she was a target? Or, was Fiona making it all up out of thin air?

"All this time, we've tried to find out who and why and you—you didn't tell anyone."

"Oh, for god's sake, Lauren, I've not had one sober day for the past two years. It was torture just to wake up in the mornings. Richard was dead. You were missing. You have to understand, alcohol was the only thing I had left."

Lauren knew the pain of facing each morning and what it had taken to live another day. It wasn't until she became immersed in her shop in London that she was able to sleep most nights without drugs.

"I do understand, Fiona. Whatever Jeffery attempts to publish, we'll stop it together. We can talk to Tully when he gets back, but for now, we'll call Schott. He can find out if Jeffery had anything to do with Dad's death or last night's shooting."

After Fiona left, Lauren went outside and sat on the patio. The air was cold and biting but offered a refreshing change. Fiona's visit had left her more puzzled than ever. It was only eleven o'clock, and already she had a dozen new questions.

What had her dad found out about Jeffery that was so alarming that he'd ask her to call off the wedding? Was Jeffery the one who shot at them last night? She couldn't imagine him with a gun or that he was sober enough to shoot straight.

Sighing, she leaned back in the lounge chair, wrapped her hands around the warm coffee cup. She remembered the sensations of Sam's hands exploring her body, and the memory made her tingle.

She heard shouting. Angry voices. Heart thumping against her ribs, she ran inside, locked the door, and frantically searched for a place to hide before recognizing Bernie's voice.

"What the hell is going on around here!" he bellowed, his face contorted in rage as he charged through the front door.

"Thank God—I heard the news, and I thought..." He folded her into his arms and started rambling, his words tumbling together. "Come live at my house. Can't sleep. Thinking of you up here and vulnerable. Someone shot at you. Christ, you could have died! I can't—I just can't take any more."

Lauren stepped back from his embrace. "Sam was here. We're fine. I'm safe." She led Bernie to the living room.

"That's bullshit! You could've died." Bernie punched the air as he roared. "Sam was supposed to protect you, and he didn't!"

"You're right, Bernie, I didn't protect her." Sam entered

from the hallway. He looked as tired and weary as Bernie. They all could use a time-out, a respite from killers, police, friends, and family.

"Well, you saved my life," Lauren interjected.

"True, but it should never have come to that. There was a breech in the security system by the back gate. We're testing it now."

"I'm taking Lauren home with me."

"Good idea."

"Whoa! Hold on a minute, you macho men. I'll decide where, when, and with whom I live. You can back off with your plans of what to do with me."

Bernie sank into a chair. Sam took the chair opposite him. Lauren folded her arms, a scolding frown on her face; she felt like a schoolmarm with two unruly kids.

"Sam will secure the premises, and they'll be doubly safe. I'll hire more security if needed. Whoever it is will be caught, and I will live here happily and safely in peace."

The men stared at her. It was all airy-fairy magical wishing, and the three of them knew it. Bernie had summed it up correctly—it was bullshit.

"Fiona was here. She said that Dad was planning on firing Jeffery and asking me to call off the wedding. You know anything about this?"

Bernie frowned, scratched at his unshaven jaw. "I'd not heard anything about it. If Jeffery were up to something dishonest, I'd have made sure he was fired. Have you asked him what was going on?"

"He's missing." She watched the men take in the information. They reached the *aha* moment at the same time.

"No one knows where he is. He may be having a little tryst with someone in the city." Lauren shrugged, knowing that she didn't sound convincing.

Bernie leaned back, closed his eyes, slowly shaking his head. He looked older than his sixty years. Tired and drawn as if all the energy had drained from his body.

"So, you're thinking—" he said.

"—that Jeffery was the shooter," Sam finished the thought.

Chapter Thirty-Seven

~~~~~

The next morning, Lauren stood in her father's study and contemplated the stack of boxes. The missing lab book might be in one of them. Box cutter in hand, she slit open the first five boxes and found volumes of antique books including the 1900 Louis Wain book of *ABC Cats*. She sat with her back against the wall. Mr. Watson curled by her feet. Turning the pages of the colorful drawings drew her back to her childhood and afternoon naps when she'd beg her grandmother to read the *ABC* book. Then she'd fall asleep, dreaming of cats.

She just knew that cats were anthropomorphic creatures as human as she. There were plenty of cats and kittens around the place when she was young. Not so many as she got older. An uneasy feeling washed over her, a memory of cats that snagged in the recesses of her thoughts and refused to come forward.

Lauren promised herself that when everything was settled, she'd get a cat, maybe two or three to hang out with Watson. And, when it was safe to ride in the hills again, she'd bring her horses back from Rand's stable.

Placing the books on the shelves and reorganizing the study, she wished her life could be restructured as easily. She longed to reset to a time when her mom was alive, when her dad was alive, when she had a life, a real life, an active life, and not one of hiding.

She'd always assumed she'd have a family—a husband, and children. She'd do mom things like soccer, ballet, and Marisa would give them art lessons. She and Risa would take the children to tea. They'd take trips to Tahoe to ski in the winter and summer vacations in Europe, as she'd done with her parents. But finding a husband now would be a challenge. Who'd want a suspected murderer, an alleged sex addict with too much wealth to be natural?

Lauren focused on the people who were now in her life. Miss Etta had arrived yesterday afternoon, white-faced and stoic. She'd heard about the shooting and refused to leave. She'd stayed overnight in the guest room. This morning, she'd gone to Rand's house to get the rest of her things.

Sam left for a run through the logging trails. He refused to let her join him. He'd planned on leaving, but with the shooting still under investigation along with the watch being found, Schott insisted that he stay until he was cleared.

Later that afternoon, Sam returned with cartons of Chinese food. The aroma made Lauren's stomach grumble.

"Food," she laughed. "I think I love you."

"Me or the food?"

"You, for bringing the food."

"You'd love *anyone* who fed you."

"Especially if they delivered Chinese."

Lauren gathered plates and napkins. Sam opened boxes of brown rice, fried rice, egg drop soup, General Tso's Chicken, Mu Shu Pork, and Beef Broccoli.

"Do you think that Jeffery was the one who shot at us?" Lauren spooned General Tso's Chicken on her plate next to the fried rice.

"No." Sam ladled the soup into two bowls, passed one to her. "Jeffery's quarrel with you is personal. He'd be in your face. The attack on us was not personal. Even if Jeffery owned a gun and knew how to use it, he was so drunk Saturday night he couldn't have loaded it without shooting himself."

"Whatever Dad found out about him—was it enough to make him commit murder?"

"No," Sam said.

"Why not?"

"Jeffery is a manipulator, a con man. He doesn't have it in him to plan a murder like your dad's. That was too professional."

"Then, we're right back with who and why. I can't come up with a reason why someone wanted to murder him or me."

"Any luck finding your dad's journal?"

"His lab book? No. I found some that dated back over the last four years, but not the last one."

Lauren reflected on how close those bullets had come to killing them. "Did I thank you for saving me the other night?"

He smiled, his eyes crinkling. "Did I thank you for taking me to the hospital?"

Lauren toyed with the rice on her plate. "Sam, on the way home from the hospital Zach mentioned you had a friend who died when you were teenagers. He said you changed after that."

Sam continued to eat as if he hadn't heard her. Finally, he looked up. He smiled, flashed white teeth and that little dimple in his cheek. His dark eyes held a desire that created a sensual burning in all her right places. Lauren let the questions go for now.

She cleared away the food and plates. He followed. She rinsed the plates in the sink, and when she turned, he was behind her. Bracing his hands on each side, he pinned her in place with a hungry look still in his eyes and a sly smile on his lips. She cupped his cheek and ran her fingers over his full lips.

"Are you just using me for sex?" he asked.

Lauren tilted her head, deliberating. "It's either food or sex. I'm still debating. You do both so well."

He gave an exaggerated sigh. "Well then, we'll just keep doing what we're doing."

He pulled her close. Slanting his head, he teased her lips, sucking, tasting, and chasing away any sensibilities.

Sensibilities that jolted back with the insistent ringing at the doorbell.

"Damn," Sam muttered and released her.

Walking to the foyer, Sam slipped the Glock out of the holster and held it at his side.

"GALLAGHER! Open up. I know you're in there," Deke shouted.

"Jeez, man," Deke said when he saw the gun. "You gonna shoot me?"

Sam holstered the Glock.

"Did you find Jeffery?" Lauren asked as she joined them.

"No sign of him. We found his cell phone in Santa Cruz. Some street kid claimed he found it." Deke huffed his skepticism. "We were able to verify that Lauren had left a message. He got a few calls after that from a burner phone which was untraceable."

"Have you eaten?" Lauren asked. "We have leftovers."

Deke looked from Sam to Lauren as if sizing up the situation between them and declined the offer. "I dropped by to check how you're doing and see if you needed anything."

"We're good so far. I've been unpacking more boxes, looking for my dad's last engineering lab book. Bernie thinks it might tell us who he was meeting and maybe why he was killed. You sure you won't have something to eat?"

"Thanks, no. Sam, did you find anything on the security video?"

"I went through the DVDs from Saturday afternoon to Sunday morning after the shooting. I can't find anything that shows how or when an intruder could have gotten past the cameras."

"Okay, I'm taking off. We'll keep searching for Jeffery. Maybe he's involved in this, maybe not."

They walked him out. "You staying?" he asked Sam.

"For now."

Deke waved goodbye and got behind the wheel of his cruiser. Security opened the gate, and he drove out of the compound.

"He was in a snarky mood," Lauren said, watching him drive away.

"You know he's in love with you."

"Deke? There's no way we'd ever get together."

"Why not?"

"He hated my cats. I could never be with a man like that. By the way, how do you feel about cats?"

Chapter Thirty-Eight

~~~~~

Marisa stood at the bedroom window and watched Detective Schott park his car. She ran downstairs and waited for him on the front steps.

Jeffery was last seen three days ago. There'd been no communication, not even a phone call. Had he finally left her? Or was he hurt and couldn't make contact?

Schott's face gave away nothing as he followed her into the living room. Angelica brought coffee, placed the tray on the ottoman, and left as mutely as she'd entered.

"Ms. Montgomery," Schott said, his demeanor solemn. He left his cup untouched. "Cyclists found an accident on Djinn road at a curve called Devil's Elbow. We've confirmed the car is your husband's Lexus."

Shock quivered through her, leaving her weak.

"I'm sorry, he did not survive. He wasn't wearing a seatbelt and was thrown from the car."

Marisa leaped to her feet, hands covering her face, and small moans emitting through her fingers. She fought to contain her emotions and prayed that Schott saw her reaction as grief.

Swiping at her tears, she rejoined Schott on the sofa. "When? When did it happen?"

"We think Sunday morning, right after he left you. Any idea why he'd be on Djinn road?"

Djinn was a narrow winding road in the Santa Cruz Mountains above Woodside. It was a favorite of bicyclists because of the challenging grade and little traffic.

"I have no idea."

"Would Jeffery have ever considered suicide?"

"Jeffery! No, good lord, no." He thought too much of himself. "Why would you think of suicide?"

"No skid marks. No indication that he'd applied the brakes before going over the side."

"Do you think he suffered?" Her voice cracked.

Schott hesitated. "He was thrown clear, and most likely, death was instantaneous."

Marisa closed her eyes. That son of a bitch didn't even suffer. Didn't lay there in pain, begging forgiveness for the abuse and endless agony he'd inflicted on her, the incessant cruelty that began on their honeymoon in Venice.

The first time he'd struck her, he claimed she'd embarrassed him in the restaurant by showing off, ordering their meal in fluent Italian, and then chatting up the waiter while he sat there like a dumbass. She'd fought back, swore she'd leave and file for divorce as soon as she got home.

Jeffery didn't beg forgiveness; instead, he stole her plane tickets, passport, cell phone, and credit cards, and took all the money she had to hold her virtually powerless. He slipped drugs into her food to make her amenable. She endured the six weeks of scheduled travel. At first, she was confident that when she got home, it would be over.

The honeymoon continued, along with the slaps and spankings that quickly turned to beatings with bruises carefully concealed. Sex became brutalized rape. He'd held her down and sodomized her when she fought him, so she stopped struggling and grew increasingly despondent.

Honeymoon nights morphed into a series of torment, breaking her will. Meanwhile, Jeffery hooked up with any woman available. Marisa had been terrified of being infected with an STD.

Resolve wilted into a haze of depression as they traveled from Italy to France to Greece. When they returned home, Jeffery convinced Kyle that she was seriously ill. For some unknown reason, her father had taken Jeffery's side, and Jeffery's abuse turned more psychological than physical.

Kyle hired Dr. Hadley to control her raging outbursts. The

doctor first administrated the pills, and then shots that kept her in a zombie-like state. It became easier for her to stay in an unconscious fog and move toward dying than it was to accept that she'd be with Jeffery the rest of her life.

But now Jeffery was dead.

And she was liberated.

What would she do now? Her world was wide open once more. "I have no idea what to do next."

"The first thing would be to select a funeral home."

She realized Schott thought she meant what to do about Jeffery. Oh, yeah, she had to bury the bastard first. How appropriate that he died going over Devil's Elbow. Her idea of a funeral service was to drive a stake through his heart and throw him in a hole.

Schott continued. "When the coroner finishes their report they'll contact the funeral home and release the body." He stood, offered his hand. "Please accept my condolences."

Marisa looked into Schott's gentle face. What a depraved person she was—she felt no guilt or remorse that Jeffery was dead, just the sweet breath of freedom.

Schott sat in his car and checked his cell phone messages. Dr. Hadley tapped on the passenger window. He leaned in when Schott rolled it down. "I heard Jeffery's car was found. Is he gone?"

"Dead? Yes."

"Accident or murder?"

"Why murder?" Schott got out of the car and walked around it to stand beside the man.

Hadley looked about before speaking. "The other night I overheard Jeffery and Marisa arguing. She wanted a divorce, and he told her the only way she'd get rid of him was if he were dead. She told him that could be arranged." Hadley smugly delivered the gossip.

"I see."

"She hated him, you know."

"Thank you. For now, it appears to have been an accident."

Schott drove away wondering if that delicate, blue-eyed, grieving widow was more cunning than she appeared? There were no skid marks on the road where the car crashed into the ravine. Had Jeffery had passed out because he was drunk or because he had no brakes?

Schott called the station. "Check the brake system on Davis' car."

~~~

On Wednesday morning, Sam stood with Jon and Flynn on the edge of the ravine.

Jon held an arrogated copy of the police report and pointed to a spot along the embankment. "He was thrown from the car and landed about there."

They made their way down a deer trail that traversed the steep slope. Black paint streaked the boulders where the car landed.

Jon continued, "The accident was ruled suspicious. Jeffery's injuries were consistent with being thrown from the vehicle, his alcohol level was very high, but they found someone had tampered with the ABS and the brake fluid leaked out. It's the type of leak that can go for a while before the brakes fail. The question is—did someone tamper with them on purpose or was it simply a malfunction?"

They searched around the crumpled weeds, but other than the streaks of black paint on the boulders found nothing new.

Jon and Flynn started up the hill to the road.

Sam hiked closer to the tree line rather than following the deer path. He stopped at the mass of trampled weeds—an old shoe, bits of cloth, papers, and trash that lay scattered among decaying beer cans.

Sam looked up when someone called his name. Coyote sat at the edge of the tree line about thirty feet away, surrounded by a haze of red.

"Hold on a minute," Sam called to Jon and Flynn and then made his way toward the animal, amazed at how normal it felt to trust these spirits. "This better be good," he groused. In front of

Coyote, a glint of silver sparkled in the grass. Sam picked it up, held it high for the others to see.

"What is it?" yelled Jon.

Sam climbed up to the road. "We may have hit pay dirt."

"What's that?" Flynn peered over Sam's shoulder.

"A thumb drive." He handed it to Jon.

"Looks like a weird key," Flynn observed.

"Which is probably why Jeffery carried it on his key ring. Hiding in plain sight." Jon turned it over in his hand.

Returning to the hotel room, Jon slipped the thumb drive into his laptop computer. The information was encrypted. "I'll take it to our guy in Milwaukee. I'll call when we have something." Jon packed his things to leave for the airport.

"I hope we can get more information than we did on that drone," Sam said. The pieces had been too small to give any evidence. The camera had taken the biggest hit from Lauren's shotgun blast.

As they waited, Flynn filled Sam in on his trip to Marrakesh and the search for the missing hostage. "Before I landed, he'd left for Germany. When I got there, he'd been eliminated."

"Eliminated?" Sam frowned. Why would a hostage who wasn't actually a hostage, be murdered? "Why?"

"Someone wants all the evidence destroyed, including the bait. Senator Phillips told me that if we don't stop investigating, then someone would get killed," Jon explained. "Sam get this Sobrantes thing settled. Whoever was responsible for the attack doesn't want any loose ends. I need you back on the job."

Chapter Thirty-Nine

~~~~~

Marisa studied the contents in Jeffery's walk-in closet.

"Marisa?" Kyle called from the doorway. "You look very pensive."

She gave what she hoped was a reassuring smile, to let her father know she was doing okay. "Do I send underwear with his suit? I can't decide."

He stepped inside the vast closet where suits, sports coats, and slacks hung on one side, sorted by colors, and on the other side were shelves and drawers for shirts, sweaters, and shoes. All organized in a precise array of colors from light to dark.

"I don't think Jeffery needs a pair of *chonies* where he's going," Kyle said.

"Probably not," she agreed. He couldn't keep them on in life so why burden him with them in death.

"Would you rather I make the selection?"

His consideration surprised her, but she declined. "It feels like this is part of the process that I should be doing." How else could she search everything?

Kyle gave her an awkward pat on the shoulder. "I know things were tough between you and Jeffery. I'm pleased to see you handling everything so well. I'll send Angelica up to give you a hand. She can drive you over to the funeral home. I'll be at the office if you need anything."

Kyle appeared to be as relieved as she that Jeffery was out of their lives. He left the room whistling under his breath. With Angelica's assistance, she selected a suit, tie, shoes, socks, but no underwear, to take to the mortuary.

191

"Now," she said, with hands on hips and a determined set to her mouth. "We're searching everything." A sense of urgency pushed her. She'd go through his things before someone else did. Why someone else would want to search Jeffery's closet wasn't logical, but this time she was determined to trust her intuition.

Marisa searched Jeffery's clothes. The boxes of cuff links, watches, and rings were examined. Marisa put aside the wedding band he'd never worn.

"Do we know what we're looking for?" quizzed Angelica.

"No, but I'll know it when I find it."

Detective Schott arrived shortly after Marisa and Angelica returned from the mortuary. Marisa found him waiting patiently in the living room.

"Detective." Marisa extended her hand. "What brings you here today?"

"Just need a little more information. Everything going well?" he asked.

"The funeral is scheduled for Saturday at 10:00. I believe we have everything in place for the funeral and graveside service. The reception will be held here." Kyle's secretary had made all the arrangements, even selecting scriptures, and someone to deliver the eulogy.

"Tell me, Ms. Montgomery, what was your relationship with your husband?"

"I'm not sure what you're asking?"

"Would you say your marriage was a loving one?"

She gave a short laugh before answering. "My husband was a very loving man to a great many loving women, but not to me."

"I see."

Did he see? Had someone told him how much she hated Jeffery? "Jeffery didn't love me. He didn't even like me. And I didn't like him."

"There must have been a time when you loved him or thought yourself to be in love with him? You married him."

"He was on the rebound after Lauren disappeared. Jeffery

and I commiserated with each other. We were married before I realized what he was really like. I knew on the honeymoon it wouldn't work."

"But you remained married, why?"

"It's complicated."

Schott let that go. "I heard that you argued before he died, and you told him his death could be arranged."

"We often argued. I may have said I wanted a divorce. I don't remember saying I'd arrange his death."

"Anyone have a complaint against your husband? Anyone threatening him?"

Marisa studied his face, which gave away nothing. Then she realized. "It wasn't an accident, was it?"

"We don't think so. The lack of skid marks made me suspicious. Forensics found the ABS brake line connector had been loosened, which allowed the brake fluid to leak out gradually over time."

The blood rushed to Marisa's head making her light-headed. *Oh, my god, none of us are safe.*

~~~

The funeral director, dressed in somber blue from head-to-toe, escorted Lauren down the hallway to where Jeffery's body *rested*. The woman's lilting voice grated Lauren's nerves raw before they reached the room.

"Please, let me see Marisa alone," Lauren said to Sam

Sam stepped inside, looked things over, and returned to the corridor. Inside, Marisa paced, circling the open ebony casket. She looked over her shoulder, nodded to Lauren, and then resumed circling. Violin music played from the speakers.

Jeffery's body was cushioned on ivory ruche silk. His face was coated with makeup that didn't cover the bruises and cuts. His hair was combed straight back. Without facial animation— the big smile, and flashing eyes, he appeared stodgy, like an old man.

"Marisa." Lauren slipped her arm around Marisa's thin shoulders.

"I'm divorcing him, you know. I was. I would have. No matter what Kyle said, I would have. Jeffery said the only way I'd get rid of him was if he were dead." Her laugh was shrill.

Lauren wondered if Marisa was spiraling out of control because of Jeffery's accident or if she were back on drugs. She talked rapidly like she'd done the day of the 49er party.

"You don't have to worry about that now," Lauren assured her.

"He was good to me at first, after you left, after your dad—after everyone was gone. Here one day and then gone. I needed someone. He was there." Her eyes darted to Jeffery and then Lauren. "You understand, don't you?" She bordered on hysteria.

"Marisa, come home with me. Miss Etta will make your favorite soup." Lauren gestured to the door.

"No. Help me, Lauren. I have to put it on his finger." Staring anxiously at Jeffery's body, she twisted the shiny gold wedding band in her hand but obviously she was reluctant to touch him.

"The funeral director can do this for you."

"No, no, we—you and me—we have to do it."

Lauren clenched her teeth. She took the ring, but sliding it on a dead man's finger was the last thing she wanted to do. Marisa watched, wide-eyed. Lauren moved to the opposite side of the casket and with a deep breath, she picked up Jeffery's cold hand, and worked the ring over the knuckle of his third finger.

Marisa gave maniacal twitter. "Wear it for eternity, you unfaithful prick." She began to ramble, "At our wedding reception, Jeffery disappeared. We waited half an hour to cut the cake. He was getting it off with my maid of honor."

They stared at Jeffery; the gold band, shiny and new, flashed his betrayals.

"You were supposed to be my maid of honor, Lauren."

"I was supposed to have married Jeffery."

"He was mean. Abusive. I'm glad he's dead."

Abusive? Lauren couldn't bear the thought of Risa being hurt. "It's over now. I'm back, and you're not alone anymore. I'm here." Lauren held her tight.

She pushed Lauren away. "You don't know what I've done."

"Whatever it is, or was, we can work it out," Lauren pleaded, worried how quickly Marisa was losing control. She reached for her again.

"No!" Marisa cowered like a trapped animal. "We can't work it out! I killed your mother."

Chapter Forty

~~~~~

Funerals should be held on dark, gloomy days, allowing the heavens to weep with the mourners. Lauren stepped out of the church and slipped on her sunglasses.

Sam pulled the Land Rover out of the parking lot of La Lumbre Village Church. They drove past the reporters and television crews that lined the entrance to the cemetery. Parking on a side street Sam took Lauren's arm, and they crossed the soft grass to the white canopy set up beside the freshly dug grave. Artificial grass covered the mound of earth. A young man handed out flowers to people as they entered the seating area.

The gathering was small—friends, family, and a few employees of RKB. Lauren wondered how many of Jeffery's conquests were among them. Not that Marisa would notice, it was clear from her stare that she was once again drug-induced.

Kyle and Marisa were in the front row with Dr. Hadley. Kyle held her close to his side. Dr. Hadley guarded the other side.

At the mortuary, Marisa had refused to tell Lauren what she'd meant when she said she'd killed Lauren's mother. The notion that she was responsible for Elizabeth's death was ludicrous. Was this what she'd meant about secrets?

The minister completed the prayers, and the casket was lowered slightly. Mourners filed by and tossed their flowers on top as they'd done at Richard's service. A few stopped to offer condolences to Kyle and Marisa. When Kyle turned to Bernie, a Lauren saw her opportunity.

"Marisa, we have to talk."

"Stay away from me," Marisa screamed, twisting away.

Kyle ordered Lauren to leave. Incessant *Shu-click Shu-click* of the cameras exploded around them. Sam threw his arm over her shoulder, and holding her tight to his side they walked rapidly toward the Land Rover.

Reporters followed, shouting questions.

"The police don't think this was an accident."

"Were you with Jeffery when he died, Ms. Sobrantes?"

Sam unlocked the passenger door. As Lauren slid into the seat, a reporter shouted, *"Did you know your bodyguard is wanted for murder in Italy?"*

"Are you wanted for murder in Italy?" Lauren asked as they drove away.

Sam gave a quick glance her way before he turned onto the on-ramp of the freeway. "You know that I work for a security company, AZEN. A client's wife received threatening letters, and her husband thought someone planned to kidnap her. He hired us for protection 24/7 while she sailed her yacht around the Aegean Sea.

"We were to provide security for six months. A month after we started, she disappeared in the middle of the night and the husband swore I'd been her lover, and when she told me to leave, I'd flown into a rage. He claimed I shot her and dumped her body overboard.

"Since he carried a lot of clout with the authorities, I was arrested and charged with her death, even though nothing was out of place, no sign of struggle, and her body was never found. The captain and crew supported his claim and testified that we'd argued violently the night before. I was held for a trial. End of story."

"So, you were acquitted?"

"Jon Malcolm got me out of the country before it got to court."

"Would you have been found guilty?"

"I'm a sniper, Lauren. I've killed to protect, but I've never murdered anyone."

Chapter Forty-One

~~~~~

By mid-week, Lauren felt stuck in the confusion of the netherworld. Whatever information Jeffery had about her father's death went to the grave with him. They determined his accident was murder, and like her dad's case, the sheriffs didn't have any suspects. Nor was there any new information on who shot at her and Sam.

Detective Schott continued to infer that she knew more than she was telling, no matter how many times she denied it.

Marisa refused to return her phone calls. Whatever secrets she'd spoken of remained secrets.

Rand reported from Hong Kong that he'd run into dead-ends in his investigation, but that he had a lead on a man who'd agreed to be an informant on the manufacturing company where he worked. He promised he'd call her after the meeting.

"Thanksgiving," she said, startling Sam, who sat across the breakfast table eating a cheese omelet.

"Less than two weeks, I believe."

"I'll have Thanksgiving dinner here. I'll invite everyone," she stated with vigorous determination.

Sam sat back and grinned. "Who's cooking?"

"I am, with Etta's help, of course. How hard can it be to cook a turkey? You just put it in the oven and... *voilà*."

He refilled their coffee from the carafe beside him. "Don't forget to take out the insides before you put it in the oven."

"It comes with insides? You mean they don't take all that out before you buy it?"

He was still laughing when the phone rang.

"I'll get it." She hoped it was Marisa, returning her call. "Hold on." She held the phone out to Sam. "It's Zach. He said he's coming over to check on you since you refuse to go to him."

Sam waved her away and walked out the door.

"Zach, he'll be here. Please, invite your dad to come too."

Sam knew that Zach would examine him and either give him a thumbs-up or thumbs-down. He needed the clearance to return to work. He also knew it was best for him to meet up with Jon and Flynn rather than get more involved with Lauren.

He knew that.

But, he didn't want to leave her. Didn't want to take a chance she'd not be fully protected. Or was he afraid that someone else could protect her better than he'd done? The security system he'd set up on the perimeter of the estate's compound was state-of-the-art. And yet, someone had breached it and gotten close enough to take a couple of shots at them.

Today the cottage was cold and gloomy. The fire went out when he'd moved in with Lauren. All signs of the shooting had been removed, but the place would have to be cleaned for Etta, and Arlo, whenever he got back from Poland.

In the security room, he sat at the computer and went over the recordings from each camera, starting with late Saturday afternoon when he and Lauren had left for the gala, through Sunday morning when the shooting took place, and the police arrived.

It was mid-morning before he found it. He studied the recordings of camera eight, the new one he'd set up by the back gate near the sycamore trees that Lauren climbed over to break-in to the Casa.

The camera pointed toward the woods. One of the sycamore trees had a single leaf on a twiggy branch. The leaf shook in the breeze.

As he watched, something wasn't right. Sam reversed it and played it in slow motion. The leaf fell off and disappeared, then it reappeared. Someone had broken through security, stopped the security camera from recording, then rewound it to appear as though it had never been tampered with.

The code clicked away the time as if there were no interruption. But there had been. The recording was reversed too far; it showed the leaf on the tree after it had already fallen off.

Clever. Absolute genius. If it weren't for that one leaf, Sam would never have realized the recording was altered. It had to have been activated remotely. Now he just had to find how and who.

Lauren met Zach at the gate and sent him to the cottage. She invited Emmett to join her for a walk around the compound, starting with the stables. Mr. Watson trotted down the path in front of them, scattering birds. Freddie joined them at a discreet distance.

"As I recall, you were quite the horsewoman, weren't you?" Emmett said.

She looked out at the pasture. "I was and then…"

"Life changed. It happens quickly, doesn't it? You think you've got it all figured out, but you don't," his voice trailed off. "I appreciate your invitation, Lauren, but Sam won't be happy I'm here. We've not talked in years.

"Sam began to withdraw from the family after his friend Andy died. Then he dropped out of college and joined the Navy when he was twenty-two. I said some awful things to him when he told me he was training to be a sniper."

Lauren stopped him. "What happened between you and your son is your business. I just know life is too precarious and uncertain to let any estrangement continue a moment longer."

They turned back toward the Casa as Zach and Sam came out of the cottage. Sam stopped when he saw his father. He turned to Zach, angrily gestured in their direction, then stormed back inside, and slammed the door.

Emmett's shoulders drooped. "I should go."

"You stay right where you are." Lauren jogged to the cottage. How stupid can such a smart man be? She threw open the door.

"What's he doing here?" Sam demanded.

"I invited him."

"You don't even know my father."

"He sat with me the night you were in the hospital. He loves you. And, you—you will forgive him for whatever he did, or what you think he did."

"This is none of your business."

"You listen to me." She stepped close, punched his chest with her fist. "Do you have any idea what I'd give to have my father back? My mother? To talk to them one more time, just to say goodbye and tell them I love them if nothing else. We almost died the other night. Your dad could die. There's no guarantee that any of us has another hour, much less another day."

She wrapped her arms around him, felt his heart beating. "Sam, please, just go out there, talk to him. Don't wait. Don't do this to yourself. Think how you'd feel if anything happened to him before you reconciled."

Without speaking, he released her and walked out the door.

His father was leaning against Zach's car in the driveway; the dog lay at his feet. He appeared to have shrunk since the last time Sam saw him. How could that be? Emmett was always the towering figure in the family.

Memories engulfed Sam, too fast to remember them all. Just flashes of his dad attending every soccer game that he and his brothers played. Celebrating their wins with pizza at Jake's and their losses the same way. His father's love and pride in his children was always evident.

Sam marched over to the car.

Stood face-to-face with Emmett.

And opened his arms.

Emmett hesitated, searching his son's face. Then, he stepped forward and was fully engulfed in Sam's tight grasp.

Emmett stepped back. He swiped his tear-streaked face with both hands, but the tears kept flowing. "Forgive me," he whispered. "Please. Forgive me."

Unable to speak, Sam pulled him close again, realizing there was nothing to forgive. His father loved him, and because he loved him, he'd tried to warn him of the damage that the profession Sam had chosen would do to him over time.

Emmett had wanted to make him understand that he'd never forget the men he killed.

Those kill shots might be a measure of one's worth in the service, but you had to live with the consequences. Sometimes, even though your job was protecting your team—you wondered if you'd be better off dead.

Chapter Forty-Two

~~~~~

Marisa pulled the folder out of her bag and checked that she had everything—Jeffery's death certificate, their marriage license, both of their birth certificates, passports, and the safe deposit key that she'd found hidden in his dresser drawer.

Before the honeymoon, she'd gone with Jeffery to open an account at the La Lumbre Bank. But she couldn't remember if she'd signed for the safe deposit box.

Squaring her shoulders, she threw a nervous smile to Angelica as they walked into the bank. "Let's do it," she said with more bravado than she felt.

At the counter, she asked for the bank manager. In his office, she handed over the documents and held her breath. Relief washed over her when he checked the file and told her that she was on the account.

Marisa was led to the vault. She gave Angelica the *okay* sign as she walked past.

The two keys were inserted into one of the larger doors. The manager pulled out the metal box and placed it in a private room, telling her to call when she was finished.

She wasn't sure why she hesitated to open the box, it wasn't like there was a viper inside ready to jump out and bite her. With shaking hands, she popped the latch and slowly began removing the contents.

Five stacks of banded 100 dollar bills—$10,000 printed on each mustard-colored band. Fifty thousand dollars? Where did Jeffery get that kind of money? She placed them in her large tote bag.

Underneath the money were several small bags of jewelry. She spilled the contents of the first one and immediately recognized a brooch that her mother used to wear, a flower of emeralds and diamonds surrounding a large ruby center stone. She picked up the sapphire ring her father had given her on her eighteenth birthday.

Why were these in this box? Had Jeffery been keeping them safe for her?

The contents of the next bag were equally surprising. She took out a ring with rubies and diamonds that had belonged to Lauren's mother. And the hair clasp that Lauren had worn in her hair the night of the funeral. These were not here for safekeeping.

Jeffery was not only abusive; he was a thief. Other bags of expensive pieces weren't familiar. How many women had he stolen from?

The jewelry was added to her bag. She sorted through the others things—her passport, marriage certificate, and his will, and several folded documents.

She opened them all and fought back a scream.

With trembling hands, she lined the documents up and laid them side-by-side.

"Oh, my God, my God…" She moaned as she read each document.

"Jeffery, what have you done? What have you done?"

~~~

Lauren searched the Internet for Thanksgiving recipes to add to the traditional turkey and dressing. She'd prove that she could put together a festive dinner. It wasn't like she had no experience cooking and besides, she had help.

She'd invited Zach and Emmett before they left and they'd agreed to invite Greg. She invited Bernie and even Fiona. As soon as she heard from Marisa, she'd extend an invitation to her and Kyle. With Miss Etta and Deke, the guest list was nicely rounded out.

Now, what to have for dessert? She searched Google for

pies. Choosing between pumpkin, apple, and chocolate cream like her grandmother used to make was tough.

She was absorbed in list making and recipes when she heard the front door open.

"Lauren?" Marisa called from the foyer.

"Risa! What a surprise." Hesitant to hug her, Lauren stood back and smiled her welcome.

Marisa clutched a large tote bag to her chest like a life preserver. She looked great in black slacks and a bulky black sweater, her hair jumbled about her shoulders in a fragile mess.

Marisa's eyes welled with tears. "I'm sorry I screamed at you at the funeral. Dr. Hadley slipped drugs in my coffee, and it sent me over the edge. I need to talk to you."

"Sit down. Tea? Coffee?" She was chattering and forced herself to stop. They settled on the sofa. Marisa gripped the bag as if afraid the contents might escape.

"What's up?" Lauren asked quietly, hoping Marisa had come to talk about her mother's death.

"When I cleaned out Jeffery's closet, I found a safe deposit key. This morning, I went to the bank." She swallowed hard. "I couldn't think of where to go, but to you. Just you."

Lauren moved closer and covered Marisa's shaky hands with hers. "We'll work it out, whatever it is." Her calm voice belied the chills rushing along her spine.

Setting her tote bag beside them, Marisa removed a jewelry sack and took out the ruby and diamond band. "Is this your mother's ring?"

Lauren took the ring her mother had worn instead of her wedding set. It represented her children—Lauren, the diamond in the center with a ruby on each side to symbolize her brothers.

"And, this." Marisa held the diamond and onyx hair clasp in the palm of her hand.

"Where did you get these?"

"They were in the box. I think Jeffery stole them."

"Oh, that son of a bitch."

The color drained from Marisa's face and Lauren immediately felt contrite over exploding so angrily. "Sweetie, please. This isn't your fault."

"There's more." Marisa pulled out additional little sacks of jewelry. "Go through these and see if there's anything else of yours or your mom's. I found the sapphire ring Kyle gave me for my eighteenth birthday and a few pieces of my mother's. I can't imagine where he got the other things."

Lauren suggested they move to the dining room where they spread the jewelry out on the table. "What the devil. Was Jeffery a kleptomaniac?"

"That's not all."

"More jewelry?"

"No, just more." She pulled out the money, placing the five stacks of 100s side-by-side.

"Fifty thousand?"

Marisa kept dragging things out and sorting them in groups—DVDs, a folder of photographs of Jeffery having sex with different women, a book with coded names, dates, and numbers. "I think Jeffery was blackmailing these women, dozens of them."

"We'll have to tell the police." Lauren flipped through the pictures searching the faces of the women and found the ones Jeffery had taken of Fiona. She put them aside until she could dispose of them.

"Yes, but I want you to see this first." Laying three official documents on the table, Marisa unfolded the first one and handed it to Lauren who quickly examined it.

"Jeffery was married before?" She found the idea bizarre.

"I think he was still married. Never divorced."

Lauren let out an edgy giggle. "Unbelievable. A thief, blackmailer, and a bigamist!" This must have been what her father had found out about Jeffery. This was why Richard told Fiona that the wedding would be canceled. Was it enough to make Jeffery kill her father?

"And there's this."

"More?" What else could he have done?

Marisa handed over the second document.

"No. Oh, no." Lauren slapped at the paper in her hand, unable to speak.

"He had a son," she said sadly. A child that he'd ignored

over the years while he was courting first her, and then Marisa, as well as the countless other women he was doing on the side, and blackmailing them.

"He *has* a son, about eleven years old now." She picked up the last document. "Jeffery left a handwritten will leaving everything to his wife, Lanh and his son, Evan."

Chapter Forty-Three

~~~~~

"I'm so not doing this!" Lauren clasped her hands behind her back, refused to take the gun from Sam. "I've taken self-defense classes. I can protect myself."

"If you're in close range and your opponent isn't armed, you might. What if he has a gun?" Sam mimicked in a falsetto voice, "Oh, excuse me, would you put that nasty gun aside so I can drop-kick you?"

"I'm not shooting anyone." She walked away from the paddock area where he'd set up the target. Mr. Watson trotted at her heels.

"You are an incredibly obstinate woman," he shouted after her. Waving a hand, she kept walking. Sam turned to the target. She could hire bodyguards. What the hell did he care? The truth was that he cared a lot more than he wanted to, or ought to, which was dangerous for them both.

He loaded the clip, raised the gun, and sensed her behind him. "Don't creep up on a man with a gun. It's not wise."

"I'm not creeping."

Lowering the gun, he waited.

"Okay," she said, grudgingly. Watson stretched out at her feet and laid his head on his paws.

"Okay, what?"

"You're going to make me say it, aren't you? You're right. I should know how to use that gun." At least it wouldn't throw her on her butt like the shotgun.

He motioned for her to stand in front of him. Wrapping his arms around her, he demonstrated how to brace the gun with her right hand, the index finger along the barrel.

"Wherever you point your finger is your aim." Sam placed his hands over hers. "Deep breath, exhale halfway, and squeeze the trigger."

The gun fired. The slight kickback pressed her against Sam. The wood on the target shattered.

"Perfect. Always aim for the bigger part of a body. If someone has a gun on you, pull the trigger. Do not hesitate. That split second could mean the difference between living or dying."

Lauren shook her head. She handed the gun to Sam. "Carrying a gun around like some NRA enthusiast, doesn't appeal to me. I'm not sure I could actually shoot someone."

Sam removed the clip and put the gun back in the box. What could he tell her? You get used to it? You see targets rather than people. The need to protect is stronger than your reluctance to take a life. He prayed that she'd never be in a situation to shoot, but he was determined that she be prepared.

Sam pulled her to him, held her close, resting his cheek on her head. "Enough for today. We'll practice again tomorrow."

A tap of a horn and a shout turned their attention toward the driveway. Deke waved from his car, then jogged down the path to the paddock.

"Good news, Lauren," he shouted, a broad grin on his face. "Good news!" Deke swung her off her feet. "I think we got him, babe. The shooter. He's in jail."

She screamed and laughed and joined in his jubilation. "Hallelujah—best news I've had yet." Mr. Watson raced in circles, barking enthusiastically.

They returned to the Casa. The shooter was in jail. This meant Sam was free to leave. Free to rejoin Jon and Flynn unless there was more than one shooter.

They gathered in the kitchen. Deke accepted coffee and a cinnamon-raisin muffin from Miss Etta. "Will you marry me, Miss Etta?"

"One husband, enough." She turned away, hiding her grin.

"Details. I want details," Lauren demanded when they settled. "Who is he? How did they find him?"

Deke smeared butter over the muffin and tucked half of it in his mouth, then washed it down with coffee. "Highway Patrol stopped a car for speeding on 85, a simple traffic violation. The car also had a taillight out. But the guy was acting strange, and they got suspicious. They looked in the back seat and saw the tip of a gun barrel poking out from under a jacket. So, they started asking questions he couldn't answer. They had him step out of the car and cuffed him.

"They hauled him in, booked him, and sure enough, the gun is the same caliber as the one used the other night. The lab is checking to see if the bullets match the ones we dug out of the wall. I've got a good feeling he's our guy."

"Did he say why he shot at us?"

"He lawyered up real fast. Not talking right now, but he will."

Sam tapped his fingers, a pensive frown settled between his eyes. "Who is he?"

Deke finished off the muffin and the last of the coffee before answering. "A local guy named Frank Grimes. He's a homeless veteran and hangs out under the bridge at Coyote Creek. He's been picked up for petty stuff—shoplifting, drunk, and disorderly. Hires out to do odd jobs for gas and drug money."

Something wasn't adding up for Sam. Yeah, an army veteran could explain the skill for a shot through the window, but homeless? Where did he get the money for an expensive high-powered rifle and a laser? Whoever hired him must have supplied the weapon.

"Could he have had anything to do with Jeffery's accident or my dad's murder?"

"We'll find out. He's got a court-appointed counsel coming this afternoon. I imagine he'll cop a plea. Hopefully, he'll give us information for a lighter sentence. Schott will work him over during interrogation. I gotta go." He shook hands with Sam, who remained at the table, deep in thought.

Lauren walked Deke to the car, hugged him goodbye. "Thanks for bringing such good news. What a relief. Don't forget—you're having Thanksgiving dinner with us."

"Wouldn't miss it. I could be on call, and if I am, I might have to leave early." He waved goodbye and drove out the gate.

Finally, things were falling into place. Tully had filed the lawsuit against the author of the *Ghost of Lauren Sobrantes* for slander, and the publisher had agreed to print a retraction and withdraw the book.

The shooter was arrested.

Sex with Sam, that gorgeous hunk of man, was far beyond expectations.

Lauren skipped a jig as she went back in the house. She kissed Sam. "With the shooter in jail, I've got my life back! No more looking over my shoulder. And if this is the same man who killed my dad? Then it's done. Truly done. This Thanksgiving will be the celebration of all celebrations!"

Later that day, Lauren found Etta with tears coursing down her pallid cheeks. "Miss Etta? What's wrong?"

"Arlo—he have a heart attack."

"Oh, no." Lauren was afraid to ask if it was fatal.

"In hospital." Etta held the phone in her hand as if it would tell her more.

Lauren took charge. "We'll get you on the first flight out. Sam and I will make all the arrangements."

"But, Thanksgiving. I have to cook for you," she protested.

"We'll do the cooking. Sam is great, not as good as you, but we'll manage." Lauren assured her.

"Sam, he's a good man."

"And that good man will drive you to the airport. I'll arrange the flight."

Lauren purchased a first class ticket to Warsaw for Miss Etta while Sam loaded her things in the Land Rover and then drove her to SFO. The tender way he cared for the older woman warmed Lauren's heart.

He *was* a good man.

A good man she had fallen in love with and who'd soon be gone.

Chapter Forty-Four

~~~~~

Lauren stood in the kitchen. A white chef's apron tied around her waist. The counter was filled with bags of flour and sugar, cans of pumpkin, apples, and a twenty-pound turkey.

There was a method to having everything ready at the same time, but never having cooked for so many people, she had no idea what it was or how to accomplish it. She'd never missed Miss Etta so much as at this moment.

The housekeeper had emailed that she'd had a safe, easy flight and that Arlo was improving. They were staying with his family until he was well enough to make the trip home.

Lauren plugged her iPod into the Bose dock and turned up the speaker. This was a happy day; a great day for giving thanks. The shooter was behind bars. No one was trying to kill her.

And all she had to do was cook this Thanksgiving dinner.

How hard could it be?

The kitchen was a disaster when Sam joined her. Lauren studied the turkey on the counter. "I have no idea what to do with this thing."

"You could cook it."

"What a clever idea." Her apron was streaked with pumpkin pie filling and flour. She returned to the recipes she'd printed out from the Internet.

He kissed her cheek. "How about I do the turkey? You know how to make the cornbread dressing, right?"

In the garden, Sam cut sprigs of the rosemary growing by the stonewall. He washed and dried the herbs, chopped and mixed them with soft butter and minced garlic. Lifting the skin on the turkey, he inserted spoonsful of the herbed mixture, and then stuffed the cavity with quartered lemons and oranges, rosemary sprigs, and garlic. Mixing olive oil, butter, lemon, and seasonings he coated the outside of the bird, placed it in the oven, and set the timer.

"Ever thought about a career as a chef?" Lauren teased, admiring his skill.

"No," his tone, emphatic. "Never considered it."

The beat of the music filled the room while a mixture of aromas—pumpkin pie, lemon, and rosemary wafted about the house. The pies cooled while the turkey cooked. Lauren chopped onions and celery to add to the cornbread Miss Etta had cooked the day before she left. She mixed in milk and butter, blending it all with poultry seasonings and sage.

She held out a spoon. "Taste this, does it need more salt?"

"More sage and pepper."

When it passed Sam's taste test, she added a couple of beaten eggs and then put the pan into the second oven. She set another timer and threw him a wicked grin, untied her apron, and raced him upstairs.

Sam stood in the shadows of the hallway watching Lauren in the dining room. She'd changed into a turquoise blouse that made her eyes luminescent or was it the afterglow of their lovemaking? He wondered if he could give up everything to live with this woman? Could he embrace family life with all the traditions and celebrations? The idea was appealing, even the notion of kids and a kids' table.

Smoothing the lace tablecloth, she looked up and laughed. "I've missed celebrating Thanksgiving." The doorbell and the oven timer rang at the same time. "You get the turkey. I'll get the door."

As Sam removed the turkey from the oven, he heard Lauren squeal. Dropping the hot pan on the counter, he ran to the foyer, gun drawn.

"I'm going to kill him."

Sam's father and his brothers were in the foyer.

"Who are you killing?" Sam holstered his gun and joined

the group.

"You rat. You lied to me."

Zach, Greg, and Emmett stood in a cluster, grinning like a Greek chorus, heads bobbing in unison.

"Sweetie, I have never lied to you," he stated with confidence.

"Cienna, the famous chef, Cienna—is she, or is she not your mother?"

Oh, hell and damnation. "Which one of you jokers told?"

Zach held a bouquet of flowers, his dad a bottle of wine. Only Greg was empty-handed.

Greg grinned. "Pay back's a bitch, brother."

"Yes, Cienna is my mother," Sam admitted.

"The international television-star and best-seller-organic chef, that Cienna."

"Uh-huh."

She slapped at him with one of his mother's cookbooks, delightedly gifted by his traitorous brother, Greg.

"You told me your mother was a terrible cook."

The men broke out in boisterous laughter.

"Oh, you didn't! Wait until mom hears this," said Zach.

Greg beamed. "And I'll be sure to tell her."

"You're in the doghouse now, Sam," added Emmett.

Sam scowled. "I never said she was a terrible cook."

"You implied it. You said you had to learn to cook for yourself if you were to survive."

"I think I said something like—with her cooking it was survival. Sometimes it was cook for yourself, or don't eat."

"That usually implies the food is inedible."

"No, it meant we were her guinea pigs. She fed the new dishes to the family first. Some were good, some great, but most were not to my liking. Besides, the food was cold after she staged and photographed it."

"Remember the night she made that Okra Mushroom Fungi shit," Greg recalled. "Sam slipped his to the dog, and the poor thing went outside and spewed."

"Or when she was on the vegan kick, and we snuck out to McDonald's and caught Dad wolfing down a Big Mac?" Zach added.

"Every man for himself," Emmett said, increasing the howls from his sons.

"Burgers were our salvation," Greg explained.

"Greg gave me her latest cookbook," Lauren teased, a mischievous glint in her eye. "Now I can cook for you, Sam, just like your mom."

The house hummed, increasing in volume as guests arrived. Marisa brought a sweet potato casserole, Deke, an apple pie, and Bernie, four bottles of *Col Vetoraz Prosecco*. Mr. Watson greeted them all with sniffs and tail wagging, and then stretched out by the fire, satisfied his job as greeter was done.

Marisa appeared relaxed and happy today, back to her old self. What a conundrum she was—screaming at Lauren at the cemetery, followed by denying she'd ever said she was responsible for Elizabeth's death. And yet, she'd trusted Lauren enough to share Jeffery's dishonesty. Lauren decided to wait until after dinner before asking if she'd given the information to Detective Schott.

Bernie poured the wine. Sam's brothers passed around the appetizer tray. The turkey was placed on the platter to rest before carving,

"Can I help?" Emmett joined them.

"No, I'm…" Sam changed his mind when he saw the hopeful look on his dad's face. "Do you still make the best gravy in the world?"

"The world? In the universe! Just show me where you keep things and move out of my way."

People wandered in and out during the last-minute dinner preparations.

"So, you work with Tully?" Marisa asked Greg.

"That old man still alive?" Kyle questioned.

"Yeah, he's doing great." Greg offered a stuffed mushroom to Marisa.

"Thank you." She took a bite. "I'd like an appointment."

"Sure, just call Tully's office."

"Why do you need an attorney?" Kyle quizzed. "We have

plenty of legal help at the office."

"They all report to you," Marisa said firmly.

"She doesn't have any money, Greg." Kyle walked away to chat with Fiona.

"I've been known to work pro bono," Greg said to Kyle's back. Marisa assured him that wasn't necessary that she could pay.

Sam glanced through the French doors to the back garden. Beyond the bronze sculpture of a young girl and her cat, Coyote paced back and forth, staring at the house. He saw Sam, and stopped, his gaze steady.

Alongside the animal, the cloud of red luminosity grew larger and redder. A woman materialized beside the coyote, her hair and translucent dress blew in an invisible wind. She hid her face in her hands. Sam was puzzled. What was their message?

"Sam?" The apparitions dissolved at the sound of Deke's voice.

"Grab the carving set, will you, Deke?"

Sam checked an incoming text on his cell phone before following Deke to the dining room. He slipped outside as the others drifted to the table. Lauren saw him leave and, curious, watched from the window. He opened the gate for a black town car that parked in the circular driveway.

Sam opened the door, and a woman stepped out and into his embrace. Her face was blocked from Lauren's view, but she could see strands of strawberry blonde hair. Sam held her for a long time.

Was this a friend? A lover? They had no agreement, but their bed was still mussed and hardly cold from this morning's lovemaking. Lauren walked outside and watched. The woman, dressed in black slacks and white blouse was quite lovely and looked familiar.

Sam caught Lauren's eye, beckoned her to join them as the town car drove away.

"Lauren, my mother, Cienna."

Damnation! She'd have preferred a long-lost lover. Lauren knew how to deal with competition, but a culinary legend? Heaven, help her.

Cienna greeted her warmly with a hug and an apology. "Lauren, I'm sorry to burst in on you like this. When Emmett called and told me Sam had invited him to dinner, well, I caught the first flight out of Heathrow."

Sam introduced his mother to the guests. Cienna hugged her family and chatted with the others.

Sam found Lauren alone in the kitchen. "Lauren?"

She pushed her fingers through her hair. "It's like asking Julia Child over for junk food. You know what I mean? Is the food passable? What about the turkey? Is it like what you had when you were—oh, my God."

He pulled her to him. "You have great food, wonderful guests, and you're a beautiful hostess. We're celebrating, so don't ruin it by worrying."

Cienna watched them with her hand over her heart, green eyes sparkling. "Everything smells wonderful. I hope I haven't upset things, barging in like this."

"I'm glad you're here," Lauren assured her. "But, today, you have to pretend you know nothing about cooking."

"Got it. I am cooking-dumb," Cienna laughed and tracked Sam with her eyes as he left the room. "I wanted to see Sam, but I also wanted to meet the woman who has so intrigued my son."

Lauren didn't know how to respond. "We're not. I mean, I'm not—"

"I know. By the way, my daughter, Brianna said to say hello. She hopes to come home for Christmas to see Sam and would love to meet you."

"That's very nice, but Sam is leaving soon."

Cienna just smiled, knowingly.

The feast was spread over the large dining room table. Lauren scanned her guests and recognized a long forgotten feeling of contentment. She stood and tapped her wine glass, to propose a toast. "To our family, those here with us and those who live in our hearts. And to good friends, good food, and new freedoms."

The dinner gathered momentum. Cienna declared the food the best she'd ever eaten and praised Lauren's culinary expertise. She was pleased to hear Sam had cooked the turkey.

After dinner, Bernie and Kyle argued over the state of the electronics industry, plus the fact that Bernie was taking a red-eye to China.

Kyle was not happy about the trip. "Bernie, we can't afford for you to keep taking off on these wild-goose chases looking for some straw man."

"Rand said he has an informant; the man's willing to tell us the name of the group that targeted RKB. Who knows, it may lead us to why Richard was…" Bernie's voice trailed off. This wasn't the place to talk about Richard's murder. By unspoken agreement, the two men suspended their argument.

Bernie joined Emmett and Fiona to compare notes on their favorite movies and plays.

Deke was called to an accident on Skyline before dessert was served.

Kyle listened to Marisa and Greg who were in a heated discussion about the environment.

Cienna and Zach debated herbs versus medicines.

Sam winked at Lauren above it all and somewhere in the back of his mind, reflected on Coyote and the lady in red. What were they trying to tell him?

Lauren was jubilant that her first Thanksgiving dinner, with Sam's assistance, was a success. She was, nonetheless, on the verge of collapse by nine o'clock and ready for bed.

"I'll leave the rest of the cleanup until tomorrow," she told Sam as they put the last of the food away. The dishwasher hummed with the first load of plates and glasses.

She stretched out on the sofa and didn't move when the doorbell rang. "Oh, who forgot what?"

"I'll get it." Sam motioned for her to stay.

Detective Schott followed Sam into the living room.

"This is a surprise." Lauren sat up and gestured to Schott to have a seat. "Have you had dinner? We have scads of leftovers. Can I offer you a piece of pumpkin pie?"

"No, thanks, I just want to ask you a few questions. Frank Grimes confessed that he shot at you and Sam on Sunday morning."

"That's great, isn't it? Did he tell you why?"

"He said someone hired him. Not to kill you, but have it look like attempted murder." Schott watched her closely.

"That's crazy."

Sam looked from one to the other, a scowl creased between his eyes. "Did he say who hired him?"

"Yes, Lauren Sobrantes."

Lauren shot to her feet. "Me? Oh, for god's sake, why would I hire him to do that? Why?"

"To take suspicion off yourself," Sam said. "To mislead the investigation and quell the rumors that you killed your dad."

Schott nodded his agreement.

"I think I'm going to be sick." She put a hand to her stomach.

"So, you deny you paid this man to shoot at you?"

"Of course, I deny it! I never hired him or anyone else. Ever!"

Sam put an arm around Lauren's shoulders. "Do you have any proof, Ed?"

Schott shook his head.

"So, it's his word against hers."

"For now." The implication hung in the air. "If there's any proof to be found, we'll find it. Lauren, come to the station tomorrow. We'll need an official statement from you that you don't know this man and that you didn't hire him."

Sam spoke up. "We'll be there with her attorney."

Schott smiled sadly. "Well, Happy Thanksgiving. Sorry to dump this on you today. I'll let myself out."

Lauren turned to Sam. "Whoever is behind this…this scheme wants to get me one way or the other. I'll either be killed or convicted. Either way, I'm screwed."

Chapter Forty-Five

~~~~~

Sam woke after mid-night, reached for Lauren but the bed was empty. Watson whined and scratched at the bathroom door.

"Lauren?" Sam opened the door.

She lay on the floor covered in vomit—her breathing shallow, pulse erratic, skin cold and clammy to the touch.

Watson, strangely quiet, watched as Sam called 911, and then his brother Zach. Working rapidly, he cleaned the vomit from Lauren's face and stripped off the soiled nightgown, replacing it with a fresh one, and wrapped her in a blanket.

Zach met them at the hospital and rushed Lauren into an exam room. Deke arrived moments behind them, breathless as if he'd run all the way.

Various scenarios sped through Sam's head as he paced the length of the waiting room. Food poisoning was the most likely, but the clamminess and shallow breathing didn't add up. Neither did the fact that he wasn't sick, nor was Deke, or Zach.

Zach reappeared to update them. "She's stabilized. Vital signs are stronger, but she's still unconscious. I've ordered blood tests. It looks like severe food poisoning." His voice trailed off.

Sam sensed he had some doubt about the diagnosis when Zach said, "We're still testing for things."

Sam took Deke to one side. "Can you go to the house and get samples of the food and drinks we had last night?" He gave him his house key and the alarm code.

"You're thinking . . . " Deke scowled.

"I'm thinking if it is food poisoning, we'll need to know which food it was and who brought it." He was confident the

220

dishes he and Lauren made yesterday were not the source, but what was? And why was no one else sick?

Ed Schott arrived at the hospital about an hour after they brought her in.

"How is she?" he asked Sam.

"Stable. Zach is waiting for the blood test results. Deke brought samples of the foods from the house."

Ed scratched his graying head. "So it might be food poisoning. Did anyone else get sick?"

"Just Lauren. I've called the others, except Kyle and Marisa. I haven't reached them yet." He threw a worried look toward her room. "Be right back."

Schott turned to Deke, who'd returned from dropping off the samples at the lab. "Something feels off."

"What do you mean?" Deke asked.

"Well, it's funny that she's the only one sick. You know Lauren, do you think she'd ever try to hurt herself?"

"Like suicide?"

Ed nodded.

Deke pursed his lips. "There was a time when I'd have said absolutely not, but how well do you know someone?"

"What about Sam?"

"Sam?"

"Would he hurt her?"

"You mean like giving her something to make her sick or poison her?"

"Yeah."

"Naw, he'd just shoot her."

Photos of Lauren, unconscious on the gurney in the emergency room, flashed across the morning news and went viral on social media.

"Sam, what the hell's happening out there?" Flynn questioned when he called. "Networks are speculating that Lauren tried to off herself or you tried to kill her."

"Zach's running blood tests and the lab's testing the foods we had at dinner. We should know something today, tomorrow at the latest."

"You all ate the same things, didn't you? Why aren't you all sick?"

"That's what we're trying to figure out."

"What does Lauren think?"

"She's confused right now. I told her it was food poisoning."

"But you don't think so."

"We'll stick with that for now."

"Soon as the pre-flight check is finished, Jon and I are taking off. We should be there by this afternoon. By the way, Sammy, you're buying the beer and dinner."

"Am I dying?" Lauren's words were slurred. She looked small and vulnerable like a child in an oversized bed. Her focus wandered from the IV in her arm to Sam.

"No, you're not dying."

"Oh." Her eyes closed. "Anyone else sick?"

"No, just you. Probably the cornbread dressing you tasted before cooking, those raw eggs."

"You ate it, too."

Sam patted his middle. "A stomach of steel."

"No one's ever coming to dinner again." Sighing, she turned her face and closed her eyes.

Sam pulled up a chair. Twice someone had attempted to kill her on his watch. Someone who had a very strong objective, and now, everyone at the dinner was suspect, even his own family.

When she woke, Sam was gone and Fiona was at her bedside.

"Good morning." Fiona, dressed in slacks and a muted striped sweater, appeared different, younger, and lighter. She leaned over the bed, straightening the sheets around Lauren, a slight frown creased between her eyes.

"Morning." Lauren's voice was hoarse. "How long...?"

"Have you been here? I think Sam brought you in just after midnight and its afternoon now." She picked up the water with a bendable straw and offered it to Lauren.

Lauren sipped slowly, then waved it away. "No, how long

have you…"

"A while. We all came as soon as we heard. We've taken turns sitting with you. How do you feel?" Fiona sounded genuinely concerned and even a little motherly.

How did she feel? Headachy. Hurting all over. "Like I've been run over by a truck. What happened? Why am I here?"

"Let's wait for the doctor, shall we?"

Lauren struggled to sit up. "Sam, where's Sam? He's not dead, is he?"

"No, he was just here with you."

"I got sick." Her memories of last night were scrambled. She'd gone downstairs for water, and afterwards, she'd begun to feel sick. She remembered stumbling into the bathroom and the cold tile on her face.

"Sam just stepped out for coffee. I promise you; he'll be right back. Any minute now."

Lauren pressed her head back on the pillows, searched Fiona's face. "Truth?"

"Truth. Do you need anything?"

"What day is it? Where's Sam?" she mumbled and closed her eyes.

Sam stood in the parking lot listening to his brother.

"There's another option." Flynn kicked the gravel with the toe of his boot. "The poison might have been slipped into one of the dishes that you washed up last night."

The blood tests had proved it was not botulism or food poisoning. The lab was running more tests.

"Which takes us back to the guests. You can eliminate your family," Jon added to the discussion. "Follow the money. The woman's worth billions, who benefits if she's dead?"

Sam paused before answering. "If the RKB principals have a survivor contract, then her stock might go to Bernie and Kyle. Or it may all go to Bernie as next of kin. But they seem to care for Lauren."

"Like those two boys in Southern Cal, who loved their parents so much that they shot them full of holes to inherit their money?" countered Jon. "Who else?"

"Any of them—Marisa, Fiona, Bernie."

"What are you thinking?" Flynn asked when Sam paused.

"Well, Marisa told Lauren that she was responsible for Lauren's mother dying. Then, she denied it. She asked for an appointment with Greg, maybe to find out what to do about Jeffery's other family.

"Then there's Fiona. At the gala, she told Lauren she planned to sue her for the Casa and the property. If Lauren died, would the place automatically go to her? She'd be the next of kin since she is still legally married to Richard."

Flynn threw up his hands. "Hold on. First things, first— where are you taking us to dinner? We'll work it out while we eat."

Chapter Forty-Six

~~~~~

Bernie checked into the hotel in Kowloon, slept for a few hours, then showered and redressed. At midnight, he met Rand in the lobby.

The informant agreed to meet them in an area most Anglos avoided, if they were smart. The taxi dropped them off, and when paid, sped away. The street bustled with food vendors, dive bars, massage parlors, and late-night partiers.

A man approached them. He refused to give his full name, telling Rand to call him *Joe—just Joe*

Joe was a tall, reed-thin man with slanted shoulders. He leaned forward and asked Rand to confirm that he was paying a large reward for the information.

"We're agreed," Joe said, looking from Bernie to Rand. "Okay?"

"Agreed," Rand said. With the exchange rate almost eight to one, Joe would be well paid. "Half now and the rest when I've confirmed your information," Rand bargained, unsure of the trustworthiness of the source and the cogency of the material.

Joe nodded and spoke rapidly. "An American paid to set up the business. The counterfeit components are manufactured after hours and shipped to companies in the United States. They go through several sources before they get there which makes it harder for Customs to trace where they came from and who produced them."

"RKB is among the companies, right?" Bernie pressed. He darted quick glances both ways on the busy street. The faster they got out of here, the better.

"Yes, RKB. There's also an investigation company that sets up phony raids and fake arrests for the people behind the counterfeit manufacturing operation. The man owns both companies. He pays off their fines and people arrested are never charged, or jailed." Joe spoke rapidly as if he, too, was concerned about the dangers of the street.

"Who is the man behind all this? The American?" Rand demanded, raising his voice over the din of the loud music and raucous laughter coming from the bar down the way.

Joe shook his head.

"I want names, Joe. I need addresses before I pay more money. And next time we meet at a safer venue."

"I'll get them. You realize this is very dangerous for me if anyone finds out?"

Rand and Bernie agreed to meet with him again the following night. Joe said he'd call and tell them the location. He took the money, tucked in his inside coat pocket. He pointed them to the safest way to get to the subway station and taxis before he casually walked in the opposite direction.

A group of men emerged from a nearby dive bar in high form, talking loudly and staggering drunkenly.

Bernie and Rand hurried toward the subway. Bernie looked back as the noise increased. Joe was engulfed in the group of partiers.

When the men scattered, Joe lay in the street.

A knife between his ribs.

Back at the hotel, Bernie opened the mini-bar in his room, poured two glasses of bourbon and handed one to Rand.

"Whoever is behind this has a lot of power." He threw back the drink and poured another. "We don't have a source or a name, and now the man is dead."

They were stunned how quickly Joe was killed. "Did those guys know that Joe was an informant?" Bernie deliberated aloud.

They'd run back to where he laid and checked for a pulse, but the man was dead. Bernie called the police. Rand checked the man's coat pockets for identification and the money. Both were gone. Was it simply a robbery? Or was he killed because he was an informant?

"It's something you never get used to, Bernie," Rand said. "There's nothing we could have done differently to protect him."

Rand's satellite phone vibrated. He checked the number before answering. "Yeah." He listened and then hung up. He tossed back his drink before he relayed the news to Bernie,

"Lauren's in the hospital. Someone tried to poison her."

Chapter Forty-Seven

~~~~~

Lauren returned home on Sunday morning. Sam helped her out of the car. She clung to him for balance. "I'm not going to bed," she declared in a tired voice.

"How about the living room? By the fire?"

She agreed. Sam settled her on the sofa with pillows behind her back and a comforter over her legs. Watson laid his head in her lap as if sensing she needed help to heal.

"What can I get you?" Sam asked.

"A glass of water—lots of water. Dr. Zach's orders."

Sam returned with a glass and a pitcher of water. "Fiona's here. I'm off to check the security system again. I won't be long."

Fiona strolled in with a grin on her face. She'd dressed in black jeans, boots, and a plaid shirt that strangely enough, suited her. She held a small wicker basket at her side.

"What's in the basket?"

"A little something for you. A welcome-home-get-well gift all in one." She placed the basket in Lauren's lap and opened the lid.

Two kittens—one black and one white curled together like a furry Yin-Yang symbol. Lauren lifted them out. They yawned, pink tongues curled, then they stretched, and blinked open round blue eyes to stare at her. Watson stuck his nose in their bellies and sniffed, lifting the kittens up. They arched and hissed. He sat back, mystified by their rejection.

Lauren was instantly in love. She beamed at Fiona. "Thank you."

Fiona's eyes sparkled. "I remembered how you love cats."

"Where did you find kittens at this time of the year?" Kittens were prevalent in the summer months and were rare at the end of the year.

"A friend had a late litter, I asked her to save a couple for me."

"Thank you for thinking of me."

"I'll get their food and litter box out of my car. Then I have to run. I have a meeting."

"Hello," Cienna sang as she breezed in. "Hi, Fiona," she called out as they passed in the hallway. "Getting through security at your gate is worse than the airport in Germany. I haven't been felt up like that since I flew out of Berlin. Oh, look at these cuties." Cienna gave the kittens a squeeze then went to the kitchen to put things in the refrigerator. She returned and picked up the black kitten that was busily attacking Lauren's fingers. "Feeling better?"

"I'm glad to be home." Lauren's voice cracked.

"I brought food, nothing fancy, just soups and light dishes to get your system back on track as prescribed by Dr. Zach. When you've had food poisoning, it takes a while regain your energy."

Fiona carried in cat food, a bag of kitty litter, and a litter box that she set up for the kittens in the downstairs bathroom. She placed food and water in their dishes. Tucking one under each arm, she showed them where everything was and assured Lauren they were box trained.

"Fiona, can you visit tomorrow?" Lauren asked. It was time to make peace with their past. "We can have lunch or tea, depending on how much energy I have."

"I'll bring the lunch." Fiona beamed at the invitation. "Don't worry about a thing." She squeezed Lauren's hand, gave each kitten a quick stroke, said goodbye to Cienna, then apologized to Watson for bringing the beasties into his domain.

Cienna made a pot of tea. Lauren relaxed with the kittens and Watson. With the warmth and the fragrance of cinnamon and spice, it was like having her mother with her again. She frowned, remembering what Marisa had said—that she was responsible for Elizabeth's death.

Cienna hovered over her, a cup of tea in hand. "Are you hurting?"

Lauren offered a reassuring smile. She hurt all right, but it would take more than a cup of tea for her to feel better.

Lauren dozed and woke to the tickle of kitty whiskers on her cheek. Cienna sat in the chair nearby, editing pages of a manuscript. She looked over her half-glasses when she saw Lauren was awake. "Have a good snooze?"

Lauren removed the white kitten from her face. "How rude of me. Where's Fiona?"

"She left, remember?"

"Oh, yeah, she's coming tomorrow and bringing lunch. And Sam?"

"Sam came in to check on you and went out again. Something about checking the fence line where the deer got into the garden."

Lauren settled the kittens in Cienna's lap and wobbled to the bathroom on shaky legs. She washed her face and finger combed her hair before returning to the sofa. The room chilled as the sunlight faded.

"I'm feeling much better," she told Cienna. "Whatever's in that tea you gave me must be working. I feel stronger."

"Old family formula. My mother always said it would either cure you or kill you." Cienna laugh was full and mellow. "I'll give you the recipe."

"Better than my dinner that *did* almost kill me."

"They still don't know what it was or how it got into your system. But it wasn't that wonderful food you and Sam prepared."

"He learned how to cook from you, didn't he?"

Cienna gazed at the kittens curled in her lap, intertwined, and giving an occasional purr when she ran her fingers over their little heads. "Sam was moderately skilled at cooking by the time he was ten. It wasn't long before he was making up new dishes, blending the ingredients that made an old dish taste new. As a teenager, he developed a keenness for knowing what herbs and spices would balance together into a unique combination that worked. He loved the challenge of it."

"But something happened..."

"He'd just turned fifteen." Cienna paused as if the memory was too much to continue. "He and his friend, Andy, planned to hike around the old quarry. Sam packed a lunch and asked me to drop them off at the entrance." She placed the black kitten on her chest, stroking its back until he purred. Watson whimpered in his sleep.

It grew dark, but neither moved to turn on a light.

"They got there around noon. Andy was stoned, plus he'd had several beers. He was unsteady and acting silly. He stumbled over the side. Sam grabbed his arm and held on, screaming for help, but he wasn't strong enough. Before help arrived, Andy slipped out of Sam's hands and fell twenty feet, broke his neck, and was dead before rescuers could rappel over the side to get him."

Cienna's tears glinted on the cat's black fur. She rubbed them away and continued. "Sam blamed himself. He felt he should have stopped Andy from smoking and drinking. He should have been able to save him. The quarry was his idea. He wanted to take photographs and search for fossils. Therefore, he was responsible for Andy's death.

"Sam lost interest in everything. It didn't help that Andy's mother publicly accused him of murder and wanted him arrested. We called in a counselor, but it didn't alleviate his guilt. He withdrew from all of us. And after high school, he enrolled in college and then dropped out and joined the Navy. My beautiful, funny, brilliant boy—was gone."

~~~

"Meet me at the gate." Flynn's voice crackled over Sam's headset. "There's a washed-out area up the hill."

Sam turned the rented motorcycle around and followed Flynn along the south perimeter of the property. Beyond the flat meadow by the orchard, the terrain roughened, and they began to climb, riding through brush and over rotted tree trunks along the back area of the fenced compound.

Flynn led up the way up an embankment and a dry wash of rocks, boulders, and gravel exposed from the storm two years before.

"This is where he got in. See where that gravel is kicked up. He had to accelerate over that hump." Flynn revved his bike. They rode farther up the wash between the exposed boulders. The sides of the gully steepened.

"Must've stopped here." Flynn pointed to the sandy area of a small plateau.

Sam examined the deep tire tracks and footprints. One bike. One person. "Looks like he was carrying something heavy."

Dismounting the motorcycles, they hung their helmets on the bars and hiked up the incline through a thicket of greasewood to the back fence. They could see the tennis court and swimming pool, yet remain out of sight of the Casa.

Sam and Flynn separated, traversing in opposite directions. About ten yards along the fence, the brush was trampled. "So, this is how he did it," Sam muttered to himself and then whistled for his brother.

A large section of the fence lay on the ground. "That sucker used an acetylene torch to cut through the metal," Flynn said, in disbelief.

"A smaller cut would have let someone crawl in. But, he needed a wider space to—"

"To carry Lauren out." Flynn completed Sam's thought. "If she'd been alone on Thanksgiving night, he would have taken her, let the poison do its job, and no one would've ever known what happened to her. We both know who'd have been up shit creek."

Chapter Forty-Eight

~~~~~

Fiona arrived at noon the next day with an assortment of light foods for Lauren and a few spicy Indian dishes for Sam to have for dinner. She set the table while Lauren reclined on the sofa.

"Are you sure you wouldn't rather have a tray?" Fiona asked for the third time.

"Zach said it was good for me to move to get my balance and energy back."

Yin and Yang chased the toy mice Fiona threw for them. "Nothing like kittens to entertain," Lauren laughed and moved slowly to sit at the table. "This chicken salad looks great."

Fiona poured a carob power shake into two glasses.

"I probably don't want to know what the media is broadcasting about my trip to the hospital, do I?"

"It's the usual no-connection-to-reality muck," Fiona said.

A difficult silence fell between the women. Lauren remembered she'd invited her stepmother over to forgive and forget. After all, as big a betrayal as it was—Fiona having sex with Jeffery saved Lauren from marrying a liar and a cheat.

"Thank you, Fiona, not only for the lunch but for something else." She explained how grateful she was to have been saved from marrying Jeffery. Then she shared what Marisa had found in the safe deposit box.

A flush covered Fiona's face. She tried to speak, but only her lips moved. She took a deep breath, struggled for control. Lauren reached out and took Fiona's hand. "I don't want this or anything else between us any longer."

"I am so ashamed, Lauren. I truly loved your dad. I would

never have done anything to dishonor Richard, but that night I'd taken tranquilizers, had a few drinks; I went into the study just to be near Richard, to feel his presence. Jeffery came in and handed me a drink, and we chatted a few minutes. And then... I was... he was..." Fiona covered her face with her hands and sobbed.

"Date rape," Lauren said with conviction. "I bet he slipped something in the drink he gave you. Marisa found a bottle hidden in his sock drawer. We're pretty sure it is Rohypnol. She sent it to a lab to be analyzed."

"I should have fought him or something. Maybe I did, I can't remember."

"Exactly! That's what the drug does. It knocks you out, makes you incapable of resisting, and you have no memory of what happened. Oh, Fiona, if only we'd known." She put her arms around her stepmother.

"One more thing," Lauren said, handing Fiona a large envelope. "I found the photos that he took of you. I wanted you to be the one to burn them, so you know for sure they're destroyed."

Fiona helped Lauren stand. Together they threw the photos into the fireplace and watched the flames turn them to ash.

"If that bastard weren't already dead, I'd kill him myself," Fiona declared, drying her tears.

Lauren chuckled, "Thank goodness, he is dead because orange is so *not* your color."

"Hmm, you're right. If those prison jumpsuits ever get fashionable, men will be running for cover."

Fiona insisted that Lauren lie down after lunch while she cleaned up. When she finished, she found Lauren asleep with the kittens curled on her stomach and Watson stretched out on the floor beside her. Fiona tiptoed out feeling lighter than she had in years.

~~~

Bernie caught the first flight out of Hong Kong. Rand stayed to investigate Joe and learn the man's real identity.

The flight to San Francisco was long. Physically and emotionally drained, Bernie took a town car to his home in Willow Glen. He called Detective Schott on the way. And then called Sam for an additional update. Both men assured him that Lauren was in good hands, recovering at home with a couple of new kittens and Fiona and Sam's family taking care of her.

The next afternoon, Bernie pondered the situation as he drove to the estate. It all started with Richard's search to determine who slipped the counterfeits into the company's packaging process. How were his murder and the attacks on Lauren connected?

Why was she a target? She'd been employed by RKB in the marketing department, but other than that, she'd not been involved with the business. She had no knowledge of the manufacturing issues.

So, what was the motive for killing her?

Bernie parked in the circular drive. Mr. Watson stood watch, guarding Lauren, who waited in the doorway. She waved, and Watson took it as permission to meet and greet.

They settled in the living room, and Bernie filled her and Sam in on what happened in Hong Kong.

"Was it robbery, or a hit?" Sam asked. Joe's death seemed too pat, too much of a coincidence to him.

"No way to tell for sure. They could've been watching us. It's hard to believe that someone randomly noticed money being handed over and decided to rob Joe and stab him."

"Rand will keep checking it out, right?" Lauren looked at both men. This could be the answer to why a hit was put out on her dad.

"If anyone can get to the bottom of it, it's Rand," Bernie assured her.

Chapter Forty-Nine

~~~~~

Lauren was bored and welcomed company when Marisa joined her for lunch. They settled at the breakfast bar. Lauren sliced tomatoes to go with the artichoke-and-spinach quiche.

"Cienna made this," she assured Marisa. "I'm sure the food is good and won't make us sick."

"You scared me, getting sick like that. I was afraid I'd lose you again."

"It was scary for me, too." Lauren removed the quiche from the oven, placed a large slice on each plate, added the tomatoes, and drizzled vinaigrette over them. "By the way, I heard from Etta. Arlo is doing great. She said she's even learning to like his mother."

She continued to talk, keeping the conversation light and inconsequential, waiting for the right time to ask questions about her mom's death.

"I found Jeffery's wife and son. They live in San Juan Bautista." Picking up her fork, she began eating.

Lauren was stunned. "They live that close?" San Juan was only an hour from La Lumbre on a good day. In traffic, it could be hours, but close enough that Jeffery could have maintained both places and both families with ease.

"Greg contacted her. We're going to his office on Thursday for a preliminary meeting. Would you go with me?"

"Of course, I'll go with you," Lauren said.

"We'll need proof they were legally married. If I'd known about her, I would have kicked him out on our honeymoon. I guess I was just his mistress for the past couple of years. As his

236

wife, Lahn is entitled to everything. Even if they're divorced, Jeffery's will leaves everything to his son."

Lauren shrugged. "I imagine there'll be an investigation into where the money came from. If only he'd told us the name of my dad's killer before he died."

"He used to drop hints; said he had proof. But he never said a name." She looked at Lauren, blue eyes large; fear in her voice. "Do you think he was blackmailing the killer?"

"It could be." The women contemplated the possibilities.

Marisa broke the silence first. "The two are related. They are—I just know it. Jeffery and your dad were murdered by the same person."

Chapter Fifty

~~~~~

Lauren felt stronger and more energetic. The lab had ruled out botulism, salmonella, listeria, and a few others she'd never heard of and finally determined that it was oleander poison.

Oleander bushes grew along the fence by the gate. Sam had trimmed them back the day she arrived, but how did it get in her food? No one else was sick, and the only thing she'd had after dinner was a few nibbles of the leftovers and a glass of water. Happily, the toxins were clearing out of her system thanks to Cienna's cooking and Angelica's herbal remedies that Marisa brought with her yesterday.

Marisa called to say she'd given Detective Schott the DVDs and photographs, plus the jewelry that didn't belong to either of them or Fiona. The bottle found in Jeffery's bathroom was analyzed and proved to be Rohypnol, just as they had suspected.

The afternoon was full of long shadows and fading light when Schott arrived. Sam led him to the living room where Lauren, casually dressed in gray sweats and a cotton t-shirt was arranging books on the book shelf.

Watson lay by the fireplace with Yin and Yang curled between his paws.

Schott sat across from Lauren. Sam leaned against the back of her chair. The quiet seemed eternal until Schott gathered his notes and thoughts before speaking.

"Frank Grimes has confessed that he killed your father."

Lauren gaped at him. Schott waited, closely observing, and judging her reaction to the news. Hands to her mouth, she

238

leaped to her feet and crossed to the windows, where she bent at the waist and screamed the unspoken pain she'd held inside for the past two years.

"Thank God. Thank God." The words repeated like a mantra between sobs.

Schott made notes.

Calmer, she wiped her tears, and asked, "What made him do it?"

"He claims he was hired to kill him."

Sam handed her a glass with a splash of scotch. Burning as it slid down her throat, the sharpness brought her back to reality. "Jeffery had always claimed someone put out a hit on Dad."

"How long have you known Grimes?" Schott asked.

"Know him? I'd never heard of him until he was arrested."

"Grimes said he'd met with you on several occasions, that you two grew quite friendly. Was it at the sex clubs?"

"He's lying. First, he says I paid him to shoot at us the night of the gala, and now he's saying we had a relationship? The man's delusional. And for the record, I've never been to a sex club in my life."

"He's writing his statement now. He said he'd give us the dates when you met and how you paid him." Schott's voice was firm.

"Why would he confess to something that's a lie? I tell you I've never met the man."

"Did he say where he met her? Or who paid him?" Sam questioned.

"He said they met here." Schott leaned forward, eyes intently watching her face. "He claims that you hired him to murder your father and that you gave him twenty thousand in cash as a retainer."

A shock wave of disbelief crashed over her. Stupefied, she stared at the detective. "You're not serious? You can't believe him. No. Of course, you don't believe him."

"What proof do you have other than his word against hers?" asked Sam.

"He says that Lauren demanded the trophies—Richard's

watch, his phone, car keys, wallet, and the ring."

"I don't have any so-called trophies." She shuddered at the thought.

"The watch was found in your bedroom. Grimes says you put the other things in the safe," Schott countered.

"The safe is empty. Sam will verify it. We opened it the night of the 49er party at Kyle's house. There was nothing in it. It was still empty when I put my jewelry there the morning after the shooting at the cottage."

"Then you won't mind if I take a look?"

Sam hesitated, but Lauren led the way to the study. It didn't take long to punch in the combination. The large door swung open. Inside was a strange box next to her jewelry case. Lauren looked at Sam before turning to Schott. "That wasn't in here before," she said weakly. "It wasn't."

The forensics team arrived within the hour. The contents of the box—Richard's phone, car keys, wallet, and ring were carefully placed in evidence bags and taken to the lab.

"Ms. Sobrantes," Schott's tone was all business. "You may call your attorney if you like and have him meet us at the station."

"Are you arresting me?"

"We need answers."

She didn't have any. Clearly, she was being set up, but who had access? The only other person who had the combination was Uncle Bernie.

He would never hurt her father or her, but who else could have put those things in the safe? And, when?

Chapter Fifty-One

~~~~~

The interrogation room at the sheriff's station was small, claustrophobic, and cold with a stale odor of cigarettes and fear. Lauren sat on an uncomfortable, straight-back chair on one side of a small desk with two equally hard chairs on the other side. Knowing she was being filmed, she feigned a calm demeanor as she waited.

The door opened. A woman of medium height dressed smartly in black pants, and a black jacket entered. Her dark hair was short, hanging in line with her square jaw. A scowl puckered between her dark eyes as she looked Lauren over.

She had an attitude. Confrontational attitude.

Lauren had experienced her kind before—people who looked at her and saw only her wealth, her social standing, rather than seeing her as a person. There would be no winning this woman over to her side.

She sat down, opened her notebook, read over her notes, before speaking. Gestures calculated to make a suspect nervous.

Finally, she spoke, "Ms. Sobrantes, I'm Detective Amelia Rodgers. I'll be asking you a few questions. This interview is being recorded. Would you like something to drink? Water? Coffee? Coke?"

Lauren declined and waited for the pleasantries to pass.

"I understand you tried to commit suicide the day after Thanksgiving. What can you tell me about that?"

Lauren strained to conceal her shock. "Your understanding is incorrect. There was no suicide attempt." She hoped her voice sounded calmer than she felt.

The woman smirked. "Let's look at the facts, Ms. Sobrantes. Your tests showed no food poisoning or any bacterial poisoning. No containers were found in the house with any trace of whatever you ingested. Now, that tells me that you took something, and then disposed of it. It made you just sick enough to be taken to the hospital. And yet, not so sick that you couldn't make a fast recovery."

Lauren let the accusation hang, neither agreeing nor disagreeing. Apparently, the information on the oleander poisoning had not reached the investigators.

Ms. Rodgers tried a new tactic. "Look, Lauren, may I call you, Lauren?" She smiled like a new best friend.

"No. You may not."

"*Ms.* Sobrantes, I understand how things can get overwhelming for someone in your position. Your first attempt for public sympathy—hiring someone to shoot at you and having it backfire when Grimes was captured and let it be known that you were the one who hired him to do it. That would be enough to make someone want to check out, wouldn't you agree?"

Lauren studied the woman. Any answer she gave would be the wrong one; like the old adage of—*do you still beat your wife?*

Lauren shifted, tucked her feet underneath her to sit in a lotus position.

The detective watched her intently, her scowl increasing.

"My shoes are new," Lauren explained.

"What?"

"I said my shoes are new and I don't want them mired in all that bullshit you're slinging."

Detective Rodgers fought back a grin. "So, you don't want to talk about the suicide attempt."

"You mean the *non-suicide* attempt. I suggest we move on or we wait for my attorney before continuing the interview."

Schott watched the exchange through the one-way window. Lauren was undeniably a Sobrantes, and he knew that Rodgers couldn't shake her composure. Personally, he didn't buy the suicide theory like the other detective. If she wanted to kill herself why wait until she came back to La Lumbre?

The Grimes confession, and then finding Richard's things in the safe that Lauren swore was empty, was troubling. Schott began to wonder if it was staged.

With all of Sam Gallagher's security cameras, how could anyone get into the Casa to hide the watch in her bedroom and put the cell phone, keys, wallet, and ring in the safe? Where would they get the combination to the safe if Lauren and Bernie were the only ones who knew it?

Ed took a deep breath and entered the integration room.

"Ms. Sobrantes." He leaned against the end of the desk next to Detective Rodgers. "For the record, do you know Frank Grimes?"

Lauren placed both feet on the floor. "For the record—I don't know anyone by that name."

"You don't remember meeting him?"

"I remember that I've *never* met him."

"How would you describe your relationship with your father?" Rodgers asked.

"It was great." Lauren smiled, sadly. "We were always close, and more so, after my mom died."

"Then he remarried."

"Yes."

"Did you argue with his new wife?"

"Sometimes."

"Did you like her?"

"Not always. We respected each other because we both loved my dad, but we didn't have a lot in common."

"Is that what caused the rift between you and your father?"

"There was no rift between my father and me."

"Perhaps it was all the sex clubbing that was the problem, plus the fact he intended to disown you, cut you out of his will."

Lauren gazed at the woman while she edited how to respond to the crazy accusations.

"Well, was it?"

Schott interrupted, "Did you ever have a membership to a sex club?"

"No, I did not."

"Numerous witnesses say differently." Detective Rodgers pushed.

"Detective Rodgers, you've evidently been gathering your facts from watching a sleazy television show and reading a book that was withdrawn by the publisher because it was fabricated. As for your alleged witnesses, if it came to swearing in a court of law that their statements were true, I doubt a single person would be willing to perjure themselves. In fact, they've already stated they were paid by the author and the show's producer to lie about my participation in the so-called sex club activity.

"Furthermore, Detective Rodgers, I suggest that you separate your facts from the media fiction and that you do so quickly before I add you, and this department, to the list of lawsuits my attorney has filed regarding that issue."

"Be that as it may, Ms. Sobrantes, there is still the matter of the confession from Grimes stating that he killed your father because you paid him to do it," Rodgers countered.

Lauren sat back in the chair, studied the detectives across from her. "I did not conspire with anyone to kill my father. I loved my father. We did not argue. He was not cutting me out of his will. I had nothing to do with his death. How things are showing up in a previously empty safe, I don't know. I just don't know," she repeated wearily.

Deke Farelle knocked, stuck his head through the door, and motioned for the detectives to step outside the room.

Schott returned with Greg Gallagher.

"Frank Grimes had a heart attack. He was still writing his confession when he went into a cardiac arrest." Schott sounded frustrated.

"It wasn't signed," interjected Greg. "It won't hold up in court. They can't hold you on hearsay evidence."

"We still have the video of his statement and the fact that Richard's things were in Lauren's safe," snapped Detective Rodgers.

Hours passed before Lauren was released. The rest of the interview after Frank Grimes was confirmed dead became a game of patience while they waited for the lab to verify Lauren's fingerprints weren't on any of the items found in the safe.

Amelia Rodgers tried her best to confuse Lauren into making a misstatement the detective could run with, but Lauren won each round of interrogation. Greg had had enough by then and told them to either charge her or release her.

The media lay in wait outside the front door of the station. A din of voices shouted questions. Lauren, escorted by Greg, held her head high as she made her way to the waiting car that Sam had sent.

When she returned to the Casa, she went upstairs without a word. Sam got updates from Greg, and then locked up, and set the alarm. He joined her in the master bathroom where earlier he'd placed candles and a chilled bottle of white wine. He turned on the water in the tub, gently undressed her, and helped her slip into the tub. She closed her eyes and sank into the warm water up to her chin.

Sam wanted to wash away her tension and worry, but all he could do was be with her, hold her hand, and assure her that things would work out.

But he knew it wasn't close to being over. A box was delivered while she was at the Sheriff station. Inside was the down payment, a photo of Lauren with the same markings as the one in the San Francisco hotel room, and a gun.

He'd opened the package very carefully to preserve any fingerprints but was sure it would be wiped clean like the drone parts. Jon would process it, but he doubted there would be anything to find.

What he didn't doubt was that the killer was escalating and would keep hiring until he succeeded, and she was dead. Sam knew he would have to act quickly to save her.

After the bath, Sam bundled her in a white terry robe and coached her downstairs where she sat in the easy chair by the fireplace.

"I felt slimed," she sighed. "Detective Rodgers kept sneering at me and asking about my sex clubbing and drugs and did I have any idea the number of men I'd had sex with? When I told her, yes, I do know, she lit up like a celebrity gossip. Then, she scoffed when I said, two. I've been intimate with two men. She didn't believe me."

The fire spiraled in low flames of red and orange. Her grandmother had taught her to fire-watch, read the flames to see the future. Gazing into the fire, the future she saw looked bleak.

Yin and Yang chased each other up and down the hallway, circling through the kitchen and back. They jumped over her lap and then down to run the route again. Watson laid his head on her knee and gave a long-suffering sigh over what he was asked to endure. She laughed at the kittens' antics and praised Watson for his patience.

"Got any marshmallows?" Sam pulled her to her feet. "Let's make S'mores."

"S'mores?"

"Soul food."

They searched the pantry and found the stash his mom left—miniature marshmallows, chocolate chips, and graham crackers. Sam showed Lauren how to improvise and melt the marshmallows in a soup ladle held over the fire.

She carefully squished the chocolate chips into the melted goo. Sam spooned it on the graham cracker and placed another one top.

"Oh, so this is soul food." She took another bite. "Wouldn't it be easier to do this in the microwave?"

"Oh, hush your mouth, woman," he teased and handed her the second one. "We'll have to go camping. Everything's better over an open fire." Sam wiped marshmallow off her chin and kissed her.

He tasted like chocolate and wood smoke and safety. She loved it. She loved that he distracted her from the ordeal of the interrogation. Loved that he was with her.

"You're leaving."

His body language confirmed she was right.

"I heard you making plans."

"Then you got sick, and I decided to stick around."

"I'm well now. I can hire personal bodyguards. It will be up to my attorneys to sort out how things keep showing up here.

I'll hire a good team of lawyers to prove that man's confession was a lie. So you're free to leave, Sam."

Lauren knew that once Sam left, he would never come back. It was best to do it sooner than later. Although, sooner wouldn't make the pain of never seeing him again any easier.

"Yes, it would seem so," Sam agreed.

What was that revolting saying about *letting go of what you love, and it'll come back?*

Chapter Fifty-Two

~~~~~

Marisa sat beside Angelica in Greg's office. It was silly of her to be so anxious, but she couldn't help it. She was relieved when Lauren and Sam arrived.

With Jeffery's death, Marisa was committed to being her own woman and re-igniting her art career. First, she had to complete things with Jeffery's wife, Lahn to sort out the inheritance issue.

Lahn and her son appeared as the clock chimed ten. Lahn was a small woman with olive skin, a broad face, and a wary look. According to Greg's research, Lahn, born in Thailand, was twenty-six years old. Which meant she was barely fifteen when she'd given birth to Jeffery's son.

Dressed in a yellow dress and gray coat, her hair pulled into a ponytail, she held tightly to the hand of a young boy who already towered above her. Evan had dark hair like his mother and green eyes like Jeffery.

Sam and Angelica excused themselves and went to the nearby Starbucks. Marisa rose from her chair, offered her hand, and introduced herself. "Welcome. Thank you for coming to meet with us." Marisa gestured to the sofa.

Lahn's son nodded, and his mother sat down and he sat beside her. "Why are we here?" asked Evan, clearly his mother's protector.

Greg began to explain, "You know that your father had an accident. And he didn't survive?"

Evan nodded. His face, inscrutable.

"Well," Greg hesitated as if unsure to whom he should

speak, the son or the mother?

"My mother understands English, but she is hesitant to speak. I will translate for her and you." Evan's words were no-nonsense and direct, reflecting a maturity beyond his years.

"Perfect, let's get started. It is our understanding that your mother, Lahn, was married to Jeffery Davis."

The boy explained to his mother, who vigorously nodded in agreement. She handed Greg the documents he'd requested when he contacted them earlier.

"Her marriage certificate." Greg passed it to Marisa. Lauren looked at it over her shoulder. The California marriage license confirmed Lahn had married Jeffery.

"Are your parents divorced?"

The boy explained in Thai.

Lahn's eyes widened in panic; she vigorously shook her head. "No divorce."

Greg turned to Evan. "And, you are the son of Lahn and Jeffery Davis?"

"I am. Is there something wrong? What is this about?"

"Nothing's wrong. Please, assure your mother that nothing is wrong. We just need to verify your mother was still married to Jeffery and that you're his son."

Marisa smiled in hopes of reassuring the woman that everything was good. There were so many things she wanted to know. Was Jeffery kind to her? Did he take good care of you? Did he love you and your son?

"Evan, can you tell us about your dad? Did he live with you?" she asked.

"My dad traveled for his work. He couldn't be with us all the time. He visited when he was in town, usually on weekends, but he couldn't stay long."

"Did he take care of you financially?" Marisa asked. "Was he supportive that way—food, clothes, school, that sort of thing?"

"He helped as much as he could. My mom works two jobs, and I work after school. I mow lawns, and during the summer, I work at a bike shop. The owner is teaching me how to repair bikes. I save my money to buy school clothes and stuff." He paused and looked at each of them. "Please, why are we here?"

Marisa looked at Greg and Lauren, knowing they were thinking the same thing, that while Jeffery lived the high life, his family was scraping by.

Greg started to explain, but Marisa interrupted, "Let me. Evan, it's rather a complicated story. Trust me that it has a happy finale for you and your mom. Your father was leading a double life."

She paused to allow the interpreting and questions from Lahn to be answered. She explained how Jeffery was once engaged to Lauren, and then after Lauren left town how she and Jeffery had married.

"My marriage to him was not legal since he was already married to your mom." She watched Evan struggle to process information that destroyed his former life and what he knew to be true about his father.

Lahn began to cry. Lauren passed tissues and a glass of water to her. Marisa moved to her side and held Lahn's hand until she regained her composure.

Marisa finished her story. "Because my marriage to your dad was not legal, you and your mother are entitled to inherit your father's estate. We have to determine there was never a divorce, and you'll need to agree to a DNA test. It's a formality to prove to the court that Jeffery was your father."

Lahn and Evan sat stunned silence. They looked from person to person.

Greg cleared his throat. "Do you understand?"

Evan nodded, then asked nervously, "I wonder, would there be money so that maybe my mom could, maybe, work just one job? And someday I could go to college?"

Marisa laughed with delight. "Honey, your mom could choose to never work again. And, you'll have enough money to do whatever the devil you want and go to any university in the country."

Greg finished the legal paperwork and swabbed the inside of Evan's mouth and then Lahn's for the DNA testing.

Lahn, obviously in shock, hugged Marisa and whispered thank you.

Evan shook her hand. They were ready to leave when Lahn turned to Marisa. "My husband gave me a box."

Marisa looked to Evan for clarification. "I don't understand."

The boy and his mother chatted for a few minutes.

"My father gave her a box to keep for him. He said never let anyone else have it. But since he's gone, she wants to give it to you."

"What's in it?"

Evan shrugged. "It's taped up. He told my mother to keep it hidden."

Chapter Fifty-Three

~~~~~

Lauren pulled the comforter over her shoulders and curled against Sam for warmth. He was lying on his back with his arm thrown wide to the side, eyes closed and sleeping. Or so, she thought until he turned over and pinned her underneath him. Morning sex with a handsome man was the best way to start your day. She would enjoy it while he was here and ignore the fact that her time with him was limited.

"I'm cleaning saddles today," Lauren called to Sam, who was in the bathroom, shaving. She pulled on jeans and a warm sweatshirt. "Would you pick up more saddle soap while you're in town?" She tugged on heavy socks and tucked in the pants legs. "Who's on security this morning?"

Sam stepped out of the bathroom, a towel around his hips. "It's Freddie's day off. Jake and Bill are on. Put them to work shoveling out the stalls." The men hated menial labor. "I'll be back in an hour or so."

Lauren went downstairs, fed Watson, and the kittens, and then slipped on her muck boots by the door. The morning air was crisp, perfect weather for trail riding when the horses felt frisky. She'd bring them home from Rand's place over the weekend. Now that she didn't have to look over her shoulder for killers, she could ride through the hills again. Humming a silly song, she waved to the security guys.

~~~

Sam parked down the block from Nick's diner. He made his

way to Jon and Flynn who were seated in a booth by the window.

A.J. waved hello as he passed the grill. A waitress brought menus, poured coffee, and threw a wide smile to Flynn.

"That gorgeous woman tired of you, yet?" Flynn goaded Sam. "I'll be glad to stop by and introduce myself." He hooted, "I wish you could see the look on your face, Sammy. You're in big trouble. Look at him, Jon. He's got woman fever all over him. You can see it in his eyes."

"Cut the crap, Flynn. What've you guys got?" Sam put the menu aside and reluctantly ordered ham and eggs.

Jon reported first. "Not much in the way of fingerprints on the package. We're still testing and trying some new techniques. There's progress on the thumb drive. It was heavily encrypted. But our tech was able to open it. Davis had money stashed in several accounts in the Caymans. Twelve million, total."

Sam whistled at the amount. "Jeffery made bank at RKB, but not that much."

Flynn flirted with the waitress when she brought their food and then grew somber when she left. "The beach house was cleaned out, man. Not even a pair of trophy panties nailed over the bed. The place was so clean it didn't even look lived in. I bet someone scrubbed it before we got there."

"So, if he'd had anything stashed there it's gone?" Sam cut into his overcooked eggs. "The question is what secret was worth twelve million in hush money?"

"Did you tell Deke about the thumb drive?" Jon buttered his toast and watched Sam concentrate on his eggs, evading the question. "Have you?"

"Not yet, I—" Coyote stood outside the café window staring at him. "I haven't yet, but I will."

The animal levitated, eye-to-eye with Sam, and then howled bone-chilling cries. Sam jumped. Shivers tore through his body.

"Sam, what is it?"

"Did you hear that?" Sam picked up his coffee with shaky hands.

Puzzled, Jon and Flynn shook their heads. "Hear what?"

Coyote howled again, raced a few yards away, and then

came back, repeating the howling and frantic running.

Lauren. Sam slammed his cup down and ran out of the diner and jumped in his car. He called Lauren, then security. No answer from either. Where was she? Where were her guards? He dialed 911. Prayed to every god and goddess he could name to protect her.

Smoke spiraled from the stable. Deke's squad car raced down the drive ahead of him. Sam and Deke pushed back the barn doors. Jake was sprawled face down, blood seeping from a large gash on the back of his head. Deke pulled him outside. Bill was nowhere to be seen.

Old hay bales and wood chips were piled up against the door of the tack room. The smoke was thick. Lauren pounded from inside, screaming for help.

Watson barked frantically, running back and forth in front of the stable.

Sam grabbed a shovel and beat at the blaze. Deke worked beside him.

In the distance, a siren wailed.

Inside, Lauren went silent.

Sam worked faster, pulling the smoldering hay away, he pried the door open and pushed back the horse blankets stuck in the doorway to keep the smoke out.

Lauren lay face down in the far corner, a blanket over her head. She was silent until he reached her. Sam was unable to speak as he held her; uncertain who shook the hardest.

"You stopped calling, I thought—"

"Saving my breath. I knew you'd rescue me."

The paramedics pushed Sam aside. They took Lauren out, slipped an oxygen mask over her face, and checked her vital signs. Jake, still unconscious was loaded into the ambulance. The firemen hosed down the burning wood and began checking the barn for other hot spots.

Then, all activity stopped. A fireman came out and talked to Deke. Among the stacks of hay, they'd discovered a gun—a Sig Sauer, like the one that killed Richard.

"I'll take it to Detective Schott," Deke told Sam.

"It's not finished, is it, Sam? Even with Frank Grimes dead, I'm not safe." Lauren's voice was raspy from the smoke. She'd refused to go to the hospital. Sam took her to the Casa. He hadn't told her about finding the gun.

"No, it's not over."

Jon and Flynn arrived and joined the search for Bill. They found him unconscious behind the barn. The estate had once again been compromised. Someone managed to break in, disable two security guards, lock her in the tack room, and set the barn on fire.

How had the killer known he'd be gone? If it hadn't been for Coyote, he'd still be having breakfast in town and Lauren would be dead.

He jumped at the loud banging.

"Sam, it's Zach. Open up."

Cienna, Greg, and Emmett crowded in behind him. Cienna hurried to Lauren's side.

Zach insisted on examining her. "I'm sure you're fine," he chided when she resisted. "Let's do this for my peace of mind."

After he confirmed she was okay, Cienna led her upstairs to shower. The men watched silently as the women left.

Emmett laid a hand on Sam's shoulder. "That was close. Now, will someone tell me what's going on? I thought Deke caught the guy who shot at the two of you. That she was safe."

"Obviously, not. I leave her with security and look what happened. She almost died in a fire."

"But, she didn't," Greg said. "Now, let's make a plan."

Sam looked at his dad, his brothers. They were ready to help him protect Lauren. They'd always been there to help him. He was the one who'd turned his back.

"This is not a game." He looked at each one of the men. He wanted to make sure they understood the peril of the situation. "You could get injured or jailed or—" Sam couldn't bring himself to say *killed*.

Zach picked up his medical bag. "Tell us what you want us to do, Sam."

Jon and Flynn returned from searching the area. They gathered with Sam in the driveway. Jon described what they'd found when they searched the security system. "The cameras were jammed, and a couple of the lenses taped over. We found new bike tracks in the dry creek."

"We swept inside the house for electronics, Sam," Flynn added. "No camera, but there are two high-tech listening devices planted in the bedroom. That's how they knew you'd be gone this morning."

Sam's jaw clenched. Someone listened to them? Listened to their intimate moments?

"Something made him take a big chance—daytime, people around, security all over the estate. Why take the risk of getting caught?"

"It's escalating, Sam. Next time, we won't be so lucky. What about a witness protection program?" Jon asked.

Sam looked away. "She wouldn't go for that. Besides, if he found her once, he'd find her again. The next time there'll be no warning. It doesn't leave me much choice."

"You planning to do what you did with Cosima?" Jon asked.

Sam nodded.

"It'll cost you this time, Sam," Jon warned. "You might end up in prison for life, or worse."

Worse meant the end of the dream he'd allowed into his imagination. A vision of a home with the woman he loved and who loved him, a dream of children running around the estate, happy, laughing. The worse would mean he failed and that she'd die.

He saw Coyote and the woman in red watching from beyond the driveway in the grove of redwoods. As Sam watched, she nodded as if giving approval to what he was about to do.

"It has to be done." Sam agreed. "There's no other choice at this point."

Chapter Fifty-Four

~~~~~

Marisa's life had fragmented into a rollercoaster of emotions. She never knew when a high or a low was coming around the corner. The drugs she'd been given over the past couple of years were slowly working their way out of her system.

Angelica assured her the remedies would cleanse her body and she'd be completely free of the residue of drugs and feel like her old self again.

What was her *old self*? She couldn't remember a time when she didn't have the burden of secrets.

Secrets that could destroy people.

Morning mist drifted over the garden as she strolled and deliberated about the past weeks since Lauren's reappearance. The attempts on Lauren's life and the shock of Jeffery's murder were surpassed when she discovered he was a blackmailer, a thief, and a bigamist.

So far, Greg had kept Jeffery's secrets quiet and the public frenzy remained focused on Lauren and not so much on Jeffery's death. The sheriffs were working to identify the women in the photographs and DVDs he'd hidden in the safe deposit box. At this point, the only thing the sheriff had on the accident was that the brakes were tampered with, but nothing else.

Angelica joined her on the path by the koi pond. "Good morning," she whispered. Their walks in the garden were the only place they could talk in English without worry of being overheard. "Dr. Hadley packed up and left early this morning."

"That's great. What made him take off without telling anyone?"

"I slipped a note to Detective Schott the other day and asked him to check on Hadley's medical license. It seems it was revoked a few years ago."

Marisa chuckled and continued to meander along the path.

"You seem troubled." Angelica fell into step beside her.

They strolled in silence stopping at the meditation garden, to sit on the low bench surrounded by overhanging ferns, and a large Kwan Yin statue.

"What if you know something? And, yet, you have no way to prove what you know. What would you do?" Marisa ruminated.

"Secrets are like cancer. They eat away at one's soul until there's nothing left. Can you share without accusing?"

Marisa let Angelica's words echo in her thoughts. Secrets, cancer, fear.

Fear had locked everything inside.

Fear that once that lock was broken, then, like Pandora's box nothing could stop the catastrophic damage.

Chapter Fifty-Five

~~~~~

Sam placed an electronic scrambler on the nightstand next to the lamp where the listening device was concealed. The listener would hear static until Sam removed it. After that, everything could be heard and recorded.

He was betting Lauren's life on it.

Finally, it was time to set his plan in motion. He drew Lauren close, making love to her with a sense of finality— saying goodbye with each caress of her soft skin, memorizing her fragrance of roses and musk. He loved her and wanted her to be a part of his life, but what he was about to do would destroy it all, along with his fantasy of a home, children, and family.

Lauren lay back against the pillows, her long hair cascading around her like a woman in an antique painting.

"Sam," she said, her voice throaty—the voice of a well-sated woman. "Let's go to London. I have to decide what to do about my store. Come with me. We'll spend Christmas there, play tourist, go to Bath, maybe fly over to Paris and Brussels."

Sam lifted his watch from the nightstand, removing the scrambling device. "I can't afford to travel right now." He stood, strapped the watch on his wrist.

"You'd be my guest. I'd pay for everything." She sat up and wrapped the sheet around her.

"Guest? Like your hired escort." He dragged on his pants. "Gigolo, boy-toy, bitch—whatever the hell they call it these days."

He sat on the bed and jerked on his socks. "I'm done. It

was fun, and I'm done. A rich piece of ass fucks just like a professional."

What an actor he was, condescending and cruel while his heart shattered. He hated seeing her face go white.

"Sam?" She reached for him. "What are you saying?"

"What am I saying? That I'm leaving. It's over. We're done. Go buy yourself another stud."

She sat up on her knees, pulled her shirt over her bare breasts. "Then, you go to hell. Get out of my house. Get out!" Confused and hurt, she redressed quickly.

Sam walked into the bathroom, shut the door, and braced himself against it. Bile filled his throat. Why had he never told her that he loved her?

Lauren's scream was chilling. "Sam! Oh God! Sam! No, no—please. SAM! Don't do this."

Sam opened the bathroom door. Lauren was backed against the wall. She pleaded with him to help her. A man dressed in black, his face covered in a mask, held a gun to her temple.

"Sam!" She reached out her hand. Eyes wide with fear, she begged him to save her. "Please. Sam!"

Sam nodded to the man, then stepped back, and closed the door.

"Please, no—" she screamed.

Pftt-pftt.

Silence.

Sam's legs buckled. He slid down the door and sat spraddle-legged on the cold tile. Numbness seeped through his body—Lauren's screams echoed in his head. Finally, he got up, cleaned the bedroom and left the Casa.

Chapter Fifty-Six

~~~~~

"Sam, we know you killed Lauren. What did you do with her body?" Schott demanded.

Sam waited. Watched. The detectives showed up after midnight and arrested him for Lauren's murder; claiming they had evidence that he'd shot her. The Casa was now a crime scene without a body.

"I have no idea what you're talking about." Sam's voice was steady. He looked Schott directly in the eyes like an innocent man.

"No idea? You don't know how you murdered Ms. Sobrantes, disposed of her body, and then returned to the cottage as if it was all in a day's work."

Sam shrugged, which seemed to infuriate Detective Rodgers.

"Gallagher, how do you explain the recording that was dropped off at the station early this morning? Lauren Sobrantes, screaming, begging you not to kill her," she asked.

Sam shrugged. "I know nothing about a recording."

"Where did you say you were last night?" Schott asked again.

"At dinner with my dad and my brother Greg. I've already explained to you, several times. Check the security cameras at the restaurant."

"What time was that?"

"I left the Casa around 7:00, maybe 7:30 and met them, oh, I'd say about 8:00 or 8:15."

"What restaurant?"

"Fish Market. El Camino and Lawrence. Dad paid the check with his American Express card. I left a hefty tip, in cash. I'm sure the server remembers me. She was cute and flirty."

"See if they have anything from the security cameras in the area and check that Amex card." Schott directed Rodgers.

Ed turned to Sam. "You know, when I put it all together, it seems to me that you've been playing us all along."

"How so, Ed?"

"You are the only one who had access to her bedroom, to the safe, to the stable. You planted those things from her dad in the safe. Things that you took when you killed Richard."

"There's just one flaw in your theory, Ed. I wasn't in the country when Sobrantes was murdered. I was living in Paris and was on assignment in Afghanistan. How did I get those trophies if I wasn't in the States?"

Deke Farelle stormed through the door. "You sonofabitch, what did you do to Lauren?" He leaned across the table stopping short of attacking Sam. Schott watched but didn't interfere.

Sam stood, slammed his fist down. "I've no idea where Lauren is or what happened to her. Last time I saw her, she was in her bedroom watching television—if she is missing, then you're wasting time with me when you could be searching for her."

Deke shoved Sam back in the chair. "How do you explain that recording? Do you want me to play it for you? Want to hear Lauren's screams before you shot her?"

"Anyone can mimic and record voices, then drop it off at the sheriff's office."

"We're authenticating the recording now," Schott said.

Deke interrupted. "Forensics examined the bedroom. Luminal showed blood on the walls. You might as well save us time and tell us what you did with her."

"There's nothing to tell," Sam said.

"Cooperate with us, Sam. You might get away with life instead of the needle." Deke stood back, frustration convulsing through his body.

"Interview's over, gentlemen." Greg and Zach strode into

the interrogation room. "No more questions without counsel, which would be me. Sam was at dinner with Dad and me last tonight. So, when you find a body or have proof that she's dead, let us know. But until then, Lauren Sobrantes is simply a missing person. She's taken off before, and she's probably taken off again."

Greg took Sam out the back where Flynn waited in an SUV with the engine running. Zach walked out the front and waded into the middle of the media frenzy where they mistook him for Sam. Before he could get down the steps, the reporters rushed him, thrusting microphones in his face.

Zach stopped and delivered a statement to the group, declaring his innocence.

Chapter Fifty-Seven

~~~~~

Blissfully dead, Lauren floated on gentle swells of ocean waves while angels sang from the clouds above. Their hands held her head; angel fingers massaged her temples.

"Slowly, slowly," a calm voice whispered in her ear. "Allow your attention to focus on your breathing. Breathing in and breathing out. You are safe. Slowly, gently, breathe. You'll sleep now, and when you awaken, you'll feel alert and happy."

Lauren drifted on the soothing voice and the easy music of babbling water. She inhaled a deep breath of perfumed air.

She thought of Sam.

Sam, who had her killed.

How can I think or take a deep breath if I'm dead? Can you breathe in the afterlife? Her thoughts faded as she sank into a contented sleep.

In the early morning hours, Lauren woke again, and sat up cautiously, looking about the dimly lit room. A large statue of Buddha stood beside a vase of flowers, fragrances of mint and lavender enveloped her. It was all very tranquil and Zen.

She checked for wounds. No bullet holes. No cuts. She had a terrible headache and a bad taste in her mouth.

What happened? She and Sam had made love. She'd asked him to go to London with her, but he'd told her he was done. Tears gathered when she recalled the horrible things he'd said about how he'd used her, how one piece of ass was just like another and how he didn't want her anymore.

Then, the gunman walked in.

And Sam... Sam nodded to him.

She'd pleaded for her life.

She'd called for Sam one last time to help her, but he didn't.

The moon glimmered through the skylight above her. A lover's moon she thought, but her lover had betrayed her, hadn't he? Why bring her here if they planned to kill her? What were they waiting for?

She had to escape. If only she knew where she was and how to get back home.

A young woman emerged from the shadows, dressed in gray tights and a gray tunic top, a long braid of blonde hair hung over her shoulder.

"My name is Ami." Her smile beamed through her warm brown eyes. She offered Lauren a small cup of tea. "It will help with your headache."

"Where am I?"

"A sanctuary." The young woman's voice was low and melodious. "You'll be our guest for a while."

"I can't stay," Lauren protested. "I have animals—cats, a dog. I can't leave my pets." Or did they kill Watson and Yin and Yang? The thought of them dead made her choke back a sob. No one knew where she was or what had happened to her. People will think she'd disappeared again. Schott wouldn't bother searching for her.

Ami sat beside her, rubbed her hand soothingly over Lauren's back. "Watson and the kittens are being cared for while you're away."

Lauren wiped her eyes. How did she know Watson's name? Who was she connected with? "Have I been kidnapped?"

"People want you out of harm's way."

"What people? Sam?" Lauren demanded.

The woman smiled compassionately, then asked if she was hungry.

Lauren ate a bowl of granola with almond milk and drank a second cup of herbal tea. She felt stronger, but her thoughts were fuzzy. Overcome with lethargy, she dozed and woke to the continuous drone of deep bells.

Cautiously, she peeked out into the hallway. The outer

room was large with wooden floors and massive redwood beams across the ceiling. Along one side were tall windows that looked out to meadows and mountains. Flowers, fruit, and incense offerings were assembled before various statues of Buddha. Groups of people walked silently through the hall toward the sound of the bells.

Ami sat outside her room, a gentle guard, but a guard nonetheless.

Lauren motioned to her. "I'd like to shower. And would you happen to have a change of clothes I could borrow?"

"Of course, I'll get them for you. We also have massage therapy, sauna, meditation, and yoga. After you shower, I'll show you around if you like."

"Yes, that would be lovely." Lauren returned the woman's smile as if she had decided to relax and enjoy her confinement.

Ami quickly returned with a towel and washcloth, soap, and shampoo. She laid out a pair of black leggings and a surplice-style tunic like her own. She opened the window and began making the bed after Lauren disappeared into the bathroom. Ami suggested leaving the door ajar to release the steam.

The shower cleared Lauren's head. Above the water, she heard the murmur of voices. Leaving the shower running, she crept to the door to listen. She leaned against the wall and peeked through the crack between the hinges and the door frame.

The man talking to Ami looked familiar. She was certain this was the same man who'd kidnapped her. Her adrenaline surged into overtime. Why was he here? To finish the job?

"Give her two of these at dinner." She heard the man tell Ami. "I'll take her out tonight."

Lauren jumped back as he turned to leave. So, that was the plan. Drug her and carry her off—to who knows where. Or to what end. She had trusted Sam to protect her. Now, the only person she could trust was herself.

Chapter Fifty-Eight

~~~~~

Rand checked his notes one more time as he approached Prince Edward Road. He'd gotten Joe's real name and an address from a contact of his at the police department. He went to the house, but the neighbors refused to give him any information until a woman whispered that Joe's wife, Ling Hau had a stall on Flower Market Road.

He passed the Yuen Po Street Bird Garden. The cage covers were off and the birds sang in an assortment of sounds. Adjacent to the Bird Garden was the Flower Market. The flowers, a mass of colors and fragrances, spilled over on the sidewalk. Rand worked his way through the crowded aisles to her stall.

Ling Hau was small of stature with thick, short white hair. Her head down, she worked with the flowers, trimming, and cleaning away dead blossoms. Rand approached cautiously. He didn't want to frighten away what might be his last and most vital resource.

~~~

Lauren watched Ami's hands rapidly move, throwing yarn over the needles as she knitted.

"I need your help. I have to go home. Please."

Ami stopped, folded her hands together, a quiet look of empathy on her face.

"I have money, I can buy you whatever you want," Lauren pleaded. "A new car, a house, money, just tell me what you want

267

to help me get out of here. I have a great deal of money."

"I know who you are. I know you have wealth, but I made a promise, and I can't break it. You are to stay here, just for a little while longer, and then someone will come for you."

Lauren didn't believe her. That man wanted her dead. Sam wanted her dead. Going home would never happen if she waited. Sitting on the edge of the bed, she nodded to Ami, knowing she'd not get anywhere with this woman. There had to be another way for her to escape.

~~~

Greg drove Sam from the Sheriff's station to the family home at the herb farm. Emmett and Zach followed in another car. Inside the house, they all gathered around the kitchen table. Watson twisted excitedly, greeting everyone, and then waited for the one person who wasn't coming. Yin and Yang raced through the throng of legs.

Zach brought out the beer.

Sam gestured to his brother with his glass. "Thanks, everyone. Zach, I owe you, buddy."

"My pleasure, Sammy. It's been a long time since we've switched identities, and while I wish the circumstances were different, but I gotta tell you it was a blast. *Cin Cin!*"

They celebrated. Now, they just had to wait for the killer to tip his hand.

~~~

Lauren watched the people come and go at the retreat house. Ami, breaking for her meal, changed places with a muscular man who was also dressed in gray. He sat in the chair outside the door eating his dinner from a small bowl.

Yoga students, apprentices, and monks roamed through the large assembly room.

Ami's knitting bag lay under the guard's chair. Would there be anything in that bag she could use as a weapon or maybe if she were lucky, a set of car keys?

When the man saw Ami walking toward him, he left his post to take his bowl to the kitchen. As they stopped to chat, a group of yoga students walked by obstructing Ami's view. Lauren grabbed the knitting bag, rummaged around inside and thanked the heavens when she found a key with the Toyota symbol.

~~~

In Ling Hau's flower stall, Rand took his time selecting flowers and engaging the woman in light conversation in Chinese before he mentioned that he'd known her husband. She watched and listened without responding when he offered his condolences.

"Ling Hau, I need some information."

"What sort of information?" Her tone was wary. She looked around to confirm they were alone.

When Rand explained that he was willing to pay for her time, she took him to the area behind her racks of flowers. There were two low stools and a brazier with glowing coals.

"Your husband said he helped someone set up a manufacturing group and an investigation group here in Hong Kong. Do you know who they were?"

"My husband was very secretive," she said, stirring the coals. "He does not tell me anything." She set a small kettle of water on the brazier. "But I knew more than he thought I did."

"Women are very clever." Rand waited as if he had all day to visit with her.

She smiled warily. "If I tell you what I know, how much will you pay?"

"Big," Rand said, without giving away an amount. "It depends on whether I can use the information. The more I can use, the more I'll pay."

She thought about that for a moment, nodding sagely.

"Your husband told me an American set up the company," Rand explained.

Ling Hau poured the water over the tea leaves. "Yes, a big man."

"Did you see him?"

269

"Yes, both of them."

"There were two?"

She nodded, poured tea into two small cups, and handed one to Rand.

"If I showed you a photo, do you think you'd recognize them?"

Ling Hau shrugged. "Maybe."

Rand took out his phone and ran through the pictures. "This one?"

She shook her head and sipped her tea.

Rand flipped through several more. She indicated no to all of them. Then cried out, "Wait. Go back."

He slid the photo back on the screen. It was a group shot taken during a picnic at the Sobrantes estate three years ago. The last event Richard had hosted.

"That one."

Rand stared at the photo. "You're sure?" She was adamant and pointed again to Jeffery Davis.

Rand paid her the balance of the money he'd promised Joe. Ling tucked the money away. "And the other one."

"The other one?"

She pointed out a second man. "They come separately. But that man is the big . . . what do you call it?"

"Big honcho?"

"Yes, he was in charge of everything."

Rand called the airport to have his plane readied for takeoff. He called Lauren's mobile phone to warn her, but his call went directly to her voicemail.

~~~

Lauren waited until it grew dark. Ami offered her food, with the drugs, no doubt. She pretended to eat which seemed to satisfy Ami. When she was gone, Lauren ran to the bathroom spit out the food and rinsed her mouth. Closing the door, she slid open the bathroom window, kicked out the screen, and squirmed her way through the small opening, landing on pine needles and rocks. Pain shot through her bare feet, but she kept moving in the shadows of the building and the surrounding trees.

She hid in the bushes until a group came out of the building laughing and chatting as they strolled to the parking lot. She slipped in with them. A disharmony of beeps sounded as cars unlocked. She pressed the button on the car keys. A Prius flashed its lights. She prayed it was the right one.

Lauren waited. Watched. But no one got into the car. Walking behind three women who were too busy talking to notice her, she opened the car door and slid into the driver's seat. Taking a deep trembling breath, Lauren pressed the starter button. The car's engine soundlessly came to life.

Slipping into the line of cars driving out of the center, Lauren turned right at the end of the driveway and sped away. Adrenaline heaved through her racing heart.

She'd escaped. She was free.

And she was hopelessly lost.

~~~

Hours later, Sam's cell phone rang. Flynn's number flashed on the screen.

"Lauren's disappeared. We've searched the grounds and discovered she'd stolen a car. She's taken off and most likely is heading back to the Casa."

Sam was out the door and in the car before Flynn hung up.

Chapter Fifty-Nine

~~~~~

Lauren arrived at a place where the GPS linked to the satellite long enough for her to read the directions to the freeway and make her way home.

Hours later, tired and hungry, she drove into the estate. Security was gone. Sam must have called them off since he expected her to be dead by now. Without their protection, she really was on her own.

Lauren slipped into the cottage through the kitchen door to search for a weapon. The shotgun was too big; she wanted one of Sam's hand guns.

Cold stillness assured her she was alone. Making her way upstairs, she searched Sam's dresser and found nothing. Returning downstairs, she went to the security room. The monitors, blank and dark, reflected her anxiety. Lauren rifled through the drawers and cabinets. Taking a knife, she pried open the locked drawer, but came up empty-handed.

In the kitchen, she tapped the adobe bricks and opened Nana's secret hiding place. Inside, there was a heavy bag of money and a photograph of her with a dramatic bull's eye written over her face. Underneath the money, she found the gun.

Everything was abruptly clear. Sam killed Richard and had been hired to kill her.

She wasn't going to hang around and let him catch her. She'd pack, drive to SFO, fly back to England, and disappear again before Sam knew she was gone.

Chapter Sixty

~~~~~

Lauren threw clothes in her suitcase and zipped it closed. She'd get her passport from the safe and leave. It was safer to wait for a flight at the airport rather than to stay here. Opening the door of her bedroom, she stepped out into the dark hallway.

And heard a low murmur.

Heart pounding against her ribs, she picked up the gun she'd taken from the cottage, released the safety and made her way down the stairs.

The voice grew louder behind the closed doors of her father's study.

Closed doors.

Voices. Angry voices.

She remembered.

The night before her father was murdered, she'd come home from dinner with Jeffrey. By the time she got into the house and started upstairs, she'd felt dizzy, nauseated, and out of control of her movements. She'd paused on the first step.

Her father had been arguing with someone.

I know what you've done. I know everything.

Had he been with his killer? She took a steadying breath and continued down the stairs.

The voice rose and fell.

She held the gun at her side. Turned the doorknob and slipped inside.

He paced on the far side of the room like a crazed stage actor—gesturing, snarling, and cursing. Then he saw her.

"I paid Gallagher to get rid of you. Why can't you just die,

273

you little bitch?"

"You murdered my dad."

A maniacal laugh burst out of him. He gestured wildly with the gun in his hand. "I didn't kill anyone."

"You hired someone. Dad said he'd tell the sheriff what you'd done, didn't he?" She was guessing, but from the shocked look on his face, she knew it was the truth.

"So, you did hear us that night. Jeffery said you did. I paid Jeffery to keep his mouth shut. But you disappeared."

"Who did your dirty work, Kyle? Who did you hire to kill my father and Jeffery?"

"You were supposed to be my daughter. My daughter! Elizabeth was in love with me, and your father stole her away with his lies."

The sudden shift stunned Lauren. Kyle was already married when he'd met her mother. "My mother didn't love you. She didn't even like you." Her mom had always avoided being alone with Kyle. Now, it was clear why.

"That's not true. It's not true." His rant exploded into rage. "She betrayed me. You all betrayed me," he declared. "Betrayers have to die."

The reality hit Lauren. "You…you murdered my mother, didn't you?"

"Oh, god," he wailed. "It was an accident. An accident, I would never hurt her. Never. I loved her."

"You gave her something." The examiner's report said Elizabeth's heart had stopped. Date rape drugs did that, she remembered from the research she'd done when they found the bottle of Rohypnol in Jeffery's stash. Odorless, it was a liquid that could be added to any drink.

Marisa's secret.

Somehow, she'd known what Kyle had done. It was the secret she'd wanted to tell.

Kyle forced Marisa to marry Jeffery to keep him quiet. He kept her drugged, so she'd stay silent.

"You can kill me Kyle, but you won't get away with it, not this time. How will you explain my death to the sheriff?"

Her fingers tightened on the Sig. She heard Sam's voice, "*If you shoot, aim for the middle. Do not hesitate. Shoot first to save your life."*

"No one would ever suspect me. They'll find your body and figure Sam did it. He's already in custody. Schott's locked him up for your murder. Now, they'll find your body. Case closed." He cackled a bizarre laugh, pointing the gun at her. "Time to join mommy and daddy—"

She fired. Kyle's bullets hit her in the neck and side. Her knees buckled. She lay on her back staring at the paneled ceiling, heart pumping wildly, spilling blood on the floor. She wanted Sam. She wanted to see him one last time before she died.

"Stay with me, Lauren," Sam shouted. She was too still. Her blood stained his hands as her life leached out onto the floor.

Deke knelt on the opposite side. He threw a towel to Sam and then applied pressure on Lauren's neck wound while Sam pressed against the wound in her ribs.

"Where the hell are those medics?" Sam cursed as the towel turned red.

"Coming. They're coming," Deke took up the chant for Lauren to stay with them.

Detective Schott rushed into the study with the paramedics. Sam watched helplessly as they lifted Lauren's body to the gurney and drove off, sirens screaming.

He'd failed her. Kyle's role in this seemed so obvious now, but somehow he'd missed all the clues.

Deke clapped a hand on his shoulder. "Lauren's tough, she won't let a couple of bullets do her in."

"What are you doing here?"

"Lauren called me. She said she needed help."

She'd called Deke, but not him. Deke had entered the study behind Sam. They'd both yelled to Kyle to stop.

"Sam," Schott joined them. "Go wash up, and then we'll talk."

He washed his hands and watched the bloody water run down the sink. His life had stopped when he saw the blast from Kyle's weapon and the kickback from Lauren's gun.

~~~

"My, you look very serious." Marisa greeted Greg.

"And, you look..." Beautiful and happy and he was about to change all that. "We need to talk." He'd driven straight to Marisa after Sam called to say Kyle was dead, and Lauren was in surgery.

"What's happened? Is this about Jeffery's wife? The money?"

"Marisa, there's been an incident." He'd never had to break the news of a death to anyone before. Was there a kind, gentle way? Was it worse to dance around it rather than just blurt it out?

Fear drained the color from her face, making her blue eyes stand out, large and round. "Tell me quickly," she whispered. "Just tell me. Who's dead? Please—not Lauren?"

"Your father."

A small gasp, and her eyes rolled back. Greg caught her as she fainted and carried her to the sofa. He yelled for help and Angelica came running.

"Kyle was shot and killed this morning," Greg explained the details as Angelica brought Marisa around.

"What happened? Was anyone else..." Marisa closed her eyes.

"Lauren is all right." Reassurance first, he decided. "But she was shot."

Holding onto the sofa with one hand and Angelica with the other, Marisa struggled to her feet.

"Sweetie, she's doing fine." Understatement of the year, but Lauren was alive after blood transfusions and surgery. She was expected to make a full recovery.

Marisa cried body-racking sobs. Angelica gently held her. Greg stood by feeling absolutely helpless.

"And, Kyle..."

"Sam, uh. . . Sam—"

"Shot him, didn't he?"

Greg nodded. "Kyle shot Lauren. Sam and Deke returned fire. And Kyle—"

"Died. I'll never forgive myself," she whispered.

Chapter Sixty-One

~~~~~

Sam paced the length of the ICU waiting room and back again. The warm taupe walls and soothing monotone furnishings did nothing to calm his anxiety. Lauren's blood, dried on his shirt and pants was a persistent reminder of his failure.

In his mind's eye, he replayed the shooting. It had all happened rapidly. Kyle fired at Lauren. Her body jerked when the bullets hit, and she went down.

Deke had come out of nowhere, yelling for Kyle to drop his gun. Instead, he shot at them. Sam and Deke returned fire in unison; the bullets smashed into Kyle's chest and head.

Sam continued to pace and pray, offering sacrifices if the gods would spare the life of the woman he loved. He wanted to talk to her, tell her how sorry he was for the things he'd said, and explain why he'd staged her murder.

Deke and Flynn entered the waiting room. A few minutes later, Zach came out, his surgical mask hanging around his neck. The family rushed to him and mutely waited for the news.

"Luckily the bullets missed anything vital. I'm keeping Lauren in the ICU for a little while. Then we'll move her to a private room."

"I want to see her," Sam demanded.

"Sorry, Sam, not until she wakes up."

"Zach, is she . . . Tell me, she'll be . . ." Sam's voice broke.

"She's good, in great shape, came through the surgery like a champ," he reassured his brother.

"Hey, Sam." Deke clapped a beefy hand on Sam's shoulder. "How about you and me run over to the station?

Schott needs a formal statement from the two of us. By the time we get back, I'll bet Lauren will be awake and ready to see you."

~~~~~

Walking into the La Lumbre Sheriff's office was easier as a free man, unlike the last time he was here when he was in handcuffs, arrested for Lauren's murder.

Schott and Amelia Rodgers joined him in the conference room. Deke helped himself to the coffee and donuts and moved on to a separate room to make his official statement. The use of deadly force even in self-defense was serious, and the proper paperwork had to be filed.

Schott started the conversation. "Sam, what happened? First, Lauren is kidnapped, then she returns, and is almost killed."

Sam explained how he and Flynn staged the pseudo-kidnapping to move Lauren to a safe place.

Amelia Rodgers spoke up. "Yeah, well, where did the blood come from that was on the wall?"

"I don't know," Sam said. "Because there was no blood; she was tranquilized." Someone got into the place and smeared blood on the wall and then cleaned it off to pin the blame on Sam for her murder.

Sam described how Zach stood in for him at the restaurant to provide the alibi. "It worked as planned until Lauren escaped. I got to the study just as Kyle fired at her. Deke was behind me. We both warned Kyle to stop. He fired at us. We fired back."

~~~

"You just missed your brother," Schott said to Greg. "He went back to the hospital with Deke."

"I told Marisa about her dad." Greg set a box on Schott's desk.

"What a mess. How's she doing? Who would have imagined that Kyle Montgomery, of all people?" Schott frowned. They still had no motive for why Kyle attempted to kill Lauren.

"Marisa's doing as well as one can, I guess. Angelica is with her."

"What's this?" Schott asked, pointing to the box.

"Marisa asked me to bring it to you. Jeffery gave it to his wife, Lahn to hide for him."

Greg left the station to catch up with Sam at the hospital.

Amelia Rodgers entered and watched Ed slit the tape with his army knife. They peered inside the banker's box. He pulled out a black book with Richard's name in gold letters embossed on the front.

"I'll be damned, the missing lab book. Jeffery had it all this time." Schott thumbed through, reading the notes Richard had written on his last day. His notes confirmed how suspicious he was of Kyle and how he planned to meet someone who had proof of Kyle's part in the counterfeit component scheme. Richard had pulled money from his safe to pay the informant.

"What happened to the money?" Amelia mused. "Jeffery?"

"He'd had a solid alibi for that day. He was with Lauren." Schott continued to empty the box. He drew out a large envelope. Inside was a photo of Kyle and an RKB engineer who'd drowned in Thailand while on vacation a decade ago. A faded newspaper article covered the accidental death.

"Why would Jeffery keep this?" Schott wondered. He took a magnifying glass out of the drawer and searched the photo. In the background, there was a reflection of the photographer.

"Damn it!" Schott's curses bounced off the walls. He threw the photo and magnifier down on the desk. "He's not going to stop. Get over to the hospital. Guard Lauren. No one in— except Zach."

Schott ran out. Jumped behind the wheel of a squad car, praying he'd be in time to prevent another murder.

Chapter Sixty-Two

~~~~~

Sam was exhausted. He laid his head against the headrest and closed his eyes as Deke drove the winding road back to the hospital.

He wanted to see Lauren. Wanted to be there and hold her hand until she woke up and turned those smoky gray eyes his way again. He'd explain what he'd done and why. Confess that he loved her and beg forgiveness for what he'd put her through.

The car slowed and then turned. Opening his eyes, he realized Deke was on Berry Falls Quarry Road, where Andy had died, years ago.

"What the hell, Deke. I thought we were going to the hospital."

Deke parked the car beside an old redwood picnic table, now gray with time and weather. "I just wanted a minute to talk, man-to-man. Find out where things stand with you and Lauren. I guess you're free to go back to work with AZEN. Are you going or you planning on staying?"

"I haven't decided. I'm not sure Lauren wants me around."

"You know, I've always liked you, Sam."

Sam waited, unsure of what Deke expected him to say. He felt drained from everything that had happened in the last twenty-four hours. A night of interrogation at the sheriff station, Deke ready to strangle him when he thought Sam had murdered Lauren, and then racing to the Casa to find Kyle Montgomery holding her at gunpoint.

Something needled at Sam.

Something Deke had said.

Deke got out of the car, motioned for Sam to join him.

Coyote sat on the rim of the quarry. Sam knew Deke couldn't see the animal, but he wasn't sure why Coyote was there. Before it had meant Lauren was in danger, but now she was safe in the ICU. Sam frowned and kept an eye on the animal as he followed Deke.

"Come on, Sam," Deke patted the table beside him. An updraft of wind sang through the pines and pine needles that floated to the ground.

A hawk soared overhead, then swooped into the quarry, reminding Sam of that day with Andy. The day a friend had died because he didn't have the strength to save him.

"Lauren called you last night. That must have been a shock since you thought she was dead and that I'd killed her."

"I tell ya, I just about crapped in my pants. I was so sure you'd offed her." Deke chortled.

Sam sat and waited.

"That Lauren, man, she's a hard woman to eliminate," Deke reflected. "She's been shot at, poisoned, locked in a burning stable, and now, shot again. I guess we'll have to wait and find out if she makes it out of intensive care, won't we?"

Coyote moved closer to the men.

Sam got it. The pieces fell into place.

"What I don't understand Deke is, why?"

"Why?"

"Why did you murder Richard?"

Deke howled, slapped his knee. "Man, I knew you were too smart. I was sure you'd figured it out a long time ago."

"Why, Deke?" Sam persisted.

"Richard Sobrantes, king of the fucking mountain. I've always hated that man." Deke's voice turned harsh, "That bastard told my dad to commit me. COMMIT ME! Just because he caught me trying to drown one of Lauren's disgusting cats."

"You killed your dad, too." Deke's pattern had been there all this time.

"Damn straight. The old fucker took off after me, riding without his helmet. Big mistake. I'd heard him tell Sobrantes that he was taking me to a doctor that afternoon—a doctor who treated psychopaths.

"It was so easy. I slipped through the trails and waited for him, scared his horse. He was thrown off. I never touched him. I just waited until his brain swelled and squeezed off his lungs so he couldn't breathe and his heart stopped. When I was sure he was brain dead, I released his horse. I took a shortcut and arrived first, so I could sound the alarm and be the hero."

"But Sobrantes knew what you'd done. Is that why you killed him?"

"Naw, man. Money. Big money. I'd already done a job for Montgomery in Thailand. Some guy who worked for RKB caught him with a young boy. Kyle was a messed-up bastard. The guy said he'd tell Richard what he'd seen when he got back stateside. I arranged an unfortunate accident, and the poor slob drowned. After that, I owned that Montgomery dude."

"Then, I don't get it. Why did Kyle want Richard dead?"

"Sobrantes had found out too much. Kyle had a dummy corporation in Asia, selling counterfeit semiconductors. There's enormous money in counterfeits. All profit. Big money! Richard found out and was threatening to expose him to the Feds. Sobrantes had to go."

"I could understand the threat that posed, but why Lauren? Why go after her? What did she have to do with the components?

"Kyle and Richard argued the night before he died. Jeffery and Lauren came home early. Jeffery heard them, and when Richard turned up dead, he put two-and-two together and began blackmailing Kyle.

"Kyle believed Lauren had heard them, too, that she knew he was the one with Richard that night. Jeffery was locked in because he was getting paid, but Lauren, she was a loose cannon." Deke shook his head. "He couldn't risk letting her live. I tell you, he was crazy paranoid. She had to be eliminated. Only that woman must have a hefty guardian angel or something because she dodged everything I tried."

"You shot at her in the orchard. Hit Watson."

"Worthless mutt. I could have ended it there if her godfather hadn't come running so fast."

It was coming together like a gigantic puzzle, and the last piece just dropped into place. "So, Kyle hired the man to push Lauren into traffic in London. When he failed, he followed her to California, and then lost her in the airport. So, you took him out and made it look like a robbery."

"You're good, Sam. Really good."

"Then, when Lauren showed up alive, Jeffery decided to trade in Marisa, but he told Lauren he had a name, and that signed his death warrant right then and there."

"Drove that sucker right off the side of the mountain."

"Who tampered with his brakes?"

"Two years of high school auto shop paid off."

"What I can't figure out is how you managed to break into the house, poison Lauren's water, and put the things in the safe."

"Well, that was easy. Jeffery worked for Richard. He had access to everything on that man's computers, because Jeffery is, was, an A-1 hacker. That boy was brilliant. Let me tell you he was one nerdy genius.

"Anyway, he broke into Sobrantes' computer files and got the safe combination. He was looking for some shit Richard had dug up on him, and he wanted it destroyed before Lauren found it. I caught him. I got the combo and let him take the papers he wanted."

"I'm surprised that Jeffery didn't try to blackmail you when stuff from the murder started showing up."

"That little fucker was greedy, but he was smart. Smart enough to know I'd blow him away in a heartbeat."

The afternoon shadows grew long as the sun dropped behind the mountains. It was now just a matter of time before Deke made his next move.

Only one of them would leave the quarry alive.

As Sam watched Coyote float away, he thought of Lauren and knew that he might never see her again.

"So, what's your plan?" Sam waited for Deke to make the next move. "Obviously, you can't let me walk away."

"I do like you, you know. Too bad you're on the wrong side of things." Deke pointed the gun at Sam's chest.

Sam exhaled a laugh at Deke's psychopathic reasoning. "Well, be that as it may, you can't just shoot me and leave me here. Schott will nail your ass in two seconds."

"That old man," Deke scoffed. "He's oblivious, so easy to outsmart. Stand up, Sam. We're taking a little walk."

Sam stood but didn't move. "No, Deke. If you're going to shoot me, you'll to have to do it right here."

Schott's computer pinged the location of Deke's squad car— Berry Falls Quarry Road. He made a left and slammed on the brakes. In the middle of the road, stood a large coyote, with an intense stare. Schott had grown up on the legends of the Dama and her *familiar*, Coyote, but he'd never had personal experience with the spirits.

"What the hell," he thought. "Let's go for it." As if Coyote understood the agreement, he trotted along the dirt road leading toward the abandoned quarry.

Schott pulled over when the animal stopped. Grabbing his shotgun, Ed eased out of the car and quietly shut the door.

The animal vanished. Doubt clouded Schott's mind, but he moved forward anyway, crouching low as he made his way toward the rim of the quarry.

"You damn well will move," Deke shouted.

Sam waited. He caught a movement behind Deke. Coyote was back. Staring at Sam as he'd done the first time in the paddock. *If you have some magic, Mr. Coyote, use it.* Behind the trees, the fading sunlight reflected a glint of metal.

"How will you convince people that I killed myself? What reason would I have?"

"Guilt. Poor Sam, he killed Richard and fell in love with his daughter, and now can't live with what he'd done. If only you'd just left town when you said you would." Deke's voice hissed with fury. "I could have had Lauren. It would have been perfect. After a few years, she'd have had a tragic accident, and I'd inherit all the money." He gestured with the gun. "Come on, start walking."

"Drop your gun, Deke," Schott shouted from the clearing,

his shotgun raised.

Deke spun around, his weapon trained on the detective.

Schott didn't flinch. "Put it down, Deke, let's make this easy for everybody."

Deke backed away, keeping the men in his sights.

"You can't take us both." Ed's voice was amazingly calm as he slowly walked toward Deke.

Deke put the gun to his temple.

Ed stepped closer. "Deke, hang on, you don't have to do that."

"You're right, Ed." Deke leveled the gun at Sam. "I'm taking this fucker with me."

Sam hit the ground. The bullet shattered the redwood.

Schott fired.

Deke spun and flew over the side of the quarry.

It was over.

Finally, it was over.

Chapter Sixty-Three

~~~~~

Lauren's doctors refused to release her. Fortunately, Kyle's aim had been reckless. His first shot grazed her neck above the collarbone. The second bullet nicked a rib. The pain was excruciatingly sharp if she turned too quickly or laughed too hard.

Detective Schott confirmed that Deke had killed Kyle, not her. She was still processing that it was Deke who shot her father and attempted to murder her at Kyle's bidding.

Reporters fixated on interviewing her to attain the *real* story of what happened used every ruse they could think of to see her. Freddie sat in a chair outside her room to make sure their missions were thwarted. He proclaimed himself her bodyguard and didn't trust anyone else to protect her.

The steady flow of family, friends, and bouquets of flowers waned after the first few days. A Do Not Disturb sign was posted with a short list of approved visitors—Bernie, Rand, and Marisa.

Sam Gallagher's name was not on the list. Cienna was added to the restricted list after she pleaded with Lauren to forgive him. Lauren believed it was best when you decide to cut ties, to cut them quickly.

While she lay in the hospital bed, she had plenty of time to think about the next phase of her life. Lauren laughed at the notion. How do you put your life together when you've given your heart to a man who not only doesn't love you, but tried to kill you?

Marisa rapped and asked, "May I come in?"

"Of course." Lauren raised the bed to a sitting position. "Please." She gestured to the chair.

"How are you?" Marisa asked, hesitantly. She stood beside Lauren's bed, her hands clenching and unclenching.

"I should be asking you the same thing, Risa. How are you?"

Marisa shook off the question, her eyes not quite meeting Lauren's gaze. "I came to tell you, I'm sorry. So, very sorry."

"Why? What do you have to be sorry for?"

"I knew. I think I've always known there was something wrong with Kyle." She covered her mouth with trembling fingers.

"He had my mother committed. Angelica used to work at the place and met her that's why she came to work at the house to be near me. For years, I was afraid he'd killed her, but he'd locked her in an institution in Arizona. My mom wrote a letter to your mother and when she came over that afternoon—" Marisa's tears spilled down her cheeks, unnoticed.

Lauren reached out to take Marisa's hand, but she jerked back. "Let me finish. Your mom and I were going shopping that day for your birthday present. Kyle was home when she picked me up, and she confronted him about my mom's letter. They had words. He was really angry. Then he apologized and made nice, offered her a cup of tea."

Marisa choked and gasped between words. Lauren could barely understand her. "I think he gave your mom one of those drugs. We were shopping when her heart just stopped. If only I'd told someone. If only I'd had dared to speak up. But, I was so scared. Afraid he'd kill me too or put me away like he did my mother."

Marisa slumped into a chair, covered her face with her hands, and rocked back and forth. "I've not been able to stop crying, Lulu. I feel so guilty that sometimes I can't breathe."

"Why?" Lauren asked incredulously. Why had Kyle, *Uncle Kyle* destroyed her family? He'd accidentally killed her mother but then paid Deke to murder her father. Why would he have such a vendetta against her family? "Why did he do that?"

"Because he couldn't have Elizabeth. He'd become

obsessed with her when they met at Stanford. He'd wanted to marry her. He believed she'd betrayed him when she refused. Marrying your dad was the ultimate insult to him."

"But wasn't he already married to your mom?"

"Yes, but he'd had it all worked out; he'd divorce my mom, then marry Elizabeth.

Lauren lay back against the pillows. Her mother would've done anything for Marisa, including confronting Kyle. Grief washed over Lauren. She felt as if she'd lost her mother all over again. If only Marisa had spoken up and told Richard what she suspected, then maybe he'd still be alive.

"Did you know that Jeffery was blackmailing Kyle?"

Marisa shook her head vigorously. "No, I had no idea. When Jeffery came around, I thought it was because he missed you. You were all we talked about. My dad pushed us together. He manipulated me to marry Jeffery. I think now it was part of Jeffery's blackmail scheme to make Kyle keep paying. Kyle wanted him close to keep an eye on him. I knew marrying him was a bad idea, but I overrode my intuition because I wanted peace. I can understand why you'd never want to talk to me again." Marisa ran out the door before Lauren could respond.

Lauren shifted to relieve her physical pain. Nothing could alleviate the pain in her heart as she reflected on the multiple betrayals of the people she'd trusted.

Kyle had been the gregarious honorary "uncle." Fun and entertaining, she'd looked forward to being with him. He'd had a manner of making everyone feel as if they were special.

But underneath, he was an angry, vindictive man who destroyed her family.

She'd also trusted Jeffery. Jeffery had been downright greedy. Resorting to a blackmail scheme that led to his death.

And Deke, a psychopath who, like Kyle, had everyone fooled. He not only killed her dad, but he'd set up Frank Grimes with promises of money, and then when his usefulness was over, he killed him and made it appear to be a heart attack.

Sam's duplicity was the hardest to accept. She'd gone over everything and wasn't sure when he'd been lying to her. When they made love? Or when he called her a rich bitch and said he was done? Was he protecting her when he set her up to be kidnapped? She still wasn't sure what would have happened if she hadn't escaped.

And now, Marisa. Heartbroken, Lauren sobbed.

~~~

Sam was packed and ready to return to his apartment in Paris. His headaches had dissipated. He'd learned to accept Coyote and the Dama as part of the mystery of life, rather than a disorder. He felt it was safe to return to work.

Bernie said there was no rush for him to move.

He could leave anytime.

On any given day.

He could. And he would.

But he waited. Lauren was released from the hospital two weeks ago and was recovering at Rand's house.

Today might be the day that she'd answer his calls and agree to see him, to let him explain why he'd had her kidnapped, that he'd done it to save her, not hurt her.

While he waited, he opened another beer and another, then killed a bottle of Johnnie Walker when the six-pack was gone. It was too painful to be sober and accept the reality that there wasn't going to be a call from Lauren. Accept that she meant it when she sent the message with Zach that she didn't want to see him.

He woke in the dark with his head pounding before realizing the pounding was also outside. When he opened the door, his brothers powered their way into the cottage, turning on lights that blinded him, and shouting in loud voices that battered his senses. They brought food—disgusting, nauseating pizza. He attempted to sneak back upstairs and hide until they got tired of waiting and left.

Flynn followed him. "You stink to high hell, worse than a camel. When was the last time you showered?"

Sam squinted, swayed on his feet; the haze floating in his skull blanking his memory.

"The shooting was weeks ago," Flynn said.

"Go away." Sam wanted to flop on the unmade bed and sink back into unconsciousness.

"No, I'm not going away, and neither are Zach and Greg. Shower first. Then food. You have to get over Lauren."

"This is none of your business." Sam pushed past his brother.

Flynn blocked him, threw an easy hammerlock over Sam's neck, walked him to the bathroom, and turned on the shower. Then caught him again as Sam slipped out the door.

"Drunks are so easy," Flynn teased. "Okay, buddy—in you go."

He pushed Sam under the spray, clothes, and all. Sam stopped resisting, and with bowed head, he braced his hands against the tile. Flynn stepped back, grabbed a towel, dried his hands, and waited. Wet clothes and swear words came flying over the shower rod.

Clean and dry, Sam went downstairs with Flynn. He sat silently while the others talked and did their best to cheer him up.

"We almost lost you, Sam," Greg started the intervention. "Deke didn't plan for you to live."

They spent the better part of the evening telling him how important he was to them. How they wanted, no, needed him in the family.

Then his brothers cleaned his bedroom, changed the sheets, and aired out the room as they'd done downstairs in the kitchen.

Zach suggested Sam sleep it off and left a small tablet in case he needed a little help. "This will relax you. You've pickled yourself with alcohol. This is mild enough not to hurt you, but you're going to sleep around the clock once it takes you under."

His sleep had been in short bursts, a few minutes here, half an hour there, nothing close to a full night's sleep for months. The cottage was strangely quiet after his brothers went home.

A soft hum filled Sam's head, like a singer warming up. Slowly he closed his eyes.

"Sam." He heard his name and rose up on his elbow.

There she was, the woman in red, standing at the foot of his bed. Coyote sat beside her. The wind blew her hair in a whirl of flames. Her red dress, a dance of filmy veils.

"Why do you do that?" he mumbled.

"Do what, Sam?"

"Always look like you're in a wind tunnel."

"Sam—I'm your apparition." The wind stopped, her hair fell like a calm red curtain past her waist. Coyote transposed into a cat and jumped on her shoulder.

"Sleep well, Sam," she sang. "Everything will work out, just like you want."

Sam closed his eyes and drifted off again.

"Sam?" He imagined another familiar voice. Lauren stood at the foot of his bed where Coyote and the woman in red had been. She was another phantom, another wishful dream.

"I've missed you." The words jammed in his throat.

"I've missed you, too." She unzipped her sweatshirt, shrugged it off her bare shoulders, and let it drop to the floor. Sam wanted to reach for her, but he was afraid she'd disappear. He'd rather have the apparition than nothing at all.

She slipped off the rest of her clothes and stood before him naked except for a piece of black lace around her hips and the small bandages on her neck and side.

"I'm so sorry," Sam said, when he saw her wounds.

"Shh." She moved to him. "We'll not talk about that now."

Pulling back the comforter and sheets, she slipped in beside him. Kissed him, her mouth soft and willing, like the rest of her body.

Sam was immediately aroused and fleetingly wondered how that could be possible, but since he was dreaming, it didn't matter. Magic happens in dreams.

Lauren slid on top of him, and slowly took him into her body, her movements gently sensual. He touched her cautiously, caressing her breasts and taut nipples as she leaned down to kiss him.

He watched her orgasm hit in full force, felt the contractions tighten; then let himself go in a powerful release. She lay on top of him, sweaty and satisfied, then curled by his side.

He was finished. In the morning, he'd tell her how much he loved her. In the morning, he'd ask her to marry him.

In the morning, Lauren was gone.

Chapter Sixty-Four

~~~~~

Sam argued with himself as he drove to RKB to meet Bernie. Lauren hadn't been a dream. She hadn't been an apparition. The woman in red and that coyote of hers may not be real, but making love to Lauren—that was real.

The scrap of black lace he'd found in between the sheets proved she'd been there. Proved that she'd made love to him.

Bernie rounded his desk and extended his hand when Sam walked in. "Glad to see you, Sam. You leaving?" He directed them to the chairs by the window.

"Not yet, I'm looking for Lauren."

"Sorry, Sam. Lauren's gone. She flew out this morning for Europe. She said to give you this." He retrieved an envelope from his desk.

Sam opened it, hoping for—for what, a note, directions on where to meet, a thank you for sex last night. Instead, it was a check with multiple zeros and a cryptic message—*thanks for everything* written in Lauren's graceful, loopy handwriting.

It was the payoff. Her way of saying it was over.

She was done with him.

He'd used her, and she'd used him back.

He tore the check into pieces, slid them in the envelope, and handed it to Bernie.

"Sam, that was big money you just ripped up."

"It's not enough." Without Lauren, it was not enough.

Chapter Sixty-Five

~~~~~

London wasn't what it used to be. Lauren found it hard returning to the daily routine of taking the Underground and strolling to her shop. Even admiring her store, Grace Delany Fine Antique Linens—none of it gave her the thrill it once had.

The morning weather matched her mood. The day was gloomy, cold, and drizzly. She'd been back six months and working with a therapist to help her move beyond the tangles of betrayal to a place where she could trust again.

Rebuilding relationships and trust wasn't easy, Lauren discovered. It was damn difficult to forgive and move on as the others had done. Miss Etta and Arlo had retired, bought a condo in Biloxi, Mississippi, near the casinos. Who knew Miss Etta was a secret gambler who liked to play roulette? Fiona had moved into the caretaker's cottage. Marisa and Angelica had flown to Flagstaff to reunite with Marisa's mother. Bernie decided to retire and was shopping for a place to live in Hawaii. Meetings with prospective buyers for RKB were ongoing. She seemed to be the only one stuck in place.

The bell jingled a cheery greeting as she entered the store.

"Morning," Meg, her store manager, sang out.

Lauren shrugged off her jacket and hung it in the closet, then strolled about the shop, as per her morning ritual. But there was no lift; the merchandise felt old and outdated rather than charming and mysterious.

"I'll be in my office," Lauren said to Meg. She climbed the stairs and closed the door. She lingered before one of the few things she'd brought with her from California; a watercolor that

Marisa had painted from a photograph. Two little girls so full sunshine and the promise of a bright and happy future and a lifetime of friendship.

The photograph had been taken the afternoon they'd sat under the sycamore trees with a needle stolen from Nana's sewing box. They'd poked each other's index fingers and smeared their blood together. Lauren repeated the words she'd heard at a wedding the weekend before—*By the power invested in me, I now pronounce us blood-sisters forever. Amen.*

She and Marisa were slowly rebuilding their relationship via Skype chats. It was easier than she'd anticipated. They were making plans to visit in some place neutral, like Greece or Spain.

Lauren missed the California sun and deliberated whether she should return to San Francisco and maybe have two shops. Let Meg run this one. She'd done an outstanding job while Lauren was away. Or sell out and move to Hawaii to join Bernie, or live in Italy near Rand and his family.

Decisions, decisions—whatever she decided, it was time to move on. Go forward, not stay in the past. But the past with Sam Gallagher, except for those attempts on her life, had been so deliciously wonderful.

So many good memories that she had to accept that her heart was still with some raggedy-assed guy in California or Afghanistan or wherever; he'd probably forgotten all about her, which was what she was trying to do with him

Forget him, she told herself.

But she was failing miserably.

She'd signed up for cooking classes because who knew—someday they might get back together. *You're one sick woman, Sobrantes.*

She knew the likelihood of them ever seeing each other again was between nil and naught.

It was close to noon when Meg buzzed her. "You have a customer. You need to come down."

"I'm busy." She wasn't ready to be social.

"I can't handle this one," Meg said firmly.

"Do we need to call security?"

"You'll have to decide."

Worried by Meg's tone, Lauren jogged down the steps.

And there he stood in the middle of the store. Momma's sexy bad boy didn't look friendly in his black leather jacket, black pants, and dark sunglasses that guarded his eyes.

She paused at the bottom of the stairs and held on to the banister for support. "What do you want?" She tried for a superior tone, but her voice trembled.

He ambled toward her with a slow, casual roll of his hips, a slight smile on his face. Her breathing was suddenly rapid, her heart slammed against her ribs, she wanted to run, but she knew, like the predator he was, he'd catch her.

"You owe me." His deep voice caressed her senses.

"Meg, run upstairs and get my checkbook, please." Her legs could barely hold her up; much less carry her back to the office.

Meg whispered as she passed. "Should I call the police?"

"No. The checkbook is in my desk."

"I didn't come for money," Sam said.

"Then what did you come for?"

"An explanation. You wouldn't see me at the hospital. You disappeared after we had sex that night."

"Have you forgotten you tried to kill me?"

Behind her, Meg gasped, "I'm calling, right now."

"No." Lauren held up a hand to stop her.

"I staged your murder to keep you safe, and you know it."

She did know. Somehow she'd always known.

He pushed his sunglasses on top of his head as he stepped closer. Intense dark eyes held her mesmerized, and like a trapped animal about to be devoured, she couldn't look away.

His hand cupped her cheek. He ran a thumb over her bottom lip. Bending forward, his lips hovered over hers. His spicy aftershave of citrus and bay rum floated over her.

He leaned back, watched her reaction. "I think these belong to you." He handed her the scrappy piece of black lace she'd left in his bed the night before she fled to London.

She heard Meg twitter, "Oh, my."

"We need to start over." Then he kissed her.

Chapter Sixty-Six

~~~~~

Lauren paused as she stepped out of the Casa. Her red silk pantsuit sparkled in the afternoon sunlight. The wedding rehearsal that morning had gone smoothly. The tables and chairs and tents for tomorrow's ceremony were set up in the garden by the gazebo. Caterers had taken over the kitchen under Miss Etta's watchful eye.

"I have to make another financial disclosure, Sam."

Sam, dressed in charcoal gray slacks and an open-collared white shirt, impatiently waited for her. "Now? We're late for the rehearsal dinner." He hustled her to the limo. "Besides, there's nothing to discuss. I've relinquished all claims to your financial empire."

Inside the limo, champagne chilled in the bucket next to two flutes, tied with white ribbons. Sam did the honors. "To you, Ms. Sobrantes. Tomorrow, Ms. Gallagher."

Lauren smiled and clinked her glass with his. "You need to know I'm not as wealthy as I was—I'm down to my last fifty..."

Sam raised an eyebrow. "I have plenty of money. Wait, your last fifty dollars?" How could she have gone through billions in six months?

Lauren laughed.

"Fifty thousand?"

"Uh...more like fifty million."

Sam eyed her over the rim of his flute before responding. "Well, I suppose we'll have to be frugal." Her laughter was music to his heart. "What did you do with your money?"

"I created a grant for the Heavens Child Foundation to

fund more research. And, I'm setting up a new foundation for homeless children and their families. The money will cover things like clothing, education, transportation, housing, and medical. In the summer, Casa de La Lumbre will host a summer camp for kids who've never been out of the city and don't know how to grow veggies, have never picked apples off a tree and who've never seen a horse, much less been on one. We should get a goat, lots of goats, rabbits, pigs, and chickens. Fiona has agreed to head the organization."

Her excitement filled him with happiness.

Chapter Sixty-Seven

~~~~~

Their wedding took place on a sunny day at the end of August. The ceremony was small and intimate with family and close friends. Marisa, as Lauren's maid of honor, led the way along the garden path strewn with rose petals. Lauren and Bernie followed. Keeping with tradition, Bernie handed her to Sam, who waited with his best man, Flynn.

Under the white canopies, the guests honored the bride and groom with toasts, speeches, laughter, and an abundance of gratitude and love. Emmett delivered a blessing that brought tears to everyone's eyes. Cienna had created a beautifully tiered wedding cake, which they'd cut after the next dance.

At sunset, the band struck up a waltz. Lauren, awash in contentment, surveyed her guests—Cienna and Emmett swayed to the music, her head on his shoulder.

Miss Etta and Arlo, who had completely recovered from his heart attack, danced slowly next to Ed Schott and his wife, together again since he'd retired from the La Lumbre Sheriff's Department. Even Amelia Rodgers and her plus one were there. Meg and Sam's sister, Brianna had flown in from Europe.

Freddie stood watch over the group. He couldn't give up his protective stance even for the wedding festivities.

Lauren's eyes skimmed over the other guests. Flynn and Zach stood drinking beer, talking to Jon J. Malcolm. Jon had said he understood why Sam would no longer take on rescue jobs with AZEN—trading action for management—but understanding didn't mean he had to like it.

Marisa laughed at something Greg said and hearing her

friend's cheerfulness made Lauren's day even brighter. She was thankful she'd been able to salvage the friendship and create a new relationship with her lifelong friend.

Bernie and Fiona sat in deep conversation at a nearby table. Fiona sipped sparkling water and busily making notes on a paper napkin. She took her job as the head of the Sobrantes Foundation very seriously, along with maintaining her sobriety.

Lauren's new family surrounded her—people she loved and trusted. She was free of fear for the first time in years. Watson wove in and among people's legs. She'd left Yin and Yang in the Casa for their safety.

Sam put an arm around her waist. "May I have this dance, Ms. Gallagher?"

"Of course, Mr. Gallagher." She turned, joyfully embraced in his arms. "I forgot to tell you a very interesting wedding gift arrived yesterday."

"Oh?" Sam said as he guided her smoothly over the dance floor.

"It was a very large and very colorful green and yellow pasta bowl and a handwritten recipe for Pasta Bolognese."

She leaned back and watched his reaction. "No name. No return address. Just a note: *Enjoy*. It was signed with a large *C*. There was a P.S. *Take good care of Sam, he's a good man, and you're lucky to have him.*"

"Words from the wise." A hint of a smile played on his lips.

Lauren knew that Cosima was alive. Whatever Sam had done, he'd protected her, and she was alive and safe.

The setting sun turned the sky a blazing red, with an illuminating glow. A collective sigh rose from the guests. Lauren turned in Sam's arms, leaned against him, and watched as the sky above the mountains morphed into a light show of red, gold, pink, and silver. At the height of the color, a chorus of coyotes sang with blood-tingling yips.

Sam enfolded Lauren in his arms and whispered, *thank you* to the Dama and the Coyote for their blessings.

Jon sipped champagne as he watched Sam laughing with Lauren.

As happy as he was for his friend, he knew he'd never be able to replace him.

Flynn, Greg, and Zach were also watching. "Looks like we have our brother back." Zach lifted his glass in Sam's direction.

Flynn was distracted by a young woman walking toward them. "Oh, momma—look a-here, look a-here."

"Careful, Flynn," warned Zach.

"No, way, you guys. I saw her first."

The petite young woman wore a short paisley dress; her golden brown hair fell past her shoulders. There was a seductive sway to her hips as she strolled toward the men. A broad smile was on her face as she came closer, her eyes riveted on Flynn.

A low moan vibrated in his throat. "Come to poppa, baby."

The men watched the drama unfold looking from the woman to Flynn.

"Flynn," Zach tried again. "Careful, now."

Flynn waved him away. "Hello, sweetness, I've been waiting for you."

"Have you now?" she laughed.

She said hello to Greg and Zach.

"Hey, Holly. How've you been?" Zach said.

Flynn's mouth dropped open. "Holly?"

Eyes twinkling, she laughed at Flynn's shock. She'd lived next door to the Gallagher's and had declared her love for Flynn when she was six years old. She'd told him to wait for her because she was going to marry him when she grew up.

"*Dinks?*" Flynn squeaked, using the nickname he'd given her when she'd trailed behind him every day after school. "Wow, you grew up."

"Yes, life has a way of doing that."

Flynn threw back his head and chortled. "Yep, life has a way of doing lots of things to you. Let's go catch up." Taking her arm, he led her away from his brothers.

Greg and Zach laughed and shook their heads. They were sure if anyone could tame Flynn, it was little *Dinks*.

Jon's satellite phone rang. He excused himself and moved away from the group.

Senator Phillips spoke hurriedly. "They're threatening me, Jon. I told them I quit. That I was done and they said they'd kill me."

"Who is threatening you? Why?"

"I'm in Brussels. Get over here, fast. I'll give you the information you wanted. If anything happens to me, find Emma O'Neal. I've given her a copy. And, Jon, if the worst happens, promise me that you'll get Emma home safely."

Before Jon could ask for details, the line went dead.

ACKNOWLEDGMENTS

Writing this novel has been an incredible journey. I am filled with gratitude for the creative people I've met along the way who willingly shared their expertise.

In 2005, I made a vow that I would not die with regrets. I knew that if I didn't act on my lifelong dream of writing a novel, it would be the biggest disappointment of my life.

I quickly discovered Redbird Studio in Milwaukee and enrolled in Judy Bridges' SHUT Up & Write classes. Judy, I still use your "alligator outline."

When I moved to Madison, I joined Laurel Yourke's critique group. She taught me how to improve the scenes and stop over-writing. Laurel, I still hear your voice telling me, *"You're starting too early."*

Laurel introduced me to Christine DeSmet. I was accepted into her Master Novel Workshop at the UW Write-by-the-Lake Conference. Chris, your encouragement gave me the confidence to finish the novel. Yeah, it has taken a while.

There were five other women in the Master Class—Barbara Belford, (Bibi Belford), Rev Blair Hull, Cheryl Hanson (Ceone Fenn), Julie Holmes (JM Holmes), and Lisa Kusko. We had such a good time together that we formed the Writing Sisters.

I had the opportunity to take a class with Julie Tallard Johnson who inspired me to enjoy the process of writing.

In the Round Table at Redbird, I met Jeannee Sacken. Jeannee's constant support, reading the pages, talking plots, and character development has been a mainstay for me. Jeannee without your friendship and encouragement, this book would still be a dream.

The Caretaker has gone through many revisions. Friends have graciously read and re-read the manuscript.

Andrea Bryan, you were the first reader outside of the family. I loved that you fell in love with Sam Gallagher, but I don't think Lauren wants to give him up anytime soon.

Evelyn Renfro Dawson, our *"buns of steel, baby"* walks over the hills of Puerto Escondido were awesome! Thank you for inviting me to Mexico to finish the book.

Diane Chamness and Ruth Ferguson, I appreciate you reading The Caretaker and encouraging me to get it published. I trust you'll like this version. Jennifer Chumbley, thank you for critiquing and your encouragement.

Jan Blasberg, your keen eye in editing is greatly appreciated, as are you, my friend. Dana Schwartz, friend, fellow writer, yoga teacher. I love our long, long lunches and discussing our characters and their challenges.

Big thanks to my friends in Betty Eiler's Yoga group, and to the awesome ladies of the F-100 club. Ladies, your support has been delightful and so important to me.

Robert Gentile P.A., thank you for answering my questions about TBIs, MRIs, and medications. And thanks to Luis Bixler for helping me with the military information.

Karen Kiefer, you came to visit us at the right time. Thank you for your artistic suggestions on the cover design.

A special thank you to my daughter, Taylor. You've encouraged me for years to write and publish a novel. Your critiques are awesome and always spot on. And thank you for the wonderful book cover design.

And a special thank you to my son, Eirik, who designed my webpage. It is amazing to have such a talented family.

I have to include the rest of my great family—Scott and Kimberly, Josh, Pierce, Zoe, and Ian. Love to you all.

Finally, to my husband, Vern—thank you for the endless hours of reading pages, discussing characters, and working out plots. I couldn't have done it without you.

ABOUT THE AUTHOR, ROI SOLBERG

Roi Solberg's debut novel, *The Caretaker* is set in the Santa Cruz Mountains above Silicon Valley, where Roi and her family live.

Roi is author of *The Spirit of Archetypes: Cards of Spiritual Guidance.*

She currently is working on the next two La Lumbre books.

Website: www.roisolberg.com
Facebook: Roisolberg, author
Twitter: Roisolberg, author